D0753609

EMPIRE OF THE MOGHUL

MOGHUL

RULER OF THE WORLD

EMPIRE OF THE MOGHUL

RULER OF THE WORLD

ALEX
RUTHERFORD

headline
review

First published in 2011 by HEADLINE REVIEW
An imprint of HEADLINE PUBLISHING GROUP

1

Cataloguing in Publication Data is available from the British Library

Hardback ISBN 978 0 7553 4757 5
Trade paperback ISBN 978 0 7553 4758 2

Typeset in Bembo by Ellipsis Books Limited, Glasgow

Printed and bound in Great Britain by CPI Mackays, Chatham ME5 8TD

Headline's policy is to use papers that are natural, renewable
and recyclable products and made from wood grown in sustainable forests.
The logging and manufacturing processes are expected to conform to
the environmental regulations of the country of origin.

HEADLINE PUBLISHING GROUP
An Hachette UK Company
338 Euston Road
London NW1 3BH

www.headline.co.uk
www.hachette.co.uk

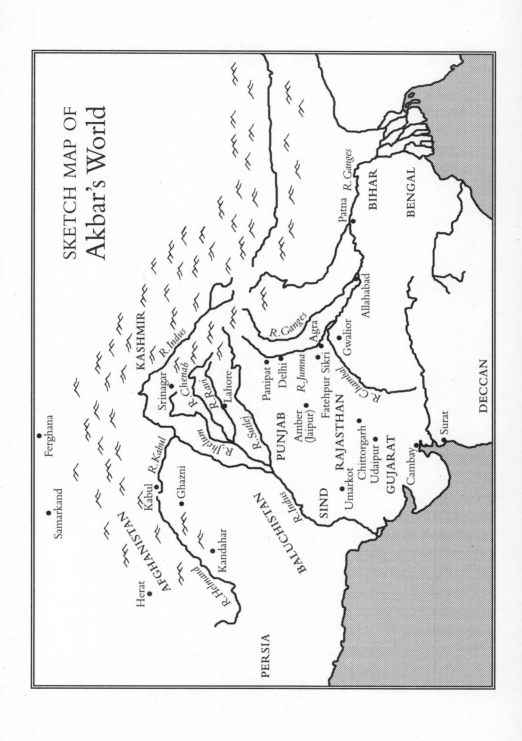

SKETCH MAP OF
Akbar's World

Main Characters

Akbar's family

Humayun, Akbar's father and the second Moghul emperor
Hamida, Akbar's mother
Gulbadan, Akbar's aunt and Humayun's half-sister
Kamran, Akbar's uncle and Humayun's eldest half-brother
Askari, Akbar's uncle and Humayun's middle half-brother
Hindal, Akbar's uncle and Humayun's youngest half-brother
Hirabai, Akbar's wife, princess of Amber and mother of Salim
Salim, Akbar's eldest son
Murad, Akbar's middle son
Daniyal, Akbar's youngest son
Man Bai, Salim's wife, mother of Khusrau and daughter of Bhagwan
   Das, Raja of Amber
Jodh Bai, Salim's wife and mother of Khurram
Sahib Jamal, Salim's wife and mother of Parvez
Khusrau, Salim's eldest son
Parvez, Salim's middle son
Khurram, Salim's youngest son

Akbar's inner circle

Bairam Khan, Akbar's guardian and first *khan-i-khanan,* commander-
   in-chief

Ahmed Khan, Akbar's chief scout and later his *khan-i-khanan*

Maham Anga, Akbar's wet-nurse (milk-mother)

Adham Khan, Akbar's milk-brother

Jauhar, Humayun's steward and later Akbar's comptroller of the household

Abul Fazl, Akbar's chief chronicler and confidant

Tardi Beg, Governor of Delhi

Muhammad Beg, a commander from Badakhshan

Ali Gul, a Tajik officer

Abdul Rahman, Akbar's *khan-i-khanan* after Ahmed Khan

Aziz Koka, one of Akbar's youngest commanders

Others at the Moghul court

Atga Khan, Akbar's chief quartermaster

Mayala, a favourite concubine of Akbar

Anarkali, 'Pomegranate Blossom', Akbar's Venetian concubine

Shaikh Ahmad, an orthodox Sunni and leader of the *ulama,* Akbar's senior Islamic spiritual advisers

Shaikh Mubarak, Islamic cleric and Abul Fazl's father

Father Francisco Henriquez, Jesuit priest, Persian by birth

Father Antonio Monserrate, a Spanish Jesuit priest

John Newberry, English merchant

Suleiman Beg, Salim's milk-brother and friend

Zahed Butt, captain of Salim's bodyguard

Zubaida, Salim's former nursemaid and attendant to Hamida

Delhi

Hemu, Hindu general who seizes Delhi from the Moghuls

Fatehpur Sikri

Shaikh Salim Chishti, a Sufi mystic

Tuhin Das, Akbar's architect

Gujarat

Ibrahim Hussain, a rival member of the Gujarati royal family

Mirza Muqim, a rival member of the Gujarati royal family
Itimad Khan, a rival member of the Gujarati royal family

Kabul
Saif Khan, Governor of Kabul
Ghiyas Beg, a Persian émigré appointed Treasurer of Kabul
Mehrunissa, Ghiyas Beg's daughter

Bengal
Sher Shah, ruler from Bengal who ejected the Moghuls from
    Hindustan in Humayun's reign
Islam Shah, Sher Shah's son
Shah Daud, vassal ruler of Bengal in Akbar's reign

Rajasthan
Rana Udai Singh, ruler of Mewar and son of Babur's enemy Rana
    Sanga
Raja Ravi Singh, a Rajasthani ruler and vassal of Akbar's
Raja Bhagwan Das, ruler of Amber, brother of Hirabai and father
    of Man Bai
Man Singh, son of Raja Bhagwan Das and nephew of Hirabai

The Moghuls' ancestors
Genghis Khan
Timur, known in the west as Tamburlaine from a corruption of
    Timur-i-Lang (Timur the Lame)
Ulugh Beg, Timur's grandson and a famous astronomer

'The rush of arrows and the clash of swords
Tore the marrow of elephants and the entrails of tigers'

Akbarnama of Abul Fazl

Part I

From Behind the Veil

Chapter 1

Sudden Danger

Northwestern India, 1556

A low rumbling growl rose from the dense acacia bushes thirty yards away. Even without it Akbar would have known the tiger was there. Its musky scent hung in the air. The beaters had done their work well. While moonlight still silvered the hills in which Akbar's army was encamped, a hundred miles northeast of Delhi, they had started towards the small forest where a large male tiger had been sighted. The village headman who had brought word of it to the camp, saying he had heard that the young Moghul emperor was fond of hunting, claimed it was a maneater that in the last few days had killed an old man labouring in the fields and two small children as they went to fetch water.

The headman had left the camp well rewarded by Akbar, who could hardly contain his excitement. Bairam Khan, his guardian and *khan-i-khanan* – commander-in-chief – had tried to dissuade him from the hunt, arguing that with the Moghuls' enemies on the move this was no time to be thinking of sport. But a tiger hunt was too good to miss, Akbar had insisted, and Bairam Khan, a faint smile lightening his lean scarred face, had finally agreed.

The beaters had employed the age-old hunting practices of the Moghul clans brought from their homelands on the steppes of Central

Asia. Moving quietly and methodically through the darkness, eight hundred men had formed a *qamargah,* a huge circle about a mile across, around the forest. Then, striking brass gongs and beating small, cylindrical drums suspended on thongs round their necks, they had begun closing in, forming a tighter and tighter human barrier and driving all kinds of game – black buck, nilgai, and squealing wild pigs – into the centre. Eventually, as the light grew stronger, some of them had spotted tiger tracks and sent word to Akbar, following the beaters on elephant-back.

The beast on which Akbar was sitting high in a jewelled canopied howdah also sensed that the tiger was close. It was swinging its great head from side to side and its trunk was coiling in alarm. Behind him Akbar could hear the elephants carrying his bodyguards and attendants also restlessly shifting their great feet. '*Mahout,* quieten the beast. Hold it steady,' he whispered to the skinny, red-turbaned man balanced on the elephant's neck. The *mahout* at once tapped the animal behind its left ear with his iron *ankas,* the rod he used to control it. At the familiar signal, the well-drilled beast slowly relaxed to stand motionless again. Taking their cue from it, the other elephants also ceased their fidgeting and a profound silence fell.

Excellent, thought Akbar. This was the moment when he felt most alive. The blood seemed to sing in his veins and he could feel his heart thump, not with fear but with exhilaration. Though not yet fourteen, he had already killed several tigers, but the battle of wits and of wills, the danger and unpredictability, always excited him. He knew that if the tiger suddenly broke cover, it would take him only an instant to pluck an arrow from the quiver on his back and fit it to his taut-stringed, double-curved bow – the weapon most hunters would use against such quarry. But Akbar was curious to see what a musket could do, especially against such a monster as this was reputed to be. He prided himself on his skill with a musket, and despite his mother's remonstrances had spent far more hours practising his marksmanship than at his studies. What did it really matter if he couldn't read when he could outshoot any soldier in his army?

4

The tiger had stopped growling and Akbar sensed its amber eyes watching him. Slowly he rested the slender engraved-steel barrel of his matchlock musket on the side of the howdah. He had already loaded the metal ball, trickled gunpowder from his silver-mounted powder horn into the pan and checked the short, thin length of fuse. His *qorchi,* his squire, half crouching close beside him, was already holding the burning taper Akbar would need to ignite the fuse.

Satisfied, Akbar aimed his musket at the densest part of the acacia bushes where he was certain the tiger was hiding, braced his shoulder to the ivory-inlaid wooden butt and squinted down the length of the long barrel. 'Hand me the taper,' he whispered to his *qorchi*, 'and signal to the beaters.' Clustered in a semicircle behind the elephants, the beaters at once broke into high-pitched yells and began striking their gongs and beating their drums. Moments later, with an answering roar, the tiger burst through the screen of acacias. Akbar saw a blur of long white teeth and gold and black fur leaping towards his elephant as he lit the fuse. There was a brilliant flash, then a deafening bang. The musket's recoil knocked Akbar backwards, almost somersaulting him out of the howdah, but not before he had seen the tiger drop to the ground, still ten yards away. As the smoke cleared, Akbar saw the animal lying motionless on its side, blood pouring from a jagged hole above its right eye.

Akbar gave a yell of triumph. Without waiting for the *mahout* to bring his mount – which had reacted with admirable calmness to the charge of the tiger and the sharp crack of the musket – to its knees, he climbed, grinning broadly, over the side of the howdah and dropped lightly to the ground. He'd made a fine kill, a perfect kill. He'd proved to the doubters who insisted a musket was too slow for killing such prey that in the hands of a good marksman it was easily fast enough. Curious to inspect the dead beast, Akbar advanced closer. The tiger's pink tongue, lolling flaccidly from its mouth, was already attracting green-black flies. Then Akbar noticed something else protruding through the thick belly fur. Teats. The tiger he'd been hunting was supposed to have been male.

The thought was swiftly followed by another that made the hairs on the back of his young neck lift. With trembling fingers Akbar yanked his bow from his shoulder and, reaching behind him, grabbed an arrow. He was still fitting it to the string when a second and massive tiger launched itself out of the acacias straight towards him. Somehow Akbar managed to fire his arrow, and then time seemed to stop for him. The clamour of warning shouts behind him faded and it was as if he and the tiger were alone. He watched his arrow very slowly part the air in its flight. The tiger too looked almost suspended in its leap, saliva-flecked lips drawn back, long canines prominent and ears flattened against its head, like the image etched on the golden ring that had once belonged to Akbar's great ancestor Timur and was now on his own shaking forefinger.

Then, suddenly, time rushed forward again and the tiger was almost on him. Akbar jumped aside, closing his eyes as he did so and expecting at any moment to feel claws ripping into his flesh or smell hot, rancid breath as sharp teeth sought his throat. Instead he heard a skidding thud and opened his eyes to see the tiger crumpled up beside him, his arrow embedded in the crimsoning fur of its throat. For a moment Akbar stood in silence, knowing he had experienced something almost unknown to him – fear – and also that he had been very, very lucky.

Still dazed, he caught the sound of rapidly approaching hoofbeats and turned to see a rider weaving through the low scrub and spindly trees towards them. It must be a messenger from the camp, no doubt sent by Bairam Khan to hurry him up. Five minutes ago he'd have been annoyed to have his sport interrupted but now he felt grateful for the distraction from thoughts of what might have happened. The crowd of beaters, guards and attendants parted to let the rider through. His tall bay horse was foamy with sweat and he himself so caked with dust that his tunic of bright Moghul green looked almost brown. Reining in before Akbar, he flung himself from the saddle, made the briefest of obeisances and said breathlessly, 'Majesty, Bairam Khan requests that you return to the camp immediately.'

'Why?'

'Delhi has fallen to an advance force of Hemu's rebels.'

• ◆ •

Four hours later, as the hunting party with Akbar at its head passed through the first of the picket lines thrown out around his camp, the sun was still high in the clear blue sky. Despite the tasselled brocade canopy shading him, Akbar's head ached. Sweat was sticking his tunic to his body, yet he barely noticed the discomfort as he pondered the disastrous news of the loss of his capital. Surely his rule was not destined to be over almost before it had begun.

It was barely ten months since, on a makeshift brick throne hastily erected on a masonry platform in the centre of a Moghul encampment, he had been proclaimed Emperor of Hindustan. Still raw with grief at the sudden death of his father, the Emperor Humayun, he had stood awkwardly but proudly beneath a silken awning to receive the homage of Bairam Khan and his other commanders.

His mother Hamida had only recently succeeded in convincing him just how desperate that time had been. How Bairam Khan, despite his Persian origins, had understood better than anyone that in the first hours and days after his father's death the danger to Akbar came from within – from ambitious commanders who, now the emperor was dead leaving only a boy as heir, might claim the throne for themselves. Most were men with no time for sentiment. Many were from the old Moghul clans who with Akbar's grandfather Babur had founded a new empire on the dry plains of Hindustan. The code of the steppes, had always been *taktya, takhta*, 'throne or coffin'. Any who felt strong enough could challenge for the crown and over the years many had done so and would do so again.

Akbar's elephant stumbled, jerking him from his recollections, but only for a moment. Staring down at the wrinkled grey neck of the beast with its sproutings of sparse coarse hair, his mind soon returned to its dark reflections. If the news was true and Delhi had indeed fallen, everything his mother and Bairam Khan had

7

done for him might have been for nothing. To win precious time, they had concealed Humayun's death for nearly two weeks, finding a loyal servant of similar build to impersonate the dead emperor. Each day at dawn, he had donned the imperial robes of green silk and Humayun's jewelled turban with its plume of white egrets' feathers and appeared as custom demanded on the riverside balcony of the imperial palace in Delhi, the Purana Qila, to show the crowds jostling each other on the banks of the Jumna that the Moghul emperor lived.

Meanwhile, Hamida and her sister-in-law Gulbadan, Akbar's aunt, had persuaded the reluctant Akbar that he must secretly leave Delhi. He could still see his mother's strained anxious face as, holding a flickering oil lamp in one hand, she had shaken him awake with the other, whispering, 'Come now – bring nothing with you – just come!' Stumbling from his bed, he had allowed her to throw a dark hooded cloak over him, like the one she was wearing. Barely awake but head reeling with questions he had followed her down narrow passageways and twisting flights of stairs through a part of the palace he had never seen to emerge into a small, grubby courtyard. He could still recall the acrid smell of urine – human or animal, he couldn't tell.

A large palanquin was waiting, and in the shadows stood Gulbadan and about twenty soldiers he recognised as Bairam Khan's men. 'Get in,' Hamida had whispered.

'Why, where are we going?' he had asked.

'Your life is in danger if you stay here. Don't question me. Just do it.'

'I don't want to run away. I'm no coward. I've already seen blood and battles . . .' he had protested.

Gulbadan had stepped forward and touching his arm had added, 'When you were a baby and in danger I risked my life for yours. Trust me now and do as your mother says . . .'

Still arguing, he had clambered in, followed by Hamida and Gulbadan who had quickly pulled the concealing curtains around them. He could still recall the coarse feel of those hangings – so different from the silks of the gilded palanquins usually used by the

8

royal family – and the lurching motion as the soldiers had lifted the supporting poles to their shoulders and carried them out into the night. Gulbadan and Hamida had sat tense and silent and some of their fear had at last communicated itself to him even though he didn't yet understand what was going on. Only when they were clear of the palace and the city had his mother told him of a plot to assassinate him before he could become emperor.

On the outskirts of Delhi, more soldiers loyal to Bairam Khan had met them and escorted them to a camp fifty miles from the city. A week later, Bairam Khan himself had joined them with the main body of his army and Akbar had been proclaimed emperor on his brick throne. Bairam Khan had then escorted Akbar in great ceremony back to Delhi where in the Friday mosque the *khutba*, the sermon, had been read in his name, confirming to all the world that he was the new emperor. Outmanoeuvred before any of them had time to plan further mischief, all the Moghul leaders had pledged their allegiance to him.

That had dealt with the enemy within but not the many beyond the Moghul frontiers, as this news about Delhi proved. The Moghuls' position in Hindustan was indeed precarious. Vassals who had only recently sworn loyalty to his father Humayun were trying to break free while enemies beyond the empire were probing its borders. But of all these only one – Hemu – had emerged as a serious menace. He was an unlikely enemy, this reputedly ugly but silver-tongued little man – a lowborn nobody who seemed to have conjured an army out of nowhere to challenge Moghul authority. He hadn't paid too much attention to him but now he wondered what kind of man this Hemu was and how he inspired his men. What lay behind his success?

• ◆ •

Akbar was entering the heart of the tented city that was the main camp. Perched high in his howdah he saw ahead, at the very centre, his own tent – bright scarlet as befitted the command tent of an emperor – and beside it, almost as magnificent with its intricate awnings, Bairam Khan's. His commander-in-chief was standing outside

9

waiting for him, and from his posture Akbar could tell how impatient he was for him to arrive.

He had barely descended from his howdah before Bairam Khan spoke. 'Majesty, you've heard the news – Hemu's forces have taken Delhi. The war council is assembled in your tent and already debating what we must do. We must join them immediately.' Following Bairam Khan inside, Akbar saw his other commanders and counsellors sitting cross-legged on the thick red and blue carpet around a low, gilded stool draped in green velvet – the emperor's chair. As Akbar took his place they rose and made brief obeisance to him, but he noticed how, as they sat down again, their eyes quickly turned to the tall, lean man standing by his side.

'Summon Tardi Beg so that he can tell the story he has already told me,' Bairam Khan ordered. Moments later, the Moghul Governor of Delhi was ushered in. Akbar had known and liked Tardi Beg all his life. He was a warrior of swaggering confidence from the mountains north of Kabul, with a booming voice to match the muscular bulk of his body. Usually his eyes held a humorous twinkle but now the lined, sun-burnished face above the thick black beard looked sombre.

'Well, Tardi Beg, account for yourself before His Majesty and the council.' Bairam Khan's tone was cold. 'Tell us how you abandoned the imperial capital to a seller of saltpetre and his rabble.'

'It was no rabble, but a powerful, well-armed force. Hemu's origins may be humble but he is an accomplished general who has won many battles for whoever would hire him. Now he is no longer a mercenary, but fighting for himself. He has raised the supporters of the old Lodi dynasty displaced by your grandfather against us, Majesty, and it seems that even the proudest and most noble will do whatever he bids them. Our spies reported a great advance party swarming towards Delhi over the plains from the west and that Hemu's main army – an even bigger force, with three hundred war elephants – was not many days behind. There was nothing we could do but withdraw from the city or face certain destruction.'

Bairam Khan's face tautened with anger. 'By fleeing Delhi you have sent a signal to every rebel and petty chieftain to turn against us. I left you with a garrison of twenty thousand men . . .'

'It wasn't enough.'

'Then you should have sent word to me and held the city until I could send reinforcements.'

Tardi Beg's eyes flashed and the fingers of his right hand sought the hilt of the ruby-studded dagger tucked into his sash. 'Bairam Khan, we have known each other many years and fought and bled side by side. Are you questioning my loyalty?'

'Your conduct is something for which you will answer on a future occasion, Tardi Beg. The question now is how to regain what you have lost. We should . . .' Bairam Khan broke off as a man with a straggling brown beard entered the tent. 'Ahmed Khan, I'm glad you have returned safely. What can you tell us?'

Akbar was always pleased to see Ahmed Khan, one of the most trusted of his father Humayun's *ichkis,* his inner circle. Humayun had appointed him Governor of Agra, but when the trouble with Hemu began Bairam Khan had recalled him and asked him to resume his former role of chief scout and intelligence gatherer. The liberal speckling of dust on his clothes suggested he had only just arrived in the camp.

'Hemu is advancing on Delhi from the northwest at the head of his main army of two hundred thousand men. If he maintains his present pace he will reach the city in about a week. According to a small band of soldiers my men intercepted as they were riding to join him, he intends to proclaim himself emperor there. He has already assumed the title of *padishah* and ordered coins to be minted in his name. What is more, he claims the Moghuls are alien interlopers in Hindustan ruled by a mere boy, and that the roots of our dynasty are so weak they will be easy to pluck out.'

His words seemed to stir the council into life, Akbar thought, watching them exchange shocked glances. 'We must strike now — before Hemu reaches Delhi and consolidates his position,' Bairam Khan was saying. 'If we are quick we can intercept him before he gets there.'

'But the risk is too great,' objected a commander from Herat

11

whose left arm ended in a stump where his hand should have been. 'If we are defeated we will lose everything. We should try to win ourselves time by negotiating . . .'

'Nonsense. Why should Hemu negotiate from a position of such strength?' said Muhammad Beg, a thickset and grizzled veteran Badakhshani with a broken nose. 'I agree with Bairam Khan.'

'You are all wrong,' cut in Ali Gul, a Tajik. 'We have only one option – to withdraw to Lahore which is still under Moghul control and regroup. Then, when we are strong enough, we can drive out our enemies.'

No one is paying me any attention, thought Akbar as the angry, anxious clamour rose around him. Bairam Khan was frowning and looking intently about him. Akbar knew he was assessing his next move. He was also sure that Bairam Khan's strategy was right – attack was the surest defence. Hadn't his father admitted that during his campaigns he had too often been prepared to delay and thus ceded the initiative to his enemies? In that moment Akbar made up his mind. He would not be driven out of Hindustan as his father had been. It was the Moghuls' destiny to rule Hindustan, but, more than that, it was *his* destiny, and rule it he would.

Almost before he realised it, he was on his feet, every eye upon him. All were used to him just sitting there, their boy emperor listening to their advice and quietly acquiescing in their decisions. 'Enough of this. How dare any of you even think of abandoning the empire?' he said loudly. 'It's not yours to surrender. I am the rightful ruler here. My duty – our duty – is to win new lands, not yield those our ancestors won to petty usurpers. We must attack Hemu at once and crush him like a melon beneath the elephant's foot. I will lead the troops myself.'

As Akbar sat down again, he looked instinctively towards Bairam Khan, whose almost imperceptible nod told him his outburst had pleased his commander-in-chief. His other counsellors and commanders were on their feet now and suddenly the great tent was filled with their voices, this time all shouting one thing: 'Mirza Akbar! Mirza Akba!' His first reaction was relief, then pride. Not only were they acknowledging him as one of the *Amirzada* – the blood-kin of Timur — but they were affirming their readiness to follow him to war in his first campaign as emperor. He had asserted himself and despite his youth they had listened. Command was sweet.

An hour later, Akbar visited his mother in the royal women's quarters. The sleeping tents and bathhouses were protected by a fence of tall, gilded wooden screens lashed together with thongs of oxhide in which there was only one well-guarded entry gate. As he entered her tent, he smelled the sweet spicy scent that ever since childhood he had associated with Hamida — sandalwood. It was coming from a silver incense burner in the centre of the floor, from which a thin wisp of smoke was curling upwards to a vent in the roof.

Hamida was lying against a bolster of flowered silk while Zainab her attendant combed her long hair, dark as Akbar's own. On one side sat his aunt Gulbadan, frowning with concentration as she plucked the strings of a somewhat battered round-bellied lute that had once belonged to Akbar's great-great-grandmother, who had carried it strapped to her back during the Moghuls' flight from Central Asia. Akbar knew the story of that lute as minutely as he knew all the family history. He also knew that his aunt, clever as she was, had no talent for lute-playing and that that annoyed her, hence her persistence.

On the other side of Hamida, embroidering a shirt, was his wet-nurse or milk-mother, Maham Anga. In Moghul society, the bond between wet-nurse and the royal child she had suckled was lifelong. It also made Maham Anga's own son Adham Khan — just a few months older than himself — his milk-brother, bound to him with ties as strong as those of blood.

At the sight of Akbar, the faces of all three women lit up. His mother Hamida, barely thirty and slender-bodied and smooth-skinned still, jumped up and hugged him. Gulbadan put down her lute and smiled. A little older than Hamida, tiny lines already wrinkled the corners of her tawny eyes, and had her long hair not been hennaed, silver threads would have run through it. Maham Anga came forward to embrace him warmly. She was taller than either Hamida or Gulbadan and handsome in a big-boned, almost masculine way.

Akbar was pleased that the three women who meant most to him were here together. 'I have come to you straight from the war council. Hemu's advance force has captured Delhi but he won't hold it long. Tomorrow I will lead our forces to intercept him and his main army before he can join his troops in Delhi. We will defeat Hemu and retake what is ours.'

While he spoke, Hamida's eyes – amber-brown like his own – were fixed on his face. As he fell silent she continued to regard him steadily. What was going through her mind? he wondered.

'My son,' his mother said at last, emotion in her voice, 'I always knew, even when I carried you in my belly, that one day you would be a great warrior and a great leader. The realisation that that time has come fills me with joy. I have something for you.' She whispered something to Zainab, who hurried off. When she returned several minutes later she was carrying an object wrapped in green velvet which she laid on the carpet at Hamida's feet. His mother knelt and threw back the velvet, and Akbar saw his father's golden breastplate and eagle-hilted sword, Alamgir, in its sapphire-studded scabbard.

The armour and the sword evoked the image of his father so powerfully that for a moment Akbar closed his eyes lest his mother see the tears in them. Hamida, helped by Maham Anga, buckled the breastplate on him. Humayun had been tall and muscular but Akbar was already nearly as broad and the armour fitted well. Now Hamida was holding Alamgir out to him. Slowly, he drew the blade from the scabbard and made a few tentative cuts through the air. The weight, the balance, felt good.

'I was waiting until I was sure you were ready,' said Hamida, as if she had read his mind. 'Now I see that you are. Tomorrow, when I watch you ride away, I will feel a mother's anxiety but also the pride of an empress. May God go with you, my son.'

Chapter 2

A Severed Head

The horizon shimmered beneath the heat haze of the late afternoon sun as Akbar stood, shifting nervously from foot to foot, on one of the few small hills on the otherwise featureless plains northwest of Delhi. Suddenly he saw emerging through the haze a troop of about fifty mounted men. As they approached, he said to Bairam Khan at his side, 'That's Ahmed Khan at their head, isn't it?'

'I can't be sure. Your young eyes are better than mine, but that is definitely a green Moghul banner that one of the leading riders is carrying.'

Soon it became clear that it was indeed Ahmed Khan returning from the scouting expedition on which Akbar, on Bairam Khan's advice, had despatched him three days previously to locate and confirm the strength of Hemu's army. About a quarter of an hour later, the familiar straggle-bearded figure approached them and, as Akbar remembered him doing so often in front of his father, briefly prostrated himself.

'Rise, Ahmed Khan. What news have you?'

'We found Hemu and his main force without difficulty. They're encamped at Panipat, only twelve miles north of here.' The name Panipat was both familiar and a source of pride to Akbar. There thirty years ago his grandfather Babur had defeated the Lodi Sultan of Delhi, Sultan Ibrahim, to found the Moghul empire. Only eighteen months before, Akbar himself had ridden through the battlefield, still littered with the great bleached bones of some of Sultan Ibrahim's war elephants, as he had accompanied his father Humayun on his victorious march to recapture Delhi and refound the empire he had lost to an ambitious ruler from Bengal, Sher Shah. Fate had not been kind to his father. After so many struggles against Sher Shah and his own traitorous half-brothers, Humayun had lived only six months after regaining his throne. Now, it seemed that it would be Akbar's turn to command a Moghul army in battle at Panipat. Young as he was he must do everything to ensure he lived up to his father's and grandfather's memories.

'How many men does Hemu have with him, Ahmed Khan?' he asked.

'We estimated more than a hundred and twenty thousand, at least half of them mounted and of good quality. And he also has around five hundred war elephants.'

'Then as we expected he will outnumber us by about twenty thousand men. How many cannon and muskets does he possess?'

'They've fewer cannon than we anticipated, perhaps thirty in total, many of them small. From what we could see, most of the foot soldiers are equipped with bows and arrows, not muskets, although they do of course have some musketeers.'

'We've got the advantage there then, Bairam Khan, haven't we?' Akbar turned to his commander-in-chief. 'There's no reason we shouldn't give battle at Panipat, is there? It is a place of good fortune for our people. Wouldn't fighting there give added confidence to our troops, even if we are outnumbered?' Akbar's expression was almost pleading.

Bairam Khan smiled at his young protégé's enthusiasm. 'Yes, Majesty, it is indeed a good site for a battle, and we can advance towards it across these barren plains quickly and without fear of ambush.'

Before Akbar could reply, Ahmed Khan interrupted. 'Your Majesty speaks of Panipat being of good omen for the Moghuls. It certainly is – but perhaps not for Hemu. We heard a story from a merchant we questioned who had been trading in Hemu's camp. He claimed he got it straight from one of Hemu's personal attendants, but it seems to be common gossip among Hemu's men because we later heard it repeated by another captive – a humble foot soldier whose ragged dress suggested he was far from being a member of Hemu's war council.'

'What is this story?' asked Akbar.

'That a couple of nights ago Hemu's own war elephant – a huge beast – was killed by lightning in its stable during a brief but violent storm. None of the other elephants was even injured. When Hemu heard the news the next morning, he confessed that he'd had a nightmare that same evening in which he had fallen from his elephant into a swollen river. He was on the point of drowning when a Moghul warrior dragged him to the bank, put him in chains and led him away with a rope around his neck. Hemu explained this away to his followers saying that in his family the reverse of what was portrayed in dreams always came about in life. Thus he would soon strike us from our high howdahs and lead us into captivity. However, he seemed clearly worried, and was later observed making lavish offerings to his Hindu gods.'

This was indeed an omen, Akbar thought. But Bairam Khan was the first to speak. 'Even if this rumour isn't true, its circulation around Hemu's camp will lower morale. It makes me even more certain that we should advance at once to Panipat.'

• ◆ •

Two days later, the bright orange flames of cooking fires punctured the grey half-light of the hour before dawn as Akbar's men grabbed a hasty meal and began to arm themselves. Nervously they tested the sharpness of their sword blades with their fingers and checked and rechecked the tightness of their horses' girths whilst muttering prayers for their safety and success in the coming battle. Elsewhere, as agreed by the war council, small cannon were being hitched to teams of twenty-four oxen so that they could accompany the army as it advanced. In the elephant lines, the *mahouts* were feeding their charges with great bundles of hay, fitting their armoured coats of overlapping steel plates and strapping the curved scimitars to their tusks. The howdahs which would carry the troops on their backs were being readied to be loaded on to them once the other preparations were complete. In their tents, the medical men – the *hakims* – were laying out their ointments and phials of pain-dulling opium and readying their saws and cauterising irons essential for the severe wounds they knew they would encounter.

Akbar himself had slept fitfully. Images of glory had been interspersed with anxiety not to let either himself or his forebears down. He had given up any pretence at sleep two hours previously. Now he was already clad in his gilded breastplate with his father's sword Alamgir slung from his studded metal belt. His helmet was encircled at its widest point by a row of rubies and a peacock feather set in gold waved at its crest, but in practical contrast to this show of magnificence a fine mesh of hard steel rings hung down at its back and sides to protect his neck in battle. At Akbar's side were Bairam Khan and the broad-shouldered, bearded figure of Tardi Beg, both also already armed and helmeted. Akbar had pressed Bairam Khan to allow Tardi Beg to take his place in the battle and have the opportunity to prove himself once more, but it had only been with great difficulty that he had persuaded him. Even now Bairam Khan's tone was harsh as he spoke. 'Tardi Beg, I trust you not to let our emperor down. It was his idea that you should lead the right wing. I had my reservations.'

'You made that clear enough at the war council. Haven't we fought side by side before? Haven't we called each other *tugan*, brother-in-arms? Only God knows what our personal fates will be today. Let us not part on bad terms. You need not fear. I will uphold my honour.' Tardi Beg's usually resonant voice was quiet.

Bairam Khan stared deep into the eyes of Tardi Beg, who steadily and unblinkingly returned his gaze. Suddenly Bairam Khan smiled, stretched out his arms and embraced the other man. 'May God be with you,' he said. 'I know you will fight well, my brother.'

'Victory will be ours,' replied Tardi Beg, before bowing to Akbar. Then without another word he turned, mounted the horse held ready for him by his groom and rode with his bodyguard towards his appointed position.

An hour and a half later, with his milk-brother Adham Khan beside him, Akbar was riding just behind the vanguard at the very centre of the mile-wide line of his advancing army. Both young men had repeatedly to rein in their horses, which seemed as eager for battle as they were, for as Bairam Khan, riding a short distance from them, had pointed out, the squadrons of horsemen on the flanks and in the vanguard must not outdistance the teams of oxen pulling the small cannon, the majestic, plodding war elephants and the ranks of archers marching behind them. Some of the bowmen had ragged clothes and many were barefoot but, like the elephants, they could still play a role in battle even in the new world of gunpowder. Their very numbers compensated for what they lacked in individual firepower, Bairam Khan had told Akbar.

The morning had dawned overcast, with scudding low clouds, but as Akbar looked up, a gap opened in them directly above him and the rising sun appeared, shining a beam of bright light on to him and his gleaming armour. Feeling the sudden warmth of its brightness on his upturned face, Akbar shouted to Bairam Khan, 'This is yet another favourable omen, isn't it? Spread the word to our men. The rising sun shines on me alone today. Only dark clouds gather over Hemu. Victory will be ours. More victories will follow. Our empire will eclipse all others until like the midday sun no one will be able to contemplate it for more than a moment without being blinded by its magnificence.'

While Bairam Khan turned to obey, Akbar drew his father's sword and waved it above his head. As he did so, the beat of his drummers grew more intense and the blare of his trumpets more strident, reverberating inside his head. 'Victory will be ours,' Akbar yelled again and heard the cry taken up in ever greater numbers all along his lines.

Then from in front of him he heard the answering, undaunted shouts of Hemu's troops. 'Hemu, Hemu, Hemu Padishah!' Standing in his stirrups, Akbar saw over the heads and through the fluttering green banners of his vanguard the glinting armour of Hemu's war elephants, no more than a mile off. He knew what it meant. Confident in his superior numbers, Hemu had scorned to draw up his men around the few low hillocks on which Akbar's grandfather Babur had positioned his troops to win his great victory all those years ago. Like Akbar, Hemu was staking his all on a frontal attack.

Excitement rising within him like an exploding volcano, Akbar kicked his tall black horse forward and galloped through the vanguard, whilst Adham Khan and his startled bodyguard followed as best they could. Lost to all thoughts but that of conflict, Akbar continued to cry, 'Victory will be ours!'

. ◆ .

'Majesty, our right flank is in chaos,' an officer gasped out as he rode up to Akbar half an hour later. His face was covered in sweat and dust and he had lost his helmet. His white horse was blowing hard and bleeding from a sword slash to its rump. Bairam Khan, who had eventually succeeded in restraining Akbar from his wild gallop at the head of his troops, was still, like Adham Khan, at his side. All three were sitting on their horses in the middle of a circle of a dozen small bronze cannon which were now being readied for action about a quarter of a mile back from the swaying, heaving front lines of the battle.

Heedless of protocol, Bairam Khan spoke before Akbar. 'Has Tardi Beg let us down?'

'Indeed he has not,' said the officer indignantly. 'His banner still flutters at the heart of the fight. However, though Hemu's forces appeared to us to be evenly distributed across his advancing battle line, they were not. Most of his best battle-inured war elephants were concentrated on the flank opposite Tardi Beg, and as the lines neared each other they rushed forward and smashed into Tardi Beg's men. The bullets of our musketeers seemed to bounce off the elephants' steel head armour. The initial charge of the elephants was followed by a rush of cavalry, many of them waving the banners of the old Lodi sultans. When I last glimpsed Tardi Beg, he had cut his way into them at the head of his bodyguard. Although hard-pressed, they were holding their own. But elsewhere on the right our horsemen are falling back, some even abandoning their comrades, throwing down their weapons and galloping for the rear.

Others, despite being more resolute, are being surrounded and killed.'

Anxiety gripped Akbar as again, standing in his stirrups, he looked in the direction of the right flank. His cavalry were indeed beginning to scatter. 'Bairam Khan, we must act quickly. Should I ride with reinforcements?'

'No. That would only cost many lives – perhaps even your own – and gain little. We must draw Hemu's men on to our centre, which remains strong and can be reinforced from the left.'

'Can we make a strong point here, around these cannon?' Akbar asked, brain racing.

'Indeed, Majesty. I will send orders to the officers of the foot archers to gather their men within the cannon circle.' He turned to an officer at his side. 'Drag as many baggage wagons as you can between the cannon and overturn them to provide protection. Order the soldiers from our vanguard to fall back on us here and summon as many from the left flank as can be spared.'

Desperate to think of anything that would help rescue the situation, Akbar had another idea. 'Bairam Khan, should we order the survivors on the right flank to retreat on us here too? If they give the impression of panic Hemu might pursue them too eagerly and expose himself to our counter-attack.'

Bairam Khan thought for a moment, then nodded. 'You have learned your military lessons well. We still have more than enough elephants and horsemen unengaged in our rear to hit Hemu and his attackers hard in the flank. Adham Khan, take a dozen men and ride to tell any officers you can find on the right flank to fall back on us here in pretended panic.'

Adham Khan wheeled his horse and pulling a band of mounted men around him disappeared into the mêlée.

Ten minutes later, Akbar, still seated on his black horse at the centre of his circle of cannon, saw some of his horsemen riding towards him. At the head was Adham Khan. As if in panic, he threw down a green Moghul banner he had got from somewhere and bending low over his horse's neck, kicked it into a wild gallop. The other riders straggled out behind him. Then Akbar heard musket shots and saw some of the horsemen fall. To his relief, Adham Khan was not among them. Above the musket smoke and the gritty dust that was drifting over the battlefield, he saw the howdahs of some of Hemu's war elephants approaching, swaying violently as their *mahouts,* sitting behind their ears, urged their mounts into an ungainly but swift trot in pursuit of Akbar's fleeing men.

'Order the artillerymen to fire when they are ready,' Akbar heard Bairam Khan shout. 'Musketeers, try to knock some of those drivers from their perches. Archers, ready your bows to fire in unison when I give the order.'

At each of the cannon which could be brought to fire towards the attackers, gunners put lighted tapers to the firing holes. Six loud explosions followed, half deafening Akbar and more acrid white smoke filled his nose and obscured his vision. When it had cleared a little, he saw that five of Hemu's elephants had been hit. The first was trumpeting piteously and trying to stand on three legs, its fourth leg just a bloody stump below the knee. Three others lay still on the ground. One in its death throes had rolled on to the howdah on its back and seemed to have crushed the occupants.

The fifth elephant had a gash in its belly from which its blue-grey intestines were protruding. As Akbar watched, its howdah fell from its back, spilling one man on to the ground but the howdah itself remained attached by some leather straps to the elephant. Still containing at least three half-conscious archers, it was dragged along behind the beast as it ran away. The elephant in its panic crossed the path of some of its fellows who were loping to the attack. One of them – a large beast with long, pointed, curved scimitars on its tusks – crashed into the wounded elephant's side, impaling it on its scimitars before both animals fell. The elephant next to them stumbled over the trailing howdah, crushing any remaining life out of the occupants before also collapsing head first to the ground, shedding its own howdah and precipitating its *mahout* over its head as it did so. More of Hemu's elephants began to slow in their charge, struggling to avoid their fallen brothers.

'Archers, fire!' Bairam Khan yelled above the noise of battle. Almost immediately arrows began to rain on to Hemu's troops.

Akbar saw several men tumble, arms flailing, from the howdahs. One arrow caught an elephant in an unprotected part of its lower face just beneath its eye and it lurched across the path of its fellow, further disrupting the attack. Then thick smoke from the second round of cannon shots obscured everything once more and the sound of their discharge rendered Akbar wholly deaf for some moments. He could see Bairam Khan's mouth moving, shouting orders, but could not hear them. However, when the acrid smoke cleared he saw what the orders must have been. His archers were firing one last volley and his own war elephants and horsemen were riding to attack Hemu's increasingly disorganised forces in the flank. He watched some green-turbaned musketeers fire from the canopied howdah on one of his own elephants and the *mahout* fall from the neck of one of Hemu's beasts to land, arms outspread, in the dust. The man twitched convulsively for a moment, clawing at the ground, and then lay still.

Elsewhere, Akbar saw a Moghul horseman, armed only with a lance, bravely charge one of Hemu's largest war elephants head on, ignoring the already bloodied scimitars on its tusks. Tugging on the reins with one hand so that his horse swerved aside at the last moment, with his other hand he thrust the lance deep between the elephant's jaws as it raised its trunk to trumpet in anger. Red blood gushing from its mouth, the beast turned and ran towards the rear.

Akbar was now bursting to join the fight and to exceed the exploits of Adham Khan, whom he could still see slashing with his sword in the middle of the action. 'Bairam Khan, shouldn't we lead our men into the battle?'

'No, you must curb your impatience. A good general, and even more a good emperor, must know when to head the charge and when, like now, to wait behind to see its effect and direct its follow-up. Battles are won by the brain as well as the sword that your milk-brother Adham Khan is wielding so mightily. See how Hemu's army is falling into confusion. Their attack has lost all impetus.'

'How can we exploit our advantage and destroy Hemu's forces?' asked Akbar, his own mind still devoid of any idea other than to charge directly into the fray.

'We should order our left wing to move across our front and encircle as many of our opponents as they can. They haven't seen much fighting as yet and should be fresh and eager. If we keep cool heads, with their help we will win a great victory where minutes ago we might have lost all. It's often so in battle.'

Akbar nodded and Bairam Khan gave the command. Soon Akbar could see movement as battalions of his cavalry and groups of his war elephants crossed from the left to attempt the encirclement. Even as they did so, green banners billowing and trumpets blaring, groups of Hemu's horsemen were already turning to flee, some stopping to pull up behind comrades who had lost their mounts. As Akbar continued to watch, a complete troop of Hemu's war elephants numbering about twenty in total also began to retreat, the archers and musketeers in their howdahs swivelling round as they did so to fire from the rear. Others simply threw down their weapons in surrender. However, Akbar could see that a little over half a mile away about a thousand of Hemu's troops – mostly horsemen – were fighting stoutly around some fallen elephants, using the carcasses as barricades and making sorties to push the Moghul attackers back. Victory was not yet his.

Before Bairam Khan could say anything, Akbar kicked his horse into a gallop and made for the group. As he galloped nearer, his bodyguard trailing behind him, some of Hemu's men seemed to recognise him. Led by an orange-turbaned officer on a tall white horse, they rode out from behind the protection of the corpses of the elephants to attack him. Akbar did not attempt to turn aside but galloped harder towards them, blood singing in his ears. Moghul musket fire brought down some of his enemies but the officer came on unscathed.

Akbar had by now outdistanced his bodyguard by at least fifty yards. Sword extended in front of him, he rode for the officer. The man swerved out of the way and slashed at Akbar, who ducked in his turn. The steel sword hissed just over Akbar's head, severing the peacock plume from his helmet. Both men turned their horses as tightly as they could and rode hard at each other again. This time, the officer's sword skidded off Akbar's gilded breastplate, and Akbar was knocked sideways. He lost one of his stirrups and only just managed to stay in the saddle. Hemu's officer wheeled his rearing horse to face him once more. Seemingly confident that he was getting the upper hand, he rashly tried to finish the fight at once, attempting to decapitate Akbar by aiming a swinging sword stroke at his throat.

Anticipating his move, Akbar dodged aside at the last moment, but the very tip of the sword nicked his throat above his Adam's apple. Oblivious of this wound, Akbar thrust his sword deep into the officer's right armpit, which he had left exposed as he lifted his arm high to slash wildly at Akbar's neck. The man fell from his white horse and lay on the ground, scarlet blood seeping from his armpit into the stony dirt. Sweating and breathing hard but relieved to be alive, Akbar looked round and saw that his bodyguard had accounted for the rest of the men who had accompanied the officer on his courageous but hopeless charge. Ahead of him some of Hemu's troops were kicking their horses and turning to flee from behind the barricades, while others were surrendering.

Akbar jumped from the saddle and ran over to the orange-turbaned officer who was still alive. Kneeling, he raised him slightly in his arms. 'You fought well,' he said.

'I recognised you as the young Emperor Akbar. I wanted to revenge my master Hemu on you,' the officer responded, the words coming with difficulty.

'How do you mean, revenge Hemu on me?'

The wounded man drew a wheezing breath and tried to speak, but at first only blood, not words, came from his mouth. Finally he succeeded in saying, 'One of your archers' arrows wounded my master in the eye just after we had vanquished your right wing. He lies mortally stricken over there, tended by the last of those who, like me, formed his personal guard.'

More blood oozed between the man's teeth and dribbled from his lips, and his head lolled back. He was clearly dead. Akbar laid his body gently back on the ground. His own bodyguards were now surrounding him, and he told them, 'See to it that this man receives the proper funeral rites according to his religion. Even if misguided in his loyalty, he fought well.'

As he realised that total victory was his, a broad smile creased Akbar's dirt-streaked face. He had succeeded in his first test. His future – the empire's future – was bright. His next campaigns would be of conquest as he expanded his empire. Akbar could see Bairam Khan riding towards him but as he drew nearer he saw that the *khan-i-khanan*'s expression was less triumphant than he might have expected.

'Why, Akbar, did you join the fight when I said we should stay where we could direct the action?' Bairam Khan began unceremoniously.

Akbar's face fell and he felt resentment surge within him. He was the emperor, even if Bairam Khan was his regent and his commander-in-chief. How dare the man speak to him like that, spoiling his moment of victory in this, his first battle as emperor? His grandfather Babur had led armies at his age. Yet how could he forget how much he owed to Bairam Khan? He bit back his anger and replied simply, 'Would you rather have an emperor who in battle felt the chill of cowardice rather than the exhilaration of hot blood and the impulse to action?'

A smile did now lighten Bairam Khan's stern features. 'No, Majesty, I dare say not.'

'This officer told me before he died that Hemu lies wounded over there, concealed behind the bodies of some of his war elephants. Let us investigate.'

Flanked by bodyguards with drawn swords, Bairam Khan and Akbar walked over to the corpses of the elephants. A foul stench was already coming from the body of one whose intestines had been mangled by a cannon ball. As Bairam Khan and Akbar passed another it suddenly moved its head and lashed its trunk in pain. Akbar's hand instinctively went to his sword but then he saw that the animal was in its death agonies from a great gash in its neck around which blue-green flies were clustering.

'Put the poor beast out of its misery,' he commanded one of his bodyguards, 'and do the same for any others that cling to life.' As he gave these orders Akbar saw that in the remains of an elephant's gilded howdah a few yards away a young man was bending over the body of a small figure in engraved steel armour which from its magnificence could only belong to Hemu. The youth was using a bloodstained cloth to dab at the left side of the face of the wounded man, who was shouting at him, 'Leave me to die. I would rather do so now on the battlefield than in some Moghul dungeon in a few days' time.'

'Seize that youth,' ordered Bairam Khan.

Immediately two tall bodyguards strode forward and, grabbing his arms, pulled him backwards from the body. With the attendant out of the way, Akbar could see the wounded man more clearly. The broken-off shaft of an arrow jutted from where his left eye had been, and blood was seeping down his face. His agony must have been extreme, but he looked almost relieved when Akbar asked, 'Are you Hemu?'

'Of course. Who else?'

'What have you to say to your rightful emperor?'

'That I have no rightful emperor and that I defy you, Moghul invader.' Hemu aimed a gob of bloody spittle towards Akbar but it fell short.

'Execute him at once, Majesty,' said Bairam Khan.

Akbar raised his sword but something made him hesitate to strike at the small, bleeding figure before him. 'Wait a moment. My father Humayun always taught me that mercy often befitted a monarch better than harsh violence . . .'

Hearing this, Hemu half-struggled to his feet and made towards Akbar, but two of Akbar's guards seized him at once. With a strength that belied both his puny frame and his severe wound, Hemu bucked and strained and struggled so much that he broke free for an instant. Staggering towards Akbar, he shouted, 'You blight and ravish our lands. You boast of your family's descent from the tyrant Timur, yet you cannot even be sure who your own father was. I hear tell your father prostituted your mother to his generals to ensure their loyalty and that she – camel-faced whore that she is – enjoy—'

Hemu got no further. With one slash of his sword, Akbar severed his head. Shaking with rage, his face spattered with Hemu's hot blood, he could not speak for some moments, but then, wiping his face with a cloth and sheathing his sword, he turned to Bairam Khan, his voice once more composed. 'You are right. We should not be merciful to the undeserving. Display this creature's body around the camp. Send his head to Delhi and set it up to rot in one of the public squares as a lesson to all other potential rebels.'

As Akbar was turning away with Bairam Khan to head back towards his own camp, Adham Khan approached. He had a bandage round the knuckles of his left hand, which had clearly suffered a cut, but seemed otherwise unscathed. Yet he too appeared less elated than Akbar thought might have been likely in this hour of victory. 'You fought well, my milk-brother. I was watching some of your deeds.'

'I hear you tasted blood too, killing the head of Hemu's bodyguard. But I've sad news to report to you and Bairam Khan. Tardi Beg is dead.'

'What? . . . How did he die?'

'When you instructed me to gather some of his troops to feign flight back towards your position, I and my men fought our way towards his command post. As we reached it, we saw from a distance that all but a very few of his bodyguard were sprawled on the ground, dead or wounded. He himself was unhorsed and surrounded by a group of Hemu's men whom he was trying valiantly to fight off. As we got nearer, hoping to save him, we heard one of his attackers calling on him to surrender. "No," Tardi Beg shouted. "I am a man of honour, true to my emperor." With that he rushed at his enemies a last time and I saw one spear him through the abdomen with a lance. As he lay impaled, twitching and clutching his guts, another of Hemu's men pulled back his head and slit his throat like a slaughterer does to an animal.'

'You died bravely, Tardi Beg, my brother, my *tugan*. May your soul rest tonight in Paradise,' murmured Bairam Khan. 'I am sorry I ever doubted you.'

After a long pause, Akbar spoke to Bairam Khan. 'In the case of Tardi Beg it was good not to execute or banish him, wasn't it? I was wrong to contemplate mercy for Hemu, but it was correct to extend it to Tardi Beg to allow him to vindicate his honour in battle.

28

My father was right, wasn't he? Mercy has as much place in the armoury of a great ruler as severity.'

'Yes, Majesty,' said Bairam Khan, and Akbar saw that a tear was running down his commander-in-chief's face.

Chapter 3

Manhood

In the palace fortress of Lahore, Akbar looked down from the marble dais. He was sitting on the high-backed throne that at Bairam Khan's suggestion he had ordered to be cast from melted-down gold coin from Hemu's treasure chests. The throne had accompanied Akbar everywhere during his six-month-long imperial progress through Hindustan. The idea of showing himself to his people in the aftermath of his triumph had been his own, but Bairam Khan had helped him orchestrate an awesome display of Moghul power.

The progress had delivered everything Akbar had hoped. How powerful, how proud, he had felt to ride at its head on his favourite black stallion with the gold-mounted saddle and bridle, wearing his father's gleaming breastplate and Alamgir at his side. Next to him had been Bairam Khan and immediately behind them those commanders who had especially distinguished themselves in the battle against Hemu, including Adham Khan his milk-brother. After that – keeping in time with the martial cacophony of trumpets and kettledrums – had come the squadrons of horsemen, green pennants fluttering and steel-tipped lances erect, then the archers, musketmen and artillerymen, some mounted and some on foot. Behind had rumbled the wagonloads of booty seized from Hemu's camp – sacks of coin, chests of jewels, bales of silks – protected by a special detachment of guards.

A quarter of a mile further behind, so that the dust rising from the road should not dim the spectacle, had followed the swaying glittering trumpeting mass of Akbar's war elephants in their steel-plate armour, some with blunted scimitars tied to their red-painted tusks. In battle those blades would be honed to a deadly sharpness, but these were merely for show. With the elephants captured from Hemu, Akbar now had over six hundred. Next trundled the gun carriages and the bullock wagons bearing Akbar's bronze cannon, then the huge baggage train carrying all the paraphernalia – tents, cooking pots, food and fuel – for the imperial encampment.

Often the crowds jostling for a sight of the Moghul procession as it passed had been so numerous that soldiers had had to hold them back with their spear shafts. Even in the remote countryside, people had come running from their fields to view the spectacle and make their obeisance. All the same, Akbar had been glad when it was finally over. It had been his particular wish that it should end here, in Lahore – the city which two years ago, on a balmy February day in 1555, his father Humayun had entered in triumph on his way to reconquer Hindustan. Akbar had been at his side and could recall everything, from the gleam of the gold thread and pearl-encrusted saddlecloth of the elephant on which they had been riding to the exultant expression on his father's face as he had turned to smile at him.

Out of respect for his father, he had ordered every detail replicated for his own entrance into Lahore, which he had made last night as the sky had crimsoned to the west. Now, gazing from his high throne on the rows of chieftains prostrated before him in the formal greeting of the *korunush*, Akbar felt a deep satisfaction. As news of the Moghul victory over Hemu had spread, they had not been able to declare their allegiance to him fast enough. Every day riders had arrived bearing unctuous messages and extravagant gifts – matched pairs of hunting dogs, doves with jewelled collars and feathers dyed in rainbow hues, jade-hilted daggers, muskets with ivory-inlaid stocks, solid gold emerald-studded incense burners and tortoiseshell boxes of fragrant frankincense – even a great ruby that its owner ingratiatingly explained had been a family heirloom for over five centuries.

He had accepted these treasures graciously but he was already shrewd enough to know that often the more lavish the present, the greater the treachery the giver had probably been contemplating. After consulting Bairam Khan, Akbar had decided to summon these supposedly loyal allies to await him at Lahore.

'You may rise.'

The sixty or so men, some sleek and plump in robes of silk and brocade in every colour from sapphire blue to saffron yellow, others – chieftains from the mountains – in coarse-woven tunics and trousers, got to their feet and waited, hands folded and heads bowed.

'I thank you for answering my summons and for your oaths of loyalty. I recall the oaths made to my father when he too passed through Lahore not long ago. Indeed, I recognise many of you.' Akbar allowed his gaze to roam slowly along the lines. Bairam Khan had briefed him well. He knew that among these chieftains were at least ten who had sworn allegiance to his father but on his death had immediately ceased sending the tribute they owed. Two had even made approaches to Hemu. They must be wondering how much Akbar knew. Did that pockmarked, pot-bellied chieftain from near Multan, who had just presented him with a fine chestnut stallion and was now regarding the carpet beneath his feet so studiously, suspect that in Akbar's possession was proof of his treachery? Ahmed Khan's men had intercepted one of his officers carrying a letter to Hemu.

On the road to Lahore, Akbar had spent many hours debating with Bairam Khan and his counsellors how best to handle those whose loyalty had been found wanting. Some had argued that in the days of his grandfather Babur there would have been no mercy. The guilty would have been stretched on the stone of execution to be crushed by the foot of an elephant until their stomachs ruptured and their intestines spilled, or else flayed alive or torn apart by stallions. But yet again – just as with Tardi Beg – Akbar could not forget the words his father had been so fond of saying to him: 'Any man can be vengeful. Only the truly great can be merciful.'

Akbar had heard enough court gossip to know that some – perhaps even his mother Hamida – believed Humayun had sometimes carried magnanimity too far. Yet instinct told Akbar his father had often been right. The Moghuls would always be warriors who would not hesitate to spill blood when necessary. But if they were to succeed in Hindustan they must rule by respect as well as fear. Too much killing led to too many blood feuds. Bairam Khan, listening gravely to the arguments and, as was his habit, saying little at first, had eventually agreed with him but had added a warning. 'Remember this. Know your enemies and listen to what our spies tell you. If, despite your attempts at reconciliation, they persist in their treachery then wipe them from the face of the earth.'

Akbar brought his mind back to the present. None of those before him seemed anxious to catch his eye. It was time to frighten them a little and he had prepared his words with care. 'I know why you are here. You perceive that the winds of war have blown in my favour. It was not luck that made this happen. My ancestor Timur conquered Hindustan and so gave the Moghuls an inalienable right to these lands. My grandfather Babur asserted that right, as did my father and as do I. Any man who challenges it will pay a heavy price, as Hemu discovered.' Here Akbar paused and then, speaking in a firm, clear voice, he said, 'Despite your fine words and gifts, I know that many of you have been traitors to me. Perhaps, even now, you are contemplating treachery. Look at me, all of you, so that I can see into your eyes.'

Slowly, the assembled chiefs raised their heads. All looked anxious, even the ones who were probably innocent of any wrong-doing. Young as he was, Akbar had learned enough from his father's struggles to know that most men craved power. Of those standing awkwardly before him, some visibly sweating, there could be few who had not at least thought of defecting from the Moghuls at some point during Hemu's rebellion.

'I have evidence that several among you have plotted against me. At a single word from me, my guards stand ready to mete out justice.' He saw the chieftains' eyes turn to the green-robed, black-turbaned men positioned on either side of the dais. 'Since I rode into Lahore I have been asking myself what I should do . . .' Akbar paused. The pockmarked man had started to shake. 'But I am young. My reign is young. I do not want to spill more blood, and so I have decided to be merciful. I will forget past transgressions and look to you — as I do to all in my empire — to give me your undivided loyalty. Do this and you will find me generous. If you do not, nothing will save you.'

As Akbar rose, the chieftains prostrated themselves once more, but not before he had seen the relief in many eyes. He felt pleased with himself. His voice had rung out clearly and he hadn't stumbled over his words. And he had sensed his power. With a single gesture he could have had any of them killed instantly. He had known it and they had known it. It was exhilarating to realise that he could alter the course of men's lives and it had made him wish to be generous. That was why on impulse — without having discussed it with his councillors or with Bairam Khan — he had decided to pardon the offenders. He had seen Bairam Khan start with surprise at his words and then frown. But Bairam Khan didn't seem to understand how his confidence had been growing. He still treated him as a mere youth. Though Akbar trusted Bairam Khan above all others, an insidious thought had begun squirming in his brain — that perhaps his regent had become so enamoured of power he couldn't bear to relinquish it . . .

Akbar was still musing when later that night, returning to his apartments, he saw an old woman waiting outside with his *qorchi*. 'Majesty, this woman has been appointed the *khawajasara,* keeper of the *haram* here in the palace, and she wishes to speak to you,' said the squire.

The old woman's raisin eyes were still bright in her wrinkled face and there was a smile on her lips. 'I served your father, Majesty, and I tended his concubines when he was a young prince,' she began. Then she paused, and it seemed to Akbar that she was scrutinising him with some interest.

'Have you something you wish to say to me?' The night air seemed hot and heavy, and Akbar was tired. For a reason he couldn't quite fathom, he felt uneasy under her penetrating gaze.

'Majesty, you now have many women in the *haram* here, sent in recent weeks by chieftains and rulers wishing to win your favour.

You have a physique that is the envy of many grown men and admired by every woman. I thought you might wish me to send one of the girls to you, or perhaps you would prefer to choose one for yourself?'

Akbar stared at her, blushing and shifting from foot to foot. It was a standing joke of his milk-brother Adham Khan that although nearly fifteen Akbar hadn't yet lost his virginity. Plenty of young women – even his mother's attendants – had tried to catch his eye in recent months. Each time he had felt bashful. He wasn't quite sure why. Was it because as emperor he didn't wish to appear inexperienced or foolish in front of anyone, even a concubine? Yet time was moving on. He had fought his first battle as emperor and was becoming a man. It was time to enjoy a man's pleasures and also to satisfy the curiosity that Adham Khan's endless smutty jokes and boasts of his own sexual prowess had roused in him. The *khawajasara*'s eyes were still fixed on him and he sensed that she too knew he'd not yet been with a woman.

'Let me choose for you, Majesty,' she said.

Akbar hesitated, but with pulses racing and a hardening in his groin, only for a moment. 'Very well,' he said in what he hoped was a measured, experienced manner.

'Will you come to the *haram*, Majesty?'

Akbar thought about all the eyes and ears that would be watching and listening if he did. The *haram* here in the Lahore palace was where all the women of the imperial household were lodged, including his mother, his aunt and his milk-mother. At the thought of their amused speculations, however affectionate, he flushed again, ardour cooling. Then he made up his mind. Now was the time. 'No. Send her here, to my apartments.'

The old woman padded briskly away down the long corridor, torchlight from sconces on the walls lighting her way. Perhaps she had been a beauty once, maybe even one of his father's concubines. Akbar had often heard that before his marriage to Hamida, whom he had loved to the exclusion of all others, Humayun had been a great lover of women, with many concubines.

Dismissing his attendants, he waited alone, pacing his apartments

36

gripped by a mixture of excitement and apprehension. As the minutes passed his nervousness began to get the upper hand. He would send word to the *haram* that he had changed his mind, he decided. He was just moving towards the tall double doors of polished mulberry when they opened and his *qorchi* stepped inside. 'Majesty, the girl is here. The keeper of the *haram* says she is a former concubine of the Raja of Talkh who prized her greatly and sent her hoping she would please you also. Her name is Mayala. Shall I send her in?'

Akbar nodded. A moment later a tall, slim form wrapped in a hooded dark purple robe slipped in through the doors, which closed behind her. The hood was pulled low so her face was in shadow as she came towards him and knelt. Akbar hesitated, then took her hands and pulled her gently to her feet. She stood motionless before him but he could hear her soft, rapid breathing. As he pushed back her hood, long black hair gleaming like silk spilled out and he caught the scent of jasmine. She was still looking down but now he took her face in his hands and raised it.

Eyes black as ebony gazed back at him and her full lips, reddened with the salve he had seen his mother apply, were smiling. After a few moments, as if she sensed his uncertainty, she gently guided his hands to the silver clasps of her robe between her breasts. As he released them, her robe fell to the floor and lay in a dark pool around her. Beneath she was naked except for a golden chain set with tiny rubies around her slender waist. Her hips were voluptuous, her breasts round and high, the nipples rimmed with henna.

As Akbar stood motionless, lost for words, she stepped back. Running her hands through the magnificent veil of hair that fell almost to her buttocks, she revolved slowly before him. 'I think you like me, Majesty,' she whispered. Akbar nodded. She stepped towards him and he felt her begin slowly, teasingly, to loosen his own garments until he too was naked. After gazing at his taut and muscular body for a moment, she smiled. 'Come, Majesty. Be my stallion.' Placing her fingers on his arm she led him to the bed, and when he lay down beside her she took his hand and guided it between her thighs. 'See, Majesty, the *mandir mandal,* the moist temple of love, which soon you will enter. This is what you must do . . .'

37

Six hours later, Akbar was lying on his back, the girl beside him, both their bodies beaded with sweat. She was sleeping now, arms and legs spread, her breasts rising and falling and her lips half parted. As he turned his head to watch her, he thought how strange it was that in such a brief time his life had changed for ever. She had introduced him into a whole new world of sensual experience in which to lose himself. They had already made love three times, from his first, tentative, then eager thrustings and almost instant climax when, under her instruction, he had pulled himself on top of her, to the other more subtle, imaginative and slightly longer-lasting ways she had begun to teach him, which seemed to give her as much sublime pleasure as him. At the thought, desire rose within him again. Reaching out, he stroked the soft velvet curve of her hip. Sleepily Mayala opened her dark eyes, then smiled languorously. No one would ever doubt his manhood, thought Akbar, young hips thrusting joyously and vigorously as he mounted her once more.

◆

The Jumna river curling away beneath the walls of the Agra fort was a faint gleam in the light of the new moon but as Akbar walked the battlements he barely noticed the beauty of the night. Over two years had passed since his triumphant progress through Hindustan after defeating Hemu. Ten days ago, on 15 October, he had celebrated his seventeenth birthday in this great brick and sandstone fortress with its courtyards, fountains and lofty *durbar* hall. His decision to make Agra – not Delhi, 120 miles upstream to the north – his capital had been deliberate. Agra had been his grandfather Babur's capital and it would have been his father Humayun's had death not robbed him of it. His mother, aunt and milk-mother had all approved his decision, as had his commanders and councillors. Only Bairam Khan had been against it, insisting that Delhi was better placed strategically to deal with any revolts or invasions. Not wanting to be seen to argue with the emperor in public, he had come to Akbar's private apartments, but Akbar had refused to be swayed, adamant that he was the emperor and of an age to take his own decisions. Bairam

Khan had stalked out pale-faced from the first real dispute they had ever had.

At the recollection, Akbar frowned. Matters hadn't improved over the intervening months. He was finding Bairam Khan increasingly irksome and interfering. It seemed that as he himself was gaining in confidence and seeking a greater role in governing, Bairam Khan was actively trying to frustrate him. With every rebuff his conviction that he must be free to take the government into his own hands was growing.

So far he had kept his thoughts to himself, conscious of all Bairam Khan had done to secure the fragile boundaries of his empire, but the need to confide in someone – someone he could trust completely – was growing overwhelming. Perhaps his mother with her astute mind would know how to advise him? Descending the winding stone staircase from the battlements he made his way through a flower-filled courtyard to the main *haram* where Hamida, as befitted the mother of the emperor, had the best apartments, with a balcony projecting out over the Jumna where she could catch the refreshing breezes. Tonight, though, the air was cool and he found her in her sleeping chamber, which was lit by oil lamps and wicks burning in *diyas,* saucers of scented oil placed in carved niches in the walls. She was reading her favourite book of Persian poems but put it aside when he entered.

'How is it with my son?' The warm sandalwood scent of her enveloped him as she embraced him. When he didn't answer, she stepped back and looked hard into his face. 'What is it? You look troubled.'

'I am, Mother.'

'Sit down and tell me.'

Hamida listened intently as he poured out his pent-up grievances and his frustrations. When he had finished she sat for a moment in silence, a frown puckering her still beautiful forehead beneath a thin gold circlet set with emeralds and pearls – one of his father's last gifts to her. When at last she looked at him, her expression was sombre.

'Even if some of your complaints are justified, how can you forget

39

what Bairam Khan has done for our family? Perhaps I need to remind you. After your father saved his life in battle, Bairam Khan pledged himself to fighting for the Moghuls. Even when our fortunes were bleakest he kept faith with us, though he could easily have returned to Persia, to the shah's service. After your father's death, as you very well know, his determination and courage saved you and our dynasty.'

'I know, but . . .'

Hamida held up her hand to silence him. 'It is natural, now that you are becoming a man, that his guidance irks you, and it is true that he can sometimes seem overbearing. But it's far better to have an adviser who does not scruple to speak the truth than one who drips honeyed agreement with your every whim. You must learn patience. When you are eighteen will be the time to think of taking power fully into your own hands and ruling without a regent. Until then, wait, watch and learn. It is only since the victory over Hemu that you have shown any interest in government. Before that, however hard I and Bairam Khan tried, you weren't interested. When there were council meetings you knew you should attend, you played truant, going off to race camels or hawking with Adham Khan. Even now you spend more time with your women than studying the real needs of your empire. I don't blame you. The pleasures of the *haram* are sweet. A young man needs to satisfy his desires and it must be flattering to have so many women competing to fulfil your every wish. But ask yourself whether you are truly ready to take full control or whether it is just the arrogance and impetuosity of youth speaking.'

'I am ready . . .'

'No, don't interrupt. Listen. That is exactly what I meant about too much haste. And perhaps your impatience – your lack of concentration – is why you still cannot read. Every tutor we appointed to teach you gave up in despair. Bairam Khan himself tried to instruct you but you wouldn't attend. Your father and his father before him were scholars as well as warriors. A good ruler should be in command of everything, including himself.'

'That's unfair.' Why had she changed the subject? How many times had he tried to explain to her that, whenever he looked at a page, the words seemed to move about, becoming such a jumble he couldn't make sense of them? But this was something his mother, a great reader herself, couldn't seem to grasp. He rose to his feet. His conversation with Hamida had not gone as he had intended. The sooner it was ended the better. He had expected her unquestioning support and instead she had first attacked, then side-tracked him. 'Thank you for your advice,' he said stiffly.

'Akbar, don't be offended. I spoke only for your own good. You will be a great emperor and I am so proud of you. You excel with every weapon. There is no better archer, rider, wrestler or swordsman than you. You are fearless, open-hearted and generous in spirit. You have the ability to make your people love you. But you must learn to be patient and tread carefully with those closer to you who do not immediately bow to your will. And above all, remember whom you have to thank for so much of the good that has come to you.'

Akbar stood silent and straight-backed as she got up and kissed his forehead. Dismay that she thought him heedless and ungrateful mingled with anger that, like Bairam Khan, she too should treat him like a thoughtless, pleasure-loving youth, grabbing for power he didn't yet fully comprehend, never mind merit. Flinging open the doors himself, he strode quickly back to his own apartments. He shouldn't resent his mother's words but he couldn't help it. Why didn't she understand? She had let him down.

He was still brooding when, a little later, his *qorchi* entered. 'What is it?'

'Maham Anga asks that you visit her.'

What did his milk-mother want? a surly-faced Akbar wondered as he approached the silverleaf-covered doors leading to her apartments. Perhaps Hamida had asked Maham Anga to join her in urging patience and moderation on him. If so, their meeting would be short – he didn't need another lecture. But Maham Anga's face as she greeted him showed only affection and concern.

'These past weeks I've noticed you've looked troubled, and my attendants tell me that earlier this evening you left your mother's apartments abruptly, as if in anger. Akbar, what is wrong?' Her clear, hazel eyes looked into his and her voice was as softly coaxing as when he'd been a child. She had always listened to him, always understood . . . He found himself pouring out his grievances anew. She listened attentively and without interrupting, just occasionally nodding her head. When at last he fell silent, Maham Anga's first question was, 'What did your mother say when you told her this?'

'Just to be patient.'

'She is right, of course. It isn't wise to act precipitately and you still have much to learn.' His milk-mother was going to agree with his mother, thought Akbar. But then Mahan Anga continued, 'That is why I wished to talk to you. I too have been growing anxious. I see that you are becoming ready to rule and that Bairam Khan – great man though he is – does not wish to acknowledge it.'

'He doesn't wish to give up his power. Since my father's death he's been emperor in all but name . . .' The words came rushing out. 'Now he feels his power slipping from him. He resents it when I assert myself, like when I decided to move my capital here, to Agra.'

'Perhaps he does think of himself as emperor. I know he makes appointments to imperial posts from among his followers without securing your permission. What is more, I hear,' she said, dropping her voice as she went on, 'he has recently been exercising even more of an emperor's privileges. Akbar, there is something you should know, but first you must promise to tell no one that this information came from me.'

'Of course. What did you mean about Bairam Khan and an emperor's privileges?'

'I am told he has been enriching himself from the imperial treasuries. In particular that he took a valuable diamond necklace with a jewelled peacock for its clasp from booty found in Hemu's camp after your great victory at Panipat. Hemu's vizier had listed it in his ledgers as among his master's greatest treasures but none of your officials could find it. As a result, some soldiers who were supposed to have been guarding the chests of booty were flogged for their negligence.'

'And you are certain that Bairam Khan took it?'

'Yes. At first I didn't believe the stories – unfounded rumours always abound at court, and in particular in the *haram* where sometimes there is little to do but gossip. But several weeks ago your milk-brother said he had a story that would amuse me. He told me of a concubine who until recently had been in Bairam Khan's *haram* and had seen this necklace with her own eyes – indeed she had worn it. It seems that Bairam Khan likes his favourite of the moment to wear it when naked in his presence. My son didn't realise the significance of his story – he just thought I'd laugh to hear about Bairam Khan's habits. I said nothing and he has no idea I recognised the necklace from his description.'

'I can't believe Bairam Khan would do such a thing.'

'Perhaps he doesn't see it as theft. Perhaps he thought it was his right. After all, he has been regent for four years, and power does strange things to people, Akbar.'

'But why take the necklace in secret? Why let others suffer?'

'A good question.'

Akbar thought for a moment. Maham Anga had no reason to lie. She had only mentioned the story after hearing of his concern. Bairam Khan was clearly becoming addicted to his power and the perquisites it brought. His mind was made up. 'Maham Anga, what you have said convinces me even more that I must break his hold over me.'

'In the time of your grandfather and father, a man would have paid with his life for deceiving the emperor.'

'What?' Akbar stared at her aghast. 'No. There is no question of that. I owe Bairam Khan everything and I would still trust him with my life. I do not even begrudge him the diamond necklace, however splendid. But I must be rid of his power over me. I must rule myself.'

Maham Anga seemed to reflect for a moment. 'Well then . . . When your father wished to be rid of your traitorous uncles he sent them on the pilgrimage to Mecca. Bairam Khan is in Delhi at the moment inspecting the defences, isn't he? Send a letter to him there. Tell him how much you value his devotion to your interests but say that you fear he has been exhausting himself in the service of the empire. Say that you wish him to make the *haj* so that his mind and body may be refreshed and he may pray for the security and prosperity of the empire he has done so much to establish. You are the emperor. He must obey.'

Akbar leaned back against a bolster of dark orange silk and pondered. Maham Anga's suggestion for getting rid of Bairam Khan was a good one. It would take him well over a year to complete the pilgrimage. He would have to travel to the coast of Gujarat, to the pilgrim port of Cambay, and there take ship to Arabia. At the other end, he would face a long overland journey through the desert to Mecca. By the time Bairam Khan eventually returned, Akbar would have taken control of every aspect of the government. He would be able to send his mentor into comfortable retirement on some rich estates that he would find for him.

But at the same time, another part of Akbar's brain told him such a plan was dishonourable. He owed it to Bairam Khan to ride to Delhi and tell him face to face how he felt. Yet he had already tried that a dozen times. On each occasion, Bairam Khan had turned the conversation, leaving him outmanoeuvred. If he had his mother's support in confronting him, it might be different, but Hamida had made her feelings clear . . . wait, wait, wait . . . . Perhaps it was time to show her as well as Bairam Khan that he had come of age, that he could think and act for himself.

'Maham Anga, be my scribe and write to Bairam Khan just as you said. But be sure to add also that I will always honour him . . . that he has been like a father to me.'

'Of course.' Akbar watched Maham Anga go to a low, brass-inlaid rosewood table on which stood a jade inkpot and a quill and sit down cross-legged before it. Within moments, candlelight flickering over her strong, handsome features, she was penning the letter he hoped would set him free. He knew he could trust her to get the words right.

Chapter 4

A Gift of Concubines

'How could you have been so unthinking and ungrateful towards Bairam Khan!' Hamida seized Akbar by the shoulders. 'Who put you up to this?'

'No one.' He had no intention of revealing Maham Anga's role. She had only had his interests at heart, and anyway it had been his decision and his alone. For a moment Akbar thought Hamida was going to slap his face. Never had he seen her so angry.

'You couldn't even wait to tell him on his return from Delhi, which wouldn't have been long. Worse, you didn't have the courage to tell me but went off hunting and left me to find out from a letter from Bairam Khan himself!'

Akbar flushed at the truth of her words. Immediately after affixing his seal to the letter and despatching his messenger to Delhi he had set off on a four-day tiger-hunting expedition. If he was honest, his decision had had far more to do with his reluctance to face his mother than any desire for the thrill of the sport. He had been intending to tell her immediately on his return . . . had even practised the words in his head. But it seemed he had miscalculated the speed with which a messenger could travel between Agra and Delhi. Hamida had been waiting for him in his apartments.

'What did Bairam Khan write?'

'That without warning or explanation you had ordered him on

the *haj* and that he regretted he had been unable to say farewell in person. I immediately wrote urging him to return to court. My messenger reached him while he was still only a few days' ride beyond Delhi. This was his reply, listen.' Voice shaking with emotion, she read: '"You are very gracious, Majesty, to ask me to return but I cannot. Your son, the emperor, has seen fit to order me on the *haj*. Just as I was ever loyal to your husband, who saved my life in battle, so I must be to your son. May God bless your house and may it rise to yet greater glory in Hindustan." Bairam Khan was the best friend, the best adviser you had, Akbar. Instead of being grateful, you have rejected and insulted him, unceremoniously dismissing him as if he were a negligent groom.'

'I will always be grateful to him, but he doesn't understand that I am ready to rule – and nor do you. When he returns he will see how well I have succeeded and I will give him an honourable place at my court.' Akbar spoke firmly, even though his own doubts – unexpressed to anyone – about the dimissal of Bairam Khan and the way he had done it were welling inside him, however much he tried to ignore them. Had he been wrong? Perhaps for the first time in his life he began to query one of his decisions as his mother continued to rebuke him.

'You have so much to learn. What makes you think a proud man like Bairam Khan would risk further humiliation at your hands? He will not return to us, and that will be your loss.'

But even while Hamida was still speaking, Akbar saw Maham Anga's face before him. She was one of his most trusted confidants, and she had agreed with Bairam Khan's dismissal . . . He must not allow his mother to weaken his resolve. If he recalled Bairam Khan he would find it even more difficult ever to assume imperial power. Besides, vacillating and showing weakness was not the way to impress – or to control – his nobles.

He looked away. Hamida hesitated a moment. 'You fool,' she whispered at last.

· ◆ ·

A month later, Akbar stirred in his sleep and moved a little closer to Mayala, whose warm, naked body was curled against his. Their love-making had been long and vigorous and now, in his semi-consciousness, a deep contentment seeped through him.

'Majesty . . . Majesty, wake up.' At the feel of a hand on his shoulder, he opened sleepy eyes to see the dry, wrinkled face of the keeper of the *haram* looking down at him.

'What is it?' Akbar looked instinctively for his dagger. Even in the *haram* the emperor must always be prepared for attack.

'A messenger has come. One of Ahmed Khan's scouts. He says he has news that will not wait.'

'Very well.' Akbar rose, wrapped a robe around him, thrust his feet into pointed red leather slippers and followed the old woman to the doors of the *haram*. Outside, beyond the guards by the entrance, he recognised the scout. He looked dirty and tired but what struck Akbar most was his expression. 'What is it?'

'Bad news, Majesty. About four weeks ago, Bairam Khan with ten of his men were attacked while out hunting near his camp on the banks of the Chambal river.'

'And Bairam Khan?' The blood was already draining from Akbar's face. He had guessed the answer.

'Killed, Majesty, along with all his hunting companions.'

'You are certain?'

'Yes. Others of his party discovered the bodies half hidden among the reeds along the Chambal.'

'I want to question them. I must know exactly what they found.'

'They are still on the road to Agra after attending to the funeral rites. I had the news from the post rider they had sent ahead, whom I encountered at a caravanserai in Dholpur. Learning who I was, he told me what had occurred and gave me this letter for you, written by Bairam Khan's senior officer.' The scout pulled a folded piece of paper from his dusty green leather satchel.

As Akbar opened it, a second folded note speckled red-brown in one corner fell to the ground. Akbar picked it up, then handed the first letter back to the scout. 'Read it to me.'

'"Majesty,"' the man began, '"it grieves me to report that Bairam

47

Khan has been murdered. We discovered his body and those of our comrades on the banks of the Chambal river. All had been killed by arrows, many shot in the back. In the case of Bairam Khan – and this is terrible to relate – the head had been hacked off. We found it some yards away at the edge of the water. All the bodies had been stripped of jewels, money and weapons. Though we searched for signs to tell us which way the attackers had gone, we could find none. Perhaps they fled by boat. As proof of what I relate I am sending a paper found on Bairam Khan's body."'

Slowly Akbar opened the second letter. He didn't need anyone to read it to him. He knew what it was – the order written by Maham Anga on his behalf to Bairam Khan to depart on the *haj*. He also knew what the dark brown stain was – Bairam Khan's blood.

· ◆ ·

Three hours later, from the balcony of his apartments Akbar watched the first shafts of sunlight warming the battlements of the Agra fort, but he didn't feel it. Instead he was shivering as if the world around him were coated with ice. He could scarcely believe Bairam Khan was dead. He would make sure the perpetrators were found and punished as savagely as they deserved, but wasn't he also guilty? If he hadn't broken with Bairam Khan and sent him away, he would still be alive. And what would his mother say? She had been angrier than he had ever seen her on hearing that he had dismissed his commander-in-chief. How would she react to his murder?

In the courtyard below he heard the timekeeper strike the brass disc that signalled the end of his watch. Soon the sun would be well above the horizon. He must not make the mistake of allowing Hamida to learn the news from anyone else as he had that of Bairam Khan's dismissal. He must go to her straight away. Splashing himself with water, he dressed quickly without the aid of his attendants whom in his black mood he had ordered not to disturb him and made his way to her apartments. Though it was barely past dawn, Hamida was already awake and he saw at once from her tear-streaked face that he was too late.

'Forgive me, Mother. You were right. I should never have sent

Bairam Khan away. God has punished me.' He waited for a torrent of anger to flow from her lips but she stood silent, eyes downcast.

'Bairam Khan was like a member of the family,' she said at last. 'His death cuts me to the heart. But I do not blame you for his murder and you should not blame yourself. You wanted to be free of his influence but you never meant him harm, I know that. Akbar . . .' She drew herself up. 'Discover everything you can about his murder. Find his killers – common bandits, hired assassins, whoever they are – find them and make them pay in blood for what they have done.'

'I will. I promise.' Akbar hesitated, half hoping, childlike, that she might embrace him, but her hands remained by her sides. He knew he was dismissed.

It was some time before he returned to his own quarters. Needing space and fresh air, he climbed to the battlements of the fort. The waters of the Jumna glinted amber in the early morning light but his mind's eye was filled with very different scenes – himself riding in triumph into Delhi with his father and Bairam Khan; Bairam Khan's hand resting on his shoulder as they stood by his father's grave; steel blades flashing as Bairam Khan taught him subtle Persian sword tricks, insisting Akbar try again and again until his technique was perfect; Bairam Khan's indigo eyes watching approvingly as he practised his musketry. How could he have ignored the bonds of trust between them and acted as he had? He had allowed himself to be influenced against Bairam Khan by Maham Anga because, thoughtlessly, selfishly, impetuously, he had wished to think badly of him because he wanted to rule. It was as simple as that.

At last, with the sun rising high into a pale blue sky patterned with clouds blowing in from the west, Akbar returned to his rooms. Almost at once he noticed an item he was sure hadn't been there earlier. Someone had placed what looked like a strip of material on top of the ivory and mother of pearl inlaid box in which Akbar kept some of his jewels. They had also taken the precaution of weighting the strip down with an ivory paperweight carved like a lotus flower. Picking up the material, Akbar saw it was a scrap of pale green silk with several lines of writing upon it. Here and there the author had allowed a few drops of blue ink to fall. It looked like the work of a child and he was about to toss it aside when some instinct told him not to. Instead, he took the piece of fabric out on to the balcony where the light was better. Why had the author chosen to write on silk not paper? Perhaps to disguise their handwriting, not that it made any difference to him, since he couldn't read it anyway. The more he looked, the more the thick, inky symbols seemed to dance about. Akbar summoned his *qorchi*.

'What does this say?'

The young man studied it for a moment then looked up, eyes startled. 'It's a warning, Majesty. It says, "Though a river of milk from the same breasts binds you, your milk-brother is not your friend. Ask Adham Khan what he knows about the murder of Bairam Khan."'

'You are certain that's what's written?' The *qorchi* nodded. 'Give it back to me.' Akbar tucked the piece of silk inside his tunic. 'Say nothing about this to anyone. It is just a piece of malice written by an enemy of Adham Khan.'

'Yes, Majesty.'

Akbar tried to put the odd message out of his mind, but couldn't. Whoever had written the warning had not had the courage to accuse Adham Khan openly. Why? Because they feared retribution or because they were trying to make mischief? Poison once poured out was hard to put back in the flask – some drops always escaped. Whatever the case, they had shattered his peace of mind, making him think the unthinkable – that the youth he had grown up with and loved as a brother might be his foe. After all, it had been Adham Khan's mother who had warned him against Bairam Khan. But he had just made one terrible error of judgement that had cost him a friend. He must not rashly make another.

• ◆ •

'Akbar, look! I told you my hawk was the best,' shouted Adham Khan. High above their heads, the bird swooped like an arrow on the pigeon it had been pursuing. 'I win!'

A few minutes later, Adham Khan held out his left arm and his yellow-eyed hawk landed on the elbow-length leather gauntlet, curved beak bloodied and more blood staining the leather jesses trailing from its legs. Still smiling triumphantly, he returned the bird to a wooden perch driven into the ground, tied the jesses to the plaited leather leash attached to the perch and placed a tufted cap inlaid with tiger eyes over the bird's head.

'I concede. Your hawk makes the faster kill,' said Akbar.

'I told you your new falconer hasn't been training your birds properly to follow the lure. Let mine have care of them for a few days, then you'll see the difference.' Adham Khan's wide-jawed, strong-featured face was split by a broad grin.

'Perhaps.' Akbar smiled back. It was as well that Adham Khan couldn't see into his mind, he thought. It was also good that his swaggering milk-brother was too conceited to wonder why Akbar had recently been seeking his company. In the aftermath of the victory over Hemu and the triumphal progress through Hindustan they had seen relatively little of each other, but as Akbar's doubts had grown about the cause of Bairam Khan's death he had deliberately invited Adham Khan hunting or hawking, or to join in games of polo on the banks of the Jumna. All the time, while seemingly focused only on the sport in hand, Akbar had been observing his milk-brother carefully, but Adham Khan had done or said nothing to rouse his suspicions. He was merely his usual boastful, ebullient self.

But in that case, whom had he so offended that they wished to damage him in Akbar's eyes with their scrawled note implying his complicity in Bairam Khan's death? Akbar frowned as he watched his milk-brother dig his heels into his horse's sides and canter over to where the falconers were waiting with fresh birds. Though he had offered a huge reward – enough to feed an entire village for ten years – even after three months there was still no intelligence about who had slaughtered Bairam Khan.

Thoughts of conspiracy – however shadowy and insubstantial – never left him, but he must learn patience. Across such a vast and in places untamed land as Hindustan, information took time to travel. Perhaps Ahmed Khan and his network of spies and scouts would soon have news. He had promised his mother he'd not rest until he'd found and punished the murderers and he would keep his word. Should he have told her about the curious warning on the piece of silk? he wondered yet again. Often he had been on the brink of it but each time had drawn back, fearing it would only distress and alarm her. And, of course, he could say nothing about it to Maham Anga either . . .

• ◆ •

The council meeting had seemed especially long and tedious. Akbar's head was aching and he wanted to hear nothing further about caravanserai construction or revenue gathering. But as he left the council chamber and made his way to the women's quarters his mood lightened. A few days ago, a new ally from the hill country beyond the Jhelum river had sent some concubines to join Akbar's *haram*. The party had reached Agra three nights ago and now Akbar was eager to see the women for himself. His first bashful though passionate love-making with Mayala seemed to belong to another life. She was still his favourite but he had found many other women to please him too. In the *haram* he felt free of court cares. At the thought of fresh pleasures ahead he quickened his step.

The elderly *khawajasara* was waiting for him and smilingly led him to a room hung with brilliant silks and ornaments of coloured glass that were also a gift from Akbar's new ally. 'The girls have been made ready and are eager to serve you. You have only to choose the one who pleases you the most.' She clapped her hands and a door in a side alcove opened. Three young women entered, dressed identically in tight-fitting bodices and wide trousers fastened at their waists with pearl tassels. Their dark hair, pulled back from their faces with jewelled clasps, gleamed with henna. Two were tall and voluptuous while the third was short and delicately formed. She was exquisite but something more than her beauty held Akbar's attention. She was standing very still and breathing rapidly like a deer that knows the hunter is there and is too afraid to move. Her vulnerability moved him and he felt a strong desire to show her she had nothing to fear from him.

52

'This one'

'She is called Shayzada. You have chosen well, Majesty.'

'Leave us, please.' As the keeper ushered the other girls from the room, Akbar saw Shayzada's eyes shining with tears. 'Don't be afraid. If you are not willing, say so. I would never force any woman.'

'I'm not afraid of you, Majesty.' She spoke the old Moghul language, Turki, but haltingly and with a strange accent Akbar had never heard.

'Then what is it?' He came closer, noting the delicate oval of her face and the unusual vivid blue of her eyes that for a moment reminded him of Bairam Khan. She looked so achingly beautiful he wanted to reach out and touch her. She hesitated, and when finally she spoke he could tell she was choosing her words with great care. 'When I was told I was to come to your court, it was a great honour and I was happy. So were my two elder sisters.'

'The two young women who were with you just now?'

'No, they are not my kin.'

'Then where are you sisters?'

Her face tightened. 'When our party was still two days from Agra, a group of Moghul soldiers stopped us. They said that they were an advance guard sent by you to inspect us and take the most beautiful to you at once. They said you were impatient and took my sisters away. When we reached Agra, I asked the keeper of the *haram* where they were but she said she knew nothing of any other women. Please, Majesty, I am frightened for my sisters . . .'

'I gave no orders for any advance guard. Who was their commander?'

'I'm not sure, but I think I heard one of the soldiers address him as Adham Khan.'

Akbar's head jerked back in surprise. 'Did you see any of their faces?'

'It was evening, and anyway the men had face cloths pulled up to their eyes.'

The tears were running down her face now and she made no effort to wipe them away, but Akbar, overcome with anger, was no longer attending to her. 'Wait here,' he said.

A few minutes later he was striding towards his milk-mother's apartments. Waving her attendants aside, he flung the silver doors open himself and burst in. Seeing the expression on his face, Maham Anga, who had been writing in a book, at once closed its ivory covers, fastened the gilt clasp and rose to her feet.

'Akbar, what's the matter?'

'Where is your son?'

'Away hunting. I haven't seen him for nearly a week.'

'Have him found — wherever he is — and tell him to return to the court immediately.'

'Of course. He is yours to command. But why?'

'A woman newly arrived in the *haram* — sent to me with several others as a token of respect and friendship by a new ally — accuses him of abducting two of them — her sisters.'

Maham Anga paled. If her son had committed such a crime she certainly knew nothing about it.

'The accusation is very serious,' Akbar said more gently, 'but let my milk-brother answer the charge. If he is innocent he has nothing to fear.'

'Of course.' Maham Anga put a hand on his arm. 'But, Akbar, there has been some mistake. My son would never . . .' Her voice faltered.

'Let us hope you are right.'

In fact, Akbar learned the fate of the missing young women three days before Adham Khan and his hunting party of other young nobles came riding up the ramp into the Agra fort in obedience to his summons. He was woken with news that two female bodies had been pulled from the Jumna river. A camel driver taking his beasts down to the water's edge to drink had found them. Both were naked, and their throats had been cut.

'What is it, Akbar? Why did you summon me to your apartments so late when I'm still tired and dusty from my journey?'

'Adham Khan, do your remember how we used to gallop our ponies through the meadows beneath the Kabul fortress?'

'Of course I do. But I don't see—'

'Those were good times. We seldom spent a day apart.'

54

'That is what a milk-brother is for.'

'It was more than that. I had no brothers or sisters of my own. Without you I would have been lonely. And when I was kidnapped from my parents by my uncles, your mother was my sole protector and you shared my captivity, suffered the same hardships, faced the same perils . . . That is what makes what I have to ask you so difficult. But we are no longer boys, and I am an emperor, and so I must.'

'What are you trying to say, Akbar?' Adham Khan's light brown eyes − so like Maham Anga's − were fixed on Akbar's face and his expression was no longer light-hearted.

'Three days ago, an old man − a camel driver − discovered the bodies of two young women floating in the river when he took his beasts to drink. He found a long stick and with its help dragged them to the bank and raised the alarm. The corpses weren't very pretty.' Akbar again saw before him the grazed, muddy bodies, already buzzing with flies, that he had insisted on viewing. Those staring eyes − a paler blue than Shayzada's − looking sightlessly out from purpling bloated faces, those gaping blood-encrusted throats, had somehow been more horrible than anything he'd witnessed on the battlefield.

Adham Khan shrugged slightly. 'I'm sorry to hear it, but what has this to do with me?'

'Be patient. I ordered my *hakim* to examine the bodies. He told me the cuts were deep and clean − probably inflicted with a sharp dagger − and that the women had not been dead for more than two or three days. He also said they had been raped.' Again Akbar's mind conjured the shameful scene: two young women, sent to what should have been a luxurious and pampered life at his court, lying blood-stained and violated on the *hakim*'s marble slab. 'Adham Khan, do you know who these women were?'

'Why should I?'

Akbar studied his milk-brother's indignant face. 'Are you certain?'

'Of course. Are you accusing me of killing them?'

'No. I'm only asking whether you knew them.'

'But why? Someone must have implicated me.'

'The women's sister, Shayzada, told me that as they were all on their way here their party was stopped by Moghul soldiers and her sisters were abducted. Shayzada heard one of the men address their commander as Adham Khan.'

'It's a lie. Someone must have bribed her to discredit me.'

'You swear to me, then, that neither you nor your men had anything to do with the abductions or the murders?'

'I swear as your milk-brother.' Adham Khan's strong hand grasped Akbar's. 'I would never violate the bond between us.'

'Then I accept what you say.'

'Where is this woman, Shayzada?'

'Here in the *haram*. I offered to send her home but she chose instead to serve my aunt who, moved by her story, has offered to take her into her household.'

Adham Khan said nothing but Akbar noticed the rapid rise and fall of his chest. 'You mustn't blame her, Adham Khan. She didn't know who you were when she named you and she must have been mistaken in what she thought she heard . . . it was understandable in the fear and confusion. I am certain she wasn't coerced or bribed to speak as she did. Now let's talk of pleasanter things. I've seen a roan stallion I'd like your opinion on . . .'

It was a relief to move on to ordinary topics. Though he'd had no choice, it had embarrassed him to question his milk-brother. Adham Khan's angry, earnest rebuttal had been a relief. All the same, Akbar knew that something had changed between them. The very fact of his asking Adham Khan to declare his innocence must surely mark the end of their old boyhood intimacy. But, as he had told his milk-brother, he was the emperor.

Chapter 5

Milk and Blood

On a humid May afternoon, Akbar slept, head cushioned by Mayala's soft, voluptuously rounded stomach, as a peacock-feather punkah pulled on a long rope by an attendant in an adjacent room stirred the hot air above them. They had just enjoyed a particularly exhausting and innovative bout of love-making and Akbar should have been dreaming of pleasurable things. Instead strange images filled his mind, causing him to stir and even cry out. Feeling a hand on his forehead he sat up with a start, but it was only Mayala trying to soothe him. It had been like this ever since the two young women's bodies had been found, though that was eight weeks ago now. Every day, despite himself, he was growing more preoccupied, more watchful, every instinct sensing a threat that seemed all the more dangerous because he didn't know when or from where it would come.

Akbar sat up and pushed back his black hair from his hot forehead. He felt Mayala kneel up behind him, pressing her naked breasts against his back and putting her arms round his neck. She was murmuring in his ear, something about a new position – the Coupling of the Lion – that might please him, but tempting as it was he gently disengaged himself and stood up. He had summoned his counsellors and courtiers to meet later that afternoon and before then he needed to think.

Since Bairam Khan's exile and death he had had no *khan-i-khanan*, no commander-in-chief. Even though he felt confident in his own judgement, it was time to select one and also to consider some other court appointments so that he could shed some of his more mundane responsibilities. At some point he must also appoint a vizier – a post it had not been necessary to fill while Bairam Khan was alive – but there was no particular hurry for that. Better to observe his counsellors carefully before making such an important decision. A corrupt or self-seeking vizier would be worse than no vizier at all. But he needed a new chief quartermaster urgently. The present one had, as a very young man, served Akbar's grandfather Babur. He was now so old he could scarcely stand and continually addressed Akbar as 'Babur', while mumbling wonderingly about how much he seemed to have changed. Akbar had also decided to revive the old Moghul post of master-of-horse to oversee the purchase of large numbers of horses for the campaigns of conquest he was planning.

He knew he must choose with care. Each of those posts conferred privileges and prestige on the holder, and all would be coveted. He had no doubt whom he wished to make *khan-i-khanan*. Ahmed Khan had demonstrated unflinching loyalty to the dynasty from the early days of Humayun's reign. He was also a shrewd military tactician. He had served Akbar's father through all his dangerous years of flight and exile and ridden at his shoulder from Kabul on the reconquest of Hindustan, as well as fighting with Akbar against Hemu. The choice of Ahmed Khan as *khan-i-khanan* might disappoint some of Akbar's generals but none could call Ahmed Khan unworthy.

But the post of chief quartermaster was problematic. The man he chose would be responsible for all the supplying of the Moghul army – from the corn to feed the horses to the gunpowder and cannon balls to feed the artillery. No other post except that of comptroller of the household, held by Humayun's one time *qorchi* and companion Jauhar in return for his years of selfless service, offered so many opportunities for corruption. When he had consulted his mother Hamida, she had suggested Atga Khan, an officer from Kabul who had escorted her to Delhi when Humayun had summoned her to join him in Hindustan. 'He is a wise and honourable man whose two daughters are in my service. He protected me on the long journey and will I am sure protect your interests as your quartermaster,' she had said, smooth brow knitted in thought. Following further enquiries – as discreet as he could make them – Akbar had decided to follow his mother's advice. It would please her, he knew.

As for his master-of-horse, Akbar had consulted no one but decided after much reflection to appoint his milk-brother. Adham Khan was an expert judge of horseflesh and it would be a way of demonstrating to all the court his confidence in his milk-brother despite the rumours that had inevitably bubbled up. Akbar knew from his *qorchi* that his questioning of Adham Khan about the deaths of the two young women was no secret.

Two hours later, to the customary blast of trumpets, Akbar entered his *durbar* hall through the arched door to the left of his throne – his gleaming golden throne forged from the molten gold of Hemu's treasuries that he had now set up in its permanent place. He had already vowed to himself to ornament it further with gems captured in future wars as a visible symbol of his greatness and success. Seating himself on the green velvet cushion, he signalled to his assembled councillors and courtiers to sit.

Before speaking, Akbar glanced up at the small grille high in the wall behind which he was sure Hamida would be sitting in the little gallery where women could watch and listen unseen. He thought he caught a glimpse of her. 'I summoned you here today because I have decided to make certain appointments. Ahmed Khan, Atga Khan and you, my milk-brother Adham Khan, approach.' As soon as all three men were before him, Akbar continued, 'Ahmed Khan, in recognition of your many years of service first to my father and now to me, I hereby appoint you my commander-in-chief, my *khan-i-khanan*.'

Ahmed Khan's smile above his long, wispy beard showed his pleasure. 'Majesty, I will serve you to the utmost of my ability.'

'I know you will. You will also retain responsibility for intelligence gathering and remain the emperor's eyes and ears.' At a signal from Akbar, attendants stepped forward to present Ahmed Khan with a green brocade robe of honour, the yak's-tail standard – an emblem of authority since the days of Genghis Khan – and a jewelled sword.

Next, Akbar turned to his milk-brother. 'Adham Khan. You have been my friend and companion since our boyhood. Now I wish to confer on you a position you richly merit and will discharge with honour.' Adham Khan's hazel eyes were shining. If he'd ever wondered about his milk-brother's ambition, Akbar thought to himself, he had his answer now. Not that ambition itself was a crime. Indeed, it was the very foundation stone of the Moghul empire.

'Step forward, my milk-brother, and let me embrace you as my new master-of-horse.' Akbar rose, and stepping down from the carved marble dais on which his throne stood he put his arms round Adham Khan's shoulders and kissed him on the cheek. But if he'd expected gratitude he was disappointed.

'Your master-of-horse?' As he spoke Adham Khan glanced for a second up at the grille in the wall. Was Maham Anga also there?

'Yes, my master-of-horse,' repeated Akbar, his smile hardening as he took in Adham Khan's angry and bewildered expression. What had his milk-brother been expecting?

As if suddenly aware of Akbar's scrutiny, Adham Khan seemed to pull himself together. 'Thank you, Majesty,' he said quietly. He acknowledged the traditional gift of jewelled bridle and saddle held out to him on velvet cushions by two attendants and stepped back, eyes on the floor.

Akbar returned to his throne. 'And you, Atga Khan. In recognition of your many services I hereby appoint you my chief quartermaster.'

Atga Khan, a tall, broad-shouldered man with a thin white scar running from his right eyebrow to his left cheekbone – a legacy of an ambush by Pashai tribesmen in the Khyber Pass many years ago – put his hand on his breast and bowed low. 'Thank you, Majesty. It is a very great honour.' When he too had been presented with a ceremonial robe and the insignia of his office – a jade seal on a thick gold chain – Akbar rose and left the *durbar* hall.

With his bodyguards preceding him two abreast he had nearly reached the doors to his apartments when Adham Khan darted out from a side corridor. He was breathing heavily – no doubt the result of having run from the *durbar* hall to intercept Akbar. Even though they could see who it was, Akbar's bodyguards at once crossed spears to stop Adham Khan coming any nearer. Their orders were to prevent anybody from getting close to the emperor without permission, and the penalty for negligence was death.

'It's all right.' Akbar nodded to the guards, who lowered their spears. 'What is it, Adham Khan?'

'You have humiliated me in front of all the court.' His milk-brother was so angry that Akbar could see a vein beating in his right temple.

'Humiliated you? Be careful what you say,' Akbar replied in a low voice, but Adham Khan seemed in no mood for restraint.

'You've made a fool of me!' His voice was even louder this time.

Akbar felt a strong desire to launch himself at him and wrestle him to the ground just as he'd done a thousand times when they were boys. Adham Khan had always had a temper, but Akbar was the better fighter and had found fists to be the best way of winning any dispute. But that was when, beneath the childish rivalry, they'd been friends. Perhaps they were so no longer . . . Looking at his milk-brother's insolent face, Akbar wondered how well he really knew him. He had thought it was very well indeed, but suddenly he was no longer sure.

Conscious of the curious glances of his bodyguards and the other attendants hovering about the entrance to his apartments, he grabbed Adham Khan's arm. 'Whatever it is you wish to say, this isn't the place. Come in here.' When the doors closed behind them, he released his arm and turned to face him. 'You forget yourself,' he said coldly.

'No, you forget who *I* am.'

'I have just made you my master-of-horse. I thought you'd be glad . . .'

'Glad to be your stable boy? I deserve something better. Since the defeat of Hemu you've changed towards me . . . we used to be companions who did everything together but you have shut me out. You never ask what I think. I have royal Moghul blood in my veins as well – my father was a cousin of your father . . .'

'What appointment were you hoping for? To be my chief quartermaster perhaps, or my *khan-i-khanan*? I chose experienced men of proven ability and loyalty . . . men I could trust . . .'

'Whom should you trust more than your milk-brother?'

'That depends on the milk-brother.' The words came out before Akbar could restrain himself.

'What do you mean?' When Akbar didn't reply Adham Khan continued, 'It's because of those kidnapped concubines, isn't it? I told you I know nothing about that. It was a plot. Whoever took them was trying to implicate and ruin me.'

'Why should they do that? You're not important enough for anyone to want to destroy . . . Bairam Khan warned me you thought too well of yourself.'

'Yes, the great Bairam Khan. If his advice was so invaluable, why did you send him away?'

The sneer on Adham Khan's lean face was too much for Akbar. Before he'd quite realised it, he'd taken a swing at him and his milk-brother was sprawling on the ground. Akbar stepped back, balancing himself on the balls of his feet in case Adham Khan, who was scrambling to his feet and wiping blood from his face, should try to come at him. But instead his milk-brother just stood very still, breathing heavily through his bleeding nose and glaring at him.

Akbar fought to master his anger. He must make Adham Khan see sense. 'My brother, we have been through much together and I can't forget what I owe your mother, who risked her life to save mine. I thought you would like to be master-of-horse and would discharge the duties with honour. I want to expand my empire, but before I can do that I must make sure my army is ready. Speed has always been one of the Moghuls' greatest strengths. Our cavalry, our mounted archers and musketmen, require the strongest and swiftest mounts, but after the campaign against Hemu our stables need replenishing. Travel through the empire – beyond, if necessary, to Turkey, Persia, Arabia – but bring me back the best.'

Akbar moved towards his milk-brother, stepping over an incense burner that Adham Khan had sent crashing to the ground as he fell.

'Let's forget what happened just now.' He took Adham Khan by the shoulders and embraced him, ignoring the blood dripping on to his pale green tunic. But Adham Khan's body was stiff and unresponsive against his own. Akbar released him and stepped back. 'I won't say anything to Maham Anga about this,' he said dispassionately. 'It would only distress her.'

'What shall I say, that I bruised myself in a fall from my horse?' Adham Khan's tone was still sneering.

'Say what you like. There's a bowl of water over there. Clean yourself up.' Akbar turned away. He should not have lost his temper like that – it was unworthy of him. He was Adham Khan's emperor now, not his equal. Both of them should remember that.

•　◆　•

The rains had come early, falling from skies so grey and heavy with clouds they looked as if they meant to engulf the sodden world beneath them. The swollen waters of the Jumna had burst their banks two weeks ago and since then an unwholesome collection of detritus had come bobbing past the fort – drowned sheep and dogs, even a camel, thin legs ludicrously splayed as the current whirled it round. It was the time of year that Akbar disliked most in Hindustan, when everything seemed rotten with moisture. Despite the summer heat, fires of camphor wood were lit for a few hours each day in the important apartments and in the *haram* to protect the sumptuous silks, brocades and velvets from damp and from the legions of insects that infested anywhere they could gain entry.

Akbar could smell the slightly acrid camphor now as he lay naked on a low red-sheeted bed in Mayala's chamber. She was massaging his back and shoulders with almond oil to relax him and rid him of the sharp headache behind his eyes that often came upon him during the monsoon, and had been troubling him all day. His father had also suffered from it. In his youth, Humayun's favourite remedy had been pellets of opium dissolved in wine, but his addiction had nearly cost him his throne and he had warned Akbar against it.

Perhaps if Humayun had had Mayala to massage him he wouldn't have needed opium. Akbar grunted with satisfaction as he felt the palms of her hands working methodically and expertly over his muscles, releasing the tension. She could also make him laugh. A sharp observer, she could mercilessly mimic every member of his court, from his comptroller of the household, Jauhar – as pursed-lipped when he was scribbling in his leather-bound ledgers as when he was playing his flute – to Ahmed Khan, unconsciously tugging at his thin little beard.

Akbar stretched out his strong body – hardened and battle-ready as any of his soldiers'– the better to enjoy Mayala's touch. The pain behind his eyes had almost gone, and, resting his forehead on his forearms and closing his eyes, he began to allow himself to drift off into sleep. But almost at once he became aware of raised voices not too far away from him. They sounded angry – very angry. Then above the shouting came a familiar sound – the clash of steel on steel. Someone was fighting. He heard female screams and, above it all, a deep voice he knew well calling, 'Akbar! Come out and fight me, you coward . . .'

Drowsiness gone, Akbar leapt up. Pausing only to grab his dagger, and heedless of his nakedness, he rushed from Mayala's chamber out into the courtyard. The rain had ceased and normally there would have been women singing, dancing or sitting by the fountain talking, but only one person was there now – Adham Khan, standing just inside the entrance to the *haram*, a sword in one hand and a dagger in the other. Beyond him, in the watery sunshine, Akbar could see the spread-eagled and bloody bodies of two *haram* guards, the legs of one still twitching. He turned his gaze back to Adham Khan.

'What are you doing?' He was so shocked he could hardly force out the words.

His milk-brother was swaying. 'I've killed that jumped-up dog Atga Khan . . .' A slur in his voice confirmed what Akbar already guessed. He had been drinking strong spirits.

'Why? Atga Khan was no enemy to you.'

'He thought himself so fine, sitting there in the gaudy robe of honour that should have been mine and dictating to his scribe a list of all the things he was planning to do. The fool even smiled at me when I entered his chamber. But he wasn't smiling when I stabbed him right through the heart . . . in fact he looked astonished, just as you do now . . .'

Akbar heard Mayala cry out behind him but he didn't take his eyes off Adham Khan. 'Get back inside your room, Mayala,' he yelled without turning his head. 'Stay there until I tell you it's safe. It seems there is a mad dog loose.'

'But Majesty . . .'

'Now!' He heard her door slam shut. At almost the same moment came the sounds of shouting and running feet approaching the *haram*. The other guards, who must have fled when Adham Khan burst in, had returned with reinforcements and now came spilling into the courtyard. Among them was an elderly servant, Rafiq, who had once served Humayun and was now Hamida's steward. The old man was brandishing a scimitar that he must have grabbed from somewhere. At one signal from Akbar they would have fallen on Adham Khan and cut him down, but Akbar had no intention of allowing anyone else to inflict death on the milk-brother who had broken the sacred bond between them. It was his duty and he would not shirk it. He waved the guards back.

'Just now, you were calling on me to fight you. Very well. Rafiq, give me that scimitar.'

Keeping a wary eye on the slightly swaying figure of Adham Khan, Rafiq tottered towards Akbar, who took the weapon and made a few swishing passes through the air. The cumbersome hilt was old-fashioned and uncomfortable, but the curved blade was sharp and bright. He knotted the length of cloth Rafiq was offering him tight round his naked waist.

'All right then, Adham Khan. We each have a sword and a dagger, so we are equal. Let's see what happens, shall we?'

Akbar moved a few paces towards Adham Khan and paused, hoping to tempt him to rush him. But though his milk-brother's wits had been slowed by drink he was still sufficiently master of himself, it seemed, not to be lured into an early blunder. As they began slowly to circle one another Akbar was reminded of the hunt, when he tried to predict what his prey would do next. Suddenly seeing an opportunity, he flung himself forward, flicking his scimitar

65

to catch the pommel of Adham Khan's sword and then giving a quick twist that sent the sword spinning from the other's grip to fall with a clatter on the stone ground. It was a Persian trick Bairam Khan had taught him long ago. Adham Khan dodged hastily back before Akbar could slice at him with the scimitar. Then he raised his dagger and flung it at Akbar, who swerved, but not quickly enough, and felt the tip of the blade slice across his cheekbone. With warm blood dripping down his neck, Akbar threw his own sword and dagger aside and taking three giant steps hurled himself on his milk-brother. As they went crashing to the ground, he could feel Adham Khan struggling to wriggle from underneath him and grasping a handful of his milk-brother's long hair he banged his head hard once, then again, against the paving stones. Then, leaning back, he smashed his right fist so hard into his face he felt the snapping of a cheekbone. 'You *batcha-i-lada*, you son of a bitch . . .' he yelled.

A bubbling, gasping noise was coming from Adham Khan as Akbar hauled him to his feet, and he could taste his own blood, metallic and salty, in his mouth. As he looked at the mangled, drooping figure of his milk-brother – only upright because he was holding him – he felt an almost overwhelming urge to pound him to a lifeless pulp, so deep was his sense of hurt and betrayal. But losing control was not how an emperor should behave. Stepping back, he reluctantly let go of Adham Khan, who crumpled to the ground.

'Before I have you executed do you have anything you wish to say?'

Adham Khan slowly raised his shattered face. 'You may have triumphed now, but I have been making a fool of you for months. Those stupid little bitches, of course it was me who took them – why should you always get the best? I killed them so they wouldn't tell.'

'And Bairam Khan?'

'What do you think?' Adham Khan's bloodied features could still approximate a triumphant sneer.

That would be his last laugh, Akbar thought as rage and anger at his own gullibility and foolishness overcame him. 'Guards. Take him and fling him from the walls.'

He watched as two guards dragged Adham Khan by his ankles across the courtyard, leaving a long smear of blood on the flagstones. Grunting with effort, they hauled him up a shallow flight of steps in one corner that led on to a narrow walkway with a low balustrade overlooking a sandstone terrace. The drop was about twenty feet. Akbar watched unmoved as, letting go of Adham Khan's ankles, they gripped him under the armpits and heaved him over head first. Akbar heard a thud. The guards peered over. 'Majesty, he's still moving.'

'Then haul him up again by his hair and throw him down a second time.'

The soldiers ran off down a sloping passageway leading to the terrace. It was some minutes before they reappeared, dragging Adham Khan's still feebly jerking body by his long dark hair. This time Akbar followed them up to the ledge and watched as once again his milk-brother was shoved over the balustrade. This time, as Adham Khan's skull hit the hard stone it cracked like a ripe nut, sending pink-grey brains spewing out. Within seconds, a kite dropped from the blue sky to peck at the corpse. Soon a dozen were feeding on what remained of the companion of Akbar's boyhood.

He didn't stay to watch. The full impact of what had happened had struck him. How could he have been so stupid? How could he have let others see his stupidity? Despite the heat, he felt cold and was beginning to shake. His mind was full of the one question he had wanted to ask Adham Khan but hadn't – perhaps because he feared the answer. How much had Maham Anga, the woman who had given him her milk and protected him when he was alone and vulnerable, known of her son's doings? The courtyard was crowded with people now – the women had come out of the chambers where they'd taken refuge and were discussing with the *haram* guards and attendants the extraordinary incident that had just taken place. Glancing round, Akbar saw Mayala watching him from the doorway of her apartment, her usually smiling face strained and anxious. He'd have liked to go and reassure her that all was well, but it wasn't, and there were things he must do. 'Fetch my robe,' he shouted to an attendant, keeping his voice as steady as he could.

A quarter of an hour later, his mind still in turmoil, Akbar made his way to Maham Anga's apartments. He had already detailed members of his personal bodyguard to search them and then to stand guard outside until he arrived. Given his semi–drunken state, Adham Khan had probably been acting alone and on impulse, even if his grievances and jealousies had been festering for a long time. Nevertheless, it was as well to be certain no further traitors lurked there. Outside, he received the brief salutation of the captain of his bodyguard. 'We have searched the chambers. It is safe for you to enter, Majesty.'

'And you've said nothing of what has occurred?'

'No, Majesty.'

'Did she mention her son?'

'Again, no, Majesty.'

As the guards swung the double doors open to admit him, Akbar knew the task ahead of him was far more distasteful than any battle. Given what the captain of his guard had said, it seemed that Maham Anga didn't yet know of his fight with Adham Khan or of her son's summary execution or the reasons for it, though it would have taken a fleet-footed attendant only five minutes to carry the news to her. Maham Anga was standing in the middle of the chamber in which in happier times she had held parties and celebrations, and where by the soft light of oil lamps she had fondly told him the stories of his youth that never bored him. Her expression now was anxious.

'Akbar, what is going on? Why am I suddenly a prisoner?' Her clear brown eyes fixed on his face were genuinely puzzled. To give himself strength, he let his mind dwell for a moment on the bloody corpse of the murdered Atga Khan, which he had inspected just a few minutes earlier and was even now being washed in camphor water and readied for burial.

'Maham Anga, all my life you have been as a mother to me. What I have to say isn't easy, so let me be direct. An hour ago your son murdered my chief quartermaster, Atga Khan, then burst armed into the *haram* intending to kill me also.'

'No.' She spoke so softly that the one word was almost inaudible. Blindly she reached out to catch at something to support her, but her flailing hand caught against a dish of marzipan sweetmeats and sent it crashing to the floor.

'There is more. Adham Khan challenged me to combat. I defeated him in a fair fight and then I ordered his immediate death – the death of a traitor.'

Maham Anga was shaking her head slowly from side to side and making a pitiful sound between a whimper and a wail. 'Tell me he isn't dead,' she sobbed at last.

Akbar came closer. 'I had no choice. I had him flung headlong from the walls. Not only did I have the evidence of my own eyes but he boasted to me of his other crimes – the girls destined for my *haram* whom he seized from spite and jealousy and then had killed. Even worse, he taunted me that he was the author of Bairam Khan's death. Such arrogance and ambition could not go unpunished . . . what else could I do but have him executed?'

'No!' This time the word was a shriek. 'I gave you my milk when you were a baby. I risked my life to protect you when your uncle ordered you to be exposed to cannon and musket fire on the walls of Kabul. And you betray me by slaughtering my only son – your own milk-brother! I have nourished a viper at my bosom, a devil.' Maham Anga fell to the floor, clawing hysterically first at the rich red rug, then at Akbar, ripping at his calves with her nails and drawing blood as red as the carpet.

'Guards!' Akbar could not bear to lay hands on her himself. 'Be gentle with her. She is hysterical with shock and grief.' Two of his men pulled Maham Anga away from him. In a moment she broke free but made no further attempt to attack him. Instead, she just knelt there, rocking back and forth, arms wrapped tightly around herself.

'Maham Anga, I must ask you this. Did you know anything of what your son had done – of his plans to kill me?'

She looked up at him through her tangled hair. 'No.'

'And when you advised me to send Bairam Khan on pilgrimage, was that because you and Adham Khan were jealous of his influence on me and at court?' This time Maham Anga was silent. 'I insist you answer, and honestly. This is probably the last time you and I will ever meet.'

'I thought that with Bairam Khan gone, you would look to others for advice.'

'Like you and your son?'

'Yes. My son felt neglected by you and I agreed with him.'

'And did you agree to Bairam Khan's murder so you could be sure your rival was never coming back?' Despite his feelings for Maham Anga, Akbar felt his anger welling up again. It would be best for them all to bring this interview to a swift close.

At the bitter edge to Akbar's voice, his milk-mother flinched. 'I never intended Bairam Khan's death . . . and I'm sure my son was not responsible, whatever he may have boasted to you.'

Nothing so blind as a mother's love, Akbar thought.

'I always loved you, Akbar,' Maham Anga said dully, as if reading his mind.

'Yes, but you loved your own son far more. Maham Anga, this is what will happen. Tomorrow, you will be taken from here to the fort in Delhi where you will live the rest of your days in seclusion. I will give you money to build a mausoleum for your son. But you will have no further contact with me or any of my family.'

As he turned and walked slowly from her apartments, he heard Maham Anga break into fresh wails. From what he could make out from her disjointed words they were not simply of grief – she was calling down God's curse on him and God's blessing on her dead son. With those anguished, vengeful cries echoing around him, Akbar made for his own mother's chambers as if he were sleep-walking. Gulbadan was with Hamida and he could tell from their faces that they already knew what had happened.

Hamida took him in her arms and clung to him. 'I thank God you are safe. I heard what that *alachi*, that devil, tried to do . . .'

'You know that he is dead? I had him thrown off the battlements. And I am exiling Maham Anga from the court.'

'She too deserves death. As your milk-mother she has betrayed a sacred trust.' Hamida's tone was harsh.

'No. Her son's execution is punishment enough. And how can I forget that when I was a child she risked her life to save mine?'

'I think you are right to spare Maham Anga,' Gulbadan said quietly.

'You have dealt decisively with the real threat and do not need to revenge yourself upon a woman. When the mother of a defeated Hindustani ruler tried to poison your grandfather, he spared her life and won much respect for it.' She turned to Hamida. 'I understand what you must be feeling, but when the anger, the shock, begin to pass you will see that I am right.'

'Perhaps,' Hamida answered in a low voice. 'But, Gulbadan, you know as well as I do the consequences of being too merciful. Again and again, my husband, your brother, forgave those he should have executed and we all suffered as a result.'

'Humayun did what he believed was right and was surely a greater man for it.'

Akbar was barely listening to the two women. The knowledge of Adham Khan's treachery couldn't at a stroke obliterate the affection – love even – he had felt for his milk-brother, whose mangled, bloodied body was now being washed for burial. Perhaps if he had understood him better he might have been able to prevent this terrible sequence of events. Was there a way he could have satisfied Adham Khan's ambitions? Or would his milk-brother's jealousy always have been a danger? In which case he had been naïve not to be aware of it . . .

Suddenly he realised his mother and aunt had stopped talking and that both were looking at him. 'I should have seen what was coming,' he said. 'I should not have taken Maham Anga's advice about Bairam Khan on trust but asked myself what her motive was. When Shayzada named Adham Khan as her sisters' abductor I should have questioned him more rigorously. I was even warned that he was responsible for the death of Bairam Khan – someone who knew left a scribbled message in my apartments.'

'I know. It was my steward. He just told me. Though elderly, Rafiq hears and sees much that goes on though people do not realise it. He overheard Adham Khan gloating about Bairam Khan's death and guessed he was responsible. Though he had no proof, he wanted to put you on your guard. He saw his chance to enter your apartments and leave a message scrawled on a piece of fabric he ripped from his sleeve because he could find no paper . . . He said he dared not

71

sign it. Akbar, he is afraid you will punish him for not having the courage to tell you his suspicions to your face.'

'No. I am doubly in his debt. Just now when I was unarmed in the *haram* he gave me a sword. Tell him I am grateful and will reward his loyalty. The fault for what happened is all mine. Despite Rafiq's warning I didn't press Adham Khan. I have been a fool . . .' Akbar brushed tears from his eyes with the back of his hand as he continued, 'I loved Adham Khan and Maham Anga and I believed they returned my affection. Now I must learn to question and doubt the motives of all around me — even those closest to me. I must accept that the role of an emperor is a lonely one, and a ruler must never give his entire trust . . .'

'If you have learned that sad truth, then perhaps the events of this day have had a purpose,' said Hamida, face grave. 'When you look back many years from now, you will realise that this was when you left your youth behind and truly became a man and an emperor. Whatever our position in the world, life holds many bitter things. You tasted some today. I pray you emerge the stronger.'

Part II

Children of Sun, Moon and Fire

Chapter 6

The Emperor Rides Out

The sky glowed with a soft pink radiance as the sun dropped, as if nature herself wished to provide a fitting backdrop for the ceremony about to be enacted, Akbar thought. So many richly coloured Persian carpets covered the parade ground beneath the Agra fort that it resembled a flower garden. On two sides of the ground his commanders and nobles were standing behind gilded wooden balustrades, while on the third were grouped some of the rulers who had sworn allegiance to him. In the centre beneath a green silk canopy stood a pair of giant golden scales on a marble platform. Two saucers five feet across, their edges set with lozenges of smooth-polished rose quartz rimmed with pearls, swayed on thick chains from an oak frame eight feet high.

Dressed in stiff green brocade robes, with a long necklace of carved emeralds round his neck and diamonds flashing in his headdress, Akbar advanced in step to a deep, rolling drumbeat towards the scales. He looked with satisfaction at the many chests of gems, sparkling in the light of the circle of torches that, with dusk falling, attendants had lit at intervals round the platform. Gold and silver chains lay coiled like snakes, while coins spilled from wide-necked brocade sacks deliberately over-stuffed to demonstrate his largesse. Bags of spices were piled on brass trays next to jewelled flasks, some of white jade, containing costly perfumes – ambergris, frankincense and aloewood. Bales of embroidered silks subtle and delicate as butterflies' wings shimmered beside jewel-bright lengths of fine-woven pashmina goat's wool.

There was also something else – twenty large iron bars. Akbar saw the many curious glances directed towards them. As he mounted the platform and approached the scales, the drummers ceased their rhythmic thumping and a trumpeter sounded a single sharp blast. At this signal, attendants picked up the bars, carried them over to the scales and stacked them on one of the giant saucers, which quickly dipped to the ground beneath the weight.

Since Adham Khan's death nearly two years ago, he had spent much time reflecting on how and why he had failed to foresee Adham Khan's treachery and how he could avoid new conspiracies among his nobles. He knew that one reason for his reluctance to suspect Adham Khan and Maham Anga had been their closeness to him since childhood. With Bairam Khan dead there was no one left in a similar position, and he would not let anyone get so close in future, or trust anyone so completely. He must rely on his own inner resources. But even if Adham Khan's and Maham Anga's intimate ties to him partly excused his blindness towards their machinations, he had also been complacent, so confident in his power and position that he thought nobody would challenge them.

A solution as to how he might minimise the chances of future unrest had come to him almost by accident as one of his *qorchis* read to him from his grandfather's memoirs. Among all Babur's wise words, two passages in particular had caught his attention: 'War and booty keep men true' and 'Be generous to your supporters. If they know they have more to gain from you than from anyone else they will stay loyal.' After all, if anyone had understood how to survive it had been Babur, and he could learn from him. That was why he had summoned his nobles here today – to tell them that very soon he would be launching wars of conquest that would fill the imperial treasuries to overflowing with gold and jewels, and also to give them a taste of the rewards that were to come. And, thanks to Gulbadan who had witnessed it during the early days of his father's reign and suggested it, he had found exactly the right occasion for his show of magnificence and ambition – a weighing ceremony. To his great satisfaction, a search of the Agra treasure vaults had produced the very scales Humayun, as a young emperor himself, had had made. Akbar allowed himself a brief smile, then raised his hands for silence.

'Like my father before me I have decided to revive the ancient custom of the rulers of Hindustan of being publicly weighed against precious stuffs. I shall hold this ceremony twice a year – on my lunar birthday, as today, and again on my solar birthday. After the weighing, the treasure will be distributed amongst those invited – as you have been today – to witness it. To show my special regard for you, I wish on this first occasion to give you more than the mere equivalent of my bodyweight. These iron bars weigh twice as much as I.' Akbar waited a moment to allow his words to sink in, then sat down cross-legged on the saucer next to the pile of iron.

Akbar's attendants at once began to load the other saucer, beginning with the most precious objects. Ten chests of gems had been stacked high before the saucer bearing Humayun began to rise slowly and shudderingly from the ground. The silence was intense and Akbar sensed every eye fixed upon him, every mind calculating what his individual share of the spoils might be. The Moghuls had come a long way, he reflected, as the jewels were replaced by the gold and silver chains and then by the sacks of gold. In former days, the moment for reward had come immediately after battle with the bloodied, still warm bodies of the Moghuls' foes as witnesses. Each clan chieftain had presented his shield to be piled with booty which he then dragged off to share with his men. But those times, with their origins in the Moghuls' nomadic past, were over. He was Emperor of Hindustan and must provide his followers with more rewards, not just for winning new territories by their feats in battle but also for retaining them through good government.

The distribution of the rich gifts took place as soon as the weighing was over. With the help of his comptroller of the household, Jauhar, Akbar had calculated what each man should receive and Jauhar had carefully recorded his wishes in his ledger. Akbar watched as Jauhar called out name after name and his nobles, commanders and allies stepped up to claim their allotted share of money and jewels and of soft silks and pashmina wools for their wives and concubines, and even gifts for their children: almonds wrapped in gold leaf, toy Moghul soldiers – horsemen, archers and musketeers – and female dolls with tiny silver earrings, necklaces and bangles. Akbar had also ordered some treasure to be reserved and sent to governors and officials of distant provinces, and for gifts of grain, rice and oil to be distributed to the granaries of the towns and cities of the empire so that even the ordinary people should share in his generosity.

That night, rosewater bubbled from the fountains in the courtyard where, seated on a golden chair on a velvet-draped dais, Akbar watched his guests feasting on the best his accomplished cooks could provide: whole sheep roasted on spits over fires of applewood, ducks and partridges stuffed with dried fruits and nuts and simmered in copper pots of saffron-spiced butter sauce, and chickens marinated in yoghourt and spices before being baked in the searing heat of the *tandoor* – the portable clay oven used by a Moghul army on the march and brought to Hindustan in Babur's time. As an extra touch of opulence, he had ordered loose gemstones to be scattered round the edges of the mounds of *zard birinj* – rice mixed with butter, raisins, dried cherries, almonds, pistachios, ginger and cinnamon – that were to be served to accompany the rich meats. He had even commanded that fragrant musk-melons and sweet-juiced grapes be packed in ice and sent down through the Khyber Pass from Kabul. The fruit had arrived two days ago in excellent condition.

Akbar waited until most had finished and were wiping their lips before rising from his chair. Now was the moment to tell them what he was planning. As he saw all the flushed, upturned faces turned towards him, a confidence possessed him that they would follow him anywhere.

'There is something I wish to say to you. It is forty years since my grandfather Babur conquered Hindustan for the Moghuls. An early death denied him the chance to expand his territories, just as it also denied my own father that opportunity. But I am young and the warrior blood of my ancestors beats strongly in my veins. It tells me my destiny is to forge an empire that will endure – an empire that cannot be lost by a single battle but will be the wonder of the world for centuries to come.

'The way to achieve that is through conquest. Today I conferred on you some of the wealth of our empire, but it was only a tiny fraction of the gold and glory I will give you in the years to come as, with your help, I push back the boundaries of the Moghul empire. My dominions will stretch from east to west, from sea to sea. Southwards, it will extend beyond the great plateau of the Deccan to the diamond mines of Golconda, the brilliant gems from which will blaze from my throne and adorn your wives and concubines. These are not idle boasts. Here, before you all, I pledge to vanquish new lands – not just those of petty chiefs along our borders who think they can defy us, but the rulers of rich and mighty kingdoms. If they will bend their proud necks to Moghul domination they will find mercy, honour and a share in our greatness. But if they resist, my armies will crush the bones of their soldiers to dust and smash their palaces and fortresses to ruins.

'So I say, prepare for war! The first who will feel our power is Rana Udai Singh of Mewar, son of Rana Sanga whom my grandfather Babur defeated forty years ago and who is just as treacherous. The ranas of Mewar claim to be the greatest of all the Rajputs. While many other Rajput princes long ago declared themselves to be my loyal vassals, Udai Singh has equivocated, seeking special privileges and finding reasons not to come to court. Now he is openly showing his hostility. His warriors recently attacked a caravan of Moghul merchants making for the coast of Gujarat. In reply to my demand for compensation Udai Singh has returned an insulting message: "You are the offspring of horse-thieves from the barbarian north while our descent is from the god Rama and through him the sun, moon and fire. You have no authority over me."

'He will learn that I have. In three months' time, when we have completed our preparations, I will ride at the head of my armies to punish him and you here tonight will play your glorious part!' As

79

a great cheer enveloped him, Akbar raised his emerald–inlaid jade drinking cup. 'To victory!'

• ◆ •

Akbar narrowed his eyes against the sun as, standing with Ahmed Khan on a balcony of the Agra fort eight weeks later, he watched a troop of cavalry galloping in single file along the dry mud bank of the Jumna river. A row of twenty spears had been stuck into the ground at five-yard intervals. As each rider approached, without lessening his breakneck pace he expertly swerved his horse between them. Reaching the last of the spears and still retaining perfect balance and control, each man rose in his stirrups to hurl his steel-tipped lance at a straw target set up some ten yards ahead. Every man hit his target spot on.

Akbar grunted. 'Impressive. How soon can the army be ready to ride out, d'you think?'

'Within another month, as we planned – perhaps sooner, although some of our gunners need further training in loading the new large cannon with stronger barrels our Turkish armourers have produced in our foundries. We're also still waiting for those supplies of extra muskets we ordered from the skilled gunsmiths of Lahore. To increase their range they can be loaded with at least twice as much gunpowder as our existing ones – even to the muzzle, I'm told – without risk of bursting. When we have them we will have the best equipped as well as the largest army within thousands of miles, stonger even than the Persian shah's.'

While a soldier yanked the line of spears from the mud, the riders re-formed. Now their task was to gallop up to a row of clay pots lying on their sides and without losing pace to scoop one up on their spear-tip. This time the performance wasn't so perfect. One rider misjudged the distance, embedding his spear in the mud and somersaulting from the saddle to land painfully on the hard-baked ground.

Akbar smiled. He too had bruises. He was training every day now, firing shot after shot from his musket and practising with sword, flail and battleaxe until they felt like living extensions of his own body.

He was also joining in wrestling bouts with his officers. At first they had treated him with too much respect, reluctant to fling their emperor into the dust, but his skill and speed and the challenges he had roared at them had quickly conquered such inhibitions.

He glanced up at the rapidly crimsoning sky. In another half-hour it would be growing dark. 'Ahmed Khan, I would like to play polo with those men down on the riverbank.'

'But the light is fading.'

'Wait and see.'

Half an hour later, dressed in simple tunic and trousers and mounted on a small, muscular chestnut horse with white fetlocks, Akbar trotted out of the fort, across the parade ground and down to the riverbank. Behind him followed attendants, some carrying *palas* – wooden balls made from dark timber – and polo sticks while four staggered under the weight of a brazier of glowing charcoals supported on two wooden poles. As he reached the bank, Akbar kicked his horse into a canter and rode up to the horsemen. Seeing their emperor, they prepared to dismount and make their salutations.

'No. Stay in the saddle. I want you to take part in an experiment,' Akbar said.

As inky purple shadows stole over the river, he ordered his attendants to distribute the polo sticks, mark out goals with torches on either side and finally place one of the wooden balls in the brazier. Almost at once the ball began to smoulder, but even after four or five minutes it hadn't burst into flames. Akbar smiled. So the story about Timur was true. On several evenings since announcing his intention to go to war, he had asked his *qorchi* to read him accounts of Timur's exploits in case there was anything he could learn from his great ancestor. One description had diverted him from thoughts of strategy to those of sport. It told how, by chance, Timur had discovered that the hard timber of the wormwood tree smouldered for many hours. He had ordered his men to play polo through the night with glowing balls of wormwood to harden and prepare them for battle. Ever since, Akbar had been eager to try it for himself.

'Throw the ball on the ground,' he ordered. As one of his attendants lifted the ball from the brazier with a pair of long, curved tongs,

Akbar kicked his horse forward and took a swing at the glowing sphere. 'Let's play,' he yelled. Soon the dark riverbank echoed to the beat of hooves and the shouts of laughing men, and the game lasted until the moon had risen high, turning the Jumna's muddy waters to liquid silver.

Later that night, as a *hakim* massaged his stiffening muscles with warm oil, Akbar again thought about Timur and why he had never once been defeated. He had favoured the shock attack, the hit-and-run raid. That was how he had smashed his way across Asia, allowing no physical or human obstacle, however mighty, to blunt his impetus. Crossing the frozen Hindu Kush he had had himself lowered down a sheer cliff of ice and brushed off attacks by cannibal tribes as easily as if they'd been fleas to be shaken from his fur-lined robes.

Timur's tactics might not be appropriate for dealing with a modern enemy like Rana Udai Singh, equipped with cannon and entrenched behind the high walls of his desert fortress, Akbar thought. But Timur's self-belief, his absolute determination to win and never to cede the initiative or be deflected from his goals, were as relevant now as two hundred years ago. The desire to emulate his warrior ancestor sent a restless energy burning through Akbar's veins so that he could hardly lie still beneath the *hakim*'s strong fingers. But it would not be long before the war drums boomed out from the gatehouse of the Agra fort and the Moghul armies advanced southwest into the pale orange deserts of Rajasthan towards Mewar and its arrogant rana. His mother had conjured those deserts for him so vividly that Akbar could almost taste the dry, gritty air and hear the harsh shrieks of the peacocks that inhabited these desolate reaches. It was not surprising Hamida should remember them so well. She had given birth to Akbar in a small desert town in Rajasthan while she and his father had been fugitives from a Rajput king who had pledged to rip Akbar living from her womb and send the unborn child as a gift to Sher Shah, the invader who had robbed Humayun of his throne.

That Rajput leader was dead, but the humbling of Udai Singh was long overdue and subduing Mewar, which straddled the route between Agra and the south, made sound strategic sense. In his mind's eye, Akbar already saw his armies battering down the gates of the great fort of Chittorgarh, capital of Udai Singh's family for over eight hundred years and symbol of their overweening arrogance. Defeating Udai Singh, head of the most powerful Rajput ruling house, would make Akbar so feared – and respected – across the Indian subcontinent that none would dare challenge him.

Chapter 7

Saffron Warriors

In the early morning of a cloudless December day Akbar stood with Ahmed Khan at his side looking towards the Rana of Mewar's great fortress-city of Chittorgarh. Its sandstone walls, over three miles long, sat high on a vast rocky outcrop soaring five hundred feet sheer from the dry Rajasthani plains below. Enclosed within them were temples, palaces, houses and markets, as well as military positions.

To Akbar's acute frustration, he and his forces had already been besieging the city for six weeks to no great effect. Initially he had been pleased with the progress they had made. They had surrounded Chittorgarh completely, cut off all food supplies and captured or killed any foraging parties the Rajputs had sent out. They had gleaned some useful information from one of their captives, a ragged scrawny child of about ten whom they had apprehended with his two elder brothers as they climbed down the exposed rock face from the fortress's outer walls in a desperate search for food. When Akbar's soldiers had separated the child from his brothers and tempted him with a piece of freshly roasted mutton he had told them, after much cajoling, that Rana Udai Singh did not command the defending army himself but had appointed two of his young generals – Jai Mal and Patti by name – to the task. The rana himself, according to the boy, was somewhere in the Aravalli range of hills where he was said to be building a new capital to be named Udaipur after him.

The reaction of his older brothers when they had found out from the child what he had revealed underlined the strictness of the Rajput code. They had attacked the boy and would have strangled him if they had not been pulled away. They had repeated their assault the next day, when the three of them had been put to work with some other captives breaking and moving stone to be used in improving Akbar's positions. This time, the eldest of the three had hit his brother with a sharp stone, inflicting a great gash to the side of his head. As he was hauled from his bleeding victim he had yelled at him, 'You gave information to the infidel attacker. You are no longer my brother. You are not even a Rajput any more.'

When Akbar had heard this story, he had ordered the child to be cleaned up, clothed and put to work in the camp kitchen, remarking as he did so that it was a fitting fate for one whose desire for food had led him to help Chittorgarh's attackers. However, the boy could not be persuaded to reveal anything about any secret routes into Chittorgarh. Nor would older captives, even when subjected to rough questioning and threatened with torture. Probably there were none.

Akbar and his generals had continued the assault, but his early hopes of success had faltered. He had ordered barrages of cannon shot to be followed up by wave after wave of attacks, attempting to charge up the single five-hundred-yard-long winding ramp leading from the plain to the city's main gateway, which was situated at the lowest point of the summit of the outcrop. But none of the attackers had even got as far as the bottom of the ramp. As soon as his soldiers had begun to ride and run towards the ramp, Akbar had been forced to watch powerless as orange-turbaned Rajputs, oblivious of cannon and musket shot, had appeared on Chittorgarh's crenellated ramparts and shot down the Moghuls with musket balls, crossbow bolts and a storm of hissing arrows. Men and horses had fallen dead or wounded, many on the exposed ground in front of the fortress. To Akbar's dismay, more of his men had been killed as they bravely rushed out to attempt to drag wounded comrades back under cover.

Eventually so many lives had been lost in such rescue attempts that Akbar had reluctantly ordered his officers only to permit them under cover of darkness. Even then, the Rajputs had killed or wounded many, so good seemed to be their hearing and vision in the moonlight. During the days following these attacks, Akbar and his soldiers were tormented by the sounds of their wounded fellows crying out for help, for water, and, in the last extremities, for their mothers and for God to release them from their agonies. The constant neighing of wounded horses was almost as pitiful. Black flies bloated from feeding on the corpses clustered everywhere and the smell from the putrescent bodies of both men and animals so polluted the air around Akbar's camp that he had ordered fires of sandalwood to be kept burning constantly in an only partially successful attempt to mask the sweet, stomach-turning stench of decay.

Determined not to be beaten, Akbar had made rounds of his vast camp morning and evening to encourage his men. He had ordered small mounds or barricades of mud and stone to be thrown up at night to provide cover for rushes by day at the walls. However, though picked bodies of men had got near to the base of the ramp they had been unable to make any further progress and had been forced to retreat again, dodging back behind the mounds and dragging with them those wounded they could.

Even now, as Akbar watched, a number of his best troops were assembling for yet another attack on the ramp leading up to Chittorgarh's gate. This time he and his commanders had decided war elephants would lead the assault. Soldiers were already climbing into the howdahs on the animals' backs. To improve the chances of success, he had had the elephants fitted with coats of thicker than normal overlapping steel plates. The howdahs had been strengthened with heavy planking to give extra cover to the musketeers and archers within. Once their howdahs were full, the *mahouts* sitting behind the elephants' ears tapped the beasts as a signal for them to rise, which they did ponderously beneath the weight of their extra armour and the reinforced howdahs and their occupants. Around them, the foot soldiers and horsemen who were to follow them into the assault were also forming up, taking advantage of what shelter the mud and stone barricades provided. The cavalrymen's horses were tossing their heads and skittering uneasily, sensing their riders' tension about the attack to come.

From his vantage point Akbar could see defenders massing on the battlements of Chittorgarh, well aware that another assault was about to be launched on their stronghold. Although his preparations were beyond musket shot, arrows fired from the battlements high into the air to secure maximum range began to plummet from the skies to fall among Akbar's men. Many had lost much of their force and did not penetrate the armour of either elephants or men; others were deflected by shields. Some, however, wounded horses or less well-protected foot soldiers. As Akbar watched, a black-feathered arrow hit an officer's tall white horse in the neck. It collapsed, crimson blood staining its coat, and its rider, a stout man wearing a domed helmet, slid from the saddle shouting for a replacement. A groom – an elderly man judging by his white hair and stiff gait – moved forward, leading another horse, this time a chestnut, but as he did so another of the defenders' lucky arrow shots caught him in the chest. He staggered and fell, dropping the reins and allowing the horse to gallop wildly out from the Moghul ranks and around the ramparts of Chittorgarh.

'Ahmed Khan, we must attack now if our assault is to succeed. Give the orders for the elephants to advance and for our cannon and archers to provide covering fire. I will take my place with the first wave of cavalry, ready to follow up the elephants' attack.'

At Ahmed Khan's signal, the elephants, encumbered by the extra weight they were carrying, began to advance, moving more slowly than usual but still they made progress over the dry, stony ground, bare except for the corpses of men and animals which lay between them and the bottom of the winding ramp. The defenders' arrows seemed to have little effect, bouncing off the elephants' steel armour or sticking harmlessly into the planking of the howdahs like quills on a porcupine. However, when the attackers came within musket shot, Akbar saw one elephant pause as if hit but then it moved forward again, stoically plodding after its companions leaving a trail of blood as it did so. Occasionally a soldier plunged from a howdah, clearly wounded, but with growing excitement Akbar realised the elephants were making better progress than in any previous attack. Soon the leading beasts would be at the foot of the ramp. Now was the time for him to ready his horsemen.

'Follow me. Chittorgarh will be ours,' he shouted as he led his riders forward at the trot, ready to charge after the elephants if they made it up the ramp to the gate. But then he saw some pots full of fire being thrown from the walls of Chittorgarh towards the elephants. All of them fell short, bursting harmlessly on the surrounding rocks. Suddenly orange-turbaned Rajputs began to emerge through a door set into the metal-studded main gate. The first man to appear put a taper to the large clay pot he was carrying and, as the pitch within caught fire, began to whirl the pot round his head while running at full pelt down the ramp towards the advancing elephants. He was followed by his companions, all similarly equipped with flaming pitch pots.

Although the noise of battle was too great for Akbar to hear the crackle of musketry, his musketeers and archers in the howdahs had clearly begun to fire. Several Rajputs fell on the ramp, dropping their fire pots, but the rest ran on, including one man whose clothes had been set afire by burning pitch after a musket ball had shattered its clay container. Eventually this human torch collapsed into a flaming heap but not before he had waved a blazing arm to encourage his fellows on. Other Rajput attackers − hit by musket balls or arrows − plunged over the low wall that formed the side of the ramp, crashing to the ground below. Yet still the rest ran on, oblivious of their comrades' deaths and the musket balls and arrows cracking and hissing around them.

A minute or two after they emerged, the leading Rajput threw his flaming pitch pot towards the first of Akbar's elephants, which had just put its front feet on to the ramp. Moments later the Rajput, hit in the forehead by a musket ball, collapsed to the ground, but his pot of burning pitch burst squarely on its target's head and its flaming contents began to run down the elephant's armour. Some of it must have seeped between the steel plates or into the animal's eyes because, maddened with pain and trumpeting wildly, it turned back from the ramp, striking the elephant behind it and setting the heavy planking of its howdah afire. Other pitch pots thrown from the walls above, as well as by the survivors of those who had run down the ramp, also found their targets.

To his horror, Akbar saw his soldiers begin to jump from the howdahs of the stricken elephants and run back towards their own lines. Some with their garments alight rolled on the dry ground to try to extinguish them. Others just ran on screaming in agony, orange flames billowing behind them, until they too fell. More elephants began to turn, streaked with flames. Akbar saw the *mahout* of one hammer into his mount's brain the large steel spike which *mahouts* carried to kill wounded elephants to prevent them rampaging among their own men. The great beast collapsed almost immediately and was instantly still. Another *mahout* was less brave and jumped from his animal's neck, leaving it to turn frenzied and riderless and run back trumpeting towards Akbar's barricades with its howdah on fire. It crashed into one barricade and stumbled over. As it fell, it exposed its unprotected belly to some of Akbar's musketeers, who despatched it with several shots. In its death throes, it rolled on its burning howdah, mercifully crushing the life from the soldiers trapped within. The pungent stench of singed and burning flesh, human and animal, now blowing across the battlefield and mingling with the acrid gunpowder smoke began to fill Akbar's nostrils, and he knew this attack – like so many others previously – had no chance of success. To save further futile casualties, with a wave of his hand he ordered his forces to fall back and turned his own horse. How was he going to break the deadlock?

• ◆ •

That evening, with the rays of the setting sun reflecting from the shoulder pieces of the gilded breastplate he now habitually wore when on campaign, Akbar was in sombre mood as he entered his scarlet command tent where his war council was assembling. His mind was still void of viable new stratagems as he took his place on a small throne placed at the centre of the semicircle in which Ahmed Khan and his other generals sat cross-legged. He had never needed their help and advice as much as he did now but he couldn't help thinking they were an ill-assorted bunch. Some, like Muhammad Beg over there in his green and red striped robes, had served even longer than Ahmed Khan and had fought at Panipat with Babur in their youth and experienced all the trials of Humayun's life and had the scars to show for it. Others, like the square-shouldered, extravagantly moustached Tajik Ali Gul, were younger and had only known Humayun's last few battles. Yet others were even newer adherents. Some, such as the large, stout, red-turbaned figure of Raja Ravi Singh, noisily crunching almonds from the engraved copper dish in front of him, were the rulers of smaller states, even – like Ravi Singh himself – of Rajput ones, who had already submitted to Akbar's suzerainty after his defeat of Hemu. Whatever their age or background, all his commanders had chastened expressions on their faces.

'What were our casualties from today's attack?' asked Akbar.

Ahmed Khan replied. 'We lost the pick of our war elephants as well as over three hundred men. Many others are so badly burned they may not survive.'

'Despite the losses it was worth trying,' said Akbar. 'We must look to the use of more innovations such as the strengthened howdahs if we do not want to allow Rana Udai time to raise a great relieving army, or perhaps even to form an alliance with other Rajput rulers, before we can take Chittorgarh.'

'He is unlikely to find allies,' put in Ravi Singh quietly. 'The ranas of Mewar have long alienated their fellow rulers with their pretensions to the leadership of all Rajasthan, and with the pompous and superior airs with which they treat their fellows.'

'That's good to hear, at least. Has Chittorgarh been conquered before, other than by treachery?'

'Yes,' answered Muhammad Beg, scratching the uneven bridge of his broken nose. 'Over two hundred years ago by a man called Alauaddin Khilji and more recently by the Gujaratis.'

'Can we learn anything from their methods?'

'I know nothing of how Alauaddin Khilji succeeded: it is too long lost in history. However, when I was in Gujarat after your father's siege of Champnir, I spoke to an old Gujarati who told me that in their attack they tried, as we have, to push strong barricades forward to allow attackers to approach nearer. They even constructed a kind of covered corridor made of thick hide – a *sabat* the man called it – which allowed them to get quite a distance up the ramp. But from what I gathered, their final victory was caused as much by deprivation and disease among the defenders as by anything else. I would have mentioned the covered corridors before if I hadn't thought that, while they were successful in offering protection against arrows, they would be easily vulnerable to musket balls as well as to cannon fire.'

'But couldn't we strengthen them by using stones and mud for the sides and heavy wooden planking for the roof?' asked Ahmed Khan.

'It would take a long time and cost many lives, Majesty,' put in Ali Gul.

'But so have all our other fruitless attacks,' Akbar pointed out. 'My grandfather Babur once said that an emperor must recognise that to win and expand an empire he has to be prepared to sacrifice lives – even potentially his own and those of his closest adherents and family. Only when victory is complete may he show compassion and compensate as best he can the families of the fallen. The idea of *sabats* is worth pursuing. Have plans drawn up. Send parties in search of more stones and supplies of timber. To give those working on the construction some protection, throw up thick hide screens as the Gujaratis did. They will stop arrows, and the Rajputs won't want to expend too much of their powder in firing cannons and muskets randomly on unseen targets, for fear of exhausting their supplies.'

• ◆ •

Akbar was feeling optimistic as he sat on his horse at the entrance of one of his two great *sabats*. They were proving quicker to construct than he had anticipated. A forest only a few miles away had provided good quantities of thick tree trunks for timbers. Prisoners had been put to the backbreaking work of quarrying stone. Chittorgarh's defenders had proved, as Akbar had predicted, reluctant to waste powder on musket and cannon fire and the hide screens had indeed provided a degree of protection from arrows. Nevertheless up to a hundred men a day – mostly poor barefoot labourers lured by the silver coin offered by Akbar – had been killed as they worked.

As he had promised he would, Akbar had had his clerks carefully record the names of the dead and wounded in leather-bound ledgers so that they or their families could receive compensation once victory was secured. The *sabat* Akbar was entering had been constructed on a huge scale. It was – as Muhammad Beg, whom he had put in charge of the works, proudly assured him – wide enough to accommodate ten horsemen riding abreast or a team of oxen pulling a small cannon, and high enough to allow even a large war elephant to get through. Akbar knew from the reports reaching him that, while the *sabats* were advancing sinuously and inexorably up and round the slopes leading to the ramp, like the tentacles of some predatory creature, they had not yet reached their target, but it could not be long . . .

'How far does this *sabat* extend at the moment, Muhammad Beg?' he asked.

'To about a hundred yards from the foot of the ramp. We had a setback three days ago when a Rajput sortie managed to set fire to some of the roof timbers. Only a display of great bravery by our labourers, who formed a bucket chain all the way from our wells to put the fire out, prevented the destruction of the forward quarter of the *sabat*.'

'Let me know the names of any who merit special reward.'

'Majesty.'

'Now let me see for myself the inside of one of these *sabats*.' Akbar kicked his black horse gently forward into the darkness of the entrance. The thick wooden roof made it cooler inside. As he went further along, a sour aroma – a combination of damp earth, smoke, and sweat, urine and faeces both animal and human – began to build up in his nostrils. Occasional torches of cloth dipped in pitch placed in holders in the walls provided the only light. By each stood a labourer with leather buckets of sand as well as water beside him, ready to douse any flame that looked like getting out of hand and setting alight the resinous wood of the roof. As Akbar passed these labourers, most of whom were dressed in little but a loincloth and a ragged shirt, they prostrated themselves before him. Sometimes he dismounted to speak briefly to them – a question about where they came from or the extent of their family, a word of encouragement and a gift of a small coin – before moving forward again.

As he was listening to a wizened, white-haired torch-bearer explain that he was the head of a large family from a hamlet called Gurgaon near Delhi, a dull thud shook the wall of the *sabat*, dislodging many small stones and one or two larger ones. The labourer flung himself to the ground but soon scrambled to his feet upon seeing Akbar still standing, holding on to his rearing horse. Shamefacedly he said, 'I apologise. I am not as brave when these cannon balls strike as you, Majesty.'

'You are sufficiently brave to stay at your post,' said Akbar. 'And remember something my father told me about battle. If you hear the sound of an impact or an explosion, you have survived it.'

The labourer smiled briefly. 'I will remember, Majesty.' Akbar slipped him some small coins, and the man raised both his hands above his head and pressed them together in the Hindu form of salutation. Then Akbar rode on through the *sabat*. Before long, despite its tortuous bends, he could see some light dimly reflected from the mouth. Occasionally he heard a musket shot, either from his own men trying to protect the workers as they laboured in the open air or from the defenders on the battlements above who were trying to pick them off. Once he heard a strangled cry which transformed into an animal-like shriek before dying away. By now, Akbar knew enough of the sounds of battle to realise that another of his labourers had died in his cause.

Soon he was at the end of the *sabat* where boulders were piled ready to extend the walls near stacks of roughly sawn tree trunks for the roof. Just within the tunnel's mouth sweating labourers were mixing buckets of water with dry earth to make mud to serve as a kind of cement to hold the walls together. Akbar and Muhammad Beg dismounted. Both men put on their helmets and with bodyguards holding large metal shields in front of them made their way across a patch of open ground towards one of the rock piles which would provide them with some protection.

'Majesty, if you come here you will have a good view of

Chittorgarh's battlements,' called an officer from a little further along the mound. His clothes and once white turban were streaked with dust and mud.

'Be careful, Majesty,' said Muhammad Beg. 'If you can see the battlements, those upon them can see you and they may recognise you from your gilded breastplate.'

'My men daily expose themselves to such risks. I shouldn't scruple to do the same,' said Akbar. He manoeuvred along to where the officer was standing pointing upwards. The top of the walls was clearly visible and there seemed to be some kind of lookout platform on them. After Akbar had watched for a minute or two, he saw two figures emerge on to the lookout and begin scanning the Moghuls' position keenly. One – a tall, black-bearded man – pointed something out to the other. From the sparkling flashes as the sun caught the rings on his fingers and from his general demeanour he was clearly an important commander. Akbar whispered to the white-turbaned officer, 'Get me two loaded muskets and a firing tripod. I want to bring down these fine fellows.'

Quickly two of the musketeers posted at the entrance to the *sabat* passed their weapons and a tripod forward to Akbar. The only way that Akbar could get sufficient elevation on the six-foot-long musket while keeping it steady on its tripod was by lowering himself on to the dusty ground and half-lying, half-crouching behind the musket. As quietly and as quickly as he could, he aligned the barrel on the jewelled man, just as if his target were a tiger in a jungle clearing. Holding his breath to keep himself as still as he was able, he fired. Coughing from the acrid smoke of the discharge, he saw the man pitch forward and plunge from the lookout platform to smash with a dull thud into the ground only a few yards away. His companion disappeared before Akbar could ready the second musket.

'Bring the body in,' he ordered. 'Let's see who we have.'

When two soldiers had dragged the broken figure over, Akbar saw that his musket ball seemed to have caught the man above the right ear, although he could not be entirely sure since much of the rest of the back of the man's head was a bloody misshapen mess from the impact of the fall.

'He is clearly a high-ranking officer,' said Muhammad Beg, 'but I don't recognise him.'

'Neither do I,' said Akbar, 'but Raja Ravi may well do so, despite the wounds, if we show the body to him. He met many of the leaders of Mewar in past years when there was less hostility between their states.'

•◆•

Akbar was standing with Raja Ravi Singh on top of one of the artificial mounds of stone and mud he had had constructed some months previously to give a slightly improved view of the city of Chittorgarh. The raja spoke. 'Majesty, since you killed Jai Mal with your fine shot the other day there has been much more activity within the fort. Despite their rejection of your offer of surrender terms when you returned the body, the defenders have clearly become unsettled by his death and the progress of the *sabats*. They've increased the number of their sorties attempting to destroy the *sabats* and the cannon we have dragged through them, but we've held them off without much difficulty. Their food must be running out too, given the number of foraging parties we've foiled recently.'

'What do you think they'll try next?'

'I don't know, Majesty.'

The two men stood in silence for a while until Akbar suddenly noticed spurts of orange flame and dark smoke beginning to spiral into the sky from several places at once within the fort. He had seen such fires previously but only coming from single points. Raja Ravi had told him that these were funeral pyres for important leaders killed in battle. The one that had followed the return of Jai Mal's body had been particularly fierce. However, these new fires springing up would clearly dwarf even that.

'What is it, Ravi?'

'The defenders must have recognised that there is no prospect of a relieving force and that defeat is inevitable. They want to choose their own moment to die. They are making *jauhar*. Those fires you see are funeral pyres. The Rajput women and girls are throwing themselves into them from specially constructed platforms to burn alive. Mothers will be clamping their babies to them as they jump. The sudden spurts of orange and yellow flame you see are when the men throw buckets of oil and *ghee* – clarified butter – on to the pyres to increase the intensity of the heat and end their families' suffering more quickly. Given courage by the knowledge that their wives and children are dead and can suffer no further pain or indignity at the hands of their enemies, in the morning the men and boys will dress themselves in their saffron battle robes. They will drink opium water from each other's palms to celebrate their brotherhood and to deaden the pain of wounds, and then they will sally forth in one last heroic charge to kill as many of us, their enemies, as they can before meeting their own deaths.'

Raja Ravi's voice was hushed and his tone admiring. After all, Ravi was a Rajput, thought Akbar. Even though such sacrifices were entirely alien and essentially abhorrent to him, Akbar too could not help but feel a degree of admiration for the heroism these women were displaying, dying inside the fortress as he watched. 'Let the fires glow white to lessen their pain,' he prayed. Then, once more the commander, he said to Ravi, 'If you are right, we must prepare for their death charge. Give orders for more cannon to be hauled through the *sabats* tonight and positioned behind what shelter we can throw up where they have a clear field of fire along the ramp. Have musketeers and archers deploy from the exit of the tunnels at dawn. Have squadrons of horsemen and war elephants standing ready to enter them as soon as we detect movement behind the fortress's gate. Horses and elephants will not wait in the dark of the *sabats* without becoming restive. It is better that they only go into them when action is close at hand.'

Early the next morning Akbar stood just outside the exit from the *sabat* which reached the nearest to the winding ramp leading to Chittorgarh's main gate. His commanders were around him and he was wearing full battle garb, his gilded breastplate strapped tightly around him, his helmet squarely on his head and his grandfather's sword Alamgir – newly sharpened and honed – at his side. During the night the defenders of Chittorgarh had fired sporadically on Akbar's men as they feverishly constructed extra barricades around and about the *sabat* exits and as near to the ramp as they dared go. The Rajputs had however succeeded in killing three of a team of a dozen oxen dragging a small bronze cannon into position and the others had stampeded in panic, overturning the cannon and injuring some archers standing nearby in their rush.

But the defenders had been content to watch the cannon righted, seemingly reserving their strength and powder for their last attack the next day. Long before dawn, drums had begun to sound out from Chittorgarh's crenellated watchtowers more loudly than Akbar had ever heard. Several hours had now passed, but their rhythm remained hypnotic, the beat incessant and accompanied by the blare and screech of long trumpets. Occasionally a great roar of voices could be heard, overtopping all other sounds, which Ravi explained was the defenders' prayers to their Hindu gods in the fortress-city's temples.

'When will they attack, Ravi?'

'It cannot be long now. They will have worked themselves into such a pitch of frenzied ecstasy that they will not be able to hold themselves back.'

A quarter of an hour later, the metal grille in front of the great iron-studded gates of Chittorgarh began slowly to wind up and behind it the wooden gates themselves started to open. As soon as there was space, a warrior on a white horse squeezed through and then, waving a curved sword above his head and with his saffron robes streaming behind him, charged down the long winding ramp. He was immediately followed by others and then by more and more riders. Soon, mixed in with them, came men and youths on foot. All were in saffron. All had weapons in their hands. All were screaming a war cry which was incomprehensible to Akbar but which Ravi hastily translated as, 'Life is cheap, honour is not.'

'Fire when you will.' Akbar gave the order to his gunners, archers and musketmen. Almost immediately the first cannon ball brought down a rider on a black horse. As he fell, another horse stumbled over him and plunged with its rider over the low wall of the ramp, falling a hundred feet on to the stony ground. Others too were hit by arrows and musket balls but the rest came on relentlessly, pushing aside the wounded, uncaring whether they tumbled from the ramp or were simply trampled by the oncoming saffron tide. The leading warrior on his white horse reached the first of Akbar's cannon just as the gunners were about to set the taper to the firing hole. Before they could do so, he cut down two of the gunners with sword slashes. Then he charged a second cannon head on. This time Akbar's artillerymen were quicker, discharging the cannon moments before he reached it. The ball hit the rider in his abdomen with its full initial force so that his upper torso was severed from his lower. Miraculously uninjured, the horse galloped on through Akbar's lines, its white coat now drenched in scarlet blood and its rider's feet still in the stirrups.

Other Rajputs had now reached the bottom of the ramp and were spreading out to attack the Moghul troops. So strong was their urge to fight and die that they kept no formation but ran at any positions that caught their eye. It took several arrows or musket balls to stop a man in his tracks. However badly wounded they were, if they reached Akbar's lines they would instantly fling themselves on to his soldiers, wrestling them to the ground and slashing at them with their heavy double-edged swords and the serrated-bladed daggers that nearly all of them grasped in their hands. Seeing that a company of his musketeers were close to being overwhelmed, Akbar ordered them to fall back to the protection of some archers while they reloaded. The ramp down from the gate was now bloodstained and clogged with the dead and dying.

Despite the many casualties they were suffering, Akbar saw to his relief and delight that his men were slowly gaining the advantage in the hand-to-hand fighting and were surrounding small groups of Rajputs. Very few were still emerging from Chittorgarh's gateway. Nearly all who did so were shot down long before they reached the foot of the ramp as they clambered over the bodies of their fallen comrades. Any who succeeded in reaching the bottom met almost immediate death by the swords of Akbar's horsemen who, having come through the *sabats*, were now riding down all Rajput stragglers. Akbar watched as his men systematically eliminated each of the small pockets of resistance. He now knew beyond all doubt that the longed-for victory, his first without the guiding hand of

Bairam Khan, was his. It would be the first of many. Yet elated as he was, he could not but be impressed by the Rajputs' raw courage, and was particularly touched by the conduct of three youths, the eldest of whom looked no more than fourteen, who embraced before rushing, swords raised above their heads, towards a group of Moghul archers, only to be shot down by a shower of hissing arrows long before they reached them. Such warriors would make better allies than foes.

Soon the battlefield was still. Akbar called Ravi Singh to him. 'Have these brave warriors cremated according to their religion. Since the senior officers refused my offer of surrender after Jai Mal's death, have any who survived executed. Death should be no hardship to them since by remaining alive they violate their own warrior code. Then raze the fortress, both to stop it being used against us again and as a warning to any other Rajput ruler who resists rather than accepts the offers of alliance I intend to make them.'

Chapter 8

Hirabai

'Majesty, Rai Surjan wishes to surrender. He offers to become your vassal and in return asks nothing but the lives of those within the walls of Ranthambhor.' The elderly Rajput's eyes were on the ground but the carriage of his tall, wiry body was proud. The words he had just spoken had not come easily to him.

Akbar suppressed a smile of triumph. Sometimes he thought of the officers executed after the fall of Chittorgarh but he had no regrets. Neither did he regret ordering the destruction of Chittorgarh itself – the orange and red flames and then the curling grey smoke had been visible across the Rajasthani deserts for days. His display of ruthlessness had had the intended effect. His siege of Ranthambhor – a fortified Rajput town known throughout Hindustan for the strength of its solid brick walls and high towers – had lasted less than a week. If Rai Surjan was ready to submit to him it meant that all the leading Rajput princes had now accepted his authority. Except, of course, Rana Udai Singh of Mewar, still skulking but defiant in the Aravalli hills after the loss of Chittorgarh and the territory around it. And it was still less than a year since the fall of Chittorgarh. With the Rajasthani princes – the most powerful rulers of northern India – and their saffron-robed warriors by his side, what couldn't he achieve?

'Tell your master I accept his offer and will spare the lives of all within Ranthambhor. Tonight he may remain with honour within its walls and tomorrow, when the sun is a spear's height above the horizon, I will receive him and his senior commanders here in my camp and we will celebrate our new alliance.'

That night Akbar summoned a scribe to his tent. Sometimes such momentous images, such potent emotions filled his mind that he truly regretted he still could not write himself. When he returned to Agra he would appoint a court chronicler – perhaps several – to record the achievements of his reign and those of his father and grandfather, but for the moment the scribe would do. He waited while the young man unstoppered the green jade ink bottle dangling from a chain round his neck and sharpened his quill, and then began to dictate.

'In this year of my reign, the flames of battle rose high in Rajasthan but seeing the might and resolution of my armies the courage of the enemy became like water and trickled away as raindrops into the sand. My victory here is complete and a fitting foundation for future glories . . .'

Long after the scribe had left and the camp had fallen silent around him, Akbar found it hard to sleep. His euphoric words had come from the heart. He had a glorious destiny – he was sure of it – and he wanted the world to know of his exploits through the court chronicles he would have compiled. But no man could live for ever. A single arrow or musket ball in battle, or an assassin's blade between his ribs, might suddenly cut off his life, and then what would happen to the Moghul dynasty? With no obvious heir the empire could soon fall apart as the Moghuls disintegrated again into a collection of petty warlords more concerned with feuding with one another than banding together to keep what they had won in Hindustan. If so, he would have failed just as surely as if, through carelessness and complacency, he allowed his armies to be defeated.

That mustn't happen. He was in his twenties now and it was his duty to secure the future of the empire and the dynasty, and to do that he should marry and produce sons. It would certainly please his mother and his aunt. They had been hinting about it for a while, even suggesting possible brides. But preoccupied with planning the conquest of Rajasthan Akbar hadn't paid much attention and, in truth, he still felt no great desire to marry. He enjoyed sex but his *haram* provided him with infinite pleasures and possibilities for that. He felt no immediate craving for the kind of close and intimate relationship Hamida had shared with Humayun. He had not fully recovered his ability to trust himself mentally to others since his betrayal by Adham Khan and Maham Anga. But sitting here restless and alone with his thoughts in the semi-darkness, he had to accept that the time for marriage had come – if not for himself, then for his empire and above all for the future of the dynasty. What mattered most, of course, was having strong, healthy sons, but marriage could also help him build alliances. He remembered some words from Babur's diary that his *qorchi* had read to him: 'I chose my wives to bind my chiefs to me.'

Outside, a sudden high-pitched squeaking announced that some small creature had been carried off by an owl or another predator. Pleased to have come to a decision, Akbar stood up and stretched. He would think as carefully about the choice of his first bride as about any military campaign. The women Hamida and Gulbadan had suggested to him belonged to the old Moghul aristocracy – one was a distant cousin of his and another was the daughter of the governor of Kabul – but were such women really the best choice for the ruler of Hindustan? Were their relations the chiefs he most wanted to bind to him?

• ◆ •

As Akbar dug his left heel hard into its coarse-haired flank, the camel shot forward, grunting even more querulously than while it had been waiting in the hot sun for the race down the wide mud bank along the Jumna to begin. The crowds held back by the spear shafts of his soldiers roared encouragement, and glancing up briefly to his right Akbar caught the brightly coloured rows of his royal guests – the red- and orange-turbaned Rajput kings who had sworn allegiance to him – assembled in the place of honour on the walls of the Agra fort. But this was no time to think of anything except winning. Right leg crooked on the base of the animal's bony neck and braced against the left, and with the rope reins looped through a brass ring in the camel's nostrils in one hand and a length of bamboo in the other, Akbar urged his mount on. The rolling, lopsided gait, so different from the smoother rhythms of a horse, was exhilarating.

He'd chosen his camel well – a young male with a coat the colour of ripe corn, strong thighs and flanks, and a tendency to snap and spit that suggested pent-up energy. Looking quickly round, he saw he was at least half a length in front of the nearest of his five rivals, but the course was two miles long and much could still happen. The ground was a blur beneath him but suddenly another camel came bumping against his and he felt its rider's thigh strike his own. It was Man Singh, the fourteen-year-old son of the Raja of Amber, his dark hair streaming out behind him. The Rajputs were legendary riders but so were the Moghuls . . . 'Hai! Hai!' Akbar yelled, raising his stick. But he had no need to use it. His own camel turned its head and as its long-lashed eyes saw its rival it surged forward with a bellow.

For a few moments the two animals were nearly level but then Akbar was ahead again, earth flying up around him and the sour smell of sweat – human and animal – in his nostrils. 'Hai! Hai!' he shouted again, as much to release his excitement as to urge his camel on. His throat was full of dust and sweat was running down his face, but all he cared about were the two spears marking the end of the course that he could see some two hundred yards in front. Twisting round he saw he was a good five yards clear of Man Singh. He felt he was flying, charging towards certain victory.

But suddenly his camel stumbled, front feet entangled in a straggle of dry brambles that Akbar, eyes fixed on the finish, hadn't seen. As the beast's front legs buckled, Akbar leaned back as hard as he could against the hump, trying to keep his balance and clamping his left leg tight against the animal's ribs. At the same time, though his every instinct screamed at him to pull tightly on them, he slackened the reins to give his mount the freedom it needed to try to right itself. With its head almost touching the ground, the camel seemed about to come crashing down. Dropping the reins entirely, Akbar flung himself forward, clinging to the nape of the beast's muscular neck and trying to guess on which side it would fall, knowing he must roll clear or be crushed.

Then, somehow, the camel struggled upright again and kicking clear of the brambles galloped on. Akbar grabbed the reins and managed to haul himself up and regain his own balance. The whole incident could only have lasted two or three moments but it had been enough for Man Singh nearly to catch up with him. They were almost thigh to thigh again. 'Hai,' Akbar yelled, 'hai!' and again his camel responded, neck almost horizontal, snorting gustily. Five strides more and Akbar shot between the two spears just a foot ahead of Man Singh. As he reined in, drummers were already beating the cylindrical drums suspended from hide thongs round their necks to acclaim his triumph. Akbar jumped down from his steaming camel, full of the sheer joy of being alive and victorious.

• ◆ •

Two hours later, as dusk was falling and the dark silhouettes of the first bats dipped and swerved through the gathering shadows, Akbar stood on a balcony of the Agra fort, freshly bathed, dressed in a green brocade tunic and pantaloons and wearing a gold chain set with thirty carved emeralds round his neck. His muscles still ached from the camel race but no matter. His Rajput guests, assembled around him, were about to witness the next stage in the festivities he had arranged in their honour. Mindful of their pride, he had determined to make the celebrations so spectacular that by the time his new allies returned to their kingdoms reports would already have reached their subjects of the great esteem in which the Moghul emperor held their rulers.

At a signal from Akbar, golden and green stars exploded into the night sky, as noisy as musket fire. Flashes of silver and red followed, then bursts of saffron yellow accompanied by a high screeching like that of a giant eagle. Next a fine mist, purple and pink, stole into the air. From all around him, and from the crowds gathered along the banks of the Jumna below, Akbar heard excited gasps. The magicians from Kashgar who had come to his court were highly skilled at such things. He had ordered them to produce their finest display and they had not disappointed him. But with the finale drawing close, Akbar was curious to see how these strange men in their long, padded coats of embroidered silk and tasselled hats would fulfil the special command he had given them. For some moments all was quiet and dark and Akbar could sense the anticipation as the crowds waited to see what fresh wonders would unfurl above them. Suddenly came a hissing and a whooshing and the heavens filled with the striped face of a great tiger, jaws yawning so wide it looked ready to swallow the universe. For a few moments it hung there, ferocious and magnificent, and then the bands of black and orange dissolved into tiny shimmering stars.

'The tiger overshadows us all now,' said Raja Bhagwan Das of Amber, a short, wiry man in his thirties with a fine-boned face and the same eagle nose and sharp black eyes as his son, Man Singh. The vermilion Hindu *tilak* mark was on his forehead.

'The tiger is the symbol of my dynasty, it's true,' Akbar replied, 'but don't we all admire the beast's courage and strength? Which of us hasn't pitted himself against the tiger's power and cunning in the hunt and felt the glory of the enterprise? My hope is that one day all Hindustan will embrace the tiger as an emblem of our collective power.'

'Perhaps it will be so, Majesty,' Bhagwan Das responded enigmatically as he again looked up into the sky, where now only stars lit the soft darkness.

'I pray that it will, and that you and I will ride to battle and to glory together many times as true brothers in arms,' Akbar persisted, and saw Bhagwan Das cast him a swift, sideways glance. Of all the Rajput leaders he had summoned to Agra – including the rulers of Bikaner, Jaisalmer and Gwalior – Bhagwan Das was the most powerful. He was also by all accounts shrewd and ambitious and no friend to the Rana of Mewar. If Udai Singh came out of the mountains and tried to retake his lost lands, Akbar wanted to have Bhagwan Das's forces on the Moghuls' side. And if tonight went as he planned, Bhagwan Das would indeed be his friend and for ever . . . Akbar put his arm around the Rajput's shoulders. 'Let us now feast together, Bhagwan Das, as true allies should.'

Akbar led Bhagwan Das and his other Rajput guests down to a large rectangular courtyard. It was lit by three eight foot high candelabras placed in the centre, in each of which burned a dozen white jasmine-scented wax candles twelve feet tall creating a star-like blaze of light. All around the courtyard, smaller candles flickered in jewelled golden candlesticks and wicks burned in *diyas* of scented oil. Silk carpets held down by weights of camel bone and silver carved into the shape of lotus leaves covered the flagstones, and low tables with plump brocade-covered bolsters for seats had been set around three sides. On the fourth stood a wide dais beneath a canopy of green velvet shot through with golden thread. A gilded throne stood upon it with divans, also gilded but slightly lower, arranged on either side.

As soon as Akbar and his Rajput guests were seated on the dais and their courtiers had arranged themselves around the tables, attendants brought dishes piled with the best food Akbar's kitchens could provide – roasted meat and game, stews simmered in spices and butter, rice scattered with dried fruits and gold and silverleaf-covered nuts, fresh-baked breads – including the Rajput delicacies of corn and millet *rotis* cooked with buttermilk – grapes, melons and sweetmeats of rosewater and marzipan. Looking around, Akbar felt confident. There was a sense of restraint, but that was only natural – after all, just a few months ago he had been at war with several of the rulers assembled here and some of them had also been at odds with each other. The purpose of this feast was to show these Rajput princes, the proudest of the proud, who claimed the sun and the moon among their ancestors, that this new-found harmony was in their interests as well as his and that as long as they remained loyal to the Moghul throne they would share in its glory.

He waited until attendants were passing round dishes of *besan* – finely ground flour in which his guests could dip their fingertips to cleanse them of grease – and brass bowls of scented water in which they could rinse their hands, and all were lying or sitting back in comfortable content. Then he rose and holding up his hands for silence began the speech that he had rehearsed so carefully, choosing words to convey both his determination to rule and his deep respect for his guests.

'My people did not come to Hindustan as ravishers to despoil it and carry its riches back to our own lands. We came to claim what is ours – like a bridegroom coming to his long promised bride. Why do I say that Hindustan belongs to the Moghuls? Because over one hundred and sixty years ago my ancestor Timur conquered it. Though he did not stay, he appointed a vassal to rule as his viceroy, but over the years usurpers took the land and, preoccupied with their own conflicts in the far north, the Moghuls could do nothing. Then, forty years ago, my grandfather Babur returned and reclaimed the empire.

'But I do not regard Hindustan as a subject land or its people as inferior to the Moghul clans. All races are equal in my eyes. Though traitors will find no mercy, those who give me their loyalty will prosper. The highest offices at court, the most powerful positions in my armies will be theirs – and yours especially, my friends from the Rajput kingdoms, the lands of warriors. To show my esteem I hereby declare that from this day forward you will number among my inner circle – my *ichkis*. I also declare that you may continue to hold your kingdoms not from me as an overlord but as *watan* – your own hereditary lands to bequeath to whichever heirs you will.'

As he sat down, Akbar glanced at Bhagwan Das, seated to his right. 'You do us honour, Majesty,' the Rajput said.

'And you honour me by your presence here. Bhagwan Das, I have something further I want to say. I wish to marry. I have heard of the beauty and accomplishment of your youngest sister, Hirabai. Will you give her to me as a wife?'

For a moment Bhagwan Das, shocked, did not answer. Eventually he said, 'Why Hirabai, Majesty? Out of all the women in your empire, why have you chosen my sister?'

'To show the esteem in which I hold the Rajputs. Of all the peoples of Hindustan you are most like the Moghuls – forged in the white heat of battle, proud and strong. And of all the Rajputs, you, Bhagwan Das of Amber, are the foremost. I have already seen the courage of your son during the camel race. Your sister will, I am sure, make a worthy empress. And – let us be frank – I wish to bind my allies to me. What better way than through marriage?'

'So that is your intention – to ally yourself with my people through ties of blood . . . ?' Bhagwan Das said slowly, as if assimilating the thought and weighing its merit.

'Yes.'

'And you will take other wives also?'

'Indeed, as a means of strengthening my empire. But I swear to you, Bhagwan Das, that I will always treat your sister with the respect due to a Rajput princess and the first of my wives.'

Bhagwan Das, though, was frowning. 'It is almost unknown for a Rajput woman to marry outside her people . . . And your own family has never broken its ancestral blood ties.'

'No. But I am the first Moghul emperor to be born in Hindustan, which is both my land and my home. Why shouldn't I seek a Hindustani wife?'

'But we Rajputs are Hindus. Even less than marry outside her people can my sister marry outside her religion. She cannot embrace your Muslim faith.'

'I would not ask it of her. I respect her religion which is indeed the religion of many of my subjects. I have never interfered with their worship, so why should I deny Hirabai that freedom?'

Bhagwan Das's aquiline face remained grave and Akbar leaned closer. 'I give you my word – the word of an emperor – that I will never force her to abandon her faith, and she may build a shrine to pray to her gods within the imperial *haram*.'

'But perhaps your own family – your nobles and your mullahs – will object?'

Akbar looked across to where some of his white-turbaned, dark-robed mullahs were seated. 'They will come to understand that it is for the good of the empire,' he said, then added with steel in his voice: 'They will also understand that it is my will.'

'Perhaps, or perhaps not . . . And my sister, though young – she is many years my junior – can be headstrong and stubborn too . . . she may not feel . . .'

'Your sister will be an empress and perhaps mother to the next Moghul emperor – as you will be his uncle. Bhagwan Das, give me your answer. Do not disappoint me, please.'

For a moment, Bhagwan Das sat back, his fingers playing with the triple-stranded necklace of pearls that fell almost to his lean waist. Then, finally, he smiled. 'Majesty, you honour my family. Hirabai is yours. May all our gods smile on the union.'

• ◆ •

She was sitting very still beneath her ruby-coloured veils, which were shot through with orange and gold thread. The only movement was the trembling of the flowers and leaves, worked in gold wire and studded with pearls, set in her headdress – a wedding gift from Akbar. The white-clad Hindu priest had finished his part in the ceremony and now it was time for Akbar's mullah to recite verses from the Koran. As the man slowly and sonorously intoned the words, Akbar could see one slender foot protruding from beneath her robes. It was decorated with henna in intricate spirals.

He glanced down at his hands, also painted with henna for good luck by his mother and aunt, who were watching the ceremony through a screen of interwoven willow wands designed to allow them to see without being seen.

Finished at last, the mullah closed the ivory covers of his book and handed it to an attendant who placed it in a carved wooden box. Then the mullah picked up a ewer of rosewater and, as Akbar held out his hands, poured the cool water over them to symbolise cleansing, then tipped what was left into a translucent agate cup. 'Drink, Majesty, to confirm the union.'

Akbar swallowed a few drops then held out his hand to Hirabai to lead her to the marriage feast, to be given by her family in accordance with Hindu custom. Akbar had given Bhagwan Das fine and richly furnished apartments in the Agra fort to house the members of his family and the retinue that had accompanied Hirabai as she travelled in her covered litter slung between two camels all the way from Amber. The celebrations tonight would signal the start of a month of gift-giving, processions, hunts, elephant fights and displays of martial skills. Yet as the wedding feast progressed, all Akbar's thoughts were on the coming night and he felt a little uncertain. The joyous giving and receiving of pleasure with his concubines was familiar and fun. In their soft, scented arms he found release from the burden of kingship. But the bedding of a virgin Rajput princess was different.

He glanced at Hirabai sitting close beside him, still hidden beneath her shimmering veils. For the hundredth time, he wondered what she would be like. Rajput women were renowned for their striking beauty, but even if she didn't please him it wasn't important, he told himself. What mattered was that by this marriage he had secured an enduring alliance with the kingdom of Amber. Other such political unions would follow, ensuring the empire's peace and stability. At least as a royal princess Hirabai would understand the cares and preoccupations that came with being a king.

Akbar tried to attend to the rituals of the feast. Dancing girls from Amber clad in peacock blue whirled before him to the wild rhythms of lean, bare-chested, orange-turbaned drummers and the wailing of brass pipes. Rajput musicians sang in high-pitched nasal voices of valour on the battlefield, acrobats tumbled through circles of flaming rope and an old man in a long coat inset with pieces of mirror glass that reflected the candle light coaxed a python from a woven basket. He let it coil itself around him and even kissed its thick, scaly body.

Then came the climax Akbar himself had planned. As the magician, uttering commands in some harsh-sounding language Akbar had never heard, returned the hissing serpent to its basket, Akbar's chief huntsman entered the chamber. He was leading a sinewy, half-grown leopard with a collar of rubies and diamonds round its tawny neck. The teardrop markings beneath its eyes had been gilded, making it look like a creature from some fable. Its tail lashed about, knocking a goblet to the ground, and the muscles in the huntsman's arms, left bare by his leather jerkin, bunched as he tightened his grip on the leash.

Akbar rose and addressed Bhagwan Das. 'This is Jala, a cub sired by my favourite hunting leopard. It is my gift to you on this auspicious occasion.' The raja's eyes gleamed. Akbar knew he loved the hunt as much as he did, but, more than that, leopards were rare and very valuable, truly imperial animals. The gift of one was a great

111

distinction. The raja seemed speechless. 'My huntsmen will continue to train him, and when he is ready I will send him to Amber.' Akbar went over to Jala and cupped the animal's graceful head between his hands. 'Be as swift and fearless in the hunt for your new master as your father has been for me.'

By the time the wedding feast was ended the moon had risen, its pale, cold light silvering the Jumna river where it flowed some thirty feet beneath the apartments in the *haram* that Akbar had chosen for Hirabai and to which, preceded by musicians, he escorted her. As his attendants began to undress him, he glanced towards the brocaded screens embroidered with flowers and stars – the product of the looms of Gujarat where the weavers excelled at such things – behind which his bride was being undressed and anointed with perfumed oils ready for the marriage bed. When the last attendant had left, Akbar drew his loose green robe around him and approached the curtains. Pulling one aside, he ducked through. Hirabai was standing with her back to him, the slim outline of her body visible through the diaphanous peach-coloured muslin of her shift. Her hair, tinted with dark red henna, hung in shining waves to the small of her back. Something about the set of her shoulders told him how tense she was.

'Hirabai . . . Don't be afraid. You have nothing to fear from me.' Akbar placed both hands on her shoulders and turned her gently to face him. Perhaps it was the expression in her eyes – wild as the leopard's had been – that gave him warning. As Hirabai twisted from his grasp and raised her right hand he was ready for her. Reacting as instinctively as on the battlefield, he wrenched her wrist back so sharply she cried out and a small, broad-bladed dagger fell to the ground.

'Why?' he demanded, still gripping her tightly by the wrist. 'Why?' he shouted again, even louder, his face inches from hers, when she didn't reply at once.

Hirabai's eyes, black as her brother's, were full of hatred. 'Because you are the enemy of my people – the slayer of countless brave Rajputs at Chittorgarh, and their women to whom you left no option but to save their honour by making *jauhar*. I wish I could

112

have been with them. I would have gone joyfully into the flames to avoid submitting to you.'

Akbar released her and she stumbled back several paces before regaining her balance and rubbing her right wrist. His eyes flickered over her, looking for any other weapons, but near naked as she was he could see there were none. 'Your brother gave you to me willingly. Does he know your feelings?' A new thought struck him. 'Perhaps he knew you meant to kill me. Was he the instigator?'

For the first time, Hirabai looked afraid. 'No. He knew nothing. He has little time for the women of his family. Even the news that I was to become your wife came to me in a letter.'

'I should call the guards. Before the sun rises you should meet your end.'

'Do it, then.'

'Is that really what you want? If the world found out what you tried to do, your brother would live the rest of his life in shame and disgrace. Who among the other Rajput rulers would wish for contact with a man whose sister had abandoned every concept of duty and honour? The Rajputs are renowned for their courage on the battlefield, not for assassination and deceit.'

Hirabai flushed. For the first time he saw how beautiful she was, oval face delicately boned as a cat's and soft skin the colour of new honey. But she held no charms for him. Striding over to her, he gripped her shoulders.

'Listen to me. I will not have my alliances with Rajput kingdoms disrupted by one woman's foolish delusions. The officers I executed after the fall of Chittorgarh met the end they wanted. Under your Rajput code it would have been shameful to them to live. Surely you understand that?' Hirabai said nothing, but he felt her body slacken as if the fight was draining from her and he relaxed his hold. 'I will tell no one what happened just now and, if you value your family's honour, neither will you. You are my wife and you will do your duty. Do you understand me?'

Hirabai nodded.

'In that case, it is time to perform your first task as my bride.' Akbar looked towards the bed. Hirabai turned away, and untying

113

the pearled cord round her waist let her robe fall to the floor. Her delicately curved body was alluring, but anger not desire was what he felt as he lowered himself on top of her and began to thrust, eyes never leaving her face. Not by a single change in her expression did she show any pain or discomfort as he moved faster and faster inside her, anxious not for pleasure but just to get the task done. This was not how he had expected his wedding night with his virgin bride to be. His new wife had violated his trust just as Adham Khan had done. Hirabai was as hostile an enemy as any he had faced on the battlefield. But they, like Adham Khan, had learned not to defy him, and so would she.

Chapter 9

Salim

'I'm sorry, Majesty, her monthly blood is flowing.' The *khawajasara* looked nervously at Akbar as if Hirabai's failure to conceive could somehow be blamed on her. 'Her Highness remains melancholy, as she has been ever since your marriage. She will hardly eat. She seldom leaves her apartments to walk in the *haram* gardens. She talks only with the maids she brought with her from Amber and keeps herself apart from the other women, never joining in with their games or entertainments. Perhaps she has a sickness . . . Should I summon a *hakim* to examine her again?'

'No.' It was only six weeks ago that an elderly doctor, a piece of cloth placed over his head to conceal the other inhabitants of the *haram* from his aged eyes, had been led by two eunuchs to Hirabai's apartments. Akbar had watched as, emerging from under the cloth like a tortoise poking its head from its shell, the *hakim* had examined Hirabai, running his hands over her body beneath her loose cotton shift. 'I can find nothing wrong, Majesty,' he had said at last. 'The entrance to her womb is strong and well formed.'

Akbar looked broodingly at the *khawajasara*, tall, big-boned, well fleshed and handsome despite her forty or so years, who had become superintendent of the *haram* on the retirement of the woman who had brought him Mayala all those years ago. But it was Hirabai he saw before his eyes. Every time he made love to her he hoped for

115

some change, but always she lay limp and unresponsive. Her passivity disturbed him more than if she had tried to fight him off. Did she still dream of stabbing him? He had ordered the *khawajasara* to ensure there was nothing sharp in the empress's apartments. The superintendent had looked at him a little curiously but had of course obeyed. It was as much for Hirabai's protection as for his own – sometimes he feared she might try to harm herself. He had had her apartments moved to a double-tiered pavilion that, though overlooking the Jumna, had windows inset with fretted marble screens from which it was impossible to jump.

'Majesty?'

He had forgotten the *khawajasara* was still there. 'You are dismissed. Come to me again next month when – God willing – you may bring better news.'

Akbar sat alone for a while. Outside the sky was fresh and clear. The rains were over and he should have been out hunting or hawking. Why did thoughts of Hirabai preoccupy him? It wasn't love, but perhaps it was pride . . . All the court must know things were amiss between the emperor and his bride. They never ate or spent time together except for his nocturnal visits to her bed. Even then, as soon as he was finished he returned to his own apartments. He had never woken in her arms as the pale dawn light came slanting in.

Perhaps his mother would have some words of wisdom – or at least of comfort. Till now he had hesitated to confide in her, hoping each month to hear that Hirabai was pregnant. But time was passing. He was being distracted from the matters that should be occupying his mind, and – if the stories the elderly Jauhar had told him were true – something yet more pernicious was gathering momentum. Bhagwan Das had been right to predict that Akbar's marriage to a non-Muslim would be criticised. The mullahs were whispering that Akbar's childless state was a punishment for marrying an infidel Hindu.

• ◆ •

Hamida was reading, but seeing Akbar she put her book of poetry down. 'What is it? You look troubled.'

'The *khawajasara* has just made her report to me.'

116

'And?'

'Hirabai has still not conceived.'

'You must be patient. Remember you have only been married six months.'

'That's what I tell myself. But how much longer will I have to wait?'

'You are a young man. You will take other wives. There will be children – sons – even if they are not Hirabai's.'

'It's not just a matter of my own impatience. Jauhar came to me two weeks ago. Since I made him my vizier he is even better informed about what is being said around the court.'

'Court gossip doesn't matter.'

'This does. Some of the senior clerics – the *ulama* – are claiming that Hirabai will never bear a child. They say it's God's judgement on me for my crime against Islam in marrying an unbeliever.'

'You rule the empire, not the *ulama*.'

'I'm not afraid of them or of their narrow prejudices. At first, I admit, I did wonder whether there was anything in their words, but the more I thought about it the more impossible I found it to believe that a merciful, compassionate God would reject people simply because they hold different beliefs. But some of my subjects may begin to heed their arguments, however absurd. This could sow hatred and division. The *ulama* know perfectly well why I married a Hindu – not only to strengthen a military alliance but to show that all can prosper under the Moghuls regardless of religion . . .'

'You are wise,' Hamida said. 'You see potential dangers early.'

'That's what my father encouraged me to do. He said he hadn't understood the threat his half-brothers posed until it was nearly too late.'

'That is true. It almost cost us our lives.'

'I mustn't make the same mistake, even though the dangers I face are different.'

'Tell me about Hirabai. I know you are unhappy . . . forgive me, but I hear things, and so does Gulbadan. Does Hirabai not please you?'

'She hates me.'

'Why should she?'

'She blames me for executing Rajput officers at Chittorgarh and for razing the fortress . . . she thinks of me as the destroyer of her people.'

'How can she, when her own brother is glad to call himself your ally?'

Akbar shrugged. 'I think she despises him for it . . . but she won't discuss her feelings.'

'Are you sure you understand her properly? Perhaps she finds our court alien and is homesick for Rajasthan. In time she may change.'

'I do understand her, Mother. On our wedding night she tried to stab me.' Akbar had not meant to say it but the words were out before he could stop them.

'She did what?' Any sympathy for her daughter-in-law vanished from Hamida's face and her eyes flashed. 'Then you should have had her executed, just as your father should have killed his brothers when they first rebelled . . . You said you had learned from his mistakes, yet you lie with a woman who wishes you dead. I don't understand.'

'I knew you wouldn't. That was why I didn't tell you. I have kept Hirabai as my wife because of what it symbolises to my people. The alliance has pleased the Rajputs. Had I rejected or executed her how could our alliance have held? And Hirabai's freedom to worship her gods is living proof that my Hindu subjects have nothing to fear from me. The wider world knows nothing of our lives at court. They see simply that the Moghul emperor has taken a royal Hindu bride and they rejoice.'

Hamida was silent, her fine brow wrinkled in thought. 'Perhaps you are right,' she said at last. 'Shock and maternal anger made me speak as I did. I will reveal to no one – not even Gulbadan – what you have just told me, but my attendants will watch Hirabai and make sure that she is doing nothing to prevent or to end a pregnancy. Many such tricks are known in the *haram* – potions of bitter herbs, sponges soaked in vinegar and pushed deep inside before intercourse, even twigs wrapped in sheep's wool and inserted afterwards to scour the womb – and the Rajput women too may have their methods.'

'She is already watched. The *khawajasara,* observing through her *jali* screen, records our couplings and is looking for signs of anything untoward . . . I only hope it isn't hatred that prevents Hirabai from conceiving. She is strong-willed and the mind can rule the body. Sometimes I worry that even if she did bear me a child such a birth could not be auspicious.'

'That is foolish, Akbar. And who knows . . . Hirabai is very young. With a child she may change . . .'

'She's not as young as you were when you married my father.'

'I was lucky. Your father chose me out of love and I loved him. Also, I was only the daughter of a nobleman. I wasn't royal like Hirabai with all the weight of an ancient lineage on my shoulders. Things were perhaps simpler for your father and me.'

'Even though you endured so much hardship and danger?'

'Perhaps because of it, who knows?' For the first time since he had told her of Hirabai's hatred of him, Hamida's face softened. She was thinking of Humayun, he was sure. Would he ever feel for a woman the kind of love that had existed between his parents?

'Akbar, perhaps I can help you. Gulbadan has told me of a Sufi mystic, Shaikh Salim Chishti. She has visited him and says that, just as my own grandfather did, he has the power to see into the future . . . Perhaps he can tell you something to ease your mind.'

'Where does this Sufi live?'

'In Sikri, not far from here.'

'I know it. I stopped there once to drink from a well while out hunting.'

'Perhaps I am wrong to suggest it. Your father in his youth became so preoccupied with what the stars could tell him about the future that he failed to see the dangers lurking around him. Sometimes it is better not to know what the future holds.'

'No, I want to know. Then I can plan for it.'

•◆•

Akbar led his small troop along the dusty road and up the plateau towards Sikri. Two of his favourite hunting dogs were running alongside, pink tongues lolling, and his only escort apart from a few bodyguards were two huntsmen and his *qorchi*. A young deer he had shot as it burst from a thicket was already on its way to Agra, slung across the saddle of another huntsman he had sent back with it. It was sensible to maintain the fiction that this was a hunting party, Akbar thought. He didn't want it known that he was consulting a mystic.

Ahead, through the shimmering midday heat haze, he saw the outline of the cluster of mud-brick houses on the edge of the plateau that was Sikri. 'We'll rest there until the heat abates a little,' he said to his *qorchi*. 'I've heard stories of a Sufi mystic who lives in this village and I'm curious to see him. Ride up there and ask him if the emperor may visit him.'

As the youth galloped ahead, Akbar followed more slowly, trotting up the steep slope and into the village where he dismounted in a pool of green-black shade beneath the dense foliage of a mango tree. A few minutes later, he saw his *qorchi* returning.

'Majesty, Shaikh Salim Chishti bids you welcome. Come this way.'

Akbar followed his squire through the village to a low single-storey house with only two slits on either side of the door for windows. Ducking inside, for a moment he found himself in darkness. Then, as his eyes adjusted, he made out an old man dressed entirely in robes of rough-spun white wool kneeling in prayer, head to the floor and facing in the direction of Mecca.

'Forgive me, Majesty, I was praying to God for guidance so that I may help you.' As he spoke the old man picked up a tinder box and with swift, efficient movements lit a candle in a clay holder. In the faint light Akbar saw a face crinkled as a walnut.

'How did you know I've come for help?' he asked, looking around him. The room was almost empty except for the dark red prayer rug, a rough-hewn wooden chest and the string charpoy that was the Sufi's bed.

'Everyone who seeks me is hoping for divine assistance, even though they may tell themselves they have only come out of curiosity. You look surprised, Majesty. Perhaps you think I claim too much for myself? I did not ask for my powers, but I know that by God's

120

divine grace I can sometimes be a conduit to him. Come and sit in front of me where I can see you.'

Akbar squatted down on a piece of woven matting. For several minutes the Sufi said nothing, but his eyes, the irises curiously luminous like an owl's, looked hard at Akbar, as if trying to divine his innermost thoughts. Then, swaying gently, long, slender hands folded against his chest, he began to intone, repeating over and over, 'Give me your wisdom, show me the way.' When was the holy man going to ask him why he'd come? Akbar wondered. But as he waited a sense of peace and tranquillity began to possess him. His eyes were closing and his body and mind beginning to relax, cares and anxieties, desires and ambitions rolling away until he felt unsullied and carefree as a child.

'We are ready to begin.' The Sufi reached out a hand and gently touched Akbar's shoulder. Akbar opened his eyes with a start, wondering how long he had been in that half-dreaming state that had been so strangely pleasurable. 'What is it you wish to know, Majesty?'

'Whether my wife will bear me a son.'

'Is that all? That is a simple question.'

'Perhaps not so simple. You know that the empress is a Hindu?'

'Of course, Majesty. All of Hindustan knows that.'

'As a Muslim yourself, do you believe her childlessness could be God's way of punishing me for marrying an unbeliever?'

'No. As a Sufi I believe there are many roads to God and that it is for each of us to find him.'

'Whatever our faith?'

'Yes. God belongs to us all.'

That was true, Akbar thought, gazing into the Sufi's searching yellow eyes. He had been foolish to wonder even for a moment whether there was any truth in what the *ulama* were alleging. Perhaps he had been equally foolish to fear that Hirabai's antipathy towards him was the reason she hadn't conceived . . . Things he'd never thought his pride or his position would allow him to reveal to a stranger came tumbling out.

'She doesn't love me. Each time I lie with her I see her contempt for me . . . I have tried to be good to her . . .'

But the Sufi raised his hand. 'Move closer.'

Akbar leaned forward and the Sufi took his face in his hands and pulled it gently towards him until Akbar's forehead was resting against his own. Again a wondrous sense of well-being flooded through Akbar and his mind felt bathed in light.

'You needn't fear, Majesty. Your wife will soon bear you a fine son. And you will have two more sons. The Moghul bloodline will flourish here in Hindustan for many generations, nourished by your conquests and your vision of a powerful and united empire.'

'Thank you, Shaikh Salim Chishti. Thank you.' Akbar bowed his head. His confidence was renewed, his self-doubts stilled. Everything would be as he wished, he was certain. He would build a mighty empire, with sons to help him, and when he died they would continue his work . . . the dynasty would flourish. 'When what you say comes to pass, I will found a great city here at Sikri to honour you. Its gardens and fountains and palaces will be a wonder of the world and I will move my court here from Agra.'

'When your wife conceives, send her here. Outside the village is a small monastery where she will be cared for, and perhaps away from the court her mind will grow calmer and she can prepare for motherhood more easily.'

'Could she practise her religion here?'

'Of course. As I told you, many paths lead to God and to the knowledge of ourselves and the universe we crave. We must each choose our own.'

'Then I will indeed send her here.' Akbar rose. 'Thank you. You have brought me comfort and hope.'

'I am glad. But there is something else I should tell you, and this time you may not welcome it.'

'What is it?' Akbar placed his hand gently on the old man's shoulder, still sinewy and strong beneath his coarse woollen robe.

'Though you will have three strong sons, remember that love of power, the desire to possess it, can poison even the closest family bonds. Do not take the love of your sons for you – or for each other – for granted.'

122

'What do you mean? Are you speaking of family rivalries like those my father endured?'

'I'm not sure, Majesty. Though I foresee that you will have sons and your empire will flourish, beyond that I see shadows. They are as yet without shape, but perhaps they carry a warning. Be vigilant, Majesty. Remember my words. Keep watch over your sons as they grow to manhood so you can dispel those shadows before they take substance and do harm . . . '

Riding back towards Agra later that day, Akbar pondered the Sufi's warning. So many times since the days of his ancestor Timur the Moghuls had almost destroyed themselves by turning on each other rather than their enemies. He would watch for the signs and be on his guard. But all that lay far off in the future. Buoyed by the thought of three sons Akbar urged his horse to a yet faster pace.

· ◆ ·

Six weeks later the *khawajasara*'s delighted face told Akbar everything he needed to know.

'Majesty, at last it has happened.'

'When will the child be born?'

'The *hakim* says in August.'

'I will go to the *haram* now.' Akbar struggled to restrain tears of joy as he half ran to the women's quarters. When he entered Hirabai's apartments he smelled the familiar sweet spiciness of the incense sticks she always kept burning in a brass pot before a statue of an unsmiling, many-armed goddess. Hirabai was sitting on a low, lacquered Rajput stool as one of her maids combed out her thick hennaed hair. It seemed to Akbar that his wife's face, grown so angular and drawn, was already softening and that her skin had a new bloom. Yet if he'd hoped for any softening in her manner to him he was disappointed. Her expression as she looked up at him was as distant and unyielding as ever.

'Leave us,' Akbar ordered the maid. As soon as they were alone, he asked, 'Is it true? You really are pregnant?'

'Yes. Surely the *khawajasara* told you.'

'I wanted to hear it from my wife as a husband should. Hirabai – you are carrying my child, perhaps the future Moghul emperor.

123

Is there nothing I can do or say to make you look more kindly on me or to make you happier?'

'The only way would be to send me back to Amber, but that is impossible.'

'You will be a mother soon. Does that mean nothing to you?'

Hirabai hesitated. 'I will love the child because the blood of my people will flow through its veins. But I will not pretend to feelings for you that I can never have. All I pray is that you take other wives and leave me in peace.'

'Bear me a healthy son and I promise never to lie with you again.' Hirabai said nothing. 'I want you to make ready for a journey a week from now.'

'Where are you sending me?' For the first time her cold demeanour faltered and she looked anxious.

'Don't be afraid. I wish you to go to a place of good omen — Sikri. I did not tell you this before because I know you distrust my religion, but a Muslim mystic lives there. He predicted you would bear me a son and asked me to send you there, to a monastery where you will be well tended until the child is born. I will send the best of my *hakims* with you and you may take all the attendants you wish. The air is good there — cooler and healthier than in Agra. It will be beneficial for you and the child you carry and you may worship your own gods there.'

Hirabai looked down at her hands folded on her lap. 'It will be as you wish, of course.'

'Shall I send word to your brother?'

Hirabai nodded. Akbar waited a few moments, hoping she might say something else. 'I will love the child,' she had said, but would she? If she hated the father, what affection could she feel for the son? For a moment he pondered the Sufi's warning. Was his wife's hostility one of the distant shadows he had glimpsed? With a last searching look at Hirabai's half-averted face, he left her. Free from the frigid aura surrounding her, he felt the warmth of his happiness returning. He was going to have a son . . .

•◆•

'I name you Salim after the holy man who predicted your birth.'

Holding the squirming body of his new-born son in the crook of his left arm, with his right hand Akbar picked up a saucer of small gold coins and poured them gently over the baby's head. Salim threshed about, flexing tiny fists, but though he screwed up his face he didn't howl. Smiling with pride, Akbar lifted Salim high so all could see him. Then he placed him on a large green velvet cushion held by his elderly vizier Jauhar. It was the turn of the black-turbaned Shaikh Ahmad, head of the *ulama*, to speak. What did he really think about blessing the child of a Hindu mother? His face, bland above his bushy dark beard, gave nothing away. Whatever his inner feelings, he and his clique had lost the battle – defeated by the birth of this child who as yet knew nothing of the tensions of the world.

After thanking God for Salim's birth, the priest said portentously: 'We whom His Imperial Majesty have summoned here to Sikri hail the auspicious birth of this world-illuminating pearl of the mansion of dominion and fortune, this night-gleaming jewel of the casket of greatness and glory. Prince Salim, may God guide you and pour an ocean of divine bounty upon you.'

Later that night, Akbar slipped from the huge many-canopied brocade tent specially erected in Sikri for the feast celebrating his son's birth. For a while he had joined in the slurred singing, circling arm in arm with Ahmed Khan and his other commanders in some semblance of the old dances of the Moghul homelands – not that many could remember the steps. But now there was something he felt he must do. Calling for his horse, he mounted and taking only a few of his guards, rode slowly through the warm night air, scented by the still-smoking dung fires over which the villagers of Sikri had cooked their evening meal, towards the nearby monastery where Hirabai was still lodged. Glancing up it seemed to him that the stars, so beloved by his own father Humayun, had never seemed so numerous or so lustrous. It was as if they had found a special radiance to shed upon the earth that now held his son – the son he must do everything to protect. Even now, at a time of so much happiness, he could not forget the Sufi's words of caution . . .

'It is the emperor!' shouted one of his guards as the arched entrance of the monastery appeared before them. Orange-clad Rajput soldiers from Amber to whom Akbar had awarded the honour of protecting the Empress stood to attention and their captain stepped forward.

'Welcome, Majesty.'

Akbar dismounted and tossing his reins to his *qorchi* walked through the gateway into a small, dimly lit courtyard. As the cry went up again, 'It is the emperor!' one of Hirabai's Rajput maids appeared through the shadows carrying an oil lamp whose tiny flame flickered and danced.

'Please take me to my wife.'

Hirabai was lying propped on blue cotton cushions on a low bed. Salim was feeding at her breast and Akbar saw a contentment in her face he had never witnessed before. It was so unexpected it made her seem almost a stranger. But as she looked at him, the glow faded. 'Why have you come? You should be at the feast attending to your guests.'

'I felt a sudden need to see my son . . . and my wife.'

Hirabai said nothing, but took Salim from her breast and handed him to her maid. The baby began to cry, angry at having his feeding so abruptly ended, but Hirabai signalled to the maid to take him away.

'Hirabai – I have come here to make one last appeal to you. For the rest of our lives Salim will be a link of flesh and blood between us. Can't we forget the past and begin again for him? Let all my sons be yours too so that in later life they can support and help one another as full brothers.'

'I have done my duty. As I have already told you, I wish you only to leave me alone. You promised that if I bore you a son you would do so. Let other women father your sons.'

'Salim's position will be less secure if he has only half-brothers. They will feel less loyalty to him. Have you considered that? Don't you owe it to your son to make his position as strong as possible?'

'My son has Rajput blood in his veins. He will trample any rival into the dust.' Hirabai raised her chin.

Frustration at such heedless, stubborn pride, such a narrow view of the world, filled Akbar. For a moment he wondered whether to tell her of the Sufi's warnings of what might lie in the future, but he knew she wouldn't listen. So be it, but he would not leave his son to be brought up by such a woman.

'Very well, I will respect your wishes. But there is a price for what you ask. Though you may see Salim whenever you wish, I intend to place him in my mother's care. Moghul princes are often reared by senior royal women rather than their birth mothers. She will appoint a milk-mother as is also the Moghul way. My son will be brought up as a Moghul prince, not a Rajput one.'

Hirabai stared at him. If he had anticipated grief, remonstrations, he was wrong. The only sign of agitation was a slight tautening of her jaw. 'You are the emperor. Your word is law.' Her tone was contemptuous, insolent even. He had come to her tonight to give her one final chance, but, as he had known in his heart, she had utterly closed her mind against him.

Chapter 10

A Wonder of the World

'You have done me a great honour and given me a great responsibility, Majesty.'

'I know you will acquit yourself well, Abul Fazl. I wish the chronicle of my reign to be a testament to future generations. You must record the truth – the bad as well as the good. Don't seek merely to flatter me.'

'I will write every word with a pen perfumed with sincerity.'

Akbar suppressed a smile as he looked at his newly appointed chief chronicler. Though he had other scribes, he had begun to feel the need for someone who would do more than just write down his words – someone he could trust to inform himself about and record all the important aspects of his reign, even when he himself was away. Abul Fazl was a bull-necked, bow-legged man a little younger than himself with a small but livid birthmark at the corner of his left eye. His father Shaikh Mubarak, a learned theologian, had brought the family to the Moghul court some years earlier. Abul Fazl's skills both as a commander and as an analyst of court politics had already caught Akbar's attention, but it was his vizier Jauhar who had recommended him for this appointment, observing to Akbar that 'although vain and an outrageous flatterer, Abul Fazl is clever and loyal. He will glory at being at the centre of events and will perform the task more ably than a more modest or retiring man.'

Certainly the beaming smile on his clean-shaven face told Akbar how gratified he was by the award of such a position of trust.

'You must take particular care in recording the reforms I intend to make to the empire's administration. One of the chief purposes of the chronicles will be to guide my successors.'

'Of course, Majesty.' Abul Fazl signalled with a richly beringed hand to an attendant who placed a carved mulberry wood writing slope before him and handed him paper, pen and ink.

'Then let us begin.' Akbar got up and paced his apartments. Through an arched opening he could see boys riding their camels along the sunlit banks of the Jumna and beyond them a group of his courtiers, one with a hawk on his wrist, going hunting. He wished he was with them, but business must come before pleasure.

'I have already made some important decisions. First, I wish to fit all my officials into a single hierarchy. Every one of them, whether they are soldiers or not, will be designated as commanders of a certain number of troops. You look startled, Abul Fazl, but with such a large and disparate empire I must find ways to make my rule uniform and consistent. Even the head of the royal kitchens will be included – he will become a commander of six hundred. You, as my adviser and chronicler, will be a commander of four thousand.'

Abul Fazl permitted himself a satisfied smile and bent over his writing again as Akbar continued. 'Next, certain lands within my empire will be designated crown property and my officials will collect the due taxes and remit them straight to my treasury. The rest of my territory will be divided into *jagirs* – fiefs – and given to my nobles and commanders to govern. They will be responsible for gathering the taxes and may keep a proportion in return for maintaining an agreed number of troops for the crown. In that way, should I need to go to war I will be able to gather a large and well-trained army quickly.'

'Can the holders bequeath their *jagirs* to their sons, Majesty?'

'No. When they die, the *jagir* will revert to me to be disposed of at my pleasure.' Akbar paused. 'By making every man of importance a servant of the empire and by being able to remove troublemakers from their *jagirs* and confiscate their property when they die, I can

130

compel my nobles' loyalty and prevent any of them from building a power base against me.' He paused, and for a few moments the only sound was the scratching of Abul Fazl's long, ivory-stemmed pen. 'Is everything clear? Have you noted down everything I said?'

'Yes, Majesty. I have written accurately and in sufficient detail for all who read my account to benefit from your great wisdom, unparalleled insight and organisational genius in bringing order to your new dominions.'

Why did Abul Fazl have to use quite so many words? Akbar wondered. He seemed to think that verbose and constant flattery was the way to Akbar's favour. Perhaps it was the Persian way, though Bairam Khan had not been like that. The memory of his old mentor and his treatment of him was still painful, and Akbar determinedly pushed it out of his mind.

'Let us go outside. We can talk further there.' He led the way from his private apartments to a courtyard where his three sons were playing. Five-year-old Salim was riding in a small cart being pulled by Murad, just eleven months younger, and three-and-a-half-year-old Daniyal. They hadn't noticed him yet, standing with Abul Fazl in the shadows beneath a neem tree, and went on with their game. Salim was growing fast. He had Hirabai's narrow, slender build and the same thick dark hair and long-lashed eyes. Murad was nearly as tall but thicker set, more like Akbar himself, but with the tawny eyes of his Rajput mother, a princess of Jaisalmer. Little Daniyal, chubby with puppy fat and trying hard to keep up with Murad, as yet resembled neither Akbar nor his beautiful Persian mother.

Akbar watched with the satisfaction he always felt when he looked at them. Just as Shaikh Salim Chishti had predicted, he had three strong sons. 'Look at them, Abul Fazl. What more could I have done to secure the succession than father three such healthy boys, and what better foundation could I have given my empire? God has been good to me.'

'Yes, indeed, Majesty. He has poured his celestial light upon you.'

The cart had come to a halt on the other side of the courtyard and Murad was trying to climb in, no doubt demanding his turn. For a moment the memory of the Sufi's warning disturbed Akbar's content. He must pay close attention to the education of his sons and be alert for any signs of rivalry or jealousy, he thought, watching them intently now. But Salim was laughing as he yielded his place in the cart to Murad who, Akbar could see, looked all smiles. They were still so young . . . He was being foolish. It would be years before he need worry – if he ever had to. He was about to walk over to join them when his *qorchi* approached.

'Majesty, the architects have arrived to discuss the plans for Sikri.'

'Excellent. I will come at once. You too, Abul Fazl. I want you to know everything about this project. I am planning a new capital at Sikri to fulfil my promise to Shaikh Salim Chishti, the Sufi priest who predicted the birth of my sons.'

'Your love of architecture is well known, Majesty. Your father's tomb in Delhi is the finest building in all Hindustan.'

Abul Fazl was for once not exaggerating, Akbar thought as they returned to his apartments. Humayun's octagonal sandstone and marble mausoleum was indeed magnificent. With its high double-skinned dome and elegant symmetry, it recalled Timur's tomb in far-off Samarkand of which Akbar had seen drawings. It was fitting that his father should rest in such a place. Of course, he himself would probably never visit blue-domed Samarkand with its soaring Turquoise Gate. For him it would remain like a dream, or the setting of some wonderful fable – spectrally beautiful but unreal. He had been born in Hindustan – its dry red soil was in his veins and his destiny was here. The thought reminded him of something important.

'You must set this down in the chronicle, Abul Fazl. Sikri will be entirely different from anything I – or my father or grandfather – have built in Hindustan. I have decided to build it in the style of my Hindu subjects. That's why I've chosen Hindu architects. I have already spent many hours questioning them. They have ancient books to guide them in which everything is written – from the best way to make bricks, to siting buildings in such a way as to bring good fortune to those who live in them.'

The two architects were waiting in Akbar's private audience chamber. One was tall and middle-aged, the other much younger and holding some long rolls of papers in his arms. They bowed as

Akbar entered but he waved at them to stand upright and addressed the elder of the two. 'Welcome, Tuhin Das. Let's dispense with ceremony. I'm eager to see what you have to show me. What are those papers your son has there?'

'Some preliminary drawings, Majesty.'

'Spread them out so I can see them.'

'Certainly. Mohan, do as His Majesty asks.'

Akbar waited as Tuhin Das's son – a slight, narrow-visaged young man with the red Hindu *tilak* mark on his forehead – laid out the sheets one by one on an ebony table, weighting each down at the corners with a few pebbles which he fished from a little bag suspended from the belt round his brown woollen robe. His fingertips were stained with ink, and Akbar noticed that they were shaking a little with nerves. Even before Mohan had finished, Akbar was leaning eagerly over the table. The pieces of paper were covered with a grid of small squares on which different buildings were marked.

'Majesty, may I suggest that we begin with this one?' Tuhin Das indicated the largest of the drawings. 'Here I have drawn the overall layout of the imperial complex. As you have already specified, it will be built up on the plateau with – as you can see – the main town below. It would be bounded by walls on three sides while on the northwestern side would be a great lake, not only to protect Sikri but to supply it with water.' Akbar nodded assent.

'I propose that the palaces, the mosque and all the other buildings of the court should be built along the line of this ridge I have sketched here, which runs from the southwest to the northeast. But please remember, Majesty, though we have tried our best to interpret your wishes these are preliminary ideas only.'

As the architect pointed at his drawing, Akbar noticed that he had lost the top joint of his right forefinger. Tuhin Das saw his glance. 'An accident, Majesty. I was once a stonemason. A slab I was working on slipped and crushed my finger. But it was good fortune not bad. Because of it I studied how to become a designer of buildings.'

'Fate acts in mysterious ways. Explain this plan further to me.'

'The palace complex would consist of a series of interconnecting courtyards. What we have brought here today are the plans for the main court buildings. If you like them, we can make wooden models to give a more detailed idea of their facades and layouts.'

'What is this?' Akbar pointed to a drawing of a large enclosed area.

'The *haram sara* – large enough for five hundred ladies to live in comfort with their attendants, just as you requested. Most of them would have apartments in this palace, the *panch mahal*.' Tuhin Das pointed to a sketch of a tall building five floors high. 'I have modelled it on buildings I saw when I travelled through Persia. There they have clever ways of designing houses and palaces with special vents and tunnels to catch and channel any cooling breezes, and I have done the same here. I have also tried to create a place of beauty – see how each floor is supported by slender sandstone columns. On the very top we have a *hawa mahal* – a palace of the winds beneath a domed canopy where the ladies may sit.'

'Good,' said Akbar. His wives and concubines must live in the luxury to be expected of the Moghul court. Among the growing number of his concubines he still visited Mayala, but perhaps more out of affection than desire after all these years. Others roused greater physical passion now. A newly arrived Russian girl – the first he had ever seen, sent as a gift by a rich Moghul merchant who traded in far-off lands – with wide sapphire eyes, pale skin and hair the colour of sunlight was absorbing much of his attention.

'Here are the drawings of the houses for your principal wives and for your mother and aunt, Majesty.'

Akbar ran his eye over Tuhin Das's sketches of a series of elegant mansions. 'Which is the one you propose for the Empress Hirabai?'

'This one. See, it has a *chattri* on the roof where she can go to observe the moon and worship our Hindu gods, just as you ordered, Majesty.'

Akbar looked carefully at the drawing. Though he hardly saw Hirabai, he wished her to be treated with the honour due to her rank as the first of his wives and the mother of his eldest son.

'Excellent. And my palace?'

'Adjacent to the *haram* and linked to it by covered walkways and subterranean passages. In front of your palace, set in a great courtyard, would be the *Anup Talao* or Peerless Pool, twelve feet deep and fed by water from the lake along a series of aqueducts, so that all the time you will hear the refreshing rippling of water.'

'You are certain there will be enough water to supply the entire city?'

'The engineers assure us so, Majesty.'

'What's this?' Akbar looked in puzzlement at a large rectangular space to one side of his proposed palace with a strange design drawn upon it.

'This would be your private terrace, Majesty, but instead of just placing ordinary stone slabs on the ground, I suggest the novelty of laying it out like the cruciform board on which we play the Hindustani game of *pachisi*. It is a little like the game of chess that I understand you play, Majesty. You and your courtiers would be able to relax here and play, using giant pieces.'

'Excellent. You have been very inventive, Tuhin Das. And this?'

'The *diwan-i-khas*, your hall of private audience. From the outside it appears to have two storeys but in reality there is only a single chamber. Mohan, show His Majesty your drawing of the interior.'

Looking more confident now, Mohan undid the leather satchel hanging from his left shoulder and drew out a small sheet of paper which he unfolded and placed carefully on the table next to the larger drawings. Akbar saw a single high-ceilinged chamber in the centre of which rose an elaborately carved column, slender at the base then swelling out to support a balustraded circular platform connected by diagonal bridges to the four corners of the room. It was beautiful, but what sort of room was it?

'I don't understand. What is the purpose of that platform so high above the ground and those narrow hanging bridges?'

'The platform is where you would sit on your throne, Majesty, while giving audience. The bridges signify that you have dominion over the four quarters of the globe. Any man invited to address you would advance along one of the bridges. The rest of your courtiers would watch and listen from the floor of the chamber.'

Akbar looked intently at the drawing. He had expected Tuhin

Das to design an audience chamber fit for an emperor, but he had surpassed himself. The more he studied the design and pondered the ideas behind it, the better he liked it.

'Where does this idea come from? Does the Persian shah have something similar?'

'No other ruler has such a chamber, Majesty. It was my idea. Does it please you?'

'Yes, I think it does . . . But this central column. Presumably it would be carved from wood? Sandalwood perhaps?'

'No, Majesty. To be strong enough to support the bridges we would need to use sandstone.'

'Impossible. The design is too intricate.'

'Forgive me for disagreeing, Majesty, but I know it can be done. The craftsmen of Hindustan are so skilled they can carve sandstone as if it were wood – no design is too detailed for them.'

'If your craftsmen can truly do as you say, then let the entire imperial complex – every column, every balustrade, every window and doorway – be of carved sandstone. We will create a rose-red city that will be a wonder of the world . . .' In his mind's eye, Akbar could already see his new capital, exquisite as a jewellery box, as durable as the stone of which it would be built. Not only would it be a fitting tribute to Shaikh Salim Chishti but a memorial to Moghul greatness.

◆

The number of labourers working on the construction of Sikri was, according to Tuhin Das whom Akbar had appointed as superintendent of construction, already over thirty thousand and still growing. Every day beneath the burning sun, a long line of men and some women toiled up and down the specially constructed road of packed earth leading to the plateau, carrying equipment up to the summit and bearing away rubble and debris in baskets balanced on their heads. From a distance they resembled lines of ants, moving with ceaseless patience and industry from the first pale light of dawn to the crimsoning sunset. They were scantily clad – the men in grimy *dhotis* and loincloths and the women in cotton saris, sometimes with an infant tied to their back. The camp where they slept on woven mats beneath awnings of dun-coloured sacking and cooked their meals of lentils, vegetables and flat bread over dung fires stretched away across the dusty plain, almost indistinguishable from it.

It was an army of quite a different sort from any he had ever commanded, Akbar thought as he rode on one of his frequent tours of inspection with Tuhin Das, who was looking around him with satisfaction. 'See, Majesty, how much progress has already been made with levelling the land ready for the building to start. Soon we will be able to dig the first foundations.'

'And the quarrying of the sandstone?'

'Two thousand rough slabs have already been cut and next week we will begin transporting them here by bullock cart so that the carvers may begin their work.'

'I've an idea that might make the work proceed even faster. We have detailed designs for everything, so why not have the main pieces carved at the quarry, building by building, and then, when they are ready, brought to Sikri to be fitted into place?'

'An excellent thought, Majesty. That should indeed make the buildings quicker to assemble and lessen the clamour and congestion on the construction site itself.'

'I want every worker well paid for their labour. Announce that I am doubling the daily wage and that, if progress continues at a good pace, once a week there will be a free distribution of corn from the imperial granaries. I wish them to go at their work with unflagging vigour, and I also intend to set an example.'

'How so, Majesty?'

'Take me to the quarries. I intend to cut stone alongside my subjects to show them their emperor does not flinch from hard manual labour . . .'

Two hours later, sweat running down his naked torso and a frown of concentration on his face, Akbar swung his pickaxe. Just as when he flung a battleaxe or a spear, his aim was good. The sharp tip found its mark again and again, biting into the line drawn with charcoal across the slab and creating a furrow into which the skilled stonemasons would then be able to hammer their chisels to cut a clean edge. It was exhausting work – tomorrow his muscles would be as tight and stiff as after a hard-fought battle – but he had seldom felt happier. Destiny intended great things for him, but for once it was good just to be an ordinary man, glorying in his youth and strength and with no worry for the future.

Chapter 11

The Pewter Sea

'Majesty, by the time you return from your campaign in Gujarat the city walls will be nearing completion,' Tuhin Das told Akbar as, together with Abul Fazl, they rode around the walls of Sikri – which currently stood only six feet high – to inspect the progress of construction.

'Take care what you promise,' Akbar responded. 'I intend my campaign to be a short one. I have learned much from Ahmed Khan and others who accompanied my father on his conquest of Gujarat nearly forty years ago. It was only because of Sher Shah that we were forced to relinquish the territory. This time I intend that Gujarat will remain Moghul for ever.'

'The holy pilgrims who cross from Cambay and Surat to Arabia will shower great praise on Your Majesty if they can travel in safety. The lawlessness that attends the rivalries in the Gujarati royal family has made life difficult for travellers, whether their purpose be spiritual or worldly,' Abul Fazl's mellifluous voice broke in. 'Once Gujarat rests in Moghul hands again, I am sure that port taxes will provide a bountiful source of revenue.'

'You are right, Abul Fazl. Gujarat is still a rich state. I intend to bring back much wealth and booty to assist in your ornamentation of Sikri, Tuhin Das.'

'Thank you, Majesty, and may good fortune accompany you on your campaign,' Tuhin Das replied.

'I trust so too, but I hope I have left little to providence in my preparations.'

With that Akbar turned, leaving Tuhin Das and Abul Fazl to decide what to record in the chronicle, and rode down towards the wide plain where his army was encamped beneath the ridge on which his new city was rising. As he approached, he could see puffs of smoke emerging from the long weapons of his musketmen as their officers drilled them to fire in mass volleys for maximum effect. Off to one side his artillerymen were toiling in the hot sun under the watchful eye of the Tajik officer Ali Gul, training to speed up their firing and reloading of the large new bronze cannon and siege mortars Akbar had ordered to be produced in his foundries. Always eager for any advantage from new innovations, he had experimented with a mortar so large and heavy that Ahmed Khan had told him it would require a team of a thousand oxen to move it. Even though Akbar knew that to be an exaggeration, he had decided not to take the monster weapon with him to Gujarat. If all went well – and he must make sure it did – any siege would be over long before it arrived and could be brought into action.

Directly in front of him Akbar saw Ahmed Khan and the bulkier figure of Muhammad Beg deep in conversation beside one of their command tents. As the two men talked, Ahmed Khan was as usual twisting the hair of his thin beard, now mostly silver, while the equally grizzled Muhammad Beg was waving his hand excitedly. Seeing Akbar ride up, the two veterans bowed.

'What are you two arguing about?'

'When we will have enough supplies to begin the campaign,' said Ahmed Khan.

'I was proposing a month's delay, Majesty,' said Muhammad Beg, 'until we can be sure we have enough grain.'

'In turn, Majesty, I was arguing that if we ride fast and light, as you intend, our requirements will be less. In any case, since we've already had promises of help from dissatisfied members of the divided Gujarati royal family, like Mirza Muqim, surely they can be counted on for some supplies. Besides, if the worst came to the worst we could live off the land.'

'I'm with you, Ahmed Khan,' said Akbar. 'Prince Muqim's call for me to intervene has already added legitimacy to our invasion – even if my father's previous conquest of Gujarat wasn't sufficient reason in itself – and I'm prepared to plan on his providing provisions and indeed troops. On that assumption when is the earliest we can move out?'

'In a week's time, Majesty,' Muhammad Beg admitted.

'So be it, then.'

• ◆ •

'Majesty, do you see that cloud of dust on the horizon? It must be a large body of men on the move,' Ahmed Khan called as he rode with Akbar at the head of an advance detachment of his army through the ripening cornfields not far from the Gujarati city of Ahmedabad.

Akbar shaded his eyes with his gauntleted hand and stared at the billowing dust. It could only be the forces of Itimad Khan, self-styled Shah of Gujarat. It seemed Mirza Muqim had been right when at their rendezvous he had suggested that if Akbar rode hard he could intercept the shah near Ahmedabad as he set out to confront the Moghul forces. 'It's Itimad Khan's men, I'm sure of it. If so, just as Mirza Muqim said, we have the advantage of surprise . . .'

'We'll soon find out, Majesty. Shall I give the order to draw weapons and deploy into battle formation?'

'Of course.'

Minutes later Akbar was galloping on his black stallion at the head of a tight phalanx of his men towards the dust cloud, flattening the golden corn as they rode. He had his domed helmet with the peacock feather at its crest on his head, gilded breastplate on his chest and his sword Alamgir in his hand. Just behind him rode two of his *qorchis*, holding great green Moghul banners which streamed out behind them. With each stride of his horse the shapes of the Gujarati horsemen in the dust cloud became more distinct. It was clear to Akbar that they had recognised that it was his forces that were approaching and had decided to meet them head on rather than retreat to the protection of the walls of Ahmedabad.

141

'How many of them do you think there are, Ahmed Khan?' shouted Akbar over the drumming of their horses' hooves.

'It's difficult to say. Perhaps five thousand, Majesty.'

'They must think they outnumber us sufficiently to be sure of victory, but we know better, don't we?'

The two columns were now less than a thousand yards apart and closing fast. At a command from Akbar his mounted archers stood in their stirrups and loosed a volley of arrows towards the Gujaratis. As they flew through the air they met an answering storm of Gujarati shafts. Ahead of him, Akbar saw the horse of one of the leading Gujaratis crash to the ground, two arrows protruding from its neck. As it fell, it catapulted its rider head over heels into the waving corn. Simultaneously another rider slipped from his saddle with an arrow in his cheek. Behind him Akbar heard a crash and an agonised shout. At least one of his own men had been hit. However, Akbar had no time to look round as the two lines of mounted men smashed into each other at speed. At the last moment one of the Gujaratis – seemingly having recognised Akbar by his gilded breastplate – swerved his chestnut into the path of Akbar's black stallion in a self-sacrificing attempt to unhorse him.

Akbar reacted quickly. Pulling hard on the reins he managed to turn his mount sufficiently to lessen the impact, but his horse's shoulder still caught the chestnut in the flank, knocking it over and sending its brave rider flying. Snorting with pain from the impact, the stallion reared up and Akbar leaned forward on its neck while gripping as hard as he could with his knees, struggling to remain aboard. He almost succeeded, but as his horse dropped its forelegs back to the ground it skittered sideways and became entangled in one of the green Moghul banners which had fallen from the dying hands of one of Akbar's *qorchis* who lay in the corn, transfixed by a Gujarati spear. This time Akbar, who had lost a stirrup in the previous struggle, could not retain his seat and slid from the saddle, but still managed to hang on to his stallion's reins with his left hand.

Within moments another Gujarati swerved towards him, aiming to run him through like his *qorchi*. At last dropping the reins, Akbar jumped aside, just avoiding the rider's lance and the hooves of his onrushing horse. As he leapt away, Akbar gave a great backhand slash with Alamgir. Despite the firmness of his grip he felt the sword judder in his gauntleted hand as it struck his opponent's mount in the flank before crunching into the bone and sinew of the rider's knee, precipitating him too from his saddle. For a moment the Gujarati attempted to stand, but his damaged knee would take no weight and as it gave way he collapsed again into the flattened corn beneath the hooves of one of Akbar's advancing cavalrymen's horses which shattered his skull.

The Moghuls' initial charge had pushed the Gujaratis back and Akbar's bodyguard were now surrounding him. His winded stallion was only a few yards off. Sheathing Alamgir and grabbing the shaft of the fallen Moghul banner, he ran to the horse and pulled himself back into the saddle. 'Forward, men. We must exploit the advantage,' he yelled. The black stallion responded to his urging and with the Moghul banner flying behind him Akbar once again charged into the mass of Gujarati horsemen. Gripping the reins in his teeth he slashed with Alamgir at a burly rider but saw the sword glance off the enemy's breastplate. His next stroke cut deep into the flesh of another Gujarati's upper arm and then he found himself on the other side of mêlée, soon to be joined once more by most of his bodyguard.

Handing the green banner to one of them, Akbar looked round as he caught his breath. The fighting was still intense, particularly near one of the Gujaratis' red flags about two hundred yards to his left. Hastily wiping away the sweat that was dripping into his eyes, he kicked his horse towards it. As he did so he suddenly saw an unhorsed, red-turbaned Gujarati stagger up from a patch of untrampled corn. He had a long dagger in his hand and pulling his arm back sent it spinning towards Akbar. His aim was good but Akbar ducked low over his horse's neck just in time and the tip of the dagger caught his helmet a glancing blow before falling harmlessly to the ground. Leaving others to deal with his assailant, Akbar urged his black stallion onwards. Soon he was pushing into the turmoil around the red banner, striking vigorously to left and right as he did so.

A tall Gujarati mounted on a brown mare charged towards him, lance extended in front of him. Seeing him only at the last moment, Akbar deflected the lance with his sword, knocking it up into the air. Pulling hard on his reins the Gujarati wheeled his horse to attack once more, but this time Akbar was ready. Swerving across the rider's charge, he plunged his sword deep into the tall man's left side, toppling him from the saddle to sprawl in the dust.

Breathing hard, Akbar reined in and saw that under the onslaught of the superior Moghul numbers he had led into the battle the Gujaratis were beginning to give way, slowly at first but then in increasing desperation, turning their horses' heads and attempting to escape back towards the safety of the walls of Ahmedabad. Akbar set off in pursuit of a group of fleeing opponents but at first his winded and blowing stallion seemed unable to gain on them. Then one of the Gujaratis' horses slipped in the mud on landing after jumping one of the small irrigation ditches that criss-crossed the cornfields. Another stumbled over it, and then another, and another. As a rider struggled to his feet to defend himself, the sword of one of Akbar's bodyguards caught him in the throat and he fell backwards into the ditch, red blood flowing from his wound into the green water over which mosquitoes were buzzing. Akbar himself closed in on a Gujarati who like several others had slowed down and was turning back to try to rescue his unhorsed comrades.

'The battle is over. Save your lives. You are surrounded by my bodyguard, and there is no shame in surrender having fought so well,' shouted Akbar. After a moment's hesitation, during which he glanced round at his remaining companions, the Gujarati, who had blood oozing from a wound to his cheek, threw down his weapon. His companions began to do likewise.

As the Moghuls were tying up their prisoners, Akbar saw Muhammad Beg approaching with some of his troops. One of them held the reins of a grey horse on which sat a slim young man wearing a ruby-encrusted breastplate over white robes. 'This is Itimad Khan, Majesty. We found him hiding in the corn near his dead horse. His bodyguard had deserted him.'

'Are you indeed Itimad Khan?' asked Akbar.

'I am and I submit myself to your mercy,' the man answered quietly, keeping his eyes on the ground.

'Are you prepared to order your armies to cease fighting and to surrender Ahmedabad and all other parts of Gujarat under your control to me? If so, I will spare your life and those of your men and allow you to retire to a small estate in a part of the country of your choosing.'

Relief flooded across Itimad Khan's smooth face, which scarcely seemed to have known a razor.

'I will do so willingly. If you release some of these prisoners they can act as my messengers.'

Akbar nodded and some of his men moved towards the captives, but before they could untie them and bring them to their leader to receive his instructions he spoke again. 'Majesty, you must understand that I do not command the coast and the hinterlands of the ports of Cambay and Surat. My rebellious cousin Ibrahim Hussain holds sway over them.' Itimad Khan paused, then continued in a low voice, 'Also, if I speak the truth I fear that not all my own commanders will obey my instructions to lay down their arms.'

'I know of the situation on the coast and will soon take my army there to force Ibrahim Hussain to accept my rule. As for your commanders, they will do well to heed your orders. Tell them from me that they will have only one chance to surrender. If they do not grasp it they will die.'

Itimad Khan nodded, soft brown eyes downcast once more. Akbar turned away, contempt for the other's weakness mingling with pity for his situation. He knew he himself had the strength of character never to allow himself to be placed in such a humiliating position, and he gave thanks for it. When his sons and then their sons read of his battles in Abul Fazl's court chronicles they would see no such shaming weaknesses or failures but rejoice in his victories and power, as he did now.

• ◆ •

The ocean was calm, lapping gently on the pale tangerine sands. Soft northerly winds were rippling the leaves of the tall palm trees fringing the beach. However, Akbar could see that about a mile and a quarter further along the shore the forces of Ibrahim Hussain were massing in and around a small fort set on a promontory and designed to protect the land and sea approaches to Cambay, itself another two or three miles up the coast. A number of ships were riding at anchor near the promontory. Akbar turned to Ahmed Khan. 'You were at Cambay with my father. What are those vessels?'

'Most are the dhows of the Arabs who transport the pilgrims to Arabia for the *haj* and at other times trade in spices and cloth. These I have seen often during my previous time in Cambay. However, I have seen nothing before like those three dark, squarer, higher-sided ships with two masts which are nearer to us.'

'Is that the barrel of a cannon protruding over the stern of one?'

'I can't be sure, Majesty.'

As Ahmed Khan spoke, sailors on the closest of the three ships began to unfurl one of its sails. As it dropped from the yardarm, Akbar saw that it had a large red cross painted on it. Other sailors were clambering into a rowing boat that had been lowered from the vessel and remained attached to it by a rope. Soon, with the help of the sailors rowing the small boat and the sail they had rigged on the main ship, the vessel was moving slowly down the coast towards Akbar's position.

In the six weeks since his defeat of Itimad Khan, Akbar had ridden hard and fast to the ocean. Leaving all his heavy equipment behind, he had defeated and scattered the forces of Ibrahim Hussain wherever he encountered them. The previous day Akbar's men had overwhelmed another small, half-derelict fort a few miles further south along the coast. Watching the approaching ship, Akbar was pleased that he had ordered draught oxen to be purchased from the peasants in the surrounding villages and the five small ancient cannon he had found inside the captured fort to be brought along in case they were of any use in the attack on Cambay.

'Deploy the cannon so that they can fire on that ship if need be. Have the musketeers prime and load their weapons,' he ordered. Half an hour later, when the dark ship with the red cross on its sail was more or less opposite Akbar's army and only a quarter of a mile

146

offshore, it anchored again. A tall man in a shining breastplate climbed down a rope ladder into the rowing boat which had been helping to pull the ship along, followed by a white-turbaned figure in flowing lilac robes. When both men had seated themselves in the stern, the sailors cast off the rope attaching the boat to the bigger vessel and began rowing strongly for the shore. As soon as the boat reached the shallows, the tall man and his lilac-clad companion climbed over the side and splashed their way out of the water up the beach. Both had their arms outstretched, presumably to show they were unarmed.

Akbar looked on, intrigued. What was their purpose in approaching him at a time when they must know battle was imminent? 'Search them for weapons and bring them to me,' he instructed the captain of his bodyguard. The captain ran quickly over to the two men, who allowed themselves to be searched. Satisfied that they were indeed unarmed the captain led them towards Akbar. As they came closer he could see that the man in lilac looked like a Gujarati but the other was paler and his eyes were dark and round. His long nose jutted over a full mouth and a thick and curly brown beard. His plain steel breastplate covered his chest, but on his lower body he wore some kind of baggy pantaloons striped in black and gold which ended just above the knee. He was wearing red stockings and on his feet calf-length, salt-marked black boots of a design Akbar had never seen before.

'Who are you?' he asked as the two men bowed low before him.

'I am Saiyid Muhammad, originally from Gujarat,' replied the man in lilac, 'and this is Don Ignacio Lopez, the Portuguese commander of those three large ships you see in the bay, whom I serve as translator.'

So the brown-bearded man was Portuguese – one of the travellers from far-off Europe who had arrived some years ago to found a trading post at Goa, a thousand miles further south down the coast, thought Akbar as he carefully appraised the newcomer. He had heard of the Portuguese, of course. They were acquiring a reputation for the supply of weapons of all sorts, and also for the fighting ability of their ships and sailors, but this was the first time he had encountered them.

147

'What do you want?' he asked.

The interpreter spoke briefly to the Portuguese in a tongue Akbar had never heard before, and listened to his reply. Then he bowed again to Akbar. 'Don Ignacio acknowledges you on behalf of his own king as a great general and mighty emperor of whose brave deeds he has heard much. Even though his three ships out there in the bay are powerful and equipped with many cannons, and despite Ibrahim Hussain's offer of chests full of jewels and gold if he would aid him against you, my master wishes to assure you of his neutrality in the battle that looms between you and Ibrahim Hussain.'

'I am glad to hear it. Is there any favour he requests in return?'

After another consultation, the translator said, 'The ability to trade through Cambay, once it is yours.'

'When the port is mine, he should approach me again and expect a favourable answer. Now you must depart. I can delay my attack on Ibrahim Hussain no longer.'

The two men bowed, turned and retraced their footsteps back down the beach and through the shallows before clambering back into the rowing boat. There were many questions Akbar would have liked to ask them but now was the time for action not reflection and he turned to Ahmed Khan. 'Order the attack. We will ride along the beach near the tree line where the sand is firmer. Ibrahim Hussain and his men will be apprehensive, knowing their approach to the Portuguese for help has been rebuffed and that we have consistently defeated their forces and now outnumber them.'

Half an hour later, Akbar was thundering along the beach, sand flying from the hooves of his black stallion. Around him were his bodyguard, four of them holding green Moghul banners, two others sounding brass trumpets. As they neared Ibrahim Hussain's defences, Akbar could see that these consisted mainly of makeshift trenches and barricades, swiftly dug from the surrounding sandy ground. The brick walls of the fort behind them were low and crumbling. However, Ibrahim Hussain clearly had some cannon, for Akbar saw orange flashes and then white smoke billowing from a two-storey building inside the fort. The first shot decapitated one of his trumpeters,

148

sending his head rolling along the sand until it came to rest a few feet from where his instrument had fallen.

Other riders fell too, hit by arrows and musket balls, but Ibrahim Hussain's men were slow in reloading their cannon and Akbar was already jumping his stallion over the first barricade and across one of the trenches while they were still ramming the next round of cannon balls down the barrels. As his stallion leapt the trench Akbar slashed down at one of the Gujaratis hiding within, who was pulling back the taut string of his double bow ready to fire. Akbar's sword caught the archer full across the mouth and he subsided, teeth exposed and face covered in blood.

Akbar heard another cannon shot and was showered with gritty sand as the ball hit the barricade in front of him. The Gujarati artillerymen had tried to depress the barrels of their weapons to fire on their advancing enemy but had only succeeded in destroying their own defences. Pulling hard on his horse's reins, Akbar was through the new gap in the barricade and past the dismembered bodies of two Gujarati musketeers that lay bleeding into the sand.

Glancing sideways, he saw that other detachments of his horsemen had likewise got into the defences. He urged his stallion forward to where a band of Moghul soldiers had already dismounted and were attempting to climb over the crumbling brick wall into the fort itself. As he approached, some of them succeeded in pushing over the top section of a stretch of the wall and scrambling through. Akbar jumped from his horse and followed, grazing his left hand on a piece of metal inserted in the wall for support as he pulled himself over. He ran, legs pumping, as hard as he could after his men who were dashing towards the two-storey strongpoint which he could now see was the only building within the fortifications.

Another burst of flame. At least one cannon remained in action in the building. One of his men fell but then staggered up again, clearly having tripped rather than been hit. Breathing hard, Akbar was by now right on the heels of the foremost of his soldiers and together they ran into the strongpoint through a doorway left open by the fleeing gunners. Struggling to adjust their eyes to the darkness inside, they made out a steep stone staircase in one corner and charged up it. At the top, a single Gujarati officer, made of stronger stuff than his comrades, was desperately trying to lift a cannon ball and roll it down into the barrel of a small bronze cannon. Hit in the back by a foot-long dagger thrown by one of Akbar's men the officer collapsed over the wooden gun carriage.

'Quickly,' Akbar shouted to two of his bodyguards behind him, 'you, plant our green banner on the roof of this building to show we occupy the fort. You, find Muhammad Beg. Tell him to order our remaining troops to ride round the fort walls as fast as they can to prevent the Gujaratis fleeing north back to Cambay.'

• ◆ •

The excitement of battle was still on Akbar, mingling with his exultation that Gujarat was now securely annexed to his growing empire, when towards evening that day he stood on top of the small sandstone watchtower at the end of the inner breakwater protecting the port of Cambay. The green Moghul banner flew above the chief buildings of the port, whose inhabitants had opened the wooden gates as soon as news of Ibrahim Hussain's defeat had been brought back by fugitives from the battle down the coast. Ibrahim Hussain, wounded in the shoulder by a battleaxe, had surrendered and was now in a dungeon awaiting his fate.

How beautiful the sea was, rippling pewter-coloured beneath a sky in which the late afternoon sun was becoming obscured by purple clouds gathering on the western horizon. Suddenly Akbar decided he must experience the ocean himself, something he had never done before.

An hour later, he was standing in the prow of a fifty-foot-long dhow which was bucking up and down in waves which were increasing in height all the time. The dhow's captain had warned Akbar that the dark clouds he had seen piling the horizon from the watchtower presaged a storm but Akbar had insisted on his putting to sea. Now the captain, a short, bandy-legged man, was shouting orders for sails to be furled and for men to lean on the tiller to keep the bows into the wind to allow the ship to ride out the squall. Beside Akbar, one of his young *qorchis* was being violently sick, his sour vomit speckling his own clothes and those of another squire next to him. A third, pale-faced and white-knuckled, was clinging for dear life to the base of the mast while muttering prayers for God's protection.

Suddenly a particularly large wave shattered over the bows, soaking Akbar and Ahmed Khan at his side, with warm foaming water. Ahmed Khan himself was looking distinctly nervous as he turned to Akbar. 'Majesty, let us move to a less exposed position. It would only be wise.'

Akbar, wet black hair blowing out behind him and legs slightly apart, braced against the unfamiliar motion, shook his head. 'The pulsing ocean fills me with awe. Besides, the captain tells me the storm will soon abate. Ignorant of the ocean's full strength I wanted to test myself on its waters and now, despite the dangers and discomforts, I am learning . . . The crashing waves and seemingly limitless power of the ocean are a salutary reminder to me not to become vainglorious and over-confident. Although I have led great armies, won great victories, filled my treasuries and come to reign over vast millions – many more than any other ruler – I am still just a man, insignificant and transitory in the face of eternal nature.'

Chapter 12

A Cauldron of Heads

'That is fine carving. The tiger looks as if it could be about to spring upon me,' Akbar said to the beaming craftsman who was standing by his side with a sharp chisel in one hand and a wooden mallet in the other. The two men were not looking at some of the excellent sandstone carving Akbar had seen on the buildings of Sikri on his return from his conquest of Gujarat. Instead, they were standing on a wooden quay on the bank of the River Jumna at Agra, gazing up at the intricately carved new figurehead of a river boat. 'With the tiger at the prow, this vessel will make an excellent flagship in my campaign in Bengal.'

Almost as soon as Akbar had reached Sikri, messages had begun to arrive from his chief general in Bengal, Munim Khan. The first said that the young Shah Daud, who now ruled the area as a vassal of Akbar after the recent death of his father, had rebelled and seized the imperial treasuries and one of the main Moghul armouries, but that the general would punish him for his presumption. The second had been short on detail, merely stating that the campaign was proving more difficult than anticipated and asking for more troops. Before these could be despatched, a third message had arrived pleading for Akbar to come himself because there was a stalemate. Daud was occupying the fortress of Patna which the general was besieging but with insufficient forces to make his blockade secure.

153

Fresh from extending his empire to the western ocean, the idea of securing Bengal and its eastern shores as a full imperial possession had instantly attracted Akbar and without even pausing to consult his advisers he had despatched an immediate response to Munim Khan's third letter. It had told him to maintain the siege as best he could without unduly hazarding his men while conserving his equipment and supplies until Akbar came. However, he had retained sufficient prudence to tell Munim Khan he would not set out until he had accumulated a sufficient force to make the outcome inevitable, as well as enough river transport to carry his army down the Jumna to Allahabad and then along the Ganges past Varanasi to Patna. This meant that he would not leave for at least three months and possibly more.

He had decided straight away that to impress those of his subjects who lived alongside the two great waterways of his empire, his fleet would be the most magnificent the rivers had ever seen. The very day he had despatched his message to Munim Khan he had called his engineers and shipbuilders to him. He had commanded the engineers to begin designing and building pontoons large enough and stable enough to transport his war elephants downriver, as well as ones strong enough to carry his largest cannon and their ammunition. He had ordered his shipbuilders to acquire as many river boats as possible for conversion into troop transports, and to build further vessels as fast as they could recruit the men and acquire the materials to do so.

Knowing his treasuries were filled not only with booty from Gujarat but also with the increased revenues from his reforms to the methods of tax collection, he had determined to fill his subjects with pleasure as well as awe and had ordered enough vessels to allow one to carry his orchestra of musicians on its deck, ready to play whenever called upon. Two others would be fitted out as floating gardens, full of bright flowers with sweet scents which the river breezes could waft to the shore. A fourth would be equipped as a platform for displays of fireworks by his magicians from Kashgar. For his own pleasure, one boat was to be modified to carry his favourite hunting dogs and leopards as well as his falcons and horses so he could go ashore to hunt whenever he pleased, and the very best craftsmen were to construct a large ship from teak to carry the favourite members of his *haram* in the greatest luxury and comfort possible. Bathtubs were to be installed in which they could bathe in warm, scented water, and large, intricately carved wooden screens running all around the boat would protect their activities from prying eyes.

Finally, he had commissioned two kitchen boats. To allow his *tandoor* ovens, cooking cauldrons and roasting spits to operate as safely as possible, one would have part of its interior lined with thin sheets of beaten copper. The other would have holds which could be filled with ice brought down from the mountains to conserve melons, grapes and other fruit. Satisfied that he had thought of everything, Akbar had settled down to wait, not very patiently, for the moment when his campaign could begin.

• ◆ •

'Majesty, we cannot sail today,' said Ahmed Khan. 'The monsoon is at its height and the ships' captains are worried that the force of the flood waters flowing so fiercely downstream will make it hazardous for us to cast off, to manoeuvre our vessels into formation and even to anchor with safety at the end of the day's journey. Also, the deep mud and swamps on the riverbank will make it difficult for the squadrons of horsemen designated to accompany our passage to keep up with us.'

Akbar thought for a moment. Ahmed Khan was growing cautious with age. 'No, I am determined that we will start today, even if we make slow progress. We will take as many precautions as we can, for example by only manoeuvring a single vessel at a time, but we will go. To set out and head down the river when others would not will only strengthen the impression of invincible power I intend to impart to all who witness our journey and to all those who come to hear of it, especially Shah Daud. Unless he is even more of a fool than I think him, he will have his spies monitoring our progress.'

An hour later, the rain had temporarily ceased and a watery sun was shining through piles of puffy white clouds. Akbar stood in the bow of his flagship, just above the ornately carved tiger's head. As he watched, rowers naked except for cotton loincloths were sweating profusely as they bent their backs over the oars, rowing against the current to hold the large vessel as still as they could in midstream while, one by one, his riverboats were rowed and pulled by small boats into the current. There had been no incidents beyond a couple of small barges bumping, and he prayed that his whole campaign would go so well. He must make sure of it. It must not falter because he failed to take sufficient care in his planning, or in his oversight of how his commanders put his plans into practice.

• ◆ •

The sheet lightning was flickering along the dark clouds piling the horizon as the line of servants carried up the ridged wooden gangplank of one of Akbar's river boats the trophies of his most recent hunting expedition. The lifeless bodies of eight tigers — one measuring at least seven foot from head to tail — were each suspended from strong bamboo poles supported on the shoulders of groups of four men. Behind them others carried the carcasses of deer, their bellies already slit and their entrails removed, ready to be skinned, spitted and cooked for the evening meal. At the end of the line, the last servants had clutches of brightly feathered ducks hanging limply from their shoulders.

Akbar himself had already washed and changed his rain-soaked and mud-spattered clothes for clean dry ones. Sipping the juice of red-fleshed watermelons, he watched as the final preparations were made for departure. They had become routine to the sailors as Akbar had insisted on hunting expeditions on most afternoons since their departure from Agra, arguing that they were a good opportunity for his horsemen to exercise their mounts and his musketeers to demonstrate their skill, as well as providing sport for himself. He had only varied the routine when, at least once a week, he ordered Muhammad Beg, Ravi Singh and others of his generals to drill his infantry on any dry ground that they could find, and when, ten days ago, he had gone ashore at Allahabad, the holy city at the confluence of the Jumna and Ganges, where he had arranged with the governor

156

to make a ceremonial procession through the streets before his Kashgar magicians organised a show of fireworks from the city walls in the evening.

He turned to Ahmed Khan, at his side. 'How many more weeks do you think it will take us to reach Patna?'

'Perhaps a month, but much will depend on the monsoon. We've been lucky so far. The only serious accident was that time when two pontoons collided and we lost three cannon to the bottom of the Jumna. However, as the Ganges begins to widen out we'll encounter more shallows and mud banks and the chances of running aground will increase. Shah Daud may even attempt ambushes to delay us. We know that he tried to bribe some river pirates to attack us.'

'But they wisely refused, didn't they?'

'Yes, Majesty. Some even brought the news to us. We'll also have to beware of the river forts defending the approaches to Patna. Our scouts tell me they are well manned and well provisioned.'

'During the passage downriver I have given a lot of thought to how to unsettle young Shah Daud and undermine his men's confidence in him. Now would seem a good time to make the attempt.'

'What do you mean, Majesty? How?' Ahmed Khan looked genuinely surprised.

'Why don't I write to him enumerating the strength of our army and offering him the opportunity to send ambassadors to witness the truth of my claims? I will go on to offer to forgo my advantage in men and equipment and to settle matters in single combat with him if he will agree.'

'But what if he says yes?'

'I'm sure he won't, but if he does all the better. I am the equal of any man in battle, never mind a callow youth as he is reputed to be. We will save many lives and much time and trouble that way.'

'How do you expect him to react, then?'

'To dismiss our offer with what he means to be a confident smile but – unless he's a braver man than I think or a better actor – will seem a nervous one to those around him. When his troops come to hear of my proposal – as we'll make sure they do – they should be impressed by our confidence. His refusal of single combat will make them think their leader something of a coward and thus undermine their morale.'

'It may work, Majesty,' said Ahmed Khan, still looking doubtful.

'It should. My own campaigns have taught me that my grandfather Babur was right when he wrote that as many battles are won in the mind before troops even come in sight of each other as are won on the field of battle itself. In any case, to make the offer costs us nothing.'

At that moment, a crack of thunder erupted overhead from the leaden clouds that had continued to fill the sky as they spoke and the warm monsoon rain began to pour down once more, millions of fat drops splashing into the Ganges and on to Akbar's fleet as it completed its preparations to cast off.

· ◆ ·

Akbar stood with Ahmed Khan on the muddy banks of the Ganges looking towards one of the forts protecting the approaches to Patna. Its strong fifty-foot-high walls, stone at the bottom and brick further up, towered over them and Akbar could see the long barrels of bronze cannon on the battlements. The weapons would have a clear field of fire over the river and across the paddy fields, bright green with rice shoots, which covered most of the banks of the Ganges at this time of year. His troops would need to cross them as fast as possible as they moved to assault the fortress's walls.

Shah Daud had – as Akbar expected – made no response to his offer of single combat. Akbar's flotilla, moving as quickly as the monsoon would allow, had reached this point on the Ganges two days ago. The previous night, after a brief war council, he had ordered part of his fleet under the command of Ravi Singh to sail under cover of darkness past the fort, and braving its guns, to land a powerful force downstream ready to attack the fort from that direction. Akbar knew how lucky he had been that the monsoon clouds had covered the moon and the rain had been incessant, so that his ships had come undetected almost abreast of the fort. However, an alert sentry had then given the alarm and the fort's cannon had begun to fire.

A pontoon carrying five war elephants had been hit and begun to sink. Amid the cannon smoke and with the river running at full spate downstream, a large boat bearing some of Akbar's best archers, recruited from his father's homelands around Kabul, had collided with the semi-submerged elephant pontoon and been holed in the prow below the waterline. As the vessel began to take in water and the intricately carved peacock at its bow dipped below the surface, the musketeers and artillerymen on the walls of the fort had started to find their range.

More cannon balls had hit the sinking pontoon, killing two of the elephants. Another, wounded in the belly, had fallen into the river where it floated on its back, thrashing its shackled legs and trumpeting in pain, blood from the gaping wound in its stomach mingling with the muddy river water. At the same time, the vessel carrying Akbar's archers had been holed again and was now itself half submerged.

Several archers had fallen dead or wounded from the stricken barge into the water. Others, stripping off their breastplates and throwing aside their weapons, had jumped into the river in an attempt to swim ashore or to other boats. Suddenly sinuous shapes had appeared in the dark waters – bright-eyed crocodiles attracted by the smell of blood. High-pitched screams had mingled with the sounds of battle as men had begun to disappear beneath the water despite the attempts by musketeers on other ships to shoot the crocodiles, whose sharp teeth had quickly reduced the wounded elephant to a hunk of bloody, mangled red meat.

At first light, Akbar's men had found dozens of partly dismembered bodies of archers, a half-eaten limb here, a bloody torso there, which had floated into the shallows downstream. They had even had to drive off packs of scrawny pariah dogs intent on finishing the feasting the crocodiles had begun. Yet despite the losses the good news had reached Akbar that the rest of Ravi Singh's ships had succeeded in avoiding the collision and passing downstream of the fort with relatively few casualties, and had soon begun transporting men and

159

equipment ashore. The strategy agreed at the war council to encircle the fort and then to attack it from all sides was working.

'Ahmed Khan, how much longer before the forces we landed upstream will have joined up with those advancing from downstream?'

'Perhaps another hour. There've been no sorties from the fort to try to disrupt them.'

'Good. Are the pontoons carrying cannon ready to float down past the fort firing as they go when I order the attack?'

'Yes. The artillerymen are aboard. The first round of shot is already loaded and the powder is being protected as best we can from the rains by oiled awnings. The troops that are to assault the river gate into the fort are in their rowing boats.'

An hour later Akbar gave the word and the sailors aboard the ten pontoons bearing the cannon cut the anchor ropes that had been holding them in midstream. Guided by the sailors' long oars, the large wooden vessels moved quickly downstream. As soon as he was in range of the fort, the officer on the leading pontoon − a tall, bushy-bearded man dressed entirely in red − signalled to the teams manning the two cannon under his command to open fire.

Carefully shielding the lit taper with their cupped hands against rain blowing under the awning, two of the artillerymen put the flame to the touchholes. Both cannon fired despite the damp, their recoil sending the pontoon swaying up and down in the fast-moving current and causing one gunner to fall into the water, only for a comrade to pull him out before any lurking crocodile could grab him. As the men tried desperately to reload on the bobbing vessel, the cannon on the other pontoons fired and a swirling layer of white smoke soon lay over the river, mingling with the rain.

Akbar was standing in an advanced position on a low mud promontory jutting out into the river. Through one of the occasional gaps in the smoke he could see that some damage had been done to the fort's water gate, which seemed to have been dislodged from one of its great hinges. Now was the time to attack, before the defenders could reinforce the damaged portion. 'Send in the boats,' he shouted, struggling to make himself heard over the din of his own cannon firing and the answering shots from Shah Daud's men within the fort.

From where he stood, Akbar could also see that on land his war elephants were trampling through the muddy water of the rice paddies towards the fort, crushing the delicate green plants beneath their large feet. Musketeers were firing from the howdahs swaying on their backs, attempting to pick off those manning the cannon on the walls. More of his soldiers ran behind the elephants, fighting the suction of the deep mud on their feet and taking what cover they could from the animals' bulk as they did so. Some carried between them long, roughly fashioned scaling ladders to assault the walls. One elephant hit in the head by a cannon ball had collapsed into a rice paddy and Moghul infantry were now using its body as a protective barricade to assemble behind before rushing to the final assault on the walls. All was going well, at least for the present.

Suddenly, turning back to the action on the fast-flowing Ganges, Akbar saw one of the rowing boats packed full of his troops going forward to attack the water gate approach within a few yards of the shore. Avoiding Ahmed Khan's restraining hand he rushed instinctively through the shallows towards it, careless of the presence of any crocodiles in his eagerness to join the attack. Recognising him by his gilded breastplate, his men cheered as they hauled him over the boat's wooden side.

Quickly scrambling to his feet, Akbar stood in the bow urging the rowers on towards the gateway. Moments later, however, he was propelled backwards as if by a giant hand pushing him in the chest. He landed awkwardly across one of the wooden struts in the bottom of the boat and lay there, winded and confused. What had happened? He could feel no running blood but his right side felt numb and he explored his breastplate with his hand. There was no hole in it but a dent beneath which a dull pain was now spreading. He must have been hit by a half-spent musket ball.

Brushing aside the attentions of his men clustering around him, he sat up to see that the boat was now only a few yards from the watergate, and that some fortunate or very well-aimed shots from his floating cannon had broken down the iron grille protecting the ten-foot-high entrance and splintered the wooden gate itself. Troops from another of his boats were already running towards it, zigzagging as they did so to put the musketeers and archers on the wall above off their aim. However, as Akbar watched, several of them fell and the rest retreated, some dragging wounded comrades with them to what little protection was afforded by a small stone hut at the end of a little jetty about ten yards from the gate.

Scrambling over the prow of the boat without waiting for it to be fully grounded, Akbar jumped into a foot of water and splashed ashore, yelling, 'Follow me into the gateway. The faster we run the less the danger.' Waving his sword he charged forward, keeping as low as he could. He was followed immediately by thirty of his men, musket balls and arrows hissing through the air around them. Seeing Akbar, the men sheltering in the hut on the jetty charged forward again too. Having a shorter distance to cover, one of them – an officer wearing a green turban – was first through the damaged gate, sword in hand, but a musket ball hit him in the forehead as he shouted to his men to follow. Spun round by the force of the impact, he collapsed just inside the fort. However, his men obeyed his last command and by the time Akbar reached the gateway himself there were a dozen or so men already there, flattening themselves against the wall to present the lowest profile to the defenders. Yet more were running up, feet sometimes slithering and sliding on the mud, from more boats which had just grounded on the shore.

Glancing upward to the walls as he caught his breath, Akbar realised that the defenders were becoming increasingly preoccupied with the assault from the landward side to have much time to spare to combat those entering through the watergate. Pointing to a stone staircase leading up to the walls about forty yards away, Akbar shouted, 'Let us climb that and take some of the defenders in the rear,' and ran forward himself, taking what cover he could by staying close to the wall. An arrow hit an infantryman running behind him in the throat and another clattered off his own breastplate but Akbar remained unscathed as, breathing hard again, he reached the base of the steep stairway and without pausing began to climb.

Suddenly the body of one of the defenders on the wall above fell, transfixed by a spear. With a thud and a crunch of bone it hit the stone staircase just above Akbar. He only just managed to dodge aside as the broken body rolled down the rest of the steps past him, skull banging on each sharp-edged step as it came. Then leaping up the remaining steps two at a time Akbar was on the battlements. He thrust at a small man who was using all his puny strength to try to dislodge one of Akbar's scaling ladders. He fell with a jagged slash to the base of his neck and Akbar cut hard at a second who was bending over the battlements to fire on the Moghuls climbing the scaling ladders. The sword stroke took him across the back of his knees, severing his tendons, and he fell over the wall, arms flailing. A third man turned to face Akbar, who easily parried his first clumsy sword swing with his own weapon and then slid the long slim-bladed dagger he held in his other hand into the man's side, deep between his ribs. As Akbar wrenched his blade free, the man collapsed, and immediately red blood frothed and welled up between his lips as well as from the wound.

Looking round, Akbar saw that by now so many of his men were either running up the staircase from the courtyard or clambering off the scaling ladders on to the battlements that they outnumbered the defenders, who for a while continued to fight bravely. But then, isolated and often wounded, more and more of them were throwing down their weapons and surrendering.

'The fort is ours,' shouted Akbar in triumph. 'Make sure none of the defenders gets away.' Another victory was his.

• ◆ •

Towards dusk that day Akbar stood in the fortress courtyard and slapped at one of the host of mosquitoes which filled the air at that time of day, infuriating man and beast alike with their sharp bites and whirring whine. Turning to Ahmed Khan at his side, he asked, 'Have we learned anything of significance from our interrogation of the prisoners?'

'One of the most senior officers told us of Shah Daud's discomfort when he received your offer of single combat. He said that the shah read it two or three times, on each occasion turning paler, before crumpling the paper, throwing it into a fire and wiping away some beads of perspiration from his forehead. It was only when one of the copies of the message that you distributed was shown to him a day or two later that he made any comment. It was to dismiss single combat as better fitting squabbles between leaders of gangs of common dacoits than disputes between rulers. However, the officer told us that Shah Daud doubled the number of his bodyguard just in case you should attempt to ambush him.'

'If young Shah Daud is susceptible to our testing of his resolve and courage, we must think how to frighten him some more.' As he spoke, Akbar's eye was caught by a party of his men under the command of a junior officer who were slinging the bodies of some of their dead enemies on to untidy piles of corpses in one corner of the courtyard. Suddenly an idea occurred to him and he went on, 'The souls of those dead men over there have already passed from their bodies so they can no longer serve them any useful purpose, can they, Ahmed Khan?'

'So our religion teaches us, Majesty.'

'Nevertheless, they may yet save the lives of some of their comrades by helping to persuade Shah Daud to surrender earlier than he might have done.'

'How?'

'Have fifty of the bodies decapitated and the heads placed in a large copper cooking cauldron. Have the cauldron covered with a fine brocade secured tightly round the rim. Then send it under a flag of truce into Patna with a message once again inviting Shah Daud to face me in single combat and telling him that if he still refuses more of his men will needlessly lose their heads and he will be their executioner.'

'Won't such an action make us appear the barbarians our enemies so often claim we are?' Ahmed Khan looked appalled.

'So much the better. We know we're not and the more fear we can induce in Shah Daud and his men the sooner they will surrender. Start hacking the heads now.'

• ◆ •

'The cauldron of heads did its task, Majesty. By the time they reached Shah Daud they were putrefying in the heat. When he had the tie around the brocade cut and lifted the material to peer inside, a cloud of black flies burst out together with an unimaginable stench. Shah Daud turned away and retched from the pit of his stomach, and he was not the only one to do so. Immediately afterwards, he gave the order for the best regiments of his army, in particular his horsemen and his mounted musketeers and archers, to prepare to leave. Only two hours later he was himself in the saddle riding through the gates of Patna.'

Akbar smiled broadly. He had been right in his assessment of Shah Daud, and the heads had indeed saved lives. So much of war was in the mind. 'How do you know all this?' he asked.

'The commander he left in the city with instructions to hold it as long as he could lost no time in sending us an offer to surrender if we would spare his life.'

'You accepted it, of course?'

'Yes.'

'Show that we are not barbarians after all. Make sure the prisoners from the garrison are treated well.' After a moment Akbar added, 'After a day or two let a few escape to carry news of their good treatment to their comrades in outlying forts. It should induce more of them to hand themselves over.'

'Majesty.'

'Where is Shah Daud headed?'

'Towards the walled city of Gumgarh at the heart of his family's ancestral lands.'

'Where is the city, and how is it fortified?'

'To the north, Majesty. It is walled, and Shah Daud might hope to hold out there while he recruits more men. Also, his older relations may have greater courage than he and stiffen his resolve, too.'

'Then we must cut him off before he gets there.'

• ◆ •

Although the heavy rain had ceased, the clouds were still low and grey as in the uncertain morning light just a fortnight after the surrender of Patna Akbar looked from beneath the dripping shelter of some tall palm trees at a low hill about three-quarters of a mile away. Shah Daud's forces were encamped in and around a small town which lay within mud walls on the hill's top. Despite its modest height, the position offered commanding views over the surrounding marshes. Shah Daud's men, when they had seen the vanguard of Akbar's force of twenty thousand of his best men including many mounted musketeers and archers approach late the previous afternoon, had not tried to continue their flight. Instead, throughout the stormy night, by the light of torches guttering in the rain and wind as well as of the almost continual sheet lightning, they had worked hard to improvise what defences they could, overturning baggage wagons to block gaps in the mud walls and trying to shore up those sections which had crumbled in the rain.

To Akbar, his opponents looked to have done a good job in the time they had had available. He was fortunate, he thought, that Shah Daud like himself had been travelling too quickly to bring any but the smallest cannon with him. Nevertheless, his forces which numbered roughly the same as his own seemed to be well supplied with muskets and his barricades, though improvised, looked strong. Akbar's scouts had reported that the men had even used the townspeople's beds and cooking pots as well as the doors of their houses as reinforcing material.

Despite his opponents' fervid work, Akbar knew that an all-out assault was the best means to capture the town and with it Shah Daud and his treasure. By doing so he would put an end to resistance in Bengal and secure this rich and fertile land with its clever, cultured and hard-working people as a new and valuable province for his empire. Ahmed Khan was as usual at Akbar's elbow and the emperor turned once more to his grizzled *khan-i-khanan*. 'Have our horsemen completed the encirclement of the town?'

'Yes. More than an hour ago.'

'Then little remains but to order our trumpeters and drummers to give the signal for a simultaneous charge at the town's defences from all sides.'

'That's true, Majesty, but there is one thing I beg of you as an old comrade-in-arms of your father and your chief general. Do not hazard yourself in the way that you did in our attack on the river fort. I remember your father Humayun ordering you to protect yourself for the sake of the dynasty and Bairam Khan advising the same in the fight against Hemu. Your sons are still young. They would be in danger if you fell. So too would the empire.'

'I know you speak with my best interests in mind, and indeed what you say is good advice. Yet I react and take risks instinctively, perhaps partly because in my heart I feel that it will not be my destiny to die in battle – certainly not so soon, not before I've expanded my empire. Indeed, I believe – and sages I've consulted confirm this – the greatest dangers to me will not lie on the battlefield.'

'But as your father came to understand, it is ultimately a man's own actions that decide his fate, not his visions and feelings about his destiny . . . Although confidence and bravery may often allow you to succeed in rash acts where others would fail, you shouldn't rely on this always being the case.'

Akbar nodded. He must guard against over-confidence in battle, just as much as he tried to when planning his campaigns with his commanders. 'Sometimes the distinction between setting an example as a leader and foolhardiness is a slim one, I know. I will remember to observe it as best I can. I had already decided that today Muhammad Beg should lead the first attack. Despite all his years he remains as eager for battle as the day he left Badakhshan to fight with my grandfather. I will hold myself and my bodyguard in reserve so that we can add our weight to support the assault wherever it is needed most.'

'Shall I give Muhammad Beg the order to begin the attack, then?'

'Yes.'

Akbar and Ahmed Khan watched as, to the sound of trumpets, the horsemen began their advance from all sides through the waterlogged fields towards the town on the hill. Although hampered by the glossy black oozing mud and the need to avoid the deepest of the pools of water, the horses slowly picked up speed. Muhammad Beg and his bodyguard were among the foremost, with several green Moghul banners fluttering in the damp breeze behind them. As they came into range, there were occasional puffs of smoke from the muskets of Shah Daud's men crouched behind the barricades. Here and there, a horse collapsed to lie twitching after throwing its rider. Sometimes a horseman fell from his saddle to disappear beneath the hooves of those following, trampled into the churned mud. Often, the fallen rider's mount, freed of his weight, outdistanced his fellows in the charge. One riderless black horse was the first to jump the outermost of the barricades that guarded the town before galloping on towards a cluster of single-storey houses above which Shah Daud's yellow banners were flying.

All seemed to be going well for his troops, Akbar thought. But then there was a sudden crackle of disciplined musketry from the section of the mud walls towards which Muhammad Beg and his men were advancing. One of the carts that blocked a hole in the wall was pushed aside and a squadron of riders emerged to charge down the hill, lances in hand and bobbing heads bent low over their horses' necks, into Muhammad Beg's advancing troops who recoiled under the impact, several of their horses being knocked together with their riders into the mud. Then the Bengalis opened further gaps in their barricades for more horsemen to pour through to join the battle. Within minutes many more of Muhammad Beg's men were down and only one of his green Moghul banners was still being held aloft.

Akbar could hold back no longer – this fight was bound to be crucial to the outcome of the battle and he must be there to lead his men in person. He pulled Alamgir from its scabbard and kicked his horse into a gallop towards the mêlée, followed immediately by his loyal bodyguard. It took him three minutes at most to cover the distance to the hill, despite his mount's slipping in the mud on landing after jumping one of the pools of water.

As he began to urge the horse up the hill towards the fighting he came within range of Shah Daud's musketeers who, recognising him from his gilded breastplate, concentrated much of their fire on him. He heard musket balls and arrows hiss past him. Then his horse staggered for a moment and he felt its warm blood soaking his right thigh. Hit in the flank by a musket ball, the horse's pace was faltering and its head was dropping. Just before it collapsed Akbar jumped from the saddle to land on his feet on the muddy ground only to

168

slip, arms flailing, as he jerked aside to avoid one of his bodyguards who was riding close behind.

Regaining his balance, he shouted for another of his men to give him his mount. Immediately a rider wheeled round and leapt from his grey horse to offer the reins to Akbar. Within moments he was back in the saddle, thrusting his mud-caked boots into the stirrups. However, the incident had blunted the momentum of his charge and that of his bodyguard. Some of Shah Daud's horsemen were almost on them. Akbar reacted only just in time to swerve his new mount away from a large Bengali whirling a spiked battle flail above his helmetless head. The man was unable to check his horse's charge because of its downhill momentum. Despite tugging hard at his reins he careered past Akbar, who slashed at the back of his head with Alamgir, feeling a grating judder in his arm as the sword bit into the man's skull.

Moments later, Akbar struck at a second man charging down the hill at him but the Bengali ducked and the sword stroke missed. The rider turned to confront Akbar once more. This time, Akbar had the advantage of the slope and before the rider could urge his horse up through the thick black mud towards him, Akbar was on him, battering his lance from his hand with a swing of his sword and then thrusting its sharp blade deep into the man's groin.

Free of immediate danger, Akbar wiped away some of the sweat dripping down his face with his arm and looked about him. The heavy fighting around Muhammad Beg's single remaining green banner was now sixty yards to his left. Gesturing to those of his bodyguard who were still with him to follow, Akbar drove the grey onward into the heaving, steaming mass of men and horses. Soon he had broken through the first circle of combatants into a scene of carnage where Muhammad Beg's charge had been halted by the musketry and cavalry of Shah Daud. The bodies of several horses lay in the mud. Akbar noticed one of them was still kicking its hind legs feebly. Beneath another he recognised the corpse of one of Muhammad Beg's *qorchis* – a youth of scarcely more than sixteen whose beardless cheek had been slashed wide open, exposing his jaw bone and perfect white teeth.

169

Fighting was still going on. Several Bengalis were trying to run through with their lances some of Muhammad Beg's unhorsed men who seemed to be protecting a mud-covered figure propped, legs widespread, head slumped, with his back against a rock. It was Muhammad Beg himself, Akbar realised with horror. Pushing his mount onwards with even greater urgency towards the combatants, who were too preoccupied with the fighting in front of them to detect his approach, Akbar struck the horse of the nearest Bengali across the rump with the flat of his sword. As he intended, it reared up, throwing its rider, who fell beneath the hooves of Akbar's own mount.

Next Akbar cut another of the Bengalis, who was about to run one of the *qorchis* through, across the nape of his neck and he fell forward, losing his grip on his lance. By now, Akbar's bodyguard had accounted for three more Bengalis and the rest, losing stomach for the fight, were turning to try to ride back up the hill through the clinging mud to the protection of the town's walls. Only one of them made it, and by the time he did so he had a throwing dagger protruding from the muscle of his upper arm.

Pausing for just a moment, Akbar shouted to one of the *qorchis*, 'What happened to Muhammad Beg?'

'The Bengalis recognised him as a general as he rode beneath our green banners. A musket ball hit him in the shoulder. When he fell from his horse he hit his head and later was wounded by a Bengal lance in the thigh.'

'Get him back to the *hakims* as soon as you can. He wouldn't have lived this long if he wasn't tough. If anyone can survive those wounds it's him.'

With that, Akbar urged his blowing horse up the hill towards the town's barricades. Some of his men had already breached them and were now pushing towards the cluster of houses with the yellow flags, dodging from the shelter of one mean mud hut to another, disturbing a few skinny chickens as they did so. Three of his musketeers were crouching behind the brick wall of a well, resting their muskets on its parapet to steady their weapons to provide covering fire for a colleague who was attempting to drag a wounded comrade behind the shelter of a steaming midden. Eventually he succeeded and the musketeers moved forward again.

Before either they or Akbar could reach the houses above which the yellow flags fluttered – surely Shah Daud's command post – Akbar saw green banners appearing over the hill behind the houses. His men had clearly breached the barricades in many places and were having much the best of the fighting. A moment or two later three men came out of one of the houses. One advanced, arms raised in surrender, towards Akbar's men. The two others first deliberately threw down the yellow banners into the mud and then raised their hands. Victory was his, thought Akbar, punching the air above his head with his fist. Realising what was happening, his men too began to cheer with a mixture of elation at victory and relief at survival.

'Order them to bring Shah Daud to me,' shouted Akbar. A look of consternation crossed the face of the Bengali to whom the command was given but he disappeared back into one of the houses, dipping his head beneath the low lintel as he entered. No one emerged for some minutes and Akbar was about to order his soldiers to force their way in when a tall, distinguished figure with a long thin face appeared in the doorway and began to walk slowly towards Akbar. When he was about fifteen feet away he prostrated himself in the mud. He was clearly at least twice the nineteen years of age Akbar knew Shah Daud to be.

'Who are you? Where is Shah Daud? If he's hiding inside, bring him to me immediately.'

'I am Ustad Ali, Shah Daud's maternal uncle. I have been his chief adviser throughout his rising. Mine is the guilt and responsibility. I sent my nephew away in disguise last night when I realised our forces faced defeat, however hard we fought. All his treasure is within these houses and I surrender it, and Bengal, to you on his behalf.'

• ◆ •

Akbar gazed out across the Bay of Bengal from the deck of a high-prowed wooden dhow. Having gone to sea on the western ocean he had been seized by the desire to do the same on the eastern and today he was fulfilling that wish. As a sudden warm gust caught the triangular red sail, the ship heaved beneath him and he planted his feet wider apart. It was only a little after midday and the sea shone silver, almost too bright to look upon, but he could taste its saltiness on his lips.

His forces had secured all the major towns and cities of Bengal, and even though they had not yet captured Shah Daud, that would be only a matter of time. Bengal was already his.

That morning he had received more good news in a despatch from Abul Fazl, his chronicler in Agra. The western part of his empire remained peaceful and the construction of Sikri was proceeding apace. Akbar smiled as he watched the waves. It was as if one part of his reign was closing. He had successfully extended his empire beyond his grandfather's, his father's and even his own ambitions. Although he would continue to expand his territories, not least to satisfy his followers' desires for booty and action, his main task now would be to consolidate his rule over his vast dominions. The empire he would one day bequeath his heir must be unassailable. To do that he knew he needed all his subjects – new and old, Hindu or Muslim – to respect him as their ruler rather than resent him as a barbarian conqueror or alien enemy of their faith. It was easier to say than to achieve, but he would rise to this new challenge.

Part III

The Power and the Glory

Chapter 13

City of Victory

'To honour our great victories in Bengal and Gujarat for posterity, I rename this city "Fatehpur Sikri", "Sikri, City of Victory". In future years those who gaze on its high red sandstone walls will remember the Moghul warriors whose deeds it commemorates. All of you here today have shared in those deeds. Your sons, your grandsons and the generations yet unborn will rejoice in the knowledge that your heroic blood runs through their veins also.' From his carved balcony overlooking the marble *Anup Talao* – the Peerless Pool whose lotus-strewn waters shone with a metallic brilliance in the late afternoon sun – Akbar, equally brilliant in a diamond-and-ruby encrusted cream silk tunic, looked down on the ranks of his commanders and officers filling the great courtyard, over which vast canopies of green silk had been erected to shade them.

A drawn Muhammad Beg was in the front row, leaning heavily on a carved ebony stick that Akbar had sent him. Thanks to the *hakims* the old warrior was well on the way to recovery, though his wounds were so severe his long years of campaigning were over. By his side stood Ahmed Khan, his long wispy beard for once carefully combed, the bulky, red-turbaned figure of Raja Ravi Singh and Akbar's brother-in-law Raja Bhagwan Das of Amber wearing diamonds in his ears, his favourite triple-stranded pearl necklace round his neck and a close-fitting orange silk coat with coral buttons.

Behind Akbar's senior commanders were the other officers, positioned according to rank. Scanning the tens of rows, Akbar's sharp eyes picked out the tall, broad-chested Ali Gul, resplendent in robes of scarlet and gold brocade rather than his usual plain cotton or wool tunic and trousers, standing among his fellow Tajiks. The Badakhshani officers next to them looked just as imposing in their bright steel breastplates, with their green standards in their hands.

As the voices of his men rose in a great roar of approbation, their faces reflected the pride welling within Akbar himself. Success was sweet. Three days ago, preceded by drummers and trumpeters riding black horses with jewelled bridles and diamond-encrusted headguards and a detachment of horsemen each bearing a yak's tail standard, and riding aboard the tallest and most stately of his war elephants in a gem-covered howdah, he had led his immaculate, victorious armies into his new capital of Sikri along a road sprinkled with rose and jasmine petals by attendants running ahead. Every blade of every weapon had been honed and shining, every bronze cannon polished and gleaming, and he had ordered the tusks of his thousand war elephants to be painted gold to show they were returning in glory from battle.

Since his return Akbar had been preparing his speech, seeking and memorising the words that would do justice to what he hoped would be a pivotal moment in his reign. He had achieved great things but he wanted his men to understand that an even more glorious future awaited the Moghul empire. Instinctively he glanced at his three sons standing to the right of his throne. Since his return he'd had little time to spend with them but he knew that some time in the future – and he hoped it would be long delayed – they would be the dynasty's upholders. Seven-year-old Salim was looking excited, his fine-boned face beneath his green silk turban eager and vital. Six-year-old Murad was also clearly enjoying himself. Of the three boys, he was the one who had changed most during Akbar's absence. He was now as tall as Salim. The left cheek and chin of his square face was bruised – the result, so his tutor had informed Akbar, of a fall from a mango tree while looking for birds' eggs. Little Daniyal was still plump and his eyes were round as he took in the mass of men below.

Akbar raised his hands, palms down, to signal he had more to say and the cheers subsided. 'You have already received the worldly tokens of my esteem – robes of honour, jewelled daggers and swords, horses swift as the wind, higher ranks to hold, richer *jagirs* to govern. Some of you have even received your bodyweight in gold. You have earned these rewards and I promise you that in the years ahead there will be more. Who can withstand us? Only yesterday, I received news from Bengal that Shah Daud, who foolishly challenged our Moghul might, has been captured and executed. Even now, his head, stuffed with straw, is on its way to Fatehpur Sikri while the trunk of his traitorous body is being nailed up in the bazaar in Bengal's chief city. Shah Daud has paid in blood for all the death and suffering caused by his treachery. Had he been loyal he would have had nothing to fear from me.

'But that is the past. Now our task is to ensure that our empire endures. History has taught us that it is easier to conquer new lands than to keep them. Nine dynasties ruled Hindustan before the arrival of my grandfather, Babur, but most were short-lived. Through indolence and conceit those rulers let what they had won trickle away like sand through their fingers. We will not make the mistakes that doomed them. With your help, the Moghul empire will become the most magnificent the world has ever seen. It will flourish not just because our armies are fearless and strong but because those who live within its borders will daily bless the fact that they are its subjects.

'I speak not only of those of my own faith but of all my people. Many Hindu rulers – like Raja Ravi Singh who I see before me – fought at my side in our recent battles. They and their men bled for the Moghul cause. It is only just that they and loyal men of every faith should find favour and advancement at my court and in my armies. It is also right and honourable that all should be free to practise their religion without hindrance or harassment.'

As he paused, Akbar looked instinctively towards two dark-robed Muslim clerics, half hidden in the shade of a covered walkway to one side of the *Anup Talao*. One of them was a stout elderly man, his hands folded over a belly round as a melon and straining against his black sash. Akbar knew him well – Shaikh Ahmad, an orthodox Sunni and leader of the *ulama,* Akbar's senior spiritual advisers. The shaikh was one of those most opposed to Akbar's marriages to Hindus. The second cleric was Abul Fazl's father Shaikh Mubarak, whose lean, pockmarked face beneath his neatly bound white turban looked thoughtful.

Akbar resumed, voice resonating with renewed determination. 'The Moghul empire will flourish only if all its subjects can prosper too. To show I mean what I say, I hereby declare an end to the *jizya* – the poll tax on non-believers. Because a man does not follow the path of Islam is no reason to impoverish him. I also abolish the ancient tax levied since before Moghul times on Hindu pilgrims visiting their holy shrines.'

Shaikh Ahmad was openly shaking his head. Well, let him. He would soon have plenty more to disapprove of. This was only the start of the changes Akbar was planning. On the leisurely journey back to Sikri he had summoned the headmen of the towns and villages he had passed and questioned them about the lives of the ordinary people. Until then he had been unaware of the oppressive taxes on the Hindu population who made up the great mass of his subjects. The more he had considered the question, the more obvious it had seemed that such taxes were not only unfair but divisive. To ensure the stability of his empire, he had taken Hindu wives and allowed them freedom of worship. Surely it was wise – as well as just – to extend tolerance and equality to all?

He was becoming more curious about the Hindu religion. In the past, if he had considered it at all, it had seemed a strange, outlandish, even childish creed centred on idol-worship and fanciful stories. But Ravi Singh had presented him with two beautifully bound Hindu texts – the *Upanishads* and the *Ramayana* – translated into Persian. Each night, as he had made his stately progress back towards his capital, he had asked his attendants to read them to him. Listening in the half-darkness he had begun to divine beneath their rich language a resonating message – that the pure in heart, whatever their religion or race, could find their way to God and inner peace.

He realised that until recently he'd scarcely thought about religion at all, not even his own. He observed the outward practices of his own faith because it was expected of him. Yet the more he listened to the wisdom in the Hindu books, the more sure he was becoming that there were universal truths, principles common to all religions, waiting to be revealed to all with open minds. Just as the Sufi Shaikh Salim Chishti, whose gentle, almost mystic Islamic beliefs he respected so much, had said, turning his luminous eyes upon him, 'God belongs to us all . . .'

Akbar rose and the four trumpeters standing behind him put their lips to their instruments, announcing by their shrill blasts that his address was over. Turning, Akbar stepped quickly through the arched sandstone doorway leading into his own apartments. He felt tired. Since returning from campaign there had been so much to attend to he had barely slept. Hamida and Gulbadan and his wives – though not Hirabai of course – had been eager to hear accounts of his triumphs and to tell him of events at court during his absence. All the time, though, his thoughts had been on his new capital. He had inspected his own quarters but was impatient to view the rest of the city. Now at last he had the opportunity.

Half an hour later, Akbar was walking around the city walls with his chief architect. 'You have indeed fulfilled your promises to me, Tuhin Das,' he said, looking up at the red sandstone parapets and ramparts that girdled his new capital.

'The labourers worked in shifts, Majesty. There was not an hour – day or night – when construction was not under way.'

'How did they manage in the hours of darkness?'

'We lit bonfires and torches. Your idea about carving pieces of sandstone at the quarry before transporting them here also speeded our progress. Come, Majesty. If we enter through this gate we can pass by the barracks and the imperial mint.'

'The Hindu carvers have excelled themselves.' Akbar gazed up at the perfect geometrical patterning of stars and hexagons on a sandstone ceiling in the mint. Indeed, wherever he looked it was almost impossible not to exclaim aloud at the perfection and detail of the craftsmen's work. *Chattris* – tiny pavilions – rested on sandstone columns so slender it seemed they might snap. Garlands of flowers and fronds of plants, tender and delicate as in life, curled round columns and over walls.

'And look at this, Majesty.' Tuhin Das pointed to a carved milk-white marble *jali*, a screen. 'The craftsmen are as skilled at working the marble as the sandstone.' He was right, Akbar thought. The *jali* looked as shining and fragile as a spider's web in a frost. It reminded him of the wonders in carved ivory brought to his court by fur-hatted, leather-coated merchants all the way from China.

Of course, for all its perfections there was still a raw, dusty newness about his city, Akbar thought. Flowers and trees would soften the outlines. 'How are the plans for the gardens going?'

'Excellently, Majesty. Over there, outside your hall of private audience, the *diwan-i-khas*, we can see some of the gardeners at work.'

Akbar followed Tuhin Das out of the mint. Again, his chief architect had done well, he thought, watching women as well as men squatting on the red earth as they planted rows of dark green cypresses in between young cedars. In another bed mango trees, sweet-smelling champa and the brilliant vermilion cockscomb his father Humayun had admired so much were already growing.

'Please enter the *diwan-i-khas*, Majesty. I hope you will be pleased. It is exactly as it appeared on the drawing.'

It was indeed, Akbar thought as he entered the graceful sandstone pavilion. In the centre of the single high chamber rose the swelling, miraculously carved column he had so admired on paper, on which rested the round platform, linked to hanging bridges, where he would sit. 'See, Majesty, you will be positioned as if at the centre of the universe . . . the place of supreme power. It is like the pattern of our Hindu *mandalas* – the column represents the axis of the world . . .'

Later that day, splashing his face with chilled water from a turquoise-inlaid silver bowl, Akbar felt a deep satisfaction. His campaigns had succeeded and his capital was as glorious as he had hoped. For the next few hours – perhaps until the dawn light warmed the stony desert plains below – he would forget about conquests and empire and visit his *haram*. Of all the buildings of Fatehpur Sikri that Tuhin Das had shown him, the complex behind its high walls, with the airy five-storey *panch mahal* where his concubines were housed and the elegant and luxurious sandstone palaces built for Hamida, Gulbadan and his wives, perhaps pleased him most.

The main entrance into the *haram* lay through a curved sandstone archway, protected, as he had ordered, by elite Rajput guards. Within the complex, the women were attended by eunuchs – the only men other than Akbar himself allowed inside it – assisted by women from Turkey and Abyssinia, selected for their physical strength. The overall running of the *haram* was under the watchful eye of the *khawajasara*, to whom he had issued detailed instructions for its smooth functioning and security. While he had been away, yet more rulers anxious for his favour had sent him women to be his concubines if they pleased him – sturdy, broad-cheekboned, almond-eyed women from as far off as Tibet, slight, green-eyed Afghan girls with skin the colour of honey, voluptuous, large-featured women from Arabia, eyes rimmed with kohl, bodies made yet more alluring by intricate patternings of henna – or so the *khawajasara* promised him.

At the thought of the sensual pleasures awaiting him in that hidden world behind its thick, metal-studded gates, Akbar's blood quickened. This new *haram* would be his private paradise – a luxurious retreat of rosewater fountains and silk-hung chambers where he could shrug off the cares of being an emperor and embrace the joys of being a man.

Whom would he make love to tonight? he wondered as he entered the torchlit subterranean passage that was his private entrance into the *haram*. His thoughts turned briefly to his wives. It would not be the Persian nor the princess from Jaisalmer . . . not tonight, anyway. As for Hirabai, he had kept his word and they had not made love since Salim's birth. However, he had paid her a courtesy visit on his return – even presented her with a diamond bracelet that had once graced the wrist of one of Shah Daud's wives. Hirabai's tone had been cold, her oval face expressionless as she had at once handed his magnificent gift to one of her Rajput attendants. He shouldn't have been surprised, but her undiminished contempt still had the power to wound.

He turned his thoughts in a more pleasurable direction. Perhaps he would order the *khawajasara* to select the pick of the new arrivals and, after they had removed their jewellery so its clinking would not betray them, he would play a game of hide and seek with them. The woman who evaded him longest would share his bed. Or perhaps he would play a game of living chess with them on the giant board he had had laid out in white and black stone in the *haram* courtyard. As he ordered each woman to move around the board in her diaphanous garments, he would have ample time to decide which one pleased his fancy most, and – unlike Hirabai – whoever he preferred would undoubtedly be delighted to be the emperor's choice . . .

· ◆ ·

Six weeks later, Akbar entered his mother's chamber. Pale pink silk hangings threaded with pearls fluttered pleasingly against the carved sandstone walls, and through the delicately arched casement he saw water bubbling from a fountain carved like a narcissus in the courtyard. His mother should be pleased with her accommodation, he thought. A little guiltily, he realised how few times he had visited her recently.

'What is it, Mother? Why did you want to see me?'

Hamida exchanged a glance with Gulbadan, seated beside her on a gold brocade bolster. 'Akbar, we have something we must say to you. We feel imprisoned in this *haram* of yours behind its gates and high walls, this city of women, guarded by so many soldiers . . .'

Akbar stared in surprise. 'It is for your own protection.'

'Of course we must be protected, but we don't need to be shut away like prisoners.'

'Our royal women have always lived in the seclusion of a *haram*.'

'Not isolated from the world like this. You forget who we are – not just royal women but Moghul women. In past times, we accompanied our warrior husbands, brothers and sons in their quest for new lands. We rode hundreds of miles on mule or camelback between makeshift encampments and remote mud-walled settlements. We ate with our menfolk. We played our part in their plans – as advisers, ambassadors, mediators.'

'Yes,' Gulbadan broke in, 'twice I crossed the lines of battle to intercede with your uncles after they had taken you prisoner . . . I risked my life like any Moghul warrior in the field and I was glad to.'

'You should be happy those times are gone . . . that we're not throneless nomads any more. I'm a powerful ruler – an emperor. It would reflect on my honour if I did not free you of such worldly worries and give you every luxury and comfort and the protection due to both your sex and your rank.'

'My rank? I am a *khanim*,' said Gulbadan, raising her chin, 'a descendant of Genghis Khan, the one they called the Oceanic Warrior because his lands once stretched from sea to sea. His blood as well as that of Timur flows in my veins and gives me strength. I think you have forgotten that, Akbar.' Her usually gentle voice was firm.

'I know what you both endured because I've often heard you speak of it – how you fled through icy mountains and across blistering deserts, how you almost starved to death. I acknowledge and honour your courage but I thought you would no longer wish to be exposed to potential dangers.'

'Why didn't you ask us first rather than assume you knew what we would want or what was good for us? We wish you to treat us like adults with adult minds – not children to be cosseted and given trinkets to keep us amused. Not all of us are content to be like your concubines, compliant, pampered and unquestioning. We have lives of our own,' responded Hamida. Rising, she came towards him and placed her hands on his shoulders. 'Yesterday I wished to visit a friend of mine – the wife of one of your commanders who lives near the western gate. I set out with several of my attendants from my palace but when I reached the gates leading from the *haram* the guards told me I could not pass . . . only the *khawajasara* could give permission for the gates to be opened. If you think this is for our benefit, for our security and protection, you're quite wrong. It is intolerable to be subject to such restrictions. You may be the emperor, Akbar, but you are also my son and I tell you I will not be treated in this way.'

'I am sorry, Mother, I hadn't realised . . . I will think about how things can be changed.'

'No. You will not. You will tell the *khawajasara* and the captain of the guard and the chief among that army of eunuchs you employ here that I, the mother of the emperor, will give the orders within the *haram*. I and your aunt will come and go as we please without let or hindrance.' Hamida released him. 'And when you go on campaign or on an imperial progress, we will accompany you if we wish to, properly concealed from impertinent or prying eyes, of course. And we will listen to council meetings as has always been our custom from behind the protection of the *jali* screens . . . and later give you any advice we see fit.'

Hamida paused and gave him a searching look. 'You have fallen in love with your power and magnificence – you think too much of the image you present to the world. Success has come easily to you – far more easily than to either your grandfather or your father. Don't let its dazzle blind you to the feelings of those close to you, whether female or male, and to the respect that is due to them as individuals, not just as elements in your hierarchy of empire . . . to do otherwise will be your loss as a man and eventually as an emperor.'

'You judge me too harshly. I do respect you, Mother – and you too, Aunt. I know without your help I might never have been emperor and I am grateful.'

'Then prove it by your behavior, not only to us but to others close to you, like your sons. You were unavoidably absent from them for many months while you were away fighting. Now you have returned you should be spending more time with them, getting to know them better rather than leaving them so much to the care of their tutors.'

Akbar nodded as if accepting her words, but inside he felt resentment stir. He needed no advice on how to govern or how to behave, and even less on how to treat his sons.

• ◆ •

'Majesty, the Christian priests you summoned here from Goa have arrived.'

'Thank you, Jauhar, I will come shortly.' Akbar turned to Abul Fazl, to whom he had been dictating an account of some new reforms to the method of tax-gathering within his empire. 'We will continue later. I want the chronicle to be as detailed as possible.'

'Indeed, Majesty. Those who come after you can learn many lessons from your manifest glorious success in every aspect of the administration of your expanding empire.'

Akbar allowed himself a quick smile. Over the years since he had appointed Abul Fazl his chronicler, he had grown used to his sometimes overblown and florid language and to his meticulous recording of every aspect of court life. When, six weeks ago, he had been gashed in the groin by the antlers of a stag while out hunting, Abul Fazl had recorded proudly that the application of a healing ointment was left 'to the writer of this book of fortune'. But he had come to realise that his chronicler was no fool. Even if Abul Fazl wrapped his advice in formulaic high-flown compliments, unlike many of his other courtiers he didn't just say what he thought the emperor wanted to hear but spoke with common sense and objectivity, and Akbar had begun consulting him more and more.

'Come with me. I want you to see these strange creatures. I hear that some of them shave their skulls almost bald, leaving just a thin circle of hair.'

'I will be interested to observe them. According to what I've heard, their own people treat them with great reverence and indeed seem almost afraid of them. If I might ask, why did you invite them to your court, Majesty?'

'I am curious about their religion. Unlike the faith of my Hindu subjects, of which I now understand a little, I know almost nothing of their god, except that they believe he was once a man who after being killed came back to life.'

'They have only one god then, like us?'

'So it would seem, except that − as I understand − they believe this god has three incarnations − they call them the father, the son and the holy ghost. Perhaps they resemble the Hindu trinity of Vishnu, Shiva and Brahma.'

Twenty minutes later, diamonds flashing in his turban, Akbar took his place on the throne placed in the balustraded, pulpit-like space at the intersection of the four slender, diagonal walkways supported by the richly-carved central column in his *diwan-i-khas*. Assembled below were the members of his council. He noticed Salim standing towards the back. It was good that the boy was here. He had probably never seen Europeans before.

'Bring in the visitors,' Akbar ordered the *qorchi* standing at his side. In a few moments, to the booming of drums from a musicians' gallery, the youth ushered the priests through a doorway that gave on to one of the balconies and out on to one of the walkways leading to where Akbar was sitting. When the two men, dark robes almost touching the floor, had advanced to within a dozen feet of Akbar, the squire signalled them to halt. Akbar saw that one man was small and sturdily built while the other was taller and paler, the skin of his bald head much freckled by the sun.

Akbar motioned the interpreter standing behind his throne to step closer. 'Tell them they are welcome at my court.' However, instead of waiting for the interpreter, the smaller of the two priests addressed Akbar directly in perfect court Persian.

'You are gracious to invite us to Fatehpur Sikri. We are Jesuit priests. My name is Father Francisco Henriquez. I am a Persian by birth and was once a follower of Islam, though now I am a Christian. My companion is Father Antonio Monserrate.'

'In your reply to my letter of invitation, you spoke of truths you wished to reveal to me. What are they?'

Father Francisco looked grave. 'They would take many hours to explain, Majesty, and you would run out of patience. But we have brought you a gift – our Christian gospels written in Latin, the language of our church. We know that you have many scholars at your court, among whom will be those able to translate them for you. Perhaps when you have had a chance to read what is written in our gospels we could talk again.'

They were well informed in some respects, Akbar thought. It was true that he employed learned men – some to translate the chronicles recounting the deeds of his Timurid ancestors from Turki into Persian, others to translate Hindu volumes from their original Sanskrit.

186

However, what the visiting priests clearly didn't know was that he himself still couldn't read. Ahmed Khan had tried to teach him during the long, rain-drenched hours sailing down the Jumna and the Ganges to fight Shah Daud, and in the year since his return Akbar had tried again, but the script still danced before his eyes. Yet frustrating as he found his failure, it had only fed his passion for books and the wisdom they contained. He always had a scholar on hand to read to him and was assembling a great library to rival any of the collections once held by his ancestors in far-off Samarkand and Herat.

'I will have your gift translated, and as soon as the first pages are ready we will talk again. I trust you will remain guests at my court until at least that time,' he said after a moment.

'We would be honoured, Majesty. We intend to spare no effort to shed the glorious light of our Saviour upon you.' As he spoke these words, Father Francisco's dark eyes gleamed and his whole face seemed possessed by a deep fervour. It would be interesting to debate religion with a man who had once followed the path of Islam but turned from it, Akbar reflected as the two priests were led away, and also to discover what these so-called gospels had to say. Father Francisco had made them sound complex and mysterious. Would they really reveal new truths? And who was this 'Saviour'? Was he another incarnation, like the father or the son or that spirit they called the 'holy ghost'? He felt impatient to know.

He was also curious to know what Salim had made of the new arrivals. He ordered an attendant to ask the prince to join him in his private apartments, and half an hour later he was looking down at his young son. 'I saw you watching the Christian priests. What did you think of them?'

'They looked strange.'

'In what way? Their clothes?'

'Yes, but more than that . . . there was something about their faces . . . almost as if they were hungry for something.'

'In a way they are. They hope to make Christians of us.'

'I heard one of our mullahs calling them foreign infidels and saying that you should never have invited them.'

'What do you think?'

Salim looked startled. 'I don't know.'

'Don't you think it's a good idea to find out as much as possible about other people's beliefs? After all, how can you show people they are wrong if you don't know what they think?'

This time Salim said nothing at all, but stared awkwardly at the ground.

'A strong, confident emperor doesn't need to fear those who hold different views, does he? Think about it, Salim. Don't your own studies make you curious to explore beyond the world you know?'

Salim looked towards the door, obviously anxious for this interview to end, and Akbar felt a surge of exasperation. He had expected more of his eldest son. Admittedly, Salim was young, but surely when he'd been that age he'd have had more to say – intelligent questions to ask. ' You must have some opinion,' he persisted. 'After all, why did you come to see the priests? I didn't see your brothers there, only you.'

'I wanted to see what Christian priests look like . . . I've heard all kinds of stories about them, and one of my tutors gave me this letter from a man who had met a priest in Delhi. It describes how the Christians worship a man nailed to a wooden cross.' Salim reached inside his orange tunic and took out a piece of folded paper. 'There's a drawing of the cross, but look what the letter says, Father – especially the last lines, about how the Christians pray.'

Akbar stared at the letter in his son's outstretched hand. Salim must know that he couldn't read . . . Slowly he took the piece of paper and unfolded it. At the top was a sketch of a skeletally thin man nailed to a cross, face creased in agony and head lolling. Beneath the drawing were some densely written lines that of course meant nothing to him. 'I will keep this and look at it later,' Akbar said, unable to help the sharp edge to his voice. 'Leave me now.'

Had his son intended to discomfit him? Akbar wondered, pacing his apartments after Salim had gone. Surely not. Why should he? But then the image of Hirabai's proud, unyielding face came into his mind. What if she was encouraging Salim to despise him, just as she did? He knew from questioning the boy's tutor that Salim was spending more and more time with his mother in her silent sandstone palace in the *haram* complex. She never saw her brother Bhagwan Das or her nephew Man Singh when they came to court, never held entertainments or gave parties, but – or so he had been told – kept herself aloof from the *haram*, spending her time reading, sewing with her Rajput waiting women and worshipping her gods. Every month at the time of the full moon, she climbed to the pavilion on the roof of her palace to gaze into the heavens and pray.

Perhaps it was simply her self-imposed isolation from him that was affecting Salim, causing the boy to start to behave towards his father as she did? Salim used to be so free and open, but not any more. Now that Akbar thought about it, this wasn't the first time he'd noticed how awkward and tongue-tied his eldest son had become in his presence. His jaw hardened. Hirabai could live as she chose but he would not allow her to influence their son. Though he wouldn't wish to prevent Salim from seeing his haughty mother, perhaps he should ensure the visits were short and the pair were not left unattended.

Chapter 14

Sun Among Women

Life was good. Akbar lay, eyes closed, feeling the air stir pleasantly around his naked body as a silk *punkah* swung rhythmically back and forth above him. He could hear the sound of water trickling down the *tattis*, the screens filled with the roots of scented *kass* grass that in summer were placed over the arched windows to cool the hot dry desert air blowing through them.

He had much enjoyed the past hours spent in the arms of a dancing girl from Delhi whose long, jasmine-scented hair fell to the curve of her buttocks. Although he was in his mid-thirties he congratulated himself he still had the vigour of any young blood. He certainly had no need of the *hakims'* aphrodisiac potions like 'the Making of the Horse' – a dark green foul-smelling concoction that supposedly gave a jaded man the sexual energy of a stallion and according to *haram* gossip was favoured by some of the more elderly members of his court. Nevertheless, he liked to explore new paths to pleasure. Sometimes he ordered one of his concubines to read to him from the centuries-old Hindu *Kama Sutra,* marvelling that there could be so many ways of making love. He smiled as he remembered the boy he had been with Mayala all those years ago. He would never have imagined then that he would acquire such a vast *haram*.

But at the thought, some of his contentment and post-coital languor ebbed. Soon he must rise and go to the *diwan-i-khas* for a meeting with members of the *ulama*. Jauhar had warned him what they wanted – to object to his intention of taking further wives because, having recently wed the daughter of an important vassal from the south, he already had four, the maximum permitted by Sunni Islam. Akbar sat up. He wouldn't tolerate any interference. Dynastic marriages were the cornerstone of his policy for pacifying and extending his empire and it was working. He would take a hundred wives, two hundred, if it would help secure his empire, whether further Rajput princesses or women from the old Moghul clans or Hindustan's Muslim nobility, whether plain or beautiful.

Of course, it had been very different for his father. Humayun had found in one woman – Hamida – the expression of his heart and soul. Sometimes he wished he himself could feel the same intense love for one woman but it had never happened and perhaps never would. At least it made it easier for him to pursue his policy of strategic alliances and left him free to enjoy an infinite variety of sexual partners. He now had over three hundred concubines. Most men would envy him, he reflected, pushing thoughts of the sour-faced *ulama* from his mind as he recalled once more the dancing girl, supple body gleaming with perfumed oil.

Two hours later, in robes of emerald silk embroidered with peacocks and with a jewelled ceremonial dagger tucked into his bright yellow sash, Akbar took his place on his throne on the circular platform atop the tall carved pillar in the *diwan-i-khas*, Abul Fazl and the now stooped figure of his vizier Jauhar behind him. On one of the balconies stood the members of his *ulama*. Shaikh Ahmad was standing slightly to the fore, obviously expecting to be invited to advance along the narrow bridge to the platform. Akbar gestured to him to remain where he was.

'Well, Shaikh Ahmad. What do you wish to say to me?'

The shaikh touched his hand to his breast but the small brown eyes he fixed on Akbar were far from humble. 'Majesty, the time has come for plain speaking. Your intention to take further wives is an affront to God.'

Akbar leaned forward. 'Be careful what you say.'

'You are defying what is written in the Koran. I have spoken to you about this many times in private but you have chosen not to listen, forcing me to protest in public. If you still will not heed me, I will preach my message from the pulpit of the great mosque at Friday prayers.' The shaikh's face was flushed and he seemed to interpret Akbar's silence as encouraging. Drawing up his portly body and with a triumphant glance over his shoulder at his colleagues, he continued, 'The Koran permits a man only four marriages – *nikah* marriages with women of the Muslim faith. Yet I hear that you plan to take many more – some not even Muslims. If you do not draw back, God will punish you and our empire.'

'I already have two Hindu wives, as you very well know. Each has borne me a son. Are you suggesting I renounce them?'

The shaikh thrust out his chin. 'Let them be concubines, Majesty. Your royal sons will still enjoy the status of royal princes. Many princes have been born to concubines . . . your own grandfather's brother, for example . . .'

Akbar looked at the mullah, wondering how it would feel to take his sword and slice through that fleshy neck. The thought came that even after being severed, that pompous, self-righteous head would probably still keep talking.

'Shaikh Ahmad, I have done you the courtesy of listening to you. Now listen to me. I am the emperor. I alone will decide what is best for my empire and for my people. I will not tolerate your meddling.'

The mullah flushed but said nothing. Akbar was about to dismiss the *ulama* when Abul Fazl's father Shaikh Mubarak stepped forward. Akbar hadn't noticed him till now.

'Majesty, if I might be permitted to speak, I might be able to propose a solution.'

'Very well.'

'Like Shaikh Ahmad, I am a Sunni Muslim, but I have spent some years studying the ways of our Shia brothers. I have come to see that they – like us – are faithful followers of the Prophet Muhammad and that we should not allow doctrinal differences to make us enemies.'

'You speak wisely, but why is this relevant to what you have just heard?'

'It could not be more relevant, Majesty. The Shias believe that the Koran permits another, lesser form of marriage – the *muta*. A man may contract a *muta* marriage with any number of women, whatever their religion, and with no need for any formal ceremony . . .'

'That is heresy . . . no true believer would follow such a path,' interrupted Shaikh Ahmad, shaking his head angrily.

'Perhaps it isn't heresy. A particular verse of the Koran – I will show it to you – appears to sanction these *muta* marriages. They are common in Persia . . .'

'Yes, and the corrupt practices of that sacrilegious land are spreading to our own. I have heard that the owners of our caravanserais now offer *muta* wives to merchants for the night as an inducement to stay there. It is no more than an excuse for prostitution!'

Shaikh Ahmad continued to rage on but Akbar was no longer listening. Shaikh Mubarak's ideas were interesting and he would like to know more. If the Koran indeed appeared to allow a man many wives, it would be useful in countering the views of the orthodox members of the *ulama* – not that he would have allowed them to frustrate his plans. But Mubarak's words had struck a deeper chord within him. Shias, Sunnis, Hindus, Christians – weren't they all seeking the same fundamental truths – certainties in an uncertain world? The rituals they enacted, the rules they followed, were all man-made. Strip all this away and what was left but man's simple quest to communicate with his god and live the best life he could?

Suddenly aware that Shaikh Ahmad had stopped ranting and that all were waiting for him to speak, Akbar raised a hand. 'You are dismissed. I will think over what I have heard. Shaikh Mubarak – you will come to me tomorrow and we will speak further. But let this be understood. I am the emperor and, as such, God's shadow upon the earth. I alone will decide how to conduct my life. I will not tolerate any interference and need no sanction from anyone for what I decide.'

The members of the *ulama* backed away. Akbar sat for a while, caught up in his musings, but after several minutes Jauhar whispered to him, 'Majesty, a stranger has arrived at court – by coincidence

194

from the very country of which we have just been speaking, Persia. He begs an audience with you.' Akbar was about to say that his patience was exhausted and he had no wish to see the man when Jauhar added, 'He has an interesting story, Majesty, and he is no common traveller.'

Akbar thought for a moment. He felt like going riding. A gallop across the desert would ease his frustration, but it was still too hot for that. 'Very well, admit him.'

Ten minutes later a tall, thin man was led on to one of the balconies. His dark purple robes hung from his emaciated body and his fingers were ringless.

'You may approach. Who are you?'

'My name is Ghiyas Beg. I am a Persian nobleman from Khurasan. My father was a courtier of the shah and my family are connected with the Persian royal family through marriage.'

'What brings you to my court?'

'A terrible blight fell upon my estates. The crops withered, my debts mounted and I and my family were reduced to poverty. I had heard of the many Persians who had come to Fatehpur Sikri and found great favour here. I therefore determined to bring my family into Hindustan and to offer you my services.' Ghiyas Beg paused and for a moment rubbed his hand over eyes beneath which were shadows so dark the skin appeared bruised. His voice was deep and musical and he spoke court Persian with the grace of the courtier he claimed to be. Though clearly destitute, his bearing was that of a man more used to commanding than seeking favours. Akbar looked at him with growing interest.

'Majesty, though I appear before you like a beggar, it was the perils of my journey that reduced me to this state. The only reason that I am not dressed in rags is that a Persian friend – one of the scholars in your library – gave me clean robes. Your inclination must be to order the poor creature that I have become from your sight, but I beg you first to hear my story.'

'Very well.'

'I brought my wife – who was well advanced in pregnancy – and my young son Asaf Khan safely across the Helmand river out of

195

Persia. It was then that our troubles began. The road to Hindustan lay through wild, lonely and mountainous country.'

'I know. My father once hazarded his life by taking that path. How did you survive?'

'To protect my family I joined a large caravan, but because of my wife's fragile condition and the poor quality of the mules carrying us, we fell behind. One night towards dusk as we descended a narrow pass, bandits swept down the steep scree slopes and attacked us. They took everything we had except for the old mule on which my wife was riding, which they left us, as they said, "for charity's sake". We struggled on, desperate to catch up with the caravan, but darkness fell and we were forced to stop for the night in the lee of a hill which gave us some protection from the weather. It was late autumn and a chill, scouring wind was already blowing down from the mountains. That night – perhaps brought on by the shock of the attack – my wife gave birth to a daughter.'

'So after all your sufferings, God was kind . . .'

Ghiyas Beg's bony face remained grave. 'In our joy, we called her Mehrunissa, "Sun Among Women", because the moment of her birth had brought light into the darkness of our lives. But our happiness was short-lived. Next morning, in the cold dawn light I was forced to confront our situation. We were starving, destitute and alone – we could not keep the child. I took Mehrunissa from the arms of my exhausted wife, who was barely conscious, and laid her in a crevice among the roots of a tall fir tree. I prayed she would die of exposure before jackals or some other wild creatures found her. I was even tempted – I confess it – to smother her myself, but that would have been too great a sin. I walked slowly away, my daughter's thin wails echoing in my ears, indeed in my very soul.'

Ghiyas Beg fell silent for a moment, as if reliving that most terrible of dilemmas. Akbar could picture the distraught father buffeted by freezing winds, seeing nothing but death and hopelessness ahead. Could he himself have abandoned one of his sons in such circumstances? As if the thought of his boys had somehow conjured one to appear, Akbar suddenly noticed Salim standing half concealed behind a sandstone pillar in the chamber below, listening intently.

196

'Continue, Ghiyas Beg,' he said.

An unexpected smile softened the Persian's face. 'It is not for us mortals to know the ways of God, but for some reason he took pity on me. A Persian merchant to whom I had been talking – he was also from Khurasan – had noticed our absence when the caravan halted for the night. He knew my wife's condition and guessed her time might have come. At first light, he and two of his servants came back to look for us. By a miracle he came across us as we were attempting to ford a stream.

'When I told him about my daughter, he at once offered me one of his attendants' horses. I galloped back – in truth we had not managed to get far – praying that Mehrunissa would still be alive. When I heard her cries above the wind I knew my plea had been answered. She was unharmed but very cold, her lips almost blue. I took the sheepskin saddlecloth of the horse and wrapped her in it. After a while, I saw the colour returning to her tiny face and from that moment hope was restored to me.

'The merchant who had helped us remained our friend, indeed our benefactor, giving us food and allowing us to ride in one of his bullock carts until four days ago we saw your great city of Fatehpur Sikri rising up before us and our hearts filled with joy. But I have taken enough of your time, Majesty. If it pleases you to find some humble task about your court, you will find me a devoted and grateful servant.'

Akbar scrutinised the tall, shabby figure before him. He didn't doubt the Persian's story of the hardships and dangers he had encountered. The man had looked truly harrowed as he had spoken of them. On the other hand, was this courtly, silver-tongued man all he claimed to be? Why had Ghiyas Beg set out with a young child and a pregnant wife on what he must have known would be a highly dangerous journey? The desire to escape poverty, the hopes of a new life that he had spoken of so eloquently might not be true. Maybe something else – corruption or rebellion – had forced him to flee . . .

As if sensing his doubts, Ghiyas Beg seemed to sag a little. That tiny, despairing gesture decided Akbar. He would give the Persian the benefit of the doubt. After all, an emperor should be generous, and he had thought of somewhere he could send him – a place where, if he was as industrious as he claimed, he could be useful, and if he was dishonest or treacherous his crime would soon be discovered.

'Ghiyas Beg, the story you have related with such candour has touched me. I believe you are a man of courage and honesty deserving of my favour. Jauhar . . .' Akbar gestured to his elderly vizier. 'A few days ago you told me that one of my assistant treasurers in Kabul had recently died, didn't you?'

'Yes, Majesty, of the spotted fever.'

'Will you take the post, Ghiyas Beg? Prove your skill and industry and it may lead to more senior appointments.'

Ghiyas Beg looked transfigured with relief. 'I will serve you in Kabul to the utmost of my ability, Majesty.'

'See that you do.'

As the Persian was ushered out, Akbar motioned to Jauhar to come closer. 'Write to my governor in Kabul about this appointment and tell him to keep an eye on Ghiyas Beg, just to be sure.' Then he looked for his son, but was not surprised to find that Salim had slipped away. Ever since the day he had questioned him about the Jesuit visitors, he had noticed how his son was avoiding him. Whenever he made an effort to seek him out – going to watch him at his lessons or practising swordplay, archery or wrestling – instead of relishing the chance to show off his skills Salim seemed awkward and nervous. His obvious unease was making it increasingly difficult for Akbar to know what to do or say. Emperor himself from a young age, he had always taken the love and admiration of those around him for granted. How should he react to his son's behaviour?

He must learn patience. If he just waited, Salim would surely start coming to him of his own accord, whatever insidious things his mother might have told him, might tell him . . . Boys needed their fathers.

• ◆ •

'I am curious. What did this man Ghiyas Beg look like?' asked Hamida.

'He was tall and thin and the robe he was wearing was too small for him. His big, bony wrists were sticking out,' Salim replied.

'And he is a Persian?'

'Yes.'

'Why has he come here?'

'To seek my father's help.'

'What did he ask for?'

'Employment in the service of the Moghuls.'

'Tell me exactly what he said.'

Hamida listened intently, and when Salim had finished was silent for a while. 'Life is a strange thing,' she said at last. 'So much that happens to us appears random, yet – like your grandfather, my husband Humayun – I have often discerned patterns running through our existence as if at the hand of a divine weaver at the loom . . . You know that a seer's blood runs in my veins. I thought that the power to see into the future had left me long ago, but while you were speaking I suddenly thought that one day this Ghiyas Beg might become important to our dynasty. There are strange parallels between his story and some of what previously befell our own family . . . You say that he has come from Persia with his fortunes in the dust after nearly abandoning his newborn child. As you know, a similar desperate plight once forced your grandfather and me to go to Persia to seek the shah's help. We too were nearly destitute. But far worse than that, your father, then just a baby, had been stolen from us.

'Picture the scene when we crossed into Persia . . . We had barely eaten for weeks and had no idea whether Shah Tahmasp would even let us remain in his kingdom. But when he learned of our arrival he sent ten thousand cavalrymen to escort us to his summer capital. Servants dressed in purple silk embroidered with gold walked ahead of us sprinkling the road with rosewater to keep the dust from rising. At night we slept in brocade tents on satin couches scented with ambergris, and attendants served us over five hundred different dishes as well as delicate sherbets chilled with ice brought down from the mountains and sweetmeats wrapped in gold and silver leaf. After every meal, we were presented with some fresh gift – singing birds with jewelled collars in cages of solid gold, an image of Timur in his summer palace in Samarkand painted on ivory that I still possess. But though we wanted the shah's assistance, we refused to behave like suppliants. Your grandfather made him a great gift – greater than anything ever presented to him before. It was the Koh-i-Nur diamond, the "Mountain of Light".'

'Why did my grandfather give the diamond to the Shah?'

Hamida smiled, a little sadly, or so it seemed to Salim. 'You must understand how it was. Indeed, it's a good lesson for you. Think how hard it was for him to throw himself on another ruler's mercy. By offering the shah the Koh-i-Nur diamond he redressed the balance, showing himself the shah's equal, even if in desperate straits, and thus retained his pride. What is a gem, however magnificent, compared with the honour of our dynasty?' Hamida's eyes were suddenly very bright.

While she had been speaking, Gulbadan had entered. Though the lines running from the corners of her mouth to her jawline gave her a severe look, it vanished when she saw Salim, to be replaced by a warm smile.

Salim smiled back. He liked to visit his grandmother and his great-aunt. With them he felt safe and secure. They didn't criticise him, and he enjoyed their stories. When they spoke of how his grandfather had won back Hindustan, he could see the pennants fluttering from the steel-tipped lances of the Moghul horsemen as they galloped across the flat, dusty plains and the clouds of white smoke rising from the Moghul cannon. He could smell the acrid fumes and hear the crackle of musket fire and the deep, harsh trumpeting of war elephants.

'Tell your great-aunt about the Persian who has arrived at court.'

'Did your father agree to help this Ghiyas Beg?' Gulbadan asked when Salim had finished.

'Yes. He gave him a post in Kabul.'

'Your father is a good judge of character,' Gulbadan said, 'but it wasn't always so. As a young man he could be rash and too easily influenced by those around him. But he has learned to be more careful. Observe him, Salim. Ask him the reasons behind his decisions . . . try to learn from him.'

That was easy for her to say, Salim thought. But what he said was, 'I often go to the audience chamber and watch my father seated on his throne on top of the carved column. But it puzzles me how anyone dares to approach him. He looks so remote – almost god-like . . .'

'It is a ruler's duty to inspire confidence, to show that he is ready to listen,' said Hamida. 'People approach him because they trust him, as you should.'

'Your grandmother is right,' said Gulbadan. 'A ruler must demonstrate to his people that he cares for them. That's why every day at dawn your father steps out on to the *jharoka* balcony to show himself to his subjects. It is to prove to them not just that their emperor still lives but also that he is concerned for them, watching over them like a father . . .'

He actually is my father, Salim thought, so why do I find it so hard to talk to him? Every time he was with Akbar it seemed to him that his father was examining and probing him, critically testing his merits and his knowledge.

'Salim, what's the matter? You look sad,' said Hamida.

'You tell me to talk to my father but it's hard . . . I don't know whether he'd welcome it. He always seems so immaculate, so perfect in dress and behaviour, and so busy, surrounded by his courtiers and his commanders. Sometimes he does come to watch me at my studies but when he asks me questions I feel confused . . . stupid . . . so worried that what I say won't be good enough that I can't answer at all. I know I disappoint him.'

'Is that all?' Hamida was smiling. 'Don't be so foolish. Remember your father is my son. He was not always this imposing presence. He was once a boy like you, grazing his knees and tearing his clothes in rough games and exercises with his companions and – if the truth be told – not half so good at his lessons or curious about the world around him as you are! And I know how proud he is of you. You should feel inferior to no one!'

Salim smiled back but said nothing. How could they understand? How could anybody, when he didn't understand his feelings himself?

• ◆ •

'I am pleased to see you, Salim. Come with me up to the roof. I was about to pray.'

Salim followed his mother up the winding flight of sandstone stairs. The light from the clay oil lamp in Hirabai's right hand was just enough for him to see where he was going, though once he turned a corner too sharply and tripped. Stepping out on to the flat roof of her palace he saw that his mother, long dark hair intertwined with white jasmine flowers, was already kneeling before a small shrine. It was a warm, windless evening and glancing up into the heavens Salim saw the pale sliver of the crescent moon.

Hirabai was bending low in prayer. Although she sometimes spoke of her Hindu beliefs, they still seemed strange to him, raised a Muslim believing in one God and unused to idols and images. At last she was finished, and rising she turned to Salim. 'Look at the moon. We Rajputs are its children by night and the offspring of the sun by day. The moon gives us our limitless endurance and the sun our indomitable courage.' Hirabai's dark eyes flickered as she looked at him. Salim could feel the intensity of her love for him and wished she would embrace him, but that was not her way and her arms remained by her sides.

'Mother, you always talk about the Rajputs, but I'm a Moghul too, aren't I?' Salim had come to his mother hoping that perhaps she might help him understand the confusions and uncertainties that seemed to be crowding in around him. And he had come alone, slipping away from the attendants who, he suspected, were under orders to report what they saw and heard to Akbar.

'To my great sorrow you have been brought up as a Moghul prince. Your tutors have stuffed your ears with tales of the valour of your great-grandfather Babur and of your grandfather Humayun – how they crossed the Indus river and conquered an empire.'

'But my father is the Moghul Emperor of Hindustan. Surely I need to know the history of his people?'

'Of course. But you also need to be told the truth. Your tutors praise the bravery and daring of the Moghul clans but never say that they stole from the Rajputs what was rightfully theirs.'

'What do you mean?'

'You have been brought up by your father to believe this land is yours – but he is deceiving you just as through blind pride and arrogance he deceives himself. The truth is that Moghuls are no more than cattle thieves who sneak among the herds at night to steal the property of others. They took advantage of a moment of weakness in Hindustan to invade. They claimed that Timur's conquest of Hindustan gave them the right to rule, but who was he but another uncouth barbarian raider from the north?

'It is my people, the Rajputs – your people too, Salim – who are the true, indeed the sacred rulers of Hindustan. Just before Babur and his hordes poured down into our land from their mountainous wildernesses, the Rajput kings under Rana Sanga of Chittorgarh were forming an alliance to depose the weak, luxury-loving Lodi rulers and take Hindustan back for our people. Perhaps we had angered the gods and the Moghul invaders were our punishment, but we have paid in blood for any offence we gave.

'Even after the Moghuls defeated the Lodi dynasty at Panipat, our people did not flinch from their warrior destiny. Babur derided them as infidels but they showed him how the Hindu warrior caste could fight. They attacked him at Khanua and nearly defeated him.' Hirabai's eyes glittered as if she too were a Rajput warrior bent on spilling blood.

'You asked me whether you are a Moghul. You are – but only in part. Never forget that you are my son as well as Akbar's and that royal Rajput blood – a thousand times more noble than Moghul blood – beats in your veins. The destiny that awaits you may not be the one you think . . . Just as your father can choose which son he names as his heir, you have a choice too . . .'

Salim stood in silence, too confused to know what he thought. Where did the truth lie between his mother's bewailing of the fate of her people and his tutors' glorious tales of the Moghuls? And where did it leave him? Was his mother hinting that his father might not choose his eldest son as his heir at the same time as suggesting that Salim might have to choose between his Moghul ancestry and his Rajput inheritance? But the latter made no sense, especially when he thought about his father's pronouncements that all were equal within the empire and about the many Rajputs who served Akbar.

'But Mother, members of your own family, the royal house of Amber, are in the service of the Moghuls — like your brother Bhagwan Das and your nephew Man Singh. They wouldn't join my father if they thought it dishonourable.'

'People can always be bought . . . even Rajput nobility. I am ashamed of my brother and my nephew.' Hirabai's voice was cold and he could see that unwittingly he had offended her. 'Leave me now, but think on my words.'

She turned away from him, back to her shrine, and kneeling down again within the halo of light from a circle of wicks burning in *diyas* began once more to pray. Salim hesitated a moment, then made his way slowly to the stone staircase and down to the courtyard below, Hirabai's contempt for his father and the Moghuls still ringing in his ears. He had hoped for some answers from her but instead his head only echoed with fresh questions about who he was and who he would become.

Part IV

Allah Akbar

Chapter 15

'You Will Be Emperor'

'Where did you get those?'

Salim glared at Murad. Two pigeons, purple throats crimson with blood, were hanging from his half-brother's silver belt, but Salim's eyes were fixed on the double bow he was holding in one hand and the gilded quiver of arrows in the other.

Murad grinned. 'I found them lying in the courtyard. I thought you didn't want them . . .'

'You mean you stole them.'

Murad's smile faded and he drew himself up. Though eleven months younger he was nearly two inches taller than Salim. 'I'm not a thief. How was I supposed to know you still wanted them? You never come to the courtyard to join us in our exercises and trials of strength as you used to. You're always skulking away somewhere. Daniyal and I hardly ever see you any more. Father says . . .'

Salim took a step closer. 'What does he say?' His voice was low and his narrowed eyes were fixed on his brother's face.

Murad looked a little taken aback. 'Nothing really . . . except that you spend too much time on your own. He was here just a while ago, watching me practise my archery. When I shot down the pigeons with this bow he said I was as skilful as he was at my age.' He beamed with pride.

'Give me back my bow and arrows.'

'Why should I? You only want them now because I like them and can use them so well.'

'I want them because they're mine.'

'Take them, then – if you can.' Murad thrust out his square jaw.

Salim felt a surge of anger, and needing no further encouragement launched himself at his half-brother. Though Murad was heavier, he was the quicker. Using his momentum he pushed Murad to the ground, then leaping on top straddled him, locking his thighs hard against Murad's ribs. Murad tried to poke his fingers into his eyes but he jerked back just in time and then got a hand on either side of his brother's face. Grabbing hold of Murad's long black hair he yanked his head up then thumped it hard against the paving stones. There was a satisfying crack and as he pulled Murad's head up again to repeat the process he saw a thin smear of dark red blood on the stones.

'Highnesses, stop!' Hearing agitated voices and feet running swiftly towards them, Salim crashed his brother's head once more against the stones. Then he felt strong arms pulling him off his brother. Glancing up, he saw it was Murad's tutor. The man carried him a few steps away then released him. Panting hard and wiping the sweat from his face, Salim had the satisfaction of seeing Murad still lying groaning on the ground. That would teach him to challenge his older brother.

Daniyal had come running into the courtyard. His eyes in his round face looked startled but it seemed to Salim that his younger half-brother was looking at him with some admiration. At least he knew how to fight . . . But as he looked round at Murad, who was sitting up now and holding his bleeding head in his hands, some of his elation began to ebb to be replaced by shame that he had lost his temper so completely. If he was honest, it wasn't the fact that Murad had taken his bow and arrows that had so enraged him, even though they had been a gift from Akbar. It was hurt that his father should criticise him to Murad – and jealousy that they could even have such a conversation.

'What has been going on?' Hearing his father's deep voice, Salim looked round and his heart began to pound.

'He called me a thief! Then he attacked me as if he wanted to kill me,' said Murad, who was now on his feet. 'All because I borrowed his bow and arrows.'

'You stole them. Then you said if I wanted them back I must take them. But keep them if they are so important to you.'

'You are brothers. Salim, you in particular as the eldest should know better. Such scuffling isn't seemly.' Akbar's tone was severe. 'You both deserve to be punished for brawling like urchins from the bazaar. This time I will overlook it, but do not let it happen again or you will not find me so lenient. As for this bow and these arrows which have caused so much trouble, let me see them.'

Murad brought them over and Akbar inspected them carefully. 'I recognise them now. These were my gift to you, Salim, weren't they? As I told you, they were crafted by a Turkish master from the very finest materials.'

'He'd just left them in the courtyard . . . he never used them . . . if it had rained they'd have been ruined.' Murad's tone was all self-righteousness.

Salim looked stonily ahead. How could he defend himself when Murad's accusation was true? He had been careless with Akbar's gift.

Akbar was looking at him, perplexed. 'I'm sorry you don't like them. I will keep them for my own use.'

Salim knew his father was waiting for him to say something, to offer some explanation. He wanted so badly to speak but somehow the words wouldn't come. All he could manage was a faint shrug of his shoulders which he was sure looked like defiance rather than regret.

• ◆ •

A week later, Akbar still couldn't shake off the sense of disquiet that had descended on him since the fight between Salim and Murad. The words spoken by the loser at the end of a game of chess – *shah mat*, 'the king is at a loss' – kept returning to his mind. That was how he had felt as he confronted Salim and he wasn't used to it. On the battlefield he always knew what to do. And governing his empire he felt the same certainty. His borders were secure, the rule of law prevailed and he was winning the loyalty of his subjects, high and low. So why didn't he have the same sure touch in his private life?

'Do not take the love of your sons for you or for each other for granted . . .' had been Shaikh Salim Chishti's parting words to him all those years ago. In the euphoria of fathering three healthy sons he had pushed the Sufi's warning from his mind. On the rare occasions he recalled it, he had comfortably dismissed it as prudent advice to any father but irrelevant to him. Now, though, the recollection of those words was making him increasingly uneasy. Were he and Salim, his eldest son, growing apart? If the bonds between them were indeed weakening, to what might it lead as Salim grew older, and what could he do to prevent it?

Several times he had felt tempted to confide his concerns to his mother and his aunt, but ever since their disagreement with him about the management of his *haram* he had felt as inhibited in discussing personal or family matters with them as Salim seemed to be in speaking to him. Instead his thoughts turned to Abul Fazl. Instinct told him that his chronicler would understand, and might even have some advice to offer . . .

Finally, one evening he summoned Abul Fazl to join him where he sat alone in a secluded courtyard lit by candles.

'I have brought my ledger and my pen and ink, Majesty. Did you wish to dictate?'

'No . . . I just want to talk. You have sons, don't you?'

'Yes, Majesty, two boys of ten and twelve.' Abul Fazl looked surprised.

'When you praise them or give them presents, how do they react?'

Abul Fazl shrugged. 'As any boy would, Majesty. They are delighted and excited.'

'Like my youngest sons Murad and Daniyal . . .'

'And Prince Salim, Majesty? Surely he is the same?' Abul Fazl probed gently.

'No, he isn't. At least not with me . . . It hurts me to say this – indeed I find it hard to admit it to myself – but it's as if an invisible wall is growing up between us. Before I went to Bengal Salim was

210

as open as either of my other sons and even more high-spirited. Now he seems quiet . . . withdrawn . . . and he avoids my company.'

'What does his tutor say?'

'That he excels in everything. He can read Persian and Turki fluently. He fights well with a sword, can fire a musket and rides his pony hard playing polo. I know this is true because I have observed it myself. But while my other sons can't wait to brag to me about their doings, Salim rarely seeks me out. I even took him tiger hunting on his own two weeks ago. When we flushed a great beast from its hiding place, I let him fire the musket. He yelled with excitement as the musket ball lodged in the animal's throat but later as we rode home he said almost nothing.'

'He is young, Majesty, barely eleven. If you are patient all will come right.'

'Perhaps.'

'All fathers worry about their children.'

'But all fathers are not emperors. Though I am young and strong and confident that God will grant me many more years, I must consider which of my sons I wish to succeed me. They are just boys, it is true, but I cannot forget that my grandfather was a king at only twelve years old. In the early years of his reign it was his own courage and resolution – fed by the knowledge that he had been brought up to rule – that helped him evade the assassin's blade and outwit rivals scheming for his throne. Whichever of my sons is to be the next Moghul emperor must feel that same sense of destiny, of duty to the dynasty. It cannot begin too early. In my heart I wish my heir to be my first-born. But if Salim is turning against me or lacks the hunger and the will to lead, what then?'

Abul Fazl was for once silent, and the two men sat wrapped in their own thoughts as one by one the candles began to gutter. Akbar signalled to his attendants not to renew them. Tonight he preferred the darkness to the light.

• ◆ •

His tutors would be anxious for his safety if they discovered what he had done but Salim didn't care. Since that strange evening with his mother he had felt even more restless and unsettled than before. For as long as he could remember, he had known that Hirabai did not love his father. As he had grown up, he had begun to understand that their marriage had been only a political alliance. But never before had he realised the depth of his mother's scorn — hatred even — for Akbar and the Moghuls. Bats swooped around Salim as he ran but he knew every inch of this path, even in the purpling dusk.

He had slipped out of the palace complex through the Agra gate, mingling with the merchants and tradesmen returning homeward as the sun had begun to slide beneath the horizon. Instead of following the crowds down to the plain where light from hundreds of dung fires was already pricking the darkness, Salim branched off down a narrow track skirting the edge of the escarpment. Another ten minutes of hard running and he thought he could see the outline of a low house. Salim stopped, his blood pounding in his ears and his breathing so loud that he was sure the old woman and the girl he could see squatting by a small fire outside the house must be able to hear him. But they went on with their work — the girl shaping dough on a flat stone and then handing the thin circles to her companion who was cooking them on a metal rack over the fire, flipping them with a piece of wood.

Salim heard the old woman exclaim in dismay as one piece fell into the fire. As he came nearer he smelled the charred bread. Somehow the very ordinariness of the scene gave him courage. He had made his decision to come here tonight without any forethought — sparked by the sight of his father walking across the sunlit *haram* courtyard with Murad and Daniyal laughing and talking beside him. Suddenly his sense of being an outsider had been so strong that something had seemed to explode within him, questioning the point of his existence. It was followed almost instinctively by the inspiration that the one person who might be able to answer his questions was the Sufi mystic who had predicted his birth and in whose honour Fatehpur Sikri had been built. Salim had never seen the Sufi for himself. All he knew was that he was very old and completely blind and that he had refused Akbar's offer to house him within the palace complex, preferring to remain in his simple house beyond the walls.

Salim's hesitant steps had brought him to the edge of the rim of light thrown out by the fire. The girl saw him first and stood up. Then the old woman followed the girl's gaze and looked up at him. 'What do you want?'

'To see Shaikh Salim Chishti.'

'My brother is very frail – too frail to be troubled by visitors who come without warning at night.'

'I'm sorry – I didn't think . . .' Salim stepped nearer. The gems round his neck and on his fingers flashed in the firelight, which also picked out the golden clasps on his green silk tunic. The old woman was studying him carefully from his leather boots – scuffed by running but richly embroidered – to the pearls hanging from his ear lobes. At last she rose.

'Halima, finish cooking the bread.' Then she gestured to Salim to follow her inside.

The lintel of the house was so low that, young as he was, Salim had to duck beneath it. In the faint light of two oil lamps he saw a figure sitting against the far wall. It looked bulky but as his eyes adjusted Salim saw that the Sufi was half cocooned in a woollen blanket. Far from being large, he looked as delicate as the Chinese porcelain the merchants brought carefully wrapped in layers of straw.

'Brother, you have a visitor. A royal prince, by his dress.' The old woman's voice, tender and soft, was quite different from the brusque tone in which she had spoken to Salim. 'Do you have the strength to talk to him?'

The old man nodded. 'He is welcome. Tell him to sit near me.'

The woman signalled to Salim to seat himself on the woven jute mat that covered the floor of beaten earth, then went back outside.

'I wondered whether one day you would come to see me, Salim. You are sitting exactly where your father did when he too visited me.'

'How did you know who I was? It might have been one of my half-brothers, Daniyal or Murad . . .'

'God has been good to me. Even though the external world is hidden from me, he reveals many things to me in my heart. I knew

213

it could only be you because you are the only one of Akbar's sons who needs my help at present.'

Suddenly tears were pricking Salim's eyelids – tears not of sorrow but of relief that here was someone who would listen and understand.

'Tell me what is troubling you,' the Sufi said gently.

'I don't understand who I am – what the purpose of my life will be. I want my father to be proud of me but I don't know what he expects of me, what he wants me to be . . . I am his eldest son. I should be the next emperor but perhaps that is not what he wants. What if he prefers one of my half-brothers to me? And even if I did become emperor, my mother would hate me for it. She says the Moghuls are barbarians who do not belong here. She . . .'

Shaikh Salim Chishti leaned forward from his shroud of blankets and took Salim's face between his dry old hands. 'No need for words. I understand what you are feeling – your doubts and fears. You look for love yet fear that by loving one parent you betray the other . . . You are envious of your half-brothers and fear they may eclipse you in your father's eyes . . . that is why you no longer seek them out. You wonder whether you were born to rule . . . I tell you this, Prince Salim: the path of the Moghuls has been hard and bloody but they have achieved greatness and there is more to come. You will be a part of that greatness – you will be emperor . . .'

The Sufi paused and with his fingertips gently probed the contours of Salim's face as if trying to find by his touch what his eyes could no longer tell him. 'You have your father's determination and strength but not yet his experience and confidence. Observe him, watch how he governs. That is the way to prepare yourself and to win his approval. But just as I once warned him, so I must warn you. Watch those around you. Be careful whom you confide in and take nothing on trust, even from those bound to you by blood – your half-brothers or even the sons you will have. I do not mean that you will always be surrounded by traitors, but you must be aware that treachery is quick to breed. Ambition is double-edged. It drives men to achieve great things but can also poison their souls – yours as much as any other man's. Be on your guard both against those around you and against your own passions and weaknesses. If you do, then you will achieve the things you yearn for.' The Sufi released him and leaned back again.

Salim closed his eyes as a scene began to take shape in his imagination: himself seated on a glittering throne, his nobles and commanders making obeisance before him. That was what he wanted – to be the next Moghul emperor. Whatever doubts his mother had put into his head vanished at the glorious vision before him. He was above all else a Moghul and he would be worthy of his inheritance. He must push aside the anxieties and uncertainties that had been tormenting him and, though still so young, learn to be a man. The Sufi was right. The way to win his father's love and respect was by showing himself worthy to rule . . .

A gentle sigh from the Sufi broke into Salim's thoughts. 'I am weary. You must go now, but I trust I have brought you comfort and hope.'

Salim tried to find the words to thank him but emotion seemed to be choking him. 'You are truly great,' he managed at last. 'I understand why my father holds you in such honour.'

'I am only a simple priest trying to divine the ways of God and of man. I am fortunate to lead a quiet, peaceful existence. That is not your fate. You will be a great ruler, but I do not envy you your life or your glory.'

Chapter 16

Heaven and Hell

Salim felt content as he approached the Agra gate of Fatehpur Sikri. It had been a good morning's hawking and his birds had performed well, swooping down through the pale early morning light on doves and rats alike. Even better, in a few weeks' time he was to accompany his father on a long hunting trip. Akbar's hunting leopards, with their jewelled collars and velvet blindfolds, would soon be being readied to go with them in their brocade-covered wicker cages, and hundreds of beaters would be making their preparations too.

Salim was pleased that his father had invited him, in preference to either of his half-brothers. Over the eight months since his night-time visit to Shaikh Salim Chishti he had done as the Sufi suggested, observing his father's daily rituals whenever he could, from his dawn appearance to his people to his daily audiences when, surrounded by courtiers and protected by his heavily armed guards, he received petitions and dispensed justice. The Sufi's words had given him confidence that whatever else happened, one day these would be his tasks. He had begun worrying less about what his father thought of him and concentrating more on what it meant to be a ruler of men. As the Sufi had predicted, this seemed to have gained him a little more of his father's approval.

If only Abul Fazl wasn't always there, scribbling in those ledgers of his and whispering in Akbar's ear. But his influence with his father remained as strong as ever. Whenever there was a problem, Abul Fazl, as he himself might put it in his ornate style, dodged between the raindrops of his father's criticism, unlike many others who failed to meet Akbar's exacting standards. It was Abul Fazl who often prompted his father to request that Salim leave meetings, arguing that the subject matter meant they should be restricted to those most closely involved. Salim also suspected that Abul Fazl was behind Akbar's stopping him from attending any meetings of his military council, much to his dismay.

'Protect His Highness, the prince! Seize those men.' The sudden shouts of the commander of Salim's bodyguard jolted him from his thoughts. Almost simultaneously a man in a scruffy dark brown robe darted straight across the path of Salim's horse, which skittered sideways in alarm. Salim pulled hard on the reins to steady it while struggling to unsheathe his sword. Just behind him he heard the neighing of his *qorchi*'s horse and the youth's muttered curses as he fought to control it. Almost at once another man – dressed strangely and with a sword in one hand and a dagger in the other – came hurtling in pursuit of the first, roaring words that Salim couldn't understand.

The first man, clearly almost out of breath and with the second gaining fast on him, vanished down a narrow, rubbish-filled alley between two rows of mud-brick houses. Four of Salim's bodyguards had already jumped from their saddles and were racing after the two men – the alleyway was too narrow for horses. Minutes later Salim heard more shouting and yelling. Soon after, the two malefactors emerged, driven from the alley by the tips of the guards' swords. The man brandishing the weapons had been disarmed but he was glaring furiously around him. The other had a bleeding cut above his left eye. The guards had clearly not been quick enough to prevent a clash between the two. Halting them a few yards in front of Salim, a guard struck them behind the knees with the flat of his sword, sending both sprawling face down to the ground. Then two more guards stood over them, feet resting in the smalls of their backs in case either should think of trying to get up.

Now that he could see them properly, Salim realised that the one in the dark robe was a Jesuit priest. The cord round his thin waist was frayed and the feet Salim could see protruding from beneath the hem of his garment were clad in the kind of thick-soled brown sandals that he had often seen the Jesuit visitors to his father's court wearing. But the other man was a puzzle. Salim stared down at the stocky, broad-shouldered figure. He was clearly also a foreigner, and among the more bizarre Salim had ever seen. His long, curly hair was a bright orange – somewhere between saffron and gold. He was wearing a short, tight-fighting leather jacket beneath which his backside was encased in billowing striped trousers that ended mid-thigh and were secured by maroon ribbons. From this curious clothing protruded long, skinny legs clad in fine-woven yellow wool stockings. On one of his feet he wore a pointed black leather shoe. The other had clearly been lost in the scuffle in the alley.

'Stand them up,' Salim ordered. As his guards hauled the two men to their feet, he leaned forward from the saddle to get a better look at the men's faces. The Jesuit he recognised – he was one of half a dozen priests sent from the Portuguese trading settlement at Goa at Akbar's request to work with his scholars on translating some of their holy books from Latin into Persian. He was a thin, gangling man with angry red pustules on one side of his face and even though some ten feet separated them Salim could smell the acrid, sweaty stench of him. It was a mystery to him why these foreigners didn't visit the bathhouses – the *hammans*. How could they endure to stink like mules?

The other man looked even odder standing up. He had a clean-shaven upper lip but a pointed beard like a billy goat's. His bulbous, pale-lashed eyes were bright blue and his complexion nearly as red as his hair – or, in the case of the shining, peeling end of his nose, even redder. He began brushing the dust from his garments.

'What has been going on?' Salim addressed the Jesuit in Persian, knowing he could probably speak it.

The priest drew himself up. 'Highness, this man insulted my religion. He called my master the Pope a scarlet whore of Babylon . . . he said—'

'Enough.' Salim had no idea what the Jesuit was talking about except that there had been a quarrel about religion. 'Where is he from?'

'From England. He is a merchant newly arrived in Fatehpur Sikri with some of his devilish companions.'

'What did you say to make him so angry he unsheathed his weapons?'

'Only the truth, Highness, that the queen of his country is a bastard whore who will rot in hell as will all his miserable heretic compatriots.'

The merchant was listening to the exchange beneath lowering brows though clearly unable to comprehend a word. Salim knew where England was. A small country on a wind-buffeted, rainwashed island on the fringes of the known world ruled by a queen with hair as red as this man's. He had even seen a miniature portrait of her brought to the court by a Turkish merchant who knew of Akbar's love of curiosities. He had sold his father the picture in its oval tortoiseshell frame studded with tiny pearls for a good sum. The queen, wearing a cream-coloured gown standing out stiffly from her body, had looked more like a doll than a woman.

'Does this merchant speak any Persian?'

'No, Highness. These English are a crude, uneducated people. They speak nothing but their own simple tongue and all they care about is trade and making money.'

'Enough. I wish to question him. As you seem to know something of his language, you will translate for me. Make sure you do so accurately.'

The Jesuit nodded glumly.

'Ask him why he makes war on the emperor's streets.'

After a brief exchange in what sounded to Salim a terse, guttural tongue, lacking the graceful cadences of Persian, the Jesuit, lip curling with contempt, replied, 'He claims he wished to avenge the insult against his queen, his country and his religion.'

'Tell him there will be no brawling on our streets and that he is lucky I do not have him thrown into prison or flogged. But I will be merciful because I can see there was blame on both sides. Tell him also to come to the court. My father will wish to question him about his country, I am sure. As for you, be careful whom you insult in our land. Like this man from England, you too are only a visitor.'

• ◆ •

'I bid you welcome to my *ibadat khana*, my hall of worship. A monarch's first duty is to preserve his borders and if possible extend them as I have done and will do again. But I believe that a great ruler should also be intent on extending the boundaries of human knowledge and understanding. He must be ever curious, ever questioning, and through knowledge seek to improve the lot of his people. That is why I have summoned not only the *ulama* and many Muslim scholars here but also the representatives of other faiths. Together we will debate questions of religion, and by exploring what is true and what is false and what is common to us all seek to shed a new light on its real meaning.'

Salim, standing towards the back of the vast hall, had seldom seen his father look more magnificent. Akbar was dressed in a bright green brocade tunic and trousers, with ropes of emeralds round his neck and on his head a turban of cloth of gold glittering with diamonds. A golden candelabra, tall as a man, stood on each side of his throne, which was positioned on a high dais approached by a flight of marble stairs. The dais itself was placed towards the back of a great sandstone platform on which were grouped the assembled clerics. The overall effect was as if his father were seated on the summit of a mountain and the men beneath him were the trees clothing its slopes.

The mullahs of the *ulama* were dressed in black – stout Shaikh Ahmad was in the front rank while Abul Fazl's father, Shaikh Mubarak, was standing a little to one side of the main group. The Jesuits were in their usual coarse dark brown robes, cords knotted round their waists and wooden crosses hanging from their necks. Salim could see among them Father Francisco Henriquez and his companion Father Antonio Monserrate who, when they had originally come to the court nearly five years ago, had been the first Christians he had ever encountered.

221

There were also five Hindu priests, calm-faced men wearing only white loincloths and a long loop of cotton thread round their left shoulders and passing beneath their right arms. Near them stood holy men whom Salim knew to be Jains and by their side fire-venerating Zoroastrians who had come to Hindustan long ago from Persia and laid their dead on the tops of 'towers of silence' to be picked clean by birds until their bones shone white. Salim recognised the tall, thin old man with a white beard and lively bright eyes standing behind the Zoroastrians as a Jew from Kashan in Persia – a scholar who had recently come to Akbar's court and found employment in his library.

On the floor of the *ibadat khana* – because he was not himself a man of God – was the red-haired English merchant Salim had encountered three months ago and whose name – it still sounded strange to him – was John Newberry. By his side were his two equally oddly dressed companions. The three Englishmen had taken lodgings in the town while they awaited a reply from his father to a petition they claimed to have brought from their queen seeking permission to trade. Just as Salim had anticipated, Akbar was keenly interested in what the strangers could tell him of their faraway world and of their religion which, though also Christian, seemed very different from the faith of the Portuguese Jesuits.

The whole scene made Salim's heart swell with pride. Though his father had said little to him about why he was constructing the *ibadat khana*, he had often gone to watch the sandstone building rising up. Having heard his father's words he now understood its purpose – to help satisfy Akbar's growing curiosity about religion. His mother had been wrong to deride the Moghuls as barbarians, Salim thought. What higher pursuit could a man follow than to enquire into matters of the mind, the very meaning of existence itself? His father in his glittering robes with his eagle-hilted sword by his side seemed the embodiment not just of physical might but of true greatness. His grandmother had spoken shrewdly when she had told him how skilled Akbar was at creating spectacle and how important was the image he projected to impress upon his audience that he was a man dazzlingly unlike any other. If he were to succeed his father, would he ever be able to reproduce such presence?

'I have heard that in far-off lands Christian men burn each other alive for reasons of religious belief,' Akbar was saying. 'I would like Father Francisco and Father Antonio to explain this to me. Let them speak up so that all can hear.'

The Jesuits exchanged a few words in low voices, then at a nod from his taller companion Father Francisco began to speak. 'You are correct, Majesty, that in Europe a battle for men's souls is being fought. A great evil has come amongst us of the Catholic faith – we call it Protestantism. Its followers have strayed from the true path and refuse to acknowledge the authority of our great spiritual leader in Rome, the Pope, who stands between us miserable sinners and God and is God's representative on earth. The Protestants reject and revile our most sacred beliefs and read heretical translations of our holy Bible in their own tongue, claiming they have no need of an intermediary between themselves and God. In good Catholic countries holy men – we call them the Inquisition – devote their lives to rooting out these heretics and, when they find them, forcing them to recant. Those who refuse are consigned living to the flames as the first taste of the torments of eternal damnation.'

'What of those who agree to return to your "true path"?' Akbar asked. His eyes, resting on the Jesuits' faces, looked very intent.

'Even if they acknowledge their error, their earthly bodies are still consigned to the flames to cleanse their souls of sin and make them worthy to enter the kingdom of heaven.'

'How do you persuade men to change their beliefs? By debate, such as we are having here?'

The fathers exchanged glances. 'Indeed, we use force of argument to bring stray sheep back to the fold, but regrettably we must sometimes also employ physical force.'

'My scholars have read to me of such things – of devices for stretching the body of a man until his joints leap from their sockets, of a great wheel on which men are spread-eagled naked and beaten with iron bars until the marrow spurts from their bones, of knotted ropes twisted tight against men's eyes until their eyeballs burst . . .'

'Sometimes it is necessary, Majesty. The torment of a few hours is nothing compared to the red-hot fires of eternal hell.'

'You torture women and children as well as men?'

'The devil casts a wide net, Majesty. Women are especially weak vessels, and tender years are no protection.'

'But how can you be sure that the tortured have truly repented and are not dissimulating to make their torments cease?'

'Our Catholic Inquisitors are skilled in such matters, Majesty, just as your investigators are. Only last week I saw two suspected thieves being buried up to their arms in hot sand to make them confess to their misdeeds. I see no difference.'

'The difference lies in whether a crime has been committed. In the case of the thieves, undoubtedly a felony had taken place and the magistrates were attempting to discover the truth. But does one religion have the right to force its opinions on another? Isn't that the question we should be addressing? In my realms, I do not distinguish between men because of their religion. My advisers, my commanders and even my wives are not all of my own faith.'

The Jesuits looked grave and Salim could see Shaikh Ahmad vigorously shaking his head and muttering something to another of the *ulama,* but no one spoke.

'Let us extend our enquiry . . .' Akbar continued, seemingly content that the import of his words had sunk in. 'You have told me your beliefs, but let us now hear from one of these Protestants you were speaking of with such disdain . . . I wish to question the Englishman John Newberry. One of my scholars, a Turk, knows his language and can translate.'

The red-headed Englishman looked as confident as a turkey cock and about as truculent, Salim thought, as he strutted forward, the Turkish interpreter by his side.

'What is your religion, John Newberry? Tell the assembled people just as you have told me in private.'

The merchant muttered a few words to the Turk who began to translate in a somewhat hesitant voice. 'I am English and a Protestant and proud to be both.'

'You told me that your queen is the head of your religion. Explain to us how that came about.'

Again more whispering between Newberry and the Turk, but the interpreter seemed to be gaining in confidence and, though having to pause every few seconds for fresh information, was soon able to keep up a smooth commentary. 'When he was very young, Her Majesty's father, our great King Henry, married a princess who had once been betrothed to his brother. However, as the years passed and she bore him only one surviving child – a daughter – he realised that by wedding his brother's affianced bride he had sinned in the eyes of God. He sought to remedy the ill by divorcing her but the Pope – whom these Jesuits revere so much – refused to allow it. Our king decided that he could not permit such interference in the governing of his kingdom. He declared himself the head of the church in England, divorced his wife and married the woman who gave birth to our present great and blessed queen, Elizabeth.'

'You have told me your religion allows a man only one wife, but I have heard that this King of England, Henry, took six wives. How? Are there different rules for a king in your country?'

'No, Majesty. Our queen's mother was found guilty of adultery – it was even said she was a witch – and executed. The king married yet again but his third queen died when her son was not two weeks old. He divorced his fourth wife – a foreign princess – because she did not please his eye. His fifth wife – young and beautiful but sadly not virtuous – also fell into the snare of adultery and was beheaded on his orders. But the king's sixth and final wife, a modest matron, outlived him.'

'Your king might have saved himself some trouble had he followed our path and taken more than one wife at a time. And it seems he did not guard his *haram* well . . .' A ripple of laughter went around the hall of worship, but neither the Englishman nor the Jesuits were smiling as the Turk translated Akbar's words.

'Tell me about your queen, John Newberry. Are the men of your country content to be ruled by a woman?'

'She is loved by our people because she protects us from the Catholic menace and keeps us free.'

'Has she no husband?'

'She glories in being a virgin. Many foreign princes have wooed her but she says England is her bridegroom.'

'Is she beautiful?'

'She is more than beautiful – she is glorious.'

Salim saw Father Antonio whispering urgently into Father Francisco's ear and after a few moments the latter stepped forward. 'If I might speak, Majesty,' he said in his smooth court Persian. 'You are in danger of being misled by this merchant. This queen of England was born of a sinful union between a king inflamed by lust and a proven whore. This Elizabeth is not the legitimate ruler of her country – which by rights should be ruled by the Catholic King of Spain – but a bastard heretic leading her country to eternal damnation. Our master the Pope in Rome has cast her out and she will burn for ever.'

The Turk was translating all this for Newberry, whose already crimson countenance was darkening as he took in what the priest had said, but Salim saw that Akbar was starting to look bored. His father enjoyed philosophical debate rather than the trading of insults, and Salim was not surprised when he rose abruptly.

'Enough. We will resume our enquiries another day,' he said, and swept from the chamber.

◆

It was a perfect autumn day. Sunlight filtered through the dense foliage of the forest as the beaters advanced, banging their gongs and shouting to drive the game ahead of them. Salim enjoyed the rhythmic motion as the elephant bearing him and his three attendants plodded on. Some ten yards ahead he could see his father's elephant, Lakna, left hind leg scored by the claws of a male tiger many years earlier. Lakna was Akbar's favourite hunting elephant. He had captured him himself, while still a youth, from a herd of wild elephants, then tamed him.

Salim had watched his father fearlessly break other elephants. It was a dangerous business requiring two men, each perched on a tame elephant on either side of the wild beast. Once in position, their task was to fling a noose of stout rope round the neck of the wild elephant and secure it to the neck of their own mount. Then, by progressively tightening the noose, they were able gradually to calm the beast and bring it under control. Salim had seen many good men killed during the process. It was easy to fall off and what chance did a man have beneath the feet of an enraged elephant? Several times he had heard the sickening squelch of a body trampled beneath a heavy grey foot. Even after the initial subduing, months of hard work remained, training the beast to advance to order by throwing fodder down on the ground before it. But Lakna had served Akbar well, and amply repaid the time he had spent.

The temperature was rising and a bead of salty sweat ran into the corner of Salim's mouth. He flicked it away with the tip of his tongue. Soon the circle of beaters, who had been closing in since dawn, would be tight enough and the hunt would begin. Glancing over his shoulder he saw his *qorchi* was following close behind on a horse and leading his own black stallion in case he should wish to exchange the elephant for a faster mount. His heart was thudding with the excitement he always felt in the hunt. He was a good marksman — equally accurate with musket or arrow — and perhaps today he would impress his father. He would like to have been riding with him on Lakna in the golden howdah festooned with green ribbons, but as usual the bulky figure of Abul Fazl was by Akbar's side.

The brief shadow that fell on Salim's spirits as he watched his father's elephant advance into a particularly thickly wooded part of the forest passed quickly. He must continue to do as Shaikh Salim Chishti had told him — wait and watch and learn and all would come right. And it was good that his father had invited him on the hunt. Hearing a sudden shouting from up ahead, Salim reached over his shoulder to check that his quiver and bow were in place and then ran his hand over the smooth steel barrel of his musket, a beautiful weapon inlaid with triangles of mother-of-pearl. Yes, he was ready.

But then he realised that the shouts were more than a cry for the hunt to begin and were growing louder. Among them he could make out the words, 'His Majesty is ill! Fetch the *hakims*!' There was a sudden thudding of hooves and two of Akbar's mounted bodyguard burst through the foliage ahead of him and galloped off towards the back of the line where the court *hakims* who always accompanied the hunt were travelling in their bullock cart.

'What is it? What's happened to my father?' Salim shouted but in the confusion no one was attending to him. Heart pounding, he climbed over the edge of his howdah and lowered himself on two gilded straps until he was close enough to the ground to jump lightly down. Dodging more riders and a group of beaters, metal gongs now silent in their hands, Salim ran forward. His father's elephant Lakna was on its knees and beside the great grey shape Salim saw a group of men clustered around a supine figure. Forcing his way through, Salim saw Akbar lying on his back, body arching as spasms rocked it. As Salim stared, he found himself repeating over and over, 'Please God, not yet.' His ambitions and his fears for the future no longer seemed to matter.

Akbar was thrashing more wildly, and red blood mingling with a dribble of spittle oozing from his mouth showed that he had bitten his tongue. Salim watched helplessly. In his mind's eye he already saw himself standing beside Murad and Daniyal at their father's funeral. He heard Hamida's and Gulbadan's wails of grief and saw the smile curving his mother's lips at the knowledge that the man she regarded as the enemy of her people was dead.

Abul Fazl was loosening the turquoise clasps of his father's tunic, fingers trembling. 'Stand back, all of you, give His Majesty some air . . .' he was saying. At that moment one of the bodyguards returned, a white-robed, white-turbaned *hakim* mounted behind him. The crowd parted to let the doctor through. He was a young, sharp-featured man whose intelligent brown eyes seemed to take in the situation at once.

Dropping to his knees beside Akbar he seized his arms and held them steady. 'You!' he shouted without ceremony to Abul Fazl. 'Hold His Majesty's legs to help calm him. And you there,' he nodded at another courtier, 'fold a clean piece of linen – handkerchief, face cloth, whatever comes to hand – and ram it hard between His Majesty's jaws or he may bite through his tongue.'

'*Hakim*, what can I do for my father?' Salim asked.

The doctor glanced round. 'Nothing,' he said tersely and turned back to his patient. Salim hesitated a moment, then getting to his feet pushed his way through the onlookers. If he couldn't help he would rather not watch.

The sunlight that had seemed so full of promise for a good day's sport barely half an hour ago as it shafted through the canopy of leaves was now lighting the forest floor with a harsh, metallic brightness. Salim wandered away through a patch of low, scrubby bushes, neither noticing nor caring where his feet were taking him. Reaching a clearing he paused, and more by instinct than anything else suddenly became aware of a pair of bright eyes watching him through some branches. It was a young deer, the velvet mantling on its antlers the very palest brown. Slowly Salim reached behind him for his bow but then stopped. What was the point? There was enough death in the world.

Almost at once the deer bounded away. Salim listened to the sounds of the frightened animal crashing through the scrub and then turned to retrace his own steps. Whatever was happening to his father, he must face up to it and any implications it had for him. He couldn't hide in the forest like a dumb beast and anyway in a few moments he would be missed – imperial princes couldn't wander off on their own unnoticed. But he dreaded what he would see as he emerged once more into the open. The *hakim* was standing up now with a crowd gathered around him, listening to what he had to say. But where was Akbar? Salim broke into a run.

As he drew closer, staring around him in panic, he saw his father sitting propped against a tree trunk, Abul Fazl holding a flask of water to his lips. His bodyguards had formed a protective circle around them but they parted as Salim ran up. 'Father . . .' He was half-sobbing with relief to see Akbar, a little paler than usual and long dark hair dishevelled, but otherwise much as usual. The bright eyes that he now turned on his son had lost none of their disconcerting penetration.

'There is no need for concern. I have had a vision – a direct communication with God. I felt my whole body shaking with joy,

229

and God revealed to me what I must do. We are abandoning the hunt and returning at once to Fatehpur Sikri, where I have an announcement to make to my people. Go now, and let me rest.'

Salim turned away, feeling that his father had somehow rebuffed him. If his father had received some divine revelation why wouldn't he share it with him? Did he think he was not to be trusted? Glancing round, he saw the man whom just a little while ago he had thought close to death whispering with Abul Fazl and realised that all the anxiety he had felt had turned to nothing more noble than resentment. He was angry with himself, but angrier still with Akbar.

◆

'I have summoned you here to the great mosque in Fatehpur Sikri to hear an important pronouncement.'

Dressed in cloth of gold and with three nodding white egrets feathers secured to his turban by a ruby clasp, Akbar gazed around at the assembled mullahs, courtiers and commanders. Salim, standing amongst them, glanced up at the small women's gallery concealed from public view by a carved *jali* where he knew that Hamida and Gulbadan were watching and listening. Did they have any idea what Akbar was going to say? He didn't. For the past three days since Akbar had returned from his hunting expedition the court had been awash with rumours. Akbar had shut himself away in his private quarters, seeing only Abul Fazl and, on two occasions, Shaikh Mubarak. Some even claimed that Akbar was about to declare himself a Christian.

'Several days ago, in his infinite goodness God spoke to me and revealed his heart. He said that he had chosen me because, like other prophets before me, I cannot read and my mind therefore remains open to hearing his voice in all its strength and purity. He told me that a true ruler must not leave the conduct of divine worship to others but take this great responsibility upon their own shoulders. Today is Friday, our day of prayer. In past times I would have asked one of our learned mullahs to mount the pulpit to lead us in our worship and to recite the *khutba*. But because of what God is asking of me, I must fulfil that task in front of you all.'

230

To gasps of surprise Akbar turned and climbed the steep carved rosewood stairs leading up to the marble pulpit. Then in his deep, resonating voice he began to recite, his voice building to a climax as the final words rang out, 'Blessed be His Majesty! *Allah Akbar!*'

Salim's head jerked back with surprise. *Allah Akbar* meant 'God is great,' but his father's words could also mean 'Akbar is God'. Was his father claiming some sort of divinity? All around him he heard a surprised buzz of conversation. But looking up again he saw his father coolly observing the effect of his ambiguous cry. He raised his hands for silence, which fell instantly. 'I have commanded my most trusted spiritual adviser Shaikh Mubarak to draw up a document that I will require every mullah in my empire to sign, which states that in any question of religious interpretation I – not they – am the final arbiter.'

Salim saw Shaikh Ahmad and the other members of the *ulama* exchange shocked glances as they took in the full import of their emperor's words – that he stood higher in the knowledge of God than any mullah. Just like that King of England, Akbar was claiming for himself not only the role of head of state but of the head of religion within his empire. Akbar was smiling a little and Salim felt a new awe for the father whom with every passing day he felt little closer to understanding.

Chapter 17

Flaming Torches

'Majesty, the Jesuit father Antonio Monserrate requests an urgent audience with you.'

Akbar looked up from the design of a new pavilion drawn by Tuhin Das that he had been studying with Abul Fazl, and Salim saw annoyance cross his father's face. The talk of the court was that the Jesuits were growing presumptuous and arrogant. Whatever Akbar allowed them to do – from processing through the streets of Fatehpur Sikri behind a giant wooden cross with candles in their hands on their saints' days, to building chapels, to aggressively seeking converts – never seemed to satisfy them. They had even petitioned Akbar to appoint Father Antonio as one of the tutors to his son Murad and from courtesy he had agreed.

'What does he want?'

'He would not say, Majesty, only that it was a matter of great urgency.'

'Very well. I'll receive him here in my private apartments.'

As always, Salim was surprised by his father's tolerance. None of his subjects, however mighty, would dare importune the emperor so frequently. He waited to see whether his father would dismiss him and was pleased when Akbar signalled to him to stay.

The Jesuit entered, bowed briefly then without waiting for Akbar to say anything burst out, 'Majesty, I heard something today that I found hard to believe. Your mullah Shaikh Mubarak says that you intend to inaugurate a new religion.'

'What you heard was the truth. At the next Friday prayers I will announce to my subjects the introduction within my empire of the *Din-i-Ilahi* – the "Religion of God".'

'What is this blasphemy!' Father Antonio's already bulbous eyes looked about to pop from his skull.

'Take care, Jesuit. You have received nothing but patience and indulgence at my court. In return what have you preached but narrow intolerance? Nothing you have said has convinced me that your Catholic church has anything particular to commend it. Indeed, no single religion seems to me to eclipse all others in truth or divinity – not even my own Muslim faith. That is why I have decided to fuse what is best in all the different religions – Hindu, Jain, Buddhist, Christian and Muslim – into a new faith.'

'And where does God sit in your structure – at your right hand, I presume, or will you allow him even that?' Father Antonio was almost choking with indignation.

'I am the focus of the *Din-i-Ilahi* as God's chosen representative, his shadow upon the earth,' Akbar said calmly but with a glint in his eye. 'I do not intend to supplant God – that would indeed be blasphemy.'

'If you persist in this misguided folly I and my fellow priests must withdraw from your court. I regret that I can no longer act as a tutor to Prince Murad.'

'Leave if that is your wish. Your closed mind disappoints me. Indeed it makes me question whether I wish men such as yourselves to have even a toehold in my empire. Do not provoke me further if you wish your European adherents to retain their trading settlements.'

'You have rejected the light and you will answer for it to one greater even than you think yourself.' Father Antonio spoke with real venom in his tone. Then he gave a slight bow, turned and walked swiftly away through the open double doors past Akbar's green-turbaned bodyguards.

Salim saw his father and Abul Fazl exchange amused smiles. Clearly they had anticipated the priest's reactions. His own mind burned with questions and for once he did not lack the courage to voice them. 'Why have you created this religion, Father? Won't it anger the *ulama*?' he asked.

It was Abul Fazl who answered. 'Let the *ulama* think what they will. It is a natural progression. His Majesty is already, of course, the head of the Muslim faith within his empire but his subjects practise many religions. By creating the new faith, the *Din-i-Ilahi*, which will be open to all and calls upon no one to renounce his existing faith, His Majesty will become accepted by all his people as one of them – their rightful sovereign – and no longer be regarded like his grandfather and father as a foreign invader. Central to the ritual is the sun as the symbol of divinity. The *Din-i-Ilahi* will embrace the Hindu principles of reincarnation and that unification with the divine is the ultimate aim of the believer. Above all, the *Din-i-llahi* will teach men kindness, compassion, tolerance and respect for all living things. In so doing it will help them seek for spiritual truth but it will also secure the Moghul dynasty.'

Content to leave Abul Fazl to deal with Salim's question, Akbar had already turned back to Tuhin Das's drawing and didn't see his son's slight frown as he contemplated Abul Fazl's words. To Salim it seemed a step too far. Surely this new 'Divine Faith' could alienate people just as easily as it could reconcile them to their Moghul rulers?

• ◆ •

'Majesty, an imperial post rider who passed by on his way to Fatehpur Sikri reports that the widow of a village headman is to be burned alive on his funeral pyre at sunset. You asked to be informed of all such incidents immediately.'

'Where is this happening?'

'In a village ten miles north of here.'

'I have given explicit orders that I will not tolerate this barbarous practice of *sati*. How dare they defy me? I will go there myself. Have my horse saddled at once and detail a detachment of my bodyguards to accompany me.'

Salim had seldom seen his father so openly angry. Without waiting for attendants to help him he was already pulling off his silk tunic ready to change into riding clothes.

'Come with me, Salim. It will be a valuable lesson. I allow my Hindu subjects complete freedom of worship except in this one thing. You know what *sati* is, of course, don't you? They call these women "flaming torches of love and fellowship" but they are just victims, often coerced to die with their husbands by relatives out of some distorted perception of family honour.' Akbar's eyes were stern. 'I thank God that our people have never practised such a thing. For the Moghuls, death on the battlefield is the most honourable thing for a man. Which of us would not, in his heart, choose to die in battle, rather than ingloriously in our beds? But which of us would find similar honour in the idea of our women committing suicide because we were no more? Don't you agree, Salim?' Akbar's attendants were now dressing him in a tunic and pantaloons and fastening a green brocade sash round his still muscular waist.

Salim nodded. What he didn't tell his father was how tales of *sati* victims both repelled and fascinated him. Death came so randomly – a friend of his own age had recently caught the spotted fever and died within two days. Mortality was hard to comprehend, especially when you were young. Perhaps that was why it held such a morbid allure. Despite himself, he always listened with half-guilty curiosity to descriptions of the women's screams rising above the crackling of the blazing pyre and even of victims trying frantically to escape, hair and clothes already alight, only to be thrown back by their husbands' relatives.

'Quickly, Salim. The sooner we get there the better chance we have of halting this crime.'

Galloping by his father's side out of Fatehpur Sikri, bodyguards in their green tunics behind them and four heralds with silver trumpets riding ahead to clear the way, Salim felt proud that his father had chosen him to accompany him, as well as a visceral thrill at the adventure ahead.

It was a hot afternoon in late March and puffs of pale dust rose from the hard-baked ground beneath the horses' hooves. Squinting up into the clear, deep blue sky, Salim saw the sun was still high. If the funeral was to take place at sunset they had time, though Akbar showed no sign of slackening the pace. His chestnut stallion beneath its gold-embroidered saddle cloth was foamy with sweat and Salim saw that the coat of his own bay mare was mottled with it. Perhaps this was a little how it felt to ride into battle – something he had never done but longed for.

They were climbing now as they followed a track over land parched a deep gold. Ahead it narrowed, winding up to the top of a steep, flat-topped hill on which Salim glimpsed a collection of simple dwellings. Beyond, a column of brown smoke was rising almost vertically into the air.

He heard Akbar shout, 'They've been warned of our coming and have fired the pyre. They'll pay for this.' Glancing at him, Salim saw his father's strong-jawed face tauten with rage and frustration. As they urged their blowing horses towards the top of the hill, Akbar shouted to his men, 'Quickly. No time to lose!'

Reaching the summit, Salim saw that they were on a plateau. To the left was a cluster of mud-brick huts around a well and on the right a larger house, also single-storeyed but enclosed by a low wall – probably the headman's dwelling. No one was there except for two young children fast asleep on a string *charpoy* beneath a neem tree and near them a puppy which regarded the new arrivals without interest through half-closed eyes. But ahead, three or four hundred yards away, Salim made out through a tangle of spiny bushes a crowd of people in dun-coloured clothes. Beyond them rose the plume of smoke, now thicker and darker, and orange flames flickered.

'Come on!' Akbar shouted, kicking his stallion hard. In a matter of moments they burst through the bushes into a clearing where a tall stack of brushwood was already well alight around the edges. On top of the pyre and not itself yet burning was a body wrapped in white muslin. Two men were leaning forward with a jar of what looked like oil or *ghee* which they were throwing over the corpse, the viscous yellow liquid arcing through the air and hissing as drops fell into the flames. At that moment the corpse's clothes caught light and Salim caught the sweet stench of flesh starting to burn. Galloping to within ten feet of the pyre, Akbar wheeled his horse to a standstill.

The crowd had been so intent on what was happening that they were slow to react.

'Surround the pyre,' Akbar shouted to his guards. Riding right up to the crowd, he demanded, 'Who is your leader?' He spoke in Hindi, the local language, in which he was as fluent as he was in Persian, the language of the court.

'I am,' replied one of the men who had been pouring the oil. 'We are cremating the body of my father, who was headman of this village. I am his eldest son, Sanjeev.'

'Do you know who I am?'

'No, Excellency.' Sanjeev shook his head. Salim saw him slowly taking in the rich trappings of Akbar's horse, the gems flashing on his fingers and round his neck, the well-armed guards in their green tunics. Puzzlement then alarm spread over his face, which was badly disfigured by smallpox scars.

'I am your emperor. I was told a widow-burning is to take place here. Is that true?'

Sanjeev once more shook his head, but Salim saw his eyes flick across to a thatched windowless shack. Akbar saw it too and at once gestured to one of his guards to check inside. Moments later the man reappeared carrying a young woman in a white sari. Her body was limp, and as the guard came nearer Salim saw that her eyes were open but unfocused.

'Lay her on the ground and one of you villagers fetch water,' Akbar commanded. A boy ran up with a small clay cup. Akbar dismounted, took it, and kneeling by the woman's side held it to her lips. The first drops ran down her chin but then she stirred and opening her mouth began to swallow. Coming closer, Salim saw the huge dark circles of her dilated pupils.

'Who is this woman? Speak or I swear I will strike off your head here and now,' Akbar said.

Sanjeev twisted his hands. 'This is my father's widow Shakuntala – he married her a year after the death of my own mother and just three months before he fell ill.'

'How old is she?'

'Fifteen, Majesty.'

'You've drugged her, haven't you?'

'I gave her opium pellets to swallow. You don't understand, Majesty. You are not a Hindu. It is a matter of family honour for a widow to follow her husband into the all-consuming heat of the flames . . . I drugged her to ease the pain.'

'You drugged her so she wouldn't resist when you put her on to the funeral pyre.'

The young woman had sat up and was looking around, confused. Behind her the flames of the pyre were now leaping higher, crackling and shooting showers of sparks into the air. The smell of burning human flesh, mingling with the aroma of the scented oils and butter with which the brushwood had been drenched, was growing ever more pungent. Suddenly aware of where she was and what was happening, Shakuntala got shakily to her feet and turned towards the pyre. At its heart the body of her dead husband was now burning like a torch. As she watched, the corpse's head burst open with a crack, followed by a frying sound as the brains were immediately incinerated.

Sanjeev glared at her, for the moment oblivious of Akbar and his entourage or of the villagers silently watching. 'It is your duty to perish in the flames consuming your husband's body. My mother would have done so had she outlived him and she would have been proud of it. You are bringing shame on my family's good name.'

'No. You are the one committing a shameful act. I have forbidden *sati* throughout my empire. Whether the widow is willing or unwilling, I will not tolerate such barbarous practices.' Akbar turned to the woman. 'You cannot stay here. You would not be safe. I am Akbar, your emperor. I offer you the chance to return with me and my men to my court where employment will be found for you as an attendant in the *haram*. Do you accept?'

'Yes, Majesty,' the woman replied. Until that moment she hadn't realised who Akbar was and Salim noticed she was scarcely able to look his father in the eye.

'As for you,' Akbar addressed the still defiant-looking Sanjeev, 'if you thought your religion required it, would you be willing to submit to the agony of being burned alive? I wonder. Guards, take hold of him and bring him over to the pyre.'

Sanjeev's pockmarked face was suddenly waxy with sweat and he started to breathe heavily. 'Majesty, please . . .' he begged as two soldiers grabbed him beneath the armpits and dragged him towards the fire. He was punily built and the guards could toss him into the flames as easily as a bale of straw, Salim thought.

Akbar strode across to the man. 'Hold him by the shoulders,' he ordered. 'Let us see how well he can bear the pain he was so ready to inflict on others.'

Then, gripping the man's right arm just above the elbow, Akbar thrust his hand into the flames. Sanjeev's screams split the air and he fought to break free but Akbar steeled himself to hold his hand in the brightly burning fire for a little longer. Sanjeev's crescendoing cries were now more animal than human. Even the young woman was no longer able to watch.

Suddenly Sanjeev passed out and apart from the crackling flames there was silence. Supporting the limp body, Akbar pulled the man's badly burned hand from the pyre and held it up for a few moments so all could see before letting him fall to the ground. Then he turned to address the villagers, who in the shock of what they had just witnessed had drawn even closer together like a knot of sheep that suspects the wolf is close.

'You have just witnessed my justice. I expect my laws to be obeyed and transgressors always to be severely punished. You are all as guilty as this man here.' He pointed to Sanjeev, who was now beginning to come round and moaning in anguish. 'You knew what was intended and did nothing to stop it. I will not make you feel the fire as he did, but I will give you ten minutes to remove your livestock and possessions. Then my men will turn your village into a pyre. Over the next weeks as you labour to rebuild your houses you will have time to contemplate the consequences of defying your emperor.'

Within minutes the settlement was ablaze. Shakuntala was mounted behind one of the guards, a scarf thrown over her head to preserve her modesty, as they rode back down the hill. Salim noticed that she did not once look back at the place which had been her home. Glancing at his father, he realised he had never felt so proud of him or so glad to be his son and a Moghul.

• ◆ •

'He was magnificent. I had never seen him dispense justice with such power and authority. It was different from watching him at court where everything is so stiff and formal and seems to take for ever.' Ever since his father's rescue of the young Hindu widow, Salim had felt buoyed by memories of it, especially of how his father had known instinctively what to say and do. That was real power.

'He was interfering with the ancient ways of our land,' Hirabai said coldly.

'But he upholds the rights of Hindus. Only a few days ago I overheard some members of the *ulama* criticising his tolerance. One mullah said he had heard that the emperor was going to pray at the Hindus' sacred place at Allahabad where the Jumna and the Ganges meet. Another was complaining that the emperor seemed prepared to venerate anything – fire, water, stones and trees . . . even the sacred cows he allows to wander freely through his towns and villages, even their very dung . . .'

'Your father only upholds what he approves of. He has no right to intervene in *sati*. It does not concern him.'

'But it does. He has forbidden it. Those villagers were defying him.'

'They were obeying a higher authority – their religion. That was not disobedience but duty.' Hirabai's words reminded Salim of what Sanjeev had said in justification of his actions, and of what the Jesuits sometimes said in justification of acts by their church that also seemed barbarous. He said nothing as Hirabai continued, 'My people – your people – the Rajputs have practised *sati* almost since time began. Many times when I was a girl I witnessed Rajput noblewomen give away their jewels and other worldly possessions and join their husbands joyfully on the funeral pyres, cradling their dead husbands' heads in their laps as the flames leapt around them, all the while smiling and uttering not a cry.'

'But it was wrong . . . why should they give up their lives before their time? What good did it do?'

'It proved their love, courage and devotion and brought honour to their families. As I have told you before, we Rajputs are the children of the sun and of fire. We perhaps more than any other Hindus believe in the power of the flame to cleanse and ennoble us. Many, many times in our history – the last was at the end of your father's siege of Chittorgarh – when it seemed that our menfolk faced certain death on the battlefield, Rajput women dressed in their finest clothes and jewels as if it was their wedding day. Then, faces transfigured by the glory that awaited them, they followed their queen in a stately procession to where a great fire had been lit. One by one, they committed the sacred rite of *jauhar*, leaping joyfully into flames which reduced their bodies to ashes and set their spirits free to rise again like phoenixes.'

Of course, no one would ever expect her to burn on Akbar's pyre since Muslims did not cremate their dead, Salim thought, though looking at the almost fanatical pride on her face he knew that had his mother been married to a Rajput she would have followed him gladly into the flames. But all Salim could think of was Shakuntala's terrified young face. Barely two years older than he, she had chosen life not death and every instinct told him she had been right. His mother's veneration of suicide seemed chilling, and proud though he was of his Rajput ancestry this was something he couldn't share. Many times when trying to judge between his father and his mother he'd been left confused and uncertain, but not this time.

Chapter 18

Warrior Prince

'I have decided that I will move the capital of the empire from this city of Fatehpur Sikri to Lahore. Preparations will begin immediately. I and the court will begin our journey to Lahore in two months' time. The council is dismissed.'

Standing at the back of the chamber, Salim felt his heart beat faster as he watched his father sweep past him and disappear through the curtained doorway into the sunlit courtyard followed by his tall green-turbaned bodyguards. By the startled look on their faces and the excited hubbub of voices, the members of his father's council were as surprised and shocked as he was by Akbar's pronouncement, which had been made at the end of a routine not to say tedious council session about the level of market taxes. Only Abul Fazl seemed unperturbed as he completed his notes of the meeting, the slight smile on his smooth fleshy face suggesting – probably intentionally – to any onlookers that Akbar had long since taken him into his confidence. Why did he so often feel like punching Abul Fazl to wipe away that supercilious smile? Salim wondered. Perhaps because he wished his father would share more of his thoughts with him. In particular, this decision to move from Fatehpur Sikri both intrigued him and worried him. His father rarely acted on impulse. He had probably calculated that to announce his decision when and how he had would indicate that his mind

243

was made up and he would brook no debate or questioning of the move.

Therefore, the relocation must be important to his father's plans. But why? As his father's eldest son, surely he should know him well enough to understand his motives. What's more, what would it mean for him? Did Akbar intend the whole court to move? Or would he leave some part of it behind in these beautiful new buildings? Would he himself accompany his father? And what about his mother Hirabai? Might she be left behind in her private sandstone palace in Fatehpur Sikri? That seemed only too likely. He still enjoyed his visits to his mother, however infrequent they had become and however often she inveighed against his father. His concern grew as he realised he might be separated from one or other of his parents. He must know what was in his father's mind. Hadn't he a right to ask?

Without pausing for reflection which might dampen his resolution, Salim pushed his way through the assembled courtiers lingering around the doorway of the room to debate the move to Lahore. As soon as he was out in the courtyard, he ran past the fountains bubbling and glinting in the noonday sun to his father's private quarters. Once through the carved wooden doors that the guards opened immediately to him, Salim saw his father unbuckling his ceremonial sword. Suddenly he felt his confidence dip and hesitated, uncertain what to say or indeed whether to leave as quickly as he had come. However, his father had seen him enter and asked, 'Salim, what do you want?'

'To know why we are leaving Fatehpur Sikri,' Salim blurted out.

'It is a good question and a fair one too. If you sit on that stool over there and wait a moment while I change my clothes I will give you the answer you deserve.'

Salim sat on the low gilded stool, nervously twisting a gold ring given to him by his mother which he habitually wore on the index finger of his right hand. His father completed his change and washed his hands and face in a gold bowl of rosewater held out by one of his young attendants before dismissing them with a wave of his hand and sitting down on another stool near his son.

'Why do you think I decided to move the court to Lahore, Salim?'

244

For a moment Salim was lost for words as if overcome by his temerity in questioning his father about a major decision. Then he stammered, 'I don't know . . . I was so surprised that you wished to leave a city that you yourself had built only recently at such cost to honour the great seer Shaikh Salim Chishti as well as to celebrate the birth of my brothers and myself and your great victories in Gujarat and Bengal . . . I could not think why. That is why I came to you . . . to find out . . . I heard one of the courtiers say something about the water supply . . .'

'It's not the water. That problem can be solved. And put out of your mind any thought of the cost of this city. Our empire is now so rich that money spent in the past should not and does not play any part in decisions about the future. I intend the consequences of my move to be greater power, greater wealth for the empire – enough to build ten, even a hundred Fatehpur Sikris.'

'What do you mean, Father?'

'Your great-grandfather Babur wrote that if a king does not offer his followers the prospect of war and plunder, their idle minds will soon turn to thoughts of rebellion against him. I have myself come to realise that if a monarch doesn't fix his mind on conquest, neighbouring rulers think him weak and it's only a matter of time before they contemplate invading his lands. The reason for the move to Lahore is that I intend to broaden the boundaries of our empire once more.'

Exhilaration mingled with relief in Salim. His father's thoughts were on conquest and external wars, nothing else. 'You must mean to expand our northern dominions if you base our command centre in Lahore. But in which direction?'

'In all directions in due course. The rulers of Sind and Baluchistan have long been a threat to us and it wounds my pride that the Shah of Persia seized Kandahar during the time Bairam Khan was regent and I have yet to recover it. Nevertheless a wise ruler, however powerful, takes on only one enemy at a time and I have decided that my first campaign should be in Kashmir.'

'Aren't the rulers relations of ours?'

'Yes. Haidar Mirza, a cousin of my father, seized the land in Sher

245

Shah's time and later ruled it as a vassal of my father. But his descendants – perhaps presuming on our shared blood – have refused to pay us homage or tribute. Now they will learn that there can be only one head of a family and that if he is to preserve his authority, not to say his throne, he must treat disrespect with equal severity, whether shown by those like the Uzbeks whose ancestors were long foes, or those closer to him.' Akbar paused and Salim saw an icy look in his eyes. Then his father went on, 'Indeed, the latter may merit harsher treatment given their disregard of their obligations. Think only of your grandfather Humayun. He would have saved himself much trouble if he had dealt more severely with his half-brothers when they first showed him disrespect.'

Even though he knew his father's words were aimed at the rulers of Kashmir, not at any closer relation, Salim felt an involuntary shiver.

• ◆ •

Salim looked out from the swaying howdah on the large elephant that was plodding at the end of the line of imperial elephants upwards through the Vale of Kashmir. Now that the early morning mists had lifted, Salim could see, over the heads of the line of horsemen flanking the elephants, glossy green-leaved rhododendron bushes bursting into pink and purple flower on the rolling hillside. Spring came late to Kashmir but when it did its beauty made the wait worthwhile. Scattered among the emerald-green grass, red tulips and mauve and purple irises stirred in the gentle breeze.

The move to Lahore had gone smoothly. Even his mother had found little to complain about in her new quarters, which were as airy as those she had left in Fatehpur Sikri and had the added advantage of overlooking the Ravi river. Taking his courage in his hands once more, he had asked his father whether he might accompany the expedition to Kashmir since at nearly fourteen years of age he wished to learn something of military matters. To his great joy and a little to his surprise, Akbar had agreed, even suggesting that he should choose one of his companions to accompany him. He had picked Suleiman Beg, one of his milk-brothers. Almost the same age as Salim, he had just returned from Bengal with his father who had been deputy governor there for some years. His mother had died in Bengal and Salim had little memory of his milk-mother. Suleiman's strength belied his slight frame and he was always ready to join Salim in trials of skill or in hunting expeditions. His ready sense of humour could always coax a laugh from the other boy, even in Salim's darker moods when he was preoccupied with what the future might hold for him.

Despite agreeing to his accompanying him, Akbar still rarely invited him into military council meetings. However, unusually, the previous evening he had done so. When he had entered his father's great scarlet command tent, he had found Akbar already speaking and the council's discussion well under way. Scarcely pausing, his father had gestured to him to take a seat at the left-hand end of the circle of commanders sitting cross-legged on some rich maroon and indigo Persian carpets in the middle of the tent.

Even before Salim had sat down, Akbar had continued, ' . . . so from these reports from our scouts and spies we can clearly expect to encounter a vanguard of the Sultan of Kashmir's army in the next day or two when the valley broadens out a little. We must be ready for them.' Turning to Abdul Rahman, the tall, muscular officer who several years ago had taken over from the ageing Ahmed Khan the role of *khan-i-khanan*, Akbar had said, 'Have the officers check their men's weapons this evening. Double the sentries round our camp tonight. Deploy a full screen of scouts about our column when we move out in the morning, which we will do much earlier than usual – an hour after dawn. You yourself will command our leading troops, which should include some of our best squadrons of horsemen and mounted musketeers.'

'Yes, Majesty. I will treble rather than double the number of sentries. And I will ensure that each sentry post has trumpets and drums to warn of any attack under cover of the mist which usually comes up in the morning. I will also order officers to make their rounds of the posts every quarter of an hour.'

'Do so, Abdul Rahman.'

'So that I can ensure your protection, Majesty, in what part of the column will you take your place tomorrow morning?'

'I will lead the war elephants, but the greatest protection should be given to the rear of the elephant column. My son Salim will ride there. It will be his first battle. He, and of course his brothers, are the future of the dynasty, the guarantee that our empire will continue to prosper. I have asked him to join us today so that he can hear us make our plans.' Salim had felt the eyes of his father's commanders swivel towards him as Akbar asked, 'Perhaps you have something to say to the council, Salim?'

Taken by surprise, Salim's mind had gone blank for a moment but then, taking courage, he had begun. 'Only that I will do my best in the battle and that I hope I can be as brave as your commanders and of course you, Father . . . and live up to what you expect of me . . .'

As Salim had stuttered to a halt, the commanders seated around his father had begun to applaud and his father had said, 'I am sure you will.'

However, as Akbar had turned quickly away from him back to a discussion of the command of the rearguard, Salim had wondered whether he had detected in his father's tone and expression a disappointment that he had not spoken better and more originally. Then excitement at the prospect of his first battle had eclipsed all other concerns in his mind.

Now, eighteen hours later, the excitement was still there as Salim gazed at the rhododendron-covered hillside. Suddenly, he saw a movement behind one of the most heavily leafed bushes. 'What's that? Is it the enemy?' he asked Suleiman Beg.

'No. It's just a deer,' his milk-brother replied. As if in confirmation, the deer sprinted out from behind the bush, to be shot down by one of the column's outriders with an arrow hastily drawn from his quiver.

'At least some of the men will eat well tonight, Suleiman Beg.'

Ten minutes later, Salim thought he again detected movement, this time on the tree-lined crest of a ridge about a mile away. Chastened by his previous mistake he tugged at Suleiman Beg's arm, pointed to the ridge and whispered, 'Do you see anything up there?'

Before Suleiman Beg could answer, it became clear that there was something and it wasn't another deer for tonight's pot. There was a blast of a trumpet from one of the Moghul scouts. Soon he appeared over the crest, hands and heels working frantically as he urged his horse down between the trees and shrubs. A musket shot crackled out from behind him. Then several other riders appeared in hot pursuit. One, on a black horse, was gaining fast on the scout despite his zigzagging, ducking and dodging beneath and through the bushes and branches. When he was only about twenty yards from the scout, the rider – without doubt a Kashmiri – pulled back his arm and moments later the Moghul fell, presumably hit by a throwing dagger.

By then, many more Kashmiri horsemen were pouring over the crest and charging towards the column, crashing down through the vegetation. The Moghul cavalry on the flanks were turning their horses to face the threat and mounted musketeers were jumping from their saddles to prime their weapons and ready their firing tripods. Somehow the Kashmiris must have evaded Abdul Rahman's screen of scouts, or perhaps killed all of them before they could get a signal away except for the man who had just fallen so bravely.

Salim's heart began to beat faster and he felt all his senses heighten. Behind him in the howdah of his war elephant, two of his bodyguards were preparing their muskets. He could see others doing the same on the elephants immediately ahead, while on each the two *mahouts* sitting behind the elephants' ears were striking the beasts' skulls to make them turn to face the attack, at the same time trying to make themselves as small a target as possible in their exposed position. Suddenly one fell, arms flailing, from the elephant two ahead of Salim's and crashed to the ground with an arrow in his neck. The following elephant carefully avoided his prone body although the man was probably already dead.

Moments later, Salim heard an arrow hiss through the air close beside him. Then he saw a phalanx of Kashmiri horsemen with steel breastplates and domed helmets ornamented with peacock feathers come crashing into the line of flanking Moghul cavalry. They unhorsed several of their rivals by the impetus of their downhill charge. Penetrating swiftly towards the elephant column, they were followed by more and more of their comrades galloping down the green hillsides, some with turquoise battle banners billowing behind them. From time to time a Kashmiri or his horse fell, hit by musket balls or arrows.

Once, a thick-set, green-turbaned Moghul officer charged at a Kashmiri banner bearer and slashed him across the eyes with his sword as they clashed, even succeeding in grabbing the Kashmiri's banner before the now sightless rider dropped from the saddle. However, a second Kashmiri thrust his lance into the officer's abdomen as he attempted to wheel his horse to re-join his comrades. With the turquoise banner flapping around him, the Moghul fell from his horse, but his foot caught in his stirrup and he was dragged head bumping along the ground a little way behind the bolting animal before his body caught beneath the hooves of some charging Kashmiri cavalry. Freed from the stirrup, it was left sprawling bloody and mangled on the stony earth.

Other Kashmiri riders were now within fifty yards or so of Salim's elephant, kicking and urging their mounts forward through the Moghul cavalry, slashing around them with their swords as they advanced. Both Salim and Suleiman Beg put arrows to their bows and fired, while behind them the muskets of their two bodyguards crackled. Salim saw his target – one of the leading Kashmiris – fall from his horse, a white-flighted arrow embedded in his cheek. Salim was exultant. That was his arrow, wasn't it? He'd brought him down. But his delight was short-lived. One of the bodyguards behind him – a black-bearded Rajput named Rajesh who had guarded him and his brothers for many years – uttered a strangled cry and fell from the howdah clutching at his throat. Moments later, one of the two *mahouts* behind his elephant's ears too collapsed to the ground. The elephant in front, turning in obedience to its own *mahouts'* urging to face the Kashmiri horsemen, couldn't help trampling the body, releasing a rank, nauseating smell as the man's stomach and intestines ruptured, bursting under the pressure of the elephant's foot.

Salim fired again at another Kashmiri cavalryman within thirty feet of his elephant. This time he missed but his arrow hit the man's horse in the neck. Thrashing its head about and whinnying in pain, it skittered sideways, causing its rider to drop his lance as he fought with both hands to control his mount. Salim heard a thump behind him and the howdah swayed violently. Glancing round, he saw that his second bodyguard lay slumped on the floor. Suleiman Beg was already trying to staunch a bullet wound to the man's right thigh that was bleeding profusely, using a yellow cotton scarf he had pulled from his own neck.

Meanwhile Salim could see a strong body of Moghul cavalry was now in turn charging into the flanks of the Kashmiris, attempting to beat them back. Several Kashmiris fell – one, a burly, heavily bearded man carried clean out of the saddle and transfixed by a well-aimed lance thrust from one of the captains of the imperial bodyguard. Another was decapitated by the heavy stroke of a Moghul battleaxe which caught him across the throat just beneath the jaw, sending his head flying backwards amid a spray of blood. The Moghuls were succeeding as he knew they would, thought Salim, but then the elephant beneath him lurched once more. The second *mahout,* a small, dark, elderly man wearing only a rough cotton loincloth, had fallen from behind its ears to the ground. Lashing its trunk, the riderless beast began to turn away from the conflict. As it did so, it knocked a Moghul horseman from his saddle. If Salim didn't do something the frightened elephant would kill more men and panic more horses.

Disregarding the noise and the fierce conflict around him, Salim climbed over the raised wooden front of the howdah. He managed to get his legs on either side of the elephant's body and to slide down on to its neck. Grabbing at the elephant's steel plate head armour to steady himself, he drew his sword. Reversing it, and despite the cuts its sharp edge made to his hand, he used its hilt instead of the *mahout's* steel rod to tap the elephant's skull to give the command for it to halt. Reassured by the weight of a rider on its neck once more, the animal began to calm and soon halted. In its panic, it had moved fifty yards away from the centre of the fight. Turning round, Salim could see that the survivors of the Kashmiri cavalry charge were breaking off the battle and retreating back through the rhododendrons up towards the ridge over which they had emerged less than an hour previously. Many did not make it. Salim saw one cream-turbaned Kashmiri, realising that he could not outride his four Moghul pursuers on his blowing black horse, turn and charge back towards them, striking one from the saddle before being cut down himself by a blow to the head.

Later that day, Salim was summoned once more to his father's war council. This time as he entered the scarlet command tent he did not find the discussion already in full flow. Rather, all eyes were turned to him as he entered and his father was conducting his commanders in applause. As he made his way towards the stool Akbar indicated to him, which was placed next to the emperor's own gilded throne, Salim was untroubled by doubts that on this occasion at least his behaviour had pleased his father.

Chapter 19

Jewel of Chastity

'You are fifteen years old. It is time you took your first wife.' Before Salim could reply, Akbar strode off to inspect the target – a log of wood on which three large clay jars had been placed on the parade ground beneath the royal palace in Lahore – at which he had just fired his musket. Even from three hundred yards away, Salim could see that his father had shattered the middle jar. Since their triumphant return from Kashmir three months ago Akbar had several times invited him hunting, hawking or to musketry practice.

Salim hurried after him. 'Father, what did you say?'

'That the time has come for you to marry. As well as helping to strengthen our dynasty it will be a celebration of our great victory in Kashmir.' Akbar smiled. Salim knew that not even Akbar had thought Kashmir would fall into his hands quite so easily. Confronted by the reality that the mountains encircling his kingdom were no barrier against his determined Moghul enemy, its ruler had rushed to sue for peace. In his mind's eye, Salim again saw the Sultan of Kashmir prostrating himself at his father's feet outside Akbar's scarlet command tent then standing meekly while the *khutba* was read in the name of the Moghul emperor. Akbar had granted the sultan life and liberty but from now on Kashmir would be firmly under Moghul control. What was more his father – never content with his

253

victories or his empire's boundaries – was already readying his forces for his invasion of Sind.

'But who am I to marry?'

'After consulting with my counsellors I have selected your cousin, Man Bai. Her father Bhagwan Das, Raja of Amber, has already given his consent.'

Salim stared at his father. Man Bai was his first cousin, the daughter of his mother's brother. He had only seen her once when they had both been children and all he could remember was a quiet, skinny, long-legged little girl with her hair bound in plaits.

'You look surprised. I thought you would be pleased to cross this threshold into manhood. I hear that you are not averse to visiting the girls in the bazaar.'

Salim flushed. He had thought he was being discreet. On the return march from Kashmir, he and his milk-brother Suleiman Beg had slipped out from the imperial quarters to find willing girls among the camp followers. He had lost his virginity one night to a cinnamon-scented Turkish woman while encamped on a mountain pass with cold winds battering the hide walls of her tent – not that he would have noticed had the tent blown away. Back in Lahore, the two youths had taken to slipping out to the town at night. There was a particular inn where Geeta, a plump dancing girl with high, round breasts, had laughingly been instructing him further in the ways of love while Suleiman Beg had been finding delight in the arms of her sister. Afterwards, sneaking back into the palace, they tried to outdo each other with exaggerated tales of their prowess. But tumbling a girl in the bazaar was very different from taking a wife.

'I am surprised. I hadn't thought of marriage at all . . .'

'Young though you are, you should have. Marrying into the houses of the most noble of our vassals, as I did, tightens our grip on our empire as surely as conquest. Such alliances give the powerful families an even greater stake in our success. They ensure that in times of trouble they will support us, not because they love us but because it is to their advantage.' Akbar paused, eyes searching Salim's face. He had seldom spoken to his son so earnestly. 'Why do you think there are so few uprisings against us and every year we grow yet richer? Why do you think that the *ulama* no longer dare to bleat openly about my policies of religious tolerance or my Hindu wives or my introduction of the *Din-i-Ilahi*, the Divine Faith? My position is unassailable and that is in good part because of the alliances I have made through marriage. Understand this, Salim. This is not about your wishes nor about pleasure. You can build yourself a *haram* of concubines for that. It is about duty. I have informed your mother of my decision.'

His father's view of marriage was a joyless one, devoid of human emotion, Salim thought, so unlike that of his grandmother who often told him of the mutual love and support she had shared with Humayun. Perhaps his father's loveless marriage to his own mother was at the root of his coldness. It had been his first union and it may have made him even more reluctant to give himself fully to succeeding brides than his self-contained self-confident nature made him already. Certainly he never spoke of any of them with great affection, being seemingly keener to list the alliances they had brought and how they had contributed to his own and the empire's glory.

Anyway, Hirabai would surely be pleased by his marriage. Any child he had by Man Bai – and a son might well be a future Moghul emperor – would be more Rajput than Moghul. But then he remembered what she had said of her brother Bhagwan Das, Man Bai's father: 'People can always be bought . . .' As so often, his mind became clouded with doubt and uncertainty, though he knew he should be pleased that his father had arranged such an important dynastic match for him. He tried to look grateful – which in his heart he was.

'When will the wedding take place?'

'In about eight weeks' time when your bride arrives from Amber.' Akbar smiled. 'That will also give time for guests to travel here from all over the empire and for others to send gifts. I intend that this will be one of the most magnificent spectacles ever witnessed in Lahore and have already been planning it with Abul Fazl. The festivities will last for a month with processions, camel races, polo matches

255

and elephant fights, and every night feasting and fireworks. Now, let us return to our target practice.'

Salim was disappointed. There was much more he would have liked to ask, but his father was already priming his musket.

• ◆ •

Man Bai was sitting beneath her layers of gold-embroidered veils in the mansion which Akbar had had specially prepared for the entourage from Amber. Two days ago towards sunset Salim had watched the arrival of the long procession bringing his bride. First had come forty Rajput warriors mounted on cream-coloured stallions, breastplates and lance tips gleaming in the light of the dying sun. Six elephants, jewels flashing in their silver headplates, had followed, bearing in gilded howdahs on their backs the personal bodyguard sent to protect Man Bai on her journey. Then had come his bride on another even more gorgeously caparisoned elephant. Silk curtains, vivid blue as a kingfisher's wing, draped over her gold-painted, turquoise-inlaid howdah concealed her from view. Immediately behind came her personal waiting women riding on camels, heavily veiled and further protected from the sun by white silk parasols embroidered with pearls held by attendants perched behind them. Next had trotted a further detachment of Rajput warriors, this time mounted on matching black horses. At the very end was the Moghul escort, green banners flying, that Akbar had sent to accompany them.

Salim had risen early to dress in readiness for the wedding procession to his bride's house where the ceremony was to take place – a Hindu custom that, as a courtesy to Bhagwan Das, Akbar had decreed should be followed. To the high-pitched wail of pipes and the beating of drums, he and his father, sitting side by side in a jewelled howdah on the back of Akbar's favourite elephant, had proceeded at a stately pace. In front had marched rows of attendants carrying trays of gifts from pearls and gems to spices, including piles of the finest saffron sent by the Sultan of Kashmir from his crocus fields.

As Shaikh Mubarak and two other mullahs began reading verses from the Koran, Salim glanced down at his hands, painted earlier that morning by his mother and her women with henna and turmeric

256

for good luck. Somewhat to his surprise – and relief – his mother had welcomed his betrothal to her niece. Maybe the consideration that any child born of the marriage would be three-quarters Rajput had outweighed her disapproval of Man Bai's father, Salim thought. He shifted position a little, conscious of the weight of the marriage diadem set with diamonds and pearls that Akbar himself had placed on his head.

When the mullahs had finally finished their intoning, Shaikh Mubarak turned to Man Bai beneath her glittering coverings to ask the customary question, 'Do you give your consent to this union?' Salim heard her muffled assent and saw the slight tilt of her head. An attendant stepped forward with a red and green enamelled ewer, and as Salim held out his hands poured rosewater over them. Then another attendant handed him a goblet of water from which to sip to confirm the union. I am a married man, Salim thought as the cool liquid ran down his throat. It seemed unreal.

As the wedding feast got under way, Salim scarcely saw the whirling Rajasthani dancing girls with their jangling anklets and gold-spangled red veils or the sinuous acrobats – muscled bodies gleaming with oil – exerting themselves to entertain him, or heard the discreet laughter of the women of the court sitting behind a carved wooden *jali* that enabled them to watch what was happening without being seen. Neither did he taste much of the food – roasted pheasants and peacocks adorned with their own gilded tail feathers, young lamb cooked with dried fruit and spices, and pistachio- and almond-flavoured sweetmeats. All the time he was thinking, I must remember this moment. This is when I became a man. From now on, I will have my own household and a bride as royal as my own mother. A new confidence was flowing through his veins, and, as he glanced at the small, glittering figure beside him, a surge of excitement at the thought of a new woman to discover.

Salim smiled to recall how Hamida – not his father – had tried to talk to him about the ways to please a woman. Of course, modesty forbade her to be explicit but he knew what she was saying – to be considerate and tender towards his young bride. He would be. Geeta had taught him well. He understood how reining in his own eager passion could add to the pleasure of both. He had gone to Geeta as an eager boy, newly initiated and as excited and unthinking as any stallion about to be put to stud, but she had made him a lover . . . Yet though he hadn't needed Hamida's hints on the art of love-making, he had been glad of her instruction on the rituals of the wedding night – how next morning the bedding would be inspected to confirm that sexual intercourse had taken place and that his bride had been a virgin.

Three hours later, Salim's attendants removed his wedding clothes and jewels in the bedchamber in the *haram* of the new apartments his father had given him. On the other side of the green brocade hangings his bride – bathed, scented and oiled by her own servants – was waiting for him in the marriage bed. When he was naked, one of his attendants fetched a green silk robe and draped it over him, fastening the emerald clasps at throat and chest. Then the servants withdrew. Salim hesitated a moment, looking at the brocade curtains gleaming in the soft light of the oil lamps burning in niches around the chamber. It wasn't that he felt nervous but rather that he wanted to fix this moment in his mind. He might one day be emperor, the Rajput princess he was about to bed perhaps the mother of a future emperor. This was no quick, joyous tumble in the bazaar but perhaps another step in his own story and that of his dynasty.

But at the thought of the woman waiting for him on the other side of those curtains desire quickened, driving out such ideas. Salim pushed the hangings aside and stepped into the bedchamber. Man Bai was sitting up, the outline of her breasts clearly visible through her almost transparent robe of peach-coloured muslin. Her long thick dark hair tumbled around her shoulders and the rubies she was wearing in her ears gleamed. Around her neck was a slender gold chain also set with rubies. But what held Salim's attention was the excited expression in those dark, long-lashed eyes and her bold, confident smile.

He had expected a shy, even bashful bride – Suleiman Beg had teased him about it, warning him not to frighten her with his brothel manners – but he could sense her anticipation. Unfastening his robe he let it fall to the ground and walked over to the bed, wishing he had fought more battles and had scars to impress her with. He sat down on the edge of the bed, close to but not touching her and suddenly unsure of himself. But Man Bai took him gently by the shoulders with her hennaed hands and pulled him down beside her. 'Welcome, cousin,' she whispered. Needing no further encouragement, Salim drew her closer and kissed her, feeling her full mouth open beneath his. Then, freeing her from her diaphanous muslin robe, he began to run his hands over the soft contours of her body. She was delicately boned with a slender waist but her hips swelled voluptuously and her breasts were large – bigger than Geeta's, Salim found himself thinking. Her hands began exploring his body, not with Geeta's assurance and expertise but eagerly and unashamedly none the less.

Parting Man Bai's thighs, he began to caress her. A quiver ran through her body and her breathing quickened. After a few moments she arched her back and eyes closed began to cry out softly, pressing herself so tightly against him he could feel the hardness of her nipples. Young though he was, he had learned enough about women to know that she did not want him to delay. Raising himself, he gently tried to enter her. She felt very tight. He had never made love to a virgin and knew he must be careful not to hurt her. But again he sensed the eagerness within his bride. Her cries were growing louder and her hands, gripping the hard muscle of his shoulders, were urging him on. He began to thrust harder, more urgently. Man Bai's cries were turning to moans but they were of pleasure not pain. Then he felt something within her ease and he was deep inside her. They were moving as one, bodies locked together and their skin dewed with sweat. Salim's eyes were clenched and his head was thrown back. He was trying to hold back for a few more moments, but he couldn't. The climax came, and mingling with his own ecstatic groans he heard Man Bai's gasps of pleasure.

Lying close to his young bride, hands cupping the lush curve of her buttocks, Salim said nothing. Her sexual hunger had stunned him a little but he was glad to have a wife who unashamedly enjoyed the sexual act and on her wedding night had been eager, not afraid. It was she who spoke first, disengaging from him, sitting up and pushing her sweat-dampened hair back from her face. 'What are you thinking, cousin?'

'That I am fortunate in my wife.'

'And I am fortunate in my husband.' She put her hands round his neck. 'They told me you were good-looking, but brides are often told lies about the men their families want them to marry. I only remembered you as a tongue-tied awkward boy.'

The next morning, the wedding sheets were duly inspected and approved, and drums were beaten to proclaim the success of the wedding night. Among those presenting themselves to pay their respects to the new bridegroom was Abul Fazl. 'I have recorded in the imperial chronicles that Your Highness was yesterday wedded to one of the brightest jewels of chastity in the empire,' he said in his usual unctuous way. Salim listened politely, as he had to, but he was glad when Abul Fazl departed.

The festivities over the days that followed were everything Akbar had promised. Wedding gifts from across the empire: gems, dishes of jade, silver and gold, high-stepping Arab horses, embroidered shawls of the softest wool – yet another gift from the chastened Sultan of Kashmir – and even a pair of lions were displayed through the streets of Lahore. Camel races were organised along the banks of the Ravi river. To his great satisfaction Salim beat both his half-brothers in one contest, successfully urging his snorting, spitting, splay-footed mount over the finishing line, the roars of the spectators in his ears. The strongest of his father's fighting elephants were pitted against one another within high earth barricades, fighting until their grey hides were lacerated and their tusks dripped with blood, while every night there was more feasting and towards midnight so many fireworks that they turned the dark world back to day.

But every evening, however spectacular and novel the entertainments, Salim's thoughts turned to the moment when he could again be in Man Bai's eager arms till the morning sun was warming the palace. Suleiman Beg joked that if he continued like this he would need ointment from the *hakims* to soothe his over-active loins.

◆

260

'I name you, my first and most beloved son, Khusrau.' So saying, Salim picked up the white jade saucer filled with tiny gold coins and poured them gently over the baby's head. 'May your life be crowned with success, in token of which I shower you with these earthly riches.' The child blinked, then looked up at Salim from the silk-fringed green velvet cushion on which he was lying. Salim expected at any moment to hear wails of protest but instead Khusrau smiled and thrashed his arms and legs. Salim picked up the cushion and raised it high so all could see his healthy young son. A polite murmuring followed as the assembled courtiers and commanders exclaimed aloud at the child's vigour and lustiness and uttered good wishes for his long life.

Salim glanced at his father standing by his side on the marble dais. This was Akbar's first grandson and his face, still handsome and firm-jawed though he was in his forties, looked both pleased and proud. The previous day Salim had received a pair of hunting leopards in velvet coats, their gilded leather collars set with emeralds – a certain sign of his father's approval. Surely now that he had become a father himself Akbar would give him some position in which he could demonstrate his abilities. Given the chance to lead a Moghul army, he could prove to everyone – not just his father – that he was a good fighter and commander and would one day make a great emperor.

His half-brothers were no rivals, Akbar must see that. Murad had married three months ago, but even at his tender age he had been drunk at his wedding feast and later had had to be half carried to his bride's bed. Salim had known of Murad's love of wine and spirits, but until his wedding his half-brother had managed to conceal his drunkenness from Akbar. Their father had been so enraged that he had ordered Murad immediately on campaign in the south. To keep an eye on him, he had sent one of his senior commanders with orders that not a drop of alcohol was to pass his son's lips. As for Daniyal, he was going the same way as Murad. Since reaching adolescence, pleasure and self-indulgence were all he seemed to care about. Salim rarely saw either of his half-brothers but he had heard the stories, particularly the one about how Daniyal had ordered the largest fountain in the marble courtyard of his apartments to be made to flow with the rich red wine of Ghazni, not water, and how he and his companions had stripped naked to frolic in it, and the one about the time a drunken Murad had dressed as a woman and danced lewdly before not only his courtiers but also an envoy sent by the Portuguese from their enclave of Goa.

Salim smiled as he gently placed his son back in the arms of one of his milk-mothers, a sister of Suleiman Beg. As he did so he vowed he would spend more time with his son than Akbar had done with him. He would have more sons too, not only by Man Bai but also by his other wives – Jodh Bai, a Rajput princess from Marwar, and Sahib Jamal, daughter of one of Akbar's commanders. He enjoyed his growing *haram*. His father was always urging on him the importance of forging alliances through marriage but really he needed little encouragement. Any new woman if she was young and good-looking was a fresh adventure, and if for political reasons it was expedient to marry a woman who was faded or ugly, well, not every wife had to be bedded more than once and she could always be found an honourable place in his *haram*. That had always been his father's policy and through his huge number of wives he had, as he so often boasted, done much to pacify and consolidate his empire. Why shouldn't he, Salim, be the same?

The only shadow, as Salim moved to take his place at the feast to celebrate his son's birth, was Man Bai. She still excited him sexually but he hadn't been prepared for her jealousy when, six months after his marriage to her, his father had announced that he wished Salim to take a further wife. Man Bai had pleaded with him not to do it, weeping copiously in her apartments and – as the day of his second wedding approached – refusing to eat. Again and again he had explained that he must obey his father but she wouldn't listen, shrieking at him that he was betraying her. Summoned by a nervous attendant to his *haram* one night, Salim had found Man Bai perched on a stone balustrade overlooking a stone-paved courtyard thirty feet below. 'You have driven me to this,' she had shouted as soon as she saw him. 'You have made me desperate. Wasn't my love enough for you? Is it because I haven't yet conceived?'

With her wild hair, red-rimmed eyes and gaunt features, Man Bai had reminded him of a mad young woman he had sometimes seen in the bazaar, going from person to person upbraiding them for some imaginary injury and being driven away by stones and dung. He had hardly recognised his beautiful Rajput wife as she clung trembling and dishevelled to the stonework. He had coaxed her down, explaining as patiently and tenderly as he could that as a royal Moghul prince he must do his father's bidding and marry again, but of course it would not affect his feelings for her.

Except that it had. Man Bai's unreasoning hysteria had made him wonder what else he didn't know about his cousin. It had also made him realise that what he felt for her wasn't love – only sexual passion. She should be happy living in the magnificence of the Moghul court surrounded by luxuries beyond those even a Rajput princess was used to. He made frequent visits to her bed where they were each other's equals in the giving and receiving of pleasure. That should surely be enough. It was foolishness to expect to be his only wife. But her unexpected jealousy had left him wary of Man Bai. His visits to her had grown less frequent and not long after her threatened suicide he had indeed married Jodh Bai. With her plump body and round face she wasn't as beautiful as Man Bai, but her wit made him laugh and he liked her company even if he didn't feel a close bond with her.

As fate would have it, four months after his marriage to Jodh Bai and just before his marriage to Sahib Jamal, Man Bai had become pregnant with Khusrau – the first of the next generation of the Moghul dynasty. The status that conferred should satisfy Man Bai, but if it didn't there was nothing he could do and he would not allow it to worry him – though it did, particularly the thought that their son might inherit some of her self-centred lack of control.

Akbar's deep voice interrupted his thoughts. 'Let us now go to feast the birth of this new prince. May he and the dynasty prosper.'

As he took his place at the feast, Salim offered up a silent prayer for his own prosperity. If he became the next Moghul emperor, what might he not be able to do for his sons?

Part V

Great Expectations

Chapter 20

The Abyss

Once again, more than three years after his first journey there, Salim was sitting in an elephant howdah as the great beast plodded its way towards Kashmir. This time, though, the circumstances were very different. Their long journey was aimed at peace and pleasure, not war and conquest. Both he and his father had fallen in love with the beauty of Kashmir, its peaceful valleys, glistening lakes and flower-strewn meadows, and above all the respite it provided from the angry summer sun of the plains. The dozen elephants preceding his carried not warriors but members of his *haram*. On the nearest was Man Bai with the two-year-old Khusrau. On the next two were Sahib Jamal with Parvez, the son she had given birth to three months earlier, and then Jodh Bai. Beyond them, further towards the front of the column, were the elephants bearing his father's *haram*. His mother was not among them, having scorned the cool of the mountains for the sun of her native lands, but his grandmother Hamida was and Salim was glad. Despite his marriages, she was still one of his closest confidantes.

Akbar was, as usual, riding at the very front of the column. Though Salim had done everything his father had asked, acquiescing in all his marriage plans for him, the closeness he had felt to Akbar after the victory over the Sultan of Kashmir had gradually ebbed. He had hoped that fathering Akbar's first grandson might have made Akbar warm towards him as well as to his grandson. To Salim's continuing frustration and disappointment, his father still seemed too preoccupied with the expansion of his empire and its smooth running, as well as with his philosophical musings, to be prepared to spend much time with his eldest son or to involve him in affairs of state. He was almost always closeted with Abul Fazl who, Salim was sure, used his smooth, flatterer's tongue to his detriment. Tasks and appointments which might have been given to Salim to prepare him to rule one day had, instead, been given to friends of Abul Fazl, who was even now sharing his father's howdah. Some court rumours claimed that he had grown fat on the bribes he had received for recommending his friends, though others said that his corpulence was solely accounted for by his excessive appetite. Salim had heard Abul Fazl's *khutmagar* – his butler – boasting to one of his own servants that Abul Fazl consumed thirty pounds of food a day and even then occasionally asked for a nocturnal snack.

Salim pushed thoughts of his father and Abul Fazl from his mind as Suleiman Beg, who was riding with him, adjusted the hangings around the howdah to keep out the rain now being driven almost horizontally by the strong north wind. If the purpose of this second journey to Kashmir was different from the first, so too was the spring weather, at least so far. It had scarcely stopped raining since they had entered the series of mountain defiles and passes. The heads of the purple rhododendrons on the hillsides were bowed low by the weight of raindrops. As Salim looked out of his howdah, he could see water streaming down some overhanging cliffs to the right before splashing into the puddles on the muddy, narrow road twisting inexorably upwards towards Kashmir. On the left-hand side of the road, the land dropped almost sheer fifty feet to the jade-green waters of the river below which, fed by snow melt as well as rainwater, was flowing fast down to the plains.

'The river level seems to rise every time I look at it,' said Suleiman Beg.

'Yes. It'll be hard for those who've gone ahead to locate a camp site and erect the tents to find somewhere free from bogs and lying water.'

Suddenly, Salim heard a crash, followed by a low rumble and then agonised human cries from round the sharp bend in the road that lay just ahead. 'What was that? Not an attack, surely.'

'No, it was a landslide, I think.' Suleiman Beg stood and gestured down into the ravine.

Salim followed his milk-brother's pointing arm. Mud and stones seemed to have partially blocked the river, which was already backing up. Wasn't that the body of an elephant he could see? '*Mahout*, make the elephant kneel!' he ordered. Even before the beast had settled fully on to its knees, both Salim and Suleiman Beg had jumped to the ground and were running forward, splashing through the wet yellow mud to see what had happened.

Rounding the bend, Salim was deeply relieved to see that all the elephants carrying his wives and his young sons were safe on the road. However, the problem was immediately apparent. Part of the rock overhang had collapsed, taking about thirty feet of the road with it as rocks and mud slid down into the river below. The body of one elephant protruded from beneath the landslide; a second lay half in and half out of the river, the water washing over it turning red with the beast's blood. Its gilded howdah lay nearby, smashed on some jagged rocks sticking out of the river. Pushing his way through those who were gathering round the site of the slide and looking down, Salim asked, 'Who was riding on these elephants?'

'Some of your grandmother's waiting-women,' one onlooker replied.

'I regret to say one of them was your old nursemaid, Zubaida. Your grandmother thought the cool mountain air would be good for her,' added a thin grizzled old man as, almost audibly creaking, he raised himself from where he had been lying peering over the very edge. Despite the mud which soaked his clothes and was splashed across his face and white beard, Salim recognised his grandmother's steward. 'I think I was able to see where her howdah landed.'

'Do you mean the one splintered by those rocks at the river's edge?'

'No, that contained four other of your grandmother's servants. I fear they are all dead. I myself saw one of their bodies washed away by the torrent, face down and arms spread. Zubaida's howdah seems to have been torn from her elephant early in its fall. I thought I could see it caught behind some trees on a ledge about three-quarters of the way down, but more of the mud was slipping away and my eyes are no longer good . . .'

'Hold my belt, Suleiman Beg,' ordered Salim as he flung himself on the ground. Oblivious of the cold wet mud soaking through his fine garments, he moved cautiously forward, propelling himself on his elbows to a point where his head and shoulders were overlooking the slide. Yes, the steward was right. The howdah had fallen away from the main landslip as the straps securing it to the elephant had burst. It had indeed caught against some scrubby trees on a ledge. But where were the occupants? The debris from the mudslide blocked his view.

'Hold on tight to me, Suleiman Beg. I'll see if I can get a better look.' As Salim edged further forward, he heard a faint cry from below. Someone was alive. What was left of the sodden overhang might give way at any moment. If those who had fallen into the ravine were to be rescued, he must act quickly. At first it looked hopeless. No one could climb down there. But then he thought he could make out a route that might just be possible. 'Bring me a rope – one of those used to pull bogged-down carts from the mud. I must try to get down there.'

'Let me go,' said Suleiman Beg.

'No, it should be me. I owe it to Zubaida to be the one to go. She took great care of me as a child. I remember she climbed a thorn tree to rescue me after I got stuck in it bird-nesting when I was about three.'

Within five minutes a rope had been brought and Salim had stripped off his outer garments and tied the rope firmly round his chest. 'Hold on tight,' he shouted to Suleiman Beg. 'Have further ropes ready to lower to pull survivors up with.' Then he disappeared over the edge.

For about the first ten feet or so he picked out hand- and footholds on the wet rocks. Then he came to a place where mud had partially covered another small ledge. As he put his foot on it, some of the loose earth and stones slipped beneath his weight. For a moment he lost all purchase. Only the rope tightening under his armpits saved him from what he realised with a shudder would inevitably have been a fatal fall. However, as he swung back and forth on the rope he retained the presence of mind to propel himself back towards the ledge and to kick away some of the mud so that he could get first one foot and then the other on to the base rock of the ledge.

After taking a deep breath, he looked down towards the considerably wider lower ledge where the howdah had caught. His view was much less obstructed now and he could see that there were two figures, both women, on it. One was lying prone on the ground and the second, who from her long grey hair he recognised as Zubaida, was kneeling beside her.

'Zubaida,' Salim shouted. She didn't hear him through the wind and rain. 'Zubaida,' he yelled again. This time to his relief the woman looked up and waved her right arm. 'I am coming,' Salim called down. 'Keep back against the rock wall so you don't get knocked off by any further falls.'

Moments later he saw Zubaida tugging at the other figure in an attempt to pull her nearer to the wall too. It would be completely beyond Zubaida's strength, but he knew she wouldn't give up and seek protection only for herself. He had no time to lose. Cautiously, so as not to dislodge any more material, he lowered himself carefully down the wet muddy slope. When he was only about twelve feet vertically and perhaps the same horizontally from the two women, he heard a noise above him and small rocks began to fall. As he looked up to see where they were coming from, a large stone struck the side of his face and he felt blood flow into his mouth.

As he spat out the metallic, salty-tasting fluid, he heard Zubaida, who had recognised him, shout, 'Go back, Highness. Save yourself. You are young. Both of us here are old and have already enjoyed a long life.' As she spoke, more stones and earth fell between him and the ledge. Glancing hastily about, Salim saw some hand- and footholds created by fissures and protuberances in the rock which might take him directly above the ledge. Quickly but carefully, testing each hold before he put his full weight on it, he manoeuvred along until he was in a position from which he could jump the ten feet or so on to the ledge. He did so, landing with a knee-jarring thump next to Zubaida.

She was in a bad state, worse than he had hoped. A large jagged cut on her swollen temple was bleeding profusely and one of the shattered bones of her left forearm was protruding bloodily through her age-mottled skin. Blood was seeping from the back of the other woman's head and staining her hennaed hair. She was unconscious, if not dead. 'You'll both soon be out of here and safe in the hands of the *hakims*,' Salim said with a little more confidence than he felt. He manoeuvred slowly forward to a position by the howdah from where he knew those on the road above could see him. Then he waved both his arms above his head in the agreed signal to throw further ropes down. Soon, two ropes snaked through the air towards the ledge. Salim grabbed one but the other fell too far away. He had to signal twice more before another rope finally descended within his reach.

He tied the first rope round Zubaida, who winced only when he accidentally caught her damaged arm. 'Be brave.' Salim smiled encouragingly at her. 'When I give the signal those on the road will pull you up on the rope. Use your feet to push yourself away from the rocks.'

'Yes, Highness, I understand.'

'When you reach the top, tell them to pull on both my rope and the remaining one at the same time. I will go up with your companion.'

Zubaida nodded and Salim moved again to the shattered howdah to signal for his old nursemaid to be hauled back up. Soon, to Salim's great relief, she was ascending the rock face, obediently pushing with her bare feet just as he had instructed.

As she disappeared from his view, Salim went over to the second woman, who somewhat to his surprise was still breathing. As he tied the rope around her, he saw her eyelids flicker. Then he quickly resecured his own rope about himself and lifted the woman in his arms. A few moments later he felt the ropes tauten. Slowly they began to be hoisted up, Salim using his feet to keep them clear of the rocks when he could. He couldn't prevent himself being swung heavily against one overhang, grazing his back through his thin tunic, but he was soon at the top, safe if bruised and blood- and mud-stained. As the *hakims* took the two elderly women away on makeshift stretchers, the first person Salim saw striding towards him was his father, the crowds parting before him. He had a broad smile on his face as he extended his arms to embrace his son.

'Salim, I am proud of you. Your strength is now the equal of mine.'

To his son, every word was as precious as gold.

• ◆ •

A soft wind was blowing through the beds of roses and some of their red petals were falling to the ground as three months later Akbar and Salim walked side by side through the Nasim Bagh near the Kashmiri capital of Srinagar. The gardens had been laid out on Akbar's orders only twelve months previously on the west bank of the Dal lake, whose blue waters lapped the edge of the lowest of the gardens' series of descending terraces. It must, thought Salim, be one of the most beautiful places in the world.

As if sensing what his son was thinking, Akbar said, 'The Persians at the court boast that their homeland has the most beautiful gardens, the closest on earth to the *charbaghs*, the gardens of Paradise, which the Koran describes as the reward of the faithful in heaven. However, for me, the whole of Kashmir is one great garden of Paradise with its meadows carpeted in spring by the mauve flowers of the saffron crocus, its babbling brooks, its tumbling waterfalls and these wonderful hills and lake.'

Salim thought, not for the first time, that he had never seen his father as relaxed as when he was in Kashmir. Although Akbar still dealt daily with the despatches brought by post messengers from Hindustan and often inspected the construction of the fast-rising Hari Parvat fort in Srinagar, he still seemed to have more time to talk to members of his family. Perhaps, thought Salim, that was because almost immediately after they had arrived in Srinagar his father had despatched Abul Fazl back to Lahore to deal with some reported problems with the running of the imperial administration.

'I was just thinking the same, Father. It is good to be among breezes and green meadows instead of the heat and rain of the monsoon in Hindustan. It makes me feel more alive.' Salim paused, pleased to share his father's mood, and then went on, 'While we've been here I've become more and more interested in nature. I've had some of the artists draw accurate pictures of crocuses and other flowers much larger than life so that I can see all the intricate details of their make-up. I have even had scholars dissect the wings of birds to see if they can understand how they fly.'

'Your grandmother has told me of your researches. I would like to see the drawings myself. Kashmir has been good for all of us. It has shown me not only how courageous you are but how strong your mind is.'

Salim said nothing for a while as the two continued to walk down through the terraces of the Nasim Bagh towards the glinting waters of the Dal lake. Then, emboldened by these moments of intimacy, he asked, 'When we return to Lahore, may I attend your council meetings, whether civil or military, more often so that I can better understand how our empire works?'

'I will certainly think about it. I shall consult Abul Fazl as to when it might be most helpful for you to do so.'

Abul Fazl, always Abul Fazl, thought Salim. He said nothing, but it was as if a shadow had passed over the warm late summer sun.

Chapter 21

'A Riband in the Cap of Royalty'

'This is good news. We should celebrate,' said Suleiman Beg. 'Perhaps it will be a third son for you in addition to Khusrau and Parvez.'

'Perhaps.'

'What's the matter? You look as if your father had appointed you inspector of the Lahore latrines, rather than a man who's just learned that his favourite wife is pregnant.'

Suleiman Beg could always lighten his mood, Salim thought. 'You're right, and I am pleased. So is Jodh Bai. It was hard for her to see me with two sons already, neither of them hers.'

'And I'm right, aren't I? She is your favourite.'

'I suppose so. At least she can always make me laugh. Like you, she knows my moods and can tease me out of them. And unlike Man Bai or some of my other wives she never complains that I don't spend enough time with her.'

'What is it then? Why the reluctance to rejoice?'

Salim's jaw tightened as he tried to answer that question as much for himself as his milk-brother. 'It's good to be the father of sons, of course it is. But what will I have to offer them? The same purposeless life that I lead? While we were with my father in Kashmir I thought he had changed towards me. He seemed to want my opinions, but since we've returned to Lahore he ignores me again. It's all Abul Fazl.

He sits at my father's right ear dripping unctuous words and I'm surer than ever he is to blame. He wants to exclude me and my half-brothers because he sees us as rivals for influence with my father.'

Suleiman Beg shrugged. 'Perhaps your father thinks you're still too young to take a hand in government.'

'I'm a grown man. I'm a father. I've proved my courage in battle. I've been patient and dutiful. What more does he want? Sometimes I think he excludes me from important debates on purpose.'

'Why should he do that?'

'Because he doesn't know whether he wants me to succeed him. He's reluctant to give me any real power or responsibility because he fears that will be a sign to me – and to others – that I am his chosen heir.'

'You don't know that. It might just be that he's wary of giving up any power to anyone. How old is he?'

'He'll be forty-nine in October.'

'There you are then. Though he looks so vigorous and strong he's not a young man any more. In his heart he'll know that and he probably resents you or anyone who might one day succeed him – he's like the old tiger driven from his haunts by a younger male.'

'How come you think you're so knowledgeable?'

Suleiman Beg shrugged, then grinned, showing very white teeth. 'My father's almost exactly the same age and he's the same. He does nothing but find fault with me, never asks my opinion about anything. I just keep out of his way. I wish your father would post him back to Bengal.'

'Perhaps you're right. Perhaps my father doesn't intentionally mean to slight me. He's certainly shown no more favour to my half-brothers. Murad and Daniyal lead the same aimless lives as I do.'

'But they continue to find ways of solacing themselves.'

'What do you mean?'

Suleiman arched an eyebrow. 'Surely you've heard the latest about their parties? Sometimes they're too drunk to get themselves to bed. Their attendants often have to carry them back to their apartments and two weeks ago Murad nearly drowned when he collapsed into one of the water channels in the garden.'

'Doesn't their behaviour make you understand how I feel? I don't want my sons to lead empty lives, not knowing what the future holds, and as a result succumb to the temptations that self-seeking people dangle before princes for their own purposes. I want to be emperor and give my sons the chance of fighting by my side as we expand and strengthen our empire.'

'You're too impatient. Your father may have many years to live.'

'I pray he does. If you think I want my father out of this world and in Paradise you're wrong. But I can't live through many more years like this, with no way of achieving anything. I might just as well be one of my concubines lying on cushions all day and growing plump on sweetmeats, or one of the fat eunuchs who never draw a dagger or a sword. I'm a young man, a warrior, I need opportunities now. If my father shuts me out I have nothing. It's not like the days of our ancestors when a Moghul prince could ride off in search of new lands where he could carve out a kingdom for himself as my great-grandfather Babur did. In his lifetime he ruled Ferghana, Samarkand and Kabul before he came near Hindustan. When he was half my age he'd already made his mark on the world.'

'Highness . . .' It was one of Salim's *qorchis*. 'Your wife Jodh Bai asks that you go to her.'

Salim nodded, and at the thought of Jodh Bai, her endearingly round little face even rounder with happiness as she'd told him the news of her pregnancy earlier that day, his own grim expression softened. He should be glad of what he had. And Suleiman Beg was right. Just as so many others had counselled him – Shaikh Salim Chishti, who now lay in a marble tomb in the courtyard of the mosque in Fatehpur Sikri, and his grandmother, and his great-aunt – he must learn patience.

'I will go to her straight away. Suleiman Beg, when I return we'll celebrate, as you suggest.'

'And don't forget one thing you already have over your father. It took him far longer than you to produce heirs . . .'

·◆·

Akbar held his new grandson in his arms. 'I name you Khurram, meaning "joyous". May your life be so and may you bring joy to all around you. But more than that, may you make our empire yet greater.' Akbar smiled down at Khurram's tiny face, wizened like all newborn babies', and tightened his grip on the small squirming body wrapped in green velvet that Salim had just placed in his arms. Then he looked up to address his courtiers and commanders. 'The court astronomers tell me that the conjunction of the planets at the moment of Khurram's birth three days ago was the same as at the birth of my great ancestor, Timur. That in itself is highly auspicious, but there is more: this is the millennium year of our Islamic calendar, while the month of my grandson's birth is the same as that of the Prophet Muhammad. This child will, as Abul Fazl here has already recorded in the chronicles, be "a riband in the cap of royalty and more resplendent than the sun".'

Salim's face flushed with pride as he looked at Khurram. His father's delight in this new grandson seemed to know no bounds. Just a few hours after the birth, having heard the astronomers' excited comparisons with Timur's birth, he had sent Salim a pair of matched black stallions and fine silks and perfume to Jodh Bai. The tenderness on his face as he held Khurram was something Salim had never witnessed and filled him with renewed hope. Surely this would bind him and his father closer together and help to assure his own succession. It seemed that God himself had spoken by bringing Khurram into the world on such a day.

Looking at his son in his father's arms, Salim wished he could roll the years forward and see what those wrinkled features, those tiny limbs, would one day become. If the stargazers were correct this child would be a great warrior, a conqueror, a ruler whose name would pass down through time when others were forgotten.

Akbar was raising jewelled hands to signal he had more to say. 'Because the omens surrounding the birth of this child are so special I have decided that I myself will rear him.'

Salim stared at Akbar as he struggled to take in what his father was saying. Surely he didn't mean . . . ? But as he continued to listen to Akbar's calm but authoritative voice, his father's intentions were becoming clearer by the moment.

'Prince Khurram will be placed in the care of one of my wives, Rukhiya Begum, in my *haram* so that I may see him at any hour of the day or night. As he begins to grow I will appoint special tutors to superintend his education but will also take a hand myself.'

Didn't his father even trust him to bring up his own son? Salim stared at the ground, willing himself not to look at Akbar because of what he might say or do. The most senior members of the court were present, he told himself, driving the nails of one hand into the palm of another so hard that he thought he had drawn blood. Causing a disturbance was unthinkable. He tried to steady his thoughts and to control his breathing, which had suddenly become jerky, as if he could not draw in enough air. Then another thought struck him with sickening force. Was his father thinking of eventually naming Khurram as his heir? Surely not . . . Glancing sideways he caught Abul Fazl watching him. The chronicler's small eyes looked interested, as if assessing how Salim was taking the news. What role had Abul Fazl played in this? Salim suddenly wondered. Was he encouraging Akbar to favour Khurram to extend the length of his time in power? He might seek to be regent if Khurram came to the throne in childhood. At the thought, such red-hot anger spurted through Salim that it was all he could do not to pull his dagger from his sash, spring forward and draw the blade across Abul Fazl's fleshy throat.

But he would not give the chronicler the satisfaction of seeing how much his father had hurt him. He forced his features to look composed, but all the time his mind was racing, trying to work out the implications of Akbar's theft of his son. It was little consolation that Khurram would have the best of everything and Rukhiya Begum was a kind woman. Salim had known her all his life. Plain-faced and grey-haired, she was Akbar's cousin — the daughter of his long-dead uncle Hindal — and at least Akbar's age.

279

She was also childless. Her marriage to Akbar – as with his marriages to so many in his vast *haram* – had probably barely been consummated. No, he need have no fears for Khurram. The victims were himself and Jodh Bai, who would be deprived of daily contact with their son . . .

At the thought of Jodh Bai, Salim's jaw tightened. She had waited a long time for a child, and to have him given completely into the care of another would hurt her badly. Rukhiya Begum would appoint the child's milk-mothers. Rukhiya Begum would be the one to watch Khurram's daily progress. As soon as the celebration feast was over, Salim slipped away to find Jodh Bai in the *haram*. Her eyes were reddened with tears but she was not hysterical as Man Bai would have been had the newborn Khusrau been taken from her. She was sitting quietly on a yellow brocade divan, hands clasped together. Salim stooped and kissed her. 'I'm sorry. I didn't know what my father was planning.'

For a moment Jodh Bai said nothing. When she did speak, her voice was calm. 'Your father has sent me another gift.' Opening her hands she revealed what she had been clutching – a magnificent gold chain set with glowing rubies and large pearls. Armies had fought for less. 'It's beautiful, but I would rather the emperor had left me my son.' She let the shining necklace trickle through her fingers on to the indigo carpet beneath her feet, where it lay like a jewelled snake.

'One day, I promise you, I will find a way of making amends for this – and so will Khurram. He won't always be a boy in his grandfather's thrall and the bonds between a mother and her son are strong, whatever the circumstances.' As he himself knew, thought Salim, as an image of Hirabai's proud face, softening as she looked at him, came into his mind.

'Is there nothing we can do?' Jodh Bai asked, then shook her head as if impatient with herself. 'Of course there isn't. Your father is the emperor and it is a great honour that he should wish to bring up our child. I shouldn't complain.'

Grief sat oddly on her round face, usually so alive with humour, and Salim felt tears prick his own eyelids – tears for her, tears of frustration at his powerlessness. But he also felt a new resolve. Hide your feelings, he told himself; be patient. Your time will come . . . You will rule.

· ◆ ·

But as Salim reflected on those words over the months ahead they seemed to him ever more empty. His situation had less to do with patience than with powerlessness, he realised. Every day he had to live with the knowledge that there was nothing he could do. He was entirely dependent on Akbar, whose delight and interest in his grandson showed no sign of diminishing. Salim knew he should be pleased his father loved Khurram so much . . . that he mustn't resent the fact that Akbar had never responded to him like that. But it was hard. So was having to endure the sight of Khurram, on his rare visits to Jodh Bai, twisting in her unfamiliar arms and bawling to be returned to the milk-mother Rukhiya Begum had appointed. Jodh Bai tried to hide her sorrow but it never left her, he was sure.

All the time, Salim's thoughts had kept returning to Abul Fazl, surely the author of so many things that had happened to frustrate his hopes. And if he'd needed any further proof that this man was his enemy, he'd just received it, Salim thought as on a warm summer's day he strode towards Abul Fazl's apartments in the Lahore fort.

'Highness, you honour me by your visit. I was just recording in the chronicle His Majesty's departure to Agra to inspect the rebuilding of the fort.' Abul Fazl rose to his feet as Salim was ushered in. A polite smile was spread across his fleshy features but the small eyes looked watchful.

'I'm surprised you haven't gone with him.'

'His Majesty will be away for nearly two months. He wished me to remain in Lahore so I could report anything of which he needed to be aware.' Abul Fazl's smooth, reasonable tone and his even smoother smile never failed to set Salim on edge but for once he felt no compulsion to hide his feelings.

'I have just heard that my half-brother Murad has been appointed Governor of Malwa and Gujarat.'

'Indeed, Highness. He is to leave Lahore to take up his new position in a month's time.'

'That is the post I asked my father to give me. He told me he would think about it. What happened?'

Abul Fazl spread his hands. 'His Majesty can best answer that question. You know that he appoints all the governors of our provinces himself.'

'I can't ask him. As you yourself observed, he isn't here. That's why I'm asking you. You are his mouth and ears. I thought you knew everything.'

Salim's tone was contemptuous. Yet he could see that instead of being offended, Abul Fazl was battling with his vanity. It hurt the man to pretend he didn't know what was going on and it seemed he was prepared to lose that battle without too much of a struggle. His heavy-featured face eased into a smile. 'What I can say is that His Majesty decided that Prince Murad would be well suited to the post.'

'Better suited than me?' If the increasingly colourful stories circulating the court were true, Murad was often too drunk to stand unaided.

'I am sure Your Highness would also make an excellent governor,' said Abul Fazl, evading the question.

'Did my father ask your advice on the appointment?'

Abul Fazl hesitated a moment. 'As I said before, His Majesty takes such decisions himself. My role is simply to record them.'

'I don't believe you.'

'Highness?' Abul Fazl looked truly shocked. It occurred to Salim that over the many years the chronicler had served his father, they had almost never been alone together. The knowledge that Akbar was far from the court was liberating and Salim persisted with what he had started, not just the frustration of this latest matter of the governorship but the resentments and suspicions of years urging him on.

'I said that I don't believe you. My father consults you on everything and will have done so over appointing a governor in Malwa and Gujarat.'

Abul Fazl's smile faded. 'My discussions with your father are confidential. It would be a breach of trust for me to say more. You should know that, Highness.'

There was no unctuousness now in Abul Fazl's voice and for the first time Salim sensed how formidable this man was. But he would not be deterred. 'I know my father holds you in high esteem.'

'As I do him. I am his loyallest subject.' Abul Fazl's voice was steely.

'But shouldn't your loyalty extend to the rest of my father's family?' Salim seized Abul Fazl by the shoulders and stared him in the face. 'I am his eldest son, but ever since I began to grow up you've schemed to keep us apart. If it wasn't for you, my father would have invited me to the meetings of his war council as a matter of course. You encouraged him to exclude me. Don't deny it.'

Abul Fazl didn't flinch but replied in a level tone, looking Salim steadily in the eye, 'I have always given His Majesty the best advice I could. If you want to know the truth, he didn't invite you because he didn't think your presence would be useful. As he himself told me, you disappoint him.'

Salim let go of Abul Fazl. Those brief but brutal words wounded him more than any weapon could ever do. Hadn't he always feared he'd never live up to his father's expectations, however hard he tried . . . ? Suddenly, just as when Akbar announced he was going to bring up Khurram, Salim became aware of Abul Fazl's hungry scrutiny, as if he wanted to observe every painful emotion passing through him. He must not let Abul Fazl feed his fears, nor must he show him his comments had hurt. Pulling himself together, he said, 'You have always tried to create mischief between me and my father, and if you hadn't always been there at his side he and I would have got to understand one another better. You may be loyal to him, as you say, but only because that best serves your interests. Know this. I see you for what you are, and the day when my father sees it as well will be a good one.'

They were eyeing each other now like enemies on the battlefield, but Salim knew that to strike Abul Fazl would only strengthen the chronicler's position when he reported their confrontation to his father. Perhaps what he'd already said had been unwise but he couldn't regret it. From now on the chronicler might be more wary of the emperor's eldest son. As for himself, he would watch Abul Fazl to find some evidence of corruption and self-interest, and when he found it he would act. Turning on his heel, he walked quickly from the apartment out into the sunlit palace courtyard. Glancing back, he saw Abul Fazl watching him from the casement window.

Chapter 22

The Battlements of Agra

'What's the matter? You've been preoccupied all afternoon. I thought you'd have so much to tell me.'

'I have. Abul Fazl will soon be returning to court from the tour of inspection in Delhi my father sent him on,' said Salim to Suleiman Beg, as they rode slowly into the shallows of the Ravi river to allow the steaming horses they had just raced along its banks to cool off. Suleiman Beg had been with his father in the Punjab and they hadn't seen one another for some months.

'So what? You're obsessed with him.'

'I have good cause.'

'Just because he's ambitious and relishes being your father's confidant doesn't make him your enemy.'

'He fears me – and my brothers – as rivals, I'm sure of it. That's why he reports every fault, every indiscretion of Murad and Daniyal to my father – don't interrupt me, Suleiman Beg, I know he does. I've heard him do it.'

'Perhaps he regards it as his duty. Your brothers are idiots.'

'That's not the point. What matters is that he tries to damage me as well in my father's eyes.'

'He's never told your father about your argument with him . . . not in the whole two years since it happened, has he?'

'My father's never said anything. But maybe Abul Fazl thought it didn't reflect well on him either.'

'Or perhaps he's learned his lesson.'

'No. He still tries to exclude me from everything. You weren't at court when my father told me that having conquered Sind he intended to send a Moghul army to seize Kandahar.' Salim's horse lowered its head to drink the muddy river water and he gently stroked its sweat-mottled neck. 'I begged my father to let me go on the campaign as one of the commanders . . . I argued that I'd proved myself in Kashmir and deserved further opportunities. I even said it was a matter of family honour – we lost Kandahar to the Persians when my grandfather Humayun died and it was right that his eldest grandson should help win it back.'

'And?'

'He was so full of his victory in Sind I thought he was going to agree but then he said he wished to consult his war council. It was Abul Fazl who next day brought me my father's decision – that I lacked the experience for such a distant campaign. My father's message ended with the usual words – "don't be impatient". But I know whose message it really was.'

'You don't know that. Maybe your father was concerned for your safety.'

'Or maybe Abul Fazl didn't want me to share in the glory . . . Nearly every day post riders have been bringing reports of the successful advance of our troops, of how they have already subdued the Baluchi tribes infesting the mountain passes leading to Kandahar and are advancing on the city itself. Last night came a despatch from Abdul Rahman, my father's *khan-i-khanan*, that the Persian commander of Kandahar was about to surrender.'

'That's wonderful news. If it's true, it means your father has extended the empire's northern frontiers yet again . . . he now rules from Kandahar down to the Deccan in the south, from Bengal in the east to Sind in the west . . . Our forces are invincible. Who can challenge the Moghuls now?' But the enthusiasm on Suleiman Beg's face died as he took in Salim's bleak expression.

'It is good news, of course it is. My father is a great man – I

286

know it and everybody else keeps telling me it. He has raised our dynasty to heights known to no other. But it would have been even better if I could have had a share in the action instead of sitting around always hoping for a chance to prove myself that never comes . . .' So saying, Salim yanked his reins so hard his horse whinnied in protest. Then, wheeling his mount in the shallow water, he kicked sharply with his heels and without waiting for Suleiman Beg set off back towards the Lahore fort where his father was no doubt already beginning his meticulous planning of the grandiose celebrations he would hold to mark the capture of Kandahar. How could a man like Akbar, who from youth had known only success and glory, possibly understand the yawning emptiness, the futility of his own existence?

• ◆ •

It was May. In just a few days the monsoon would begin and the heat was intense as musicians playing long brass pipes and beating drums suspended on thongs round their necks led the procession from the *haram* quarters within the Lahore palace out into the city. Next marched the eight bodyguards assigned to guard Akbar's beloved grandson Khurram from the day of his birth. Then, mounted on matching cream-coloured ponies, came eight-year-old Khusrau and six-year-old Parvez, egrets' feathers nodding in their tightly bound silk turbans.

Standing with some of Akbar's most senior courtiers and commanders to the left-hand side of the carved sandstone entrance to the imperial school, Salim thought how serious his two elder sons looked, how stiffly they sat in their saddles. They weren't used to such ceremonials. Much as their grandfather loved them, he had never put on such a show to mark the start of their formal education which, in line with Moghul tradition for the rearing of royal princes, began at the age of four years, four months and four days – Khurram's exact age today. Beyond Khusrau and Parvez, Salim could see the baby elephant on which Khurram was riding and which Akbar himself was leading with a golden chain attached to the animal's jewelled headplate. Immediately behind came the captain of Akbar's

287

own bodyguard, carrying the yak's tail standard that since early times had been a symbol of Moghul rule.

Khurram himself was in an open howdah of beaten silver set with turquoises – a stone that Timur himself had loved to wear. A parasol of green silk embroidered with pearls and held aloft by the attendant riding behind him in the howdah protected him from the hot sunlight shafting down from a completely clear blue sky. Salim felt sweat running between his shoulder blades, though he too was protected by a silk canopy. But as the procession drew nearer, Salim realised that despite the heat his youngest son was relishing the occasion. Unlike his elder brothers he didn't seem to find his elaborate clothes – a gold brocade coat and green pantaloons – uncomfortable. Gems sparkled round his neck and on his fingers and in the tiny ceremonial dagger tucked into his sash. Though he looked like a little bejewelled doll he was clearly enjoying himself, smiling and looking anything but nervous, waving to the straining, cheering crowds being held back by soldiers.

A large red and blue Persian carpet had been spread out in front of the school steps. Some twenty paces away from them, the musicians fell silent and the procession divided to one side or the other leaving Akbar and Khurram on his baby elephant alone in front of the school. Akbar advanced to the very centre of the carpet, and after a quick glance at his grandson to assure himself that the boy was seated securely, addressed Salim and the assembled members of his court.

'I have invited you here to witness an important event. My beloved grandson Prince Khurram will today begin his education. I have assembled the best scholars from within my empire and beyond. They will instruct him in every subject from literature and mathematics to astronomy and the history of his forebears, and will guide him on the journey from boyhood to manhood.'

Yes, thought Salim, and they included Abul Fazl's father Shaikh Mubarak, who was to instruct Khurram about religion. Abul Fazl himself was standing just a few paces away, his usual leather-bound ledger beneath his right arm, doubtless ready to compose some florid verses about the occasion. As if aware of Salim's scrutiny, the chronicler returned his stare, then looked away again. Salim returned his attention to his father.

'The prince has already shown signs of exceptional ability,' Akbar was saying. 'My astrologers predict that he will achieve great things. Come, Khurram, it is time.'

He released the catches fastening the side of the howdah and lifted Khurram down. Then, taking the child by the hand, he walked slowly towards the high, arched entrance. As they passed within a few feet of Salim, Khurram gave him a quick smile but Akbar continued to look straight ahead. Another few moments and they had vanished inside. Salim tried to compose his thoughts. A father should be able to do things for his sons. He, not Akbar, should have taken Khurram to school on his first day, just as he had taken Khusrau and Parvez. He not Akbar should have chosen his son's tutors. But Akbar had robbed him of all that . . .

The familiar heaviness that always came when he thought about Khurram settled around his heart. He loved him but he didn't know him and perhaps never would. When the ties between parent and child were broken so early perhaps they could never be mended . . . Hamida had once told him that his great-grandfather Babur had been moved by his love for one wife to give her the child of another. Akbar had deprived him and Jodh Bai of their son as surely as Babur had robbed that mother of her child. For a moment he stared at the archway into the school, tempted to enter, but what would be the point? Akbar, he was pretty sure, didn't want him there. Khurram didn't need him.

'Highness, your other sons and the rest of the procession are about to return to the palace. Only your father's bodyguards are remaining here. Shall we go back?' Suleiman Beg's voice forced Salim back to the present. Like himself, his friend was sweating. The heat was becoming unbearable. Salim nodded. It would be good to return to the cool and shade of the palace and Jodh Bai would be eager to hear how well Khurram had conducted himself.

'Your father certainly knows how to put on a spectacle. The crowds were almost hysterical,' Suleiman Beg went on as, with Salim's own bodyguard behind them, and fanned by attendants wielding giant peacock-feather fans, they slowly retraced their steps.

'He likes to show the people his wealth and splendour. He thinks it makes them proud to be citizens of the Moghul empire – and proud to be his subjects.'

'He's right. Didn't you hear their shouts of "Allah Akbar"? They love him.'

'Yes.' Salim's head was beginning to ache and the sun's glare – so relentlessly bright – was hurting his eyes. Everyone loved Akbar. He began to walk more quickly, suddenly desperate to be back in his own apartments and alone with his thoughts.

•➤•

His father was sensible to have waited for the cool weather to return before making the journey south from Lahore to inspect the newly reconstructed fort at Agra, Salim reflected as, six months later, the imperial party rode on elephant-back up the steep, twisting ramp with its right-angled turns designed to slow down and frustrate attackers and through the fort's towering gateway, the great gates studded with spikes to wound any elephant which tried to batter them down. Akbar was on the leading elephant, Khurram as usual by his side.

'Majesty, you have surpassed yourself,' said Abul Fazl when they descended from their howdahs a few minutes later, gazing up at the seventy-foot-high sandstone battlements snaking a mile and a half around the reconstructed fort.

For once Abul Fazl wasn't exaggerating, Salim had to admit. Unlike Akbar, he hadn't visited the fort while the work had been under way but he had seen the plans drawn up by his father's architects and knew that Akbar had remodelled the Agra fort almost completely, strengthening its external defences, beautifying its interior and massively extending it to make it more imposing and imperial. The old building constructed by the Lodi dynasty and seized from them by Babur had been of brick as much as of sandstone. Akbar had used only sandstone, employing Hindu craftsmen to carve it just as he had at Fatehpur Sikri. New courtyards and gardens were enclosed by elegant colonnades. Over one hundred sandstone columns supported the roof of the new *durbar* hall.

'Well, Salim, what do you think?' Akbar was almost visibly swelling with pride as he looked about him.

'It's magnificent,' said Salim, doing no more than speak his thoughts. All around him the courtiers Akbar had brought with him from Lahore on this tour of inspection were also murmuring their admiration.

'So it should be, given the cost, but our coffers are deep. I could build a hundred such forts.' Akbar ran a hand over a carved frieze of narcissi and irises so delicate and detailed they appeared to be bending in the wind. 'What about you, Khurram? Do you think the builders have done well?'

Khurram's young eyes didn't look that impressed. 'They've just done what you told them to do, Grandfather.'

Akbar threw back his head and laughed. 'You are hard to please; that's not a bad thing in a prince. But I think I can impress even you.' Akbar stripped off his silk tunic and the fine muslin shirt beneath it. Despite his age, he was still magnificently muscled, his torso lean and hard as that of a man half his age. 'You two, come over here,' he shouted to two of the youngest of his bodyguards. They exchanged a startled look then hurried forward. 'Put down your weapons and strip off like me.'

The men hurriedly did as they were told. What was his father doing? wondered Salim. All around, people were staring at the emperor in astonishment, but Akbar was grinning. 'Now come over here so I can look at you properly.' As the two young men stood before him, Akbar ran his hands over their arms and shoulders, feeling their muscles. 'Not bad, but I wish I had chosen bigger stronger men.' Then, without warning, he punched the bigger of the two guards in the stomach. The youth gasped and doubled over, clutching himself and breathing in great, wheezy gasps. 'You need to toughen up. Where are you from?'

'Delhi, Majesty,' he managed to gulp out.

'If you were of the old Moghul clans you could have taken a blow twice as hard without flinching. Let me show you what I am made of.' Akbar lunged forward, grabbed the youth round the waist and shoving him under his left arm lifted him from the ground. Then, satisfied, he let the guard's feet touch the ground again. 'You, come to my other side,' he ordered the second youth, who a moment later was gripped tight by Akbar's right arm. Bracing his legs apart, Akbar took a deep breath and lifted both young men off the ground at once.

Khurram let out a delighted shriek, but Akbar hadn't finished. Lifting the men yet higher so that his arm muscles bulged and the veins stood out among the whitened battle scars, he began to run towards the battlements. 'What are you waiting for, Khurram?' he shouted over his shoulder. 'Come with me.' Khurram at once trotted after his grandfather. After a moment's hesitation Salim followed, his other sons and the rest of the courtiers close behind. Akbar had gone insane, he was thinking as he saw his father climb the flight of sandstone steps to the battlements, accidentally banging the head of one of the men he was clutching, and begin running along them.

Watching that dogged figure, Salim guessed what Akbar was intending to do – run the whole mile and a half. Sure enough, though running slowly, Akbar didn't falter until he had completed the entire circuit and descended to the courtyard once more. His breathing was ragged and sweat was pouring off his body as he released the two soldiers, one of whom indeed had a fine bruise on his forehead, but his expression was triumphant.

'Majesty, you still have the strength of your youth,' said Abul Fazl, who had followed Akbar round the battlements and was not as out of breath as Salim expected. He was fitter than he looked.

'Well, Khurram? What do you say now? Have I impressed you?'

The child nodded. 'You are the strongest man I know, Grandfather. Are you going to teach me how to hunt like you promised?'

'Of course. And more than that I am going to teach you how we make war. When you are just a little older you will attend the meetings of my war council and I will take you on campaign. I have created a great empire but all that will be for nothing if my descendants cannot make it greater still. Such an education cannot begin too early.'

Chapter 23

Pomegranate Blossom

Dusk had fallen on the eighth day of the Nauruz, the New Year festival which celebrated the sun's entry into Aries. In a few minutes the feasting would begin again in the palace courtyard, where servants were lighting candles and arranging cushions around low tables. Salim, already dressed for the evening's entertainment, eyed the scene without enthusiasm. The Nauruz was a Persian custom that Akbar had introduced into Hindustan. Apart from the emperor's birthday, it was the most lavish of all spectacles at a court where shows of opulence and extravagance were the rule, and his father attended to every detail himself.

Each day so far had brought camel races and elephant fights, singing and dancing, fireworks and acrobatics and the heaping of money and fresh honours on Akbar's loyal commanders and courtiers. Each night the emperor had been the guest of a different noble, but tonight was his own feast for his special favourites which must, of course, surpass all others. Guests would drink from jade cups inlaid with rubies and emeralds. Standing in the shadow of a sandstone column, Salim watched the fortunate few beginning to arrive, eyes lingering on the gleaming cups, doubtless calculating whether they would be allowed to keep them at the end of the evening's revelry. In the centre of the courtyard, on a dais draped with cloth of gold, stood the green velvet, pearl–embroidered canopy supported on silver poles beneath which Akbar himself would sit on a low throne.

The Nauruz was not a time of rest for the cooks. They had been busy since dawn. The rich, savoury aroma of roasting fowl and of whole sheep basted with a mixture of saffron, cloves, cumin seed and ghee as they turned on the spit was already filling the air. It wasn't long before three trumpet blasts announced the arrival of the emperor. Salim scrutinised the magnificent gold-clad figure moving through the ranks of courtiers as they bowed low before him, like a field of bright Kashmiri flowers bending to the wind. Not even Timur himself could have presented such an image. Tonight Akbar, the absolute ruler of all he surveyed, would sit alone in his magnificence on his dais. A table below and to the right had been prepared for Salim and his half-brother Daniyal. Abul Fazl and Abdul Rahman would sit at an identical table positioned symmetrically to the left.

Seeing that his father was now seated, Salim moved through the guests to take his place beside Daniyal. Akbar acknowledged him with a brief nod then returned his attention to a dish that his food taster had just presented to him. As always, his father ate sparingly. Salim had often heard him criticise commanders for getting soft and fat. 'With a belly like that you could never have ridden with my grandfather on his conquest of Hindustan, though the clan chiefs might have employed you as a jester,' he had recently rebuked a corpulent Tajik officer at least fifteen years his junior as he patted him on his round stomach. Akbar had been smiling, but Salim knew him well enough to know it wasn't a joke and sure enough the officer had soon been ordered to a remote outpost in Bengal where he would sweat off his fat among the swamps and mosquitoes.

Sometimes Salim watched Akbar as he exercised. Thrusting and parrying with a sword, bending his favourite bow of white poplar to shoot down a pigeon, or wrestling, he could still beat men half his age. Salim glanced at Daniyal, whose flushed and sweating face revealed he had not come to the feast entirely sober. His dilated pupils and foolish half-grin as he looked about him suggested he had also taken opium. Daniyal was weak, Salim thought. But as he saw his brother's shaking hands trying and failing to hold his drinking cup steady he felt some pity. He could understand the temptation.

Sometimes in his frustration he too drank to excess or found consolation in *bhang* – cannabis – or a few pellets of opium dissolved in rosewater. But those times were rare. He wanted to keep himself sharp in mind and body just in case his father should give him a military command or some other responsibility he craved.

Daniyal, though, seemed to have abandoned thoughts of anything but pleasure, while if the rumours from Malwa and Gujarat were true Murad was growing ever fonder of drinking and squandering his chance to impress his father in the post that Salim had so desired. Surely he had deserved the opportunity more, he thought. Why had his father and Abul Fazl deprived him of it? He was more of a man than his half-brothers and as much of a man as his father, despite all the latter's exercising. All he wanted was to prove himself so.

Salim's resentful eyes returned again and again to the glittering figure of Akbar as the feast progressed. Musicians from Gwalior, famed for their skill, were coaxing soft, haunting sounds from their flutes and their stringed instruments, the big-bellied *tanpura* and the two-bowl *rudra-vina*. Every few minutes a *qorchi* ushered forward a courtier wishing to present a Nauruz gift to the emperor. The attendants were bringing yet more food – almonds and pistachios wrapped in gold and silver leaf, pale green grapes and wedges of orange-fleshed musk melon resting on crushed ice from the fort's ice house where giant chunks carried by mules down the passes from the distant northern mountains were stored – and ewers of cool, scented sherbets. Salim looked up into the soft night sky and at the sliver of moon whose silvery light was far outshone by the mass of candles arranged around the courtyard. Sometimes these feasts could go on until dawn. He wondered how soon he would be able to slip away.

The musicians were putting down their instruments and bowing low before Akbar. It must be time for some other entertainment, thought Salim – fire-eaters or rope-climbers or perhaps a fight between wild beasts released into the same cage.

Akbar rose, and instantly a hush fell across the courtyard. 'Tonight is the high point of our Nauruz celebrations. Though we have already exchanged many gifts of jewels, I have one priceless gem

295

I wish for a short while to share with you. Two months ago, the Turkish sultan sent me a dancing girl of rare skill and beauty from Italy, a land far from our own. I have called her Anarkali, "Pomegranate Blossom".' He turned to the attendant at his side. 'Summon Anarkali.'

Even when Akbar had sat down, the silence continued as the guests waited, eyes bright with anticipation. Salim's own curiosity was whetted and he decided to remain for a while longer. He had only seen portraits of European women before, presented to his father by travellers. He had of course heard of Italy from the Jesuits, some of whom had been born there, but had learned little of its luxuries – or its women – from their ascetic sectarian discourses.

Glancing at his father, Salim saw a well-pleased, even self-satisfied smile curve his lips as he listened to the excited buzz of anticipation from his courtiers while attendants spread yet more carpets over the fine kilims already covering the courtyard. As soon as they were finished, other servants carrying gilt incense burners suspended from chains on their wrists began running round and round the courtyard, pale fragrant smoke trailing behind them until they had created such a cloud that Salim could barely make out his father on his dais. Suddenly, at a signal from Akbar, further attendants darted forward and extinguished all the candles. No one spoke in the soft scented darkness. Then, just as abruptly, the candelabras were again ablaze and there in the centre of the courtyard, amid the remaining wisps of smoke, stood Anarkali, wreathed in a long veil of semi-transparent gauze which emphasised rather than concealed the outline of her full breasts and opulent hips. Her head beneath the circlet of pearls securing the veil was erect.

She raised her arms and began to sway. No music accompanied the sinuous motion of her body, only the clash of her heavy bracelets and anklets. Her movements became freer and wilder. She began tossing her head from side to side and then started to spin, breasts swaying and bare feet stamping on the dark red carpet as she turned. Salim watched mesmerised, like all the guests. First one man, then another, began beating on the table before him with his fist. The noise grew thunderous as Anarkali whirled yet faster, arms outspread. Then with a cry she ripped the veil from her body.

There was a collective gasp. It was not just the perfection of her voluptuous body, naked except for her tight jewelled bodice and almost sheer muslin pantaloons. It was her hair. The colour of palest gold and falling to her waist, it flew out in a shimmering mass around her as she continued to whirl. Suddenly, dramatically, she stopped. She was smiling, fully aware of the sensation she had caused. Then, approaching the dais, she dropped slowly to her knees before Akbar and with two flicks of her head sent her glorious hair flying first forward over her breasts and then back. Arms outstretched towards the emperor, she leaned further and further backwards, arching her supple spine until her head touched the ground behind her.

In the flickering candlelight Salim was close enough to make out Anarkali's features. Her face was oval with a cleft chin and a small straight nose, and above them the most beautiful eyes he had ever seen — somewhere between dark blue and violet. He also saw his father's fond complacent gaze as it rested on his prized possession. Salim's own pulses were pounding and his mouth was dry. He must have Anarkali, he would have her . . .

• ◆ •

'Highness, the risk . . . Anarkali is at present your father's favourite concubine. Discovery would mean death beneath the elephant's foot or worse for me and for her. In the seven years I have been superintendent of your father's *haram* no one has ever asked such a thing of me.' The *khawajasara*, a small, beak-nosed woman, looked terrified. Salim could see a vein beating in her right temple beneath her thinning grey hair, but he could also see how tempted she was.

'Name your price. I'll give you whatever you ask.' Salim reached inside his tunic for a silk pouch hanging round his neck from a hide thong. Loosening it, he drew out a ruby. As he held it up to the light of an oil lamp burning in a niche in the small court behind the elephants' stables to which he had summoned the *khawajasara*, the uncut gem glowed. 'This is the pick of my jewels — a ruby of the first water worth one thousand gold *mohurs*. Do what I ask and

297

it is yours. You and your family will be wealthy for generations.'

'But how can I, Highness?' The *khawajasara* stared at the gem as if unable to tear her eyes away. 'Only the emperor can enter the imperial *haram*.'

'You are the superintendent and go to and from the *haram* all the time. You could smuggle Anarkali out disguised as your attendant. The guards will not suspect or challenge you.'

'Highness, I'm not sure . . ' the *khawajasara* said miserably. 'The emperor sends for her all the time . . .'

'Three days from now my father departs on a long hunting expedition. Bring her to me the first night he is away and the ruby is yours.' As Salim waited, he turned the gem so that its heart flashed like fire. The *khawajasara* bit her lip but then seemed to make up her mind.

'Very well, I will do as you ask.' Pulling her dark shawl over her head as she spoke, she immediately turned and hurried away, merging into the purple shadows, her bare feet padding away over the stone paving still warm from the day's heat.

• ◆ •

The time before Akbar's departure passed slowly. Salim could think of little but Anarkali — those violet eyes, that golden hair. She was like a jewel herself but one made of soft, living flesh, not hard stone. He half expected his father to change his plans but at dawn on the third morning he watched Akbar, accompanied by Abul Fazl and a few of his inner circle, ride through the palace gates to the deep booming of the gatehouse drums. He was planning to be away for three weeks and fifty bullock carts loaded with tents, cooking pots, chests of clothes, bows, arrows and muskets followed the procession of guards, huntsmen and beaters, raising a cloud of white dust that spiralled into the air long after the procession had wound out of the city and into the plains.

That night Salim waited in his apartments. The candles his attendants always lit at sunset — fetching the flame from the palace fire-pot, the *agingir* — were half melted and the palace had fallen still and quiet around him when, an hour after midnight, he at last heard a gentle knocking on the door.

'Highness.' It was one of his guards, face creased with the sleep from which he had just been roused. 'Two women are here.' Salim had told his men that he had summoned a girl from the bazaar. It was not the first time he had done so and they had not looked surprised.

'Send them in.'

Moments later, two heavily veiled women stood before him. The *khawajasara* at once uncovered her face and Salim saw sweat beading it. 'All went as it should, Highness. No one questioned me.'

'You've done well. Now leave us and return an hour before dawn.'

'My reward, Highness . . .'

Eyes fixed on the motionless figure of Anarkali, Salim pulled the pouch containing the ruby from his neck. 'Take it.'

He scarcely noticed as the *khawajasara* hastened from the room. Anarkali was wearing a plain black robe that was slightly too long for her so that the hem was coated with dust. The *khawajasara* had done well. Who would have guessed that such drab garments concealed his father's favourite concubine, the cherished companion of his most intimate moments?

'You sent for me, Highness?' Anarkali spoke in Persian that was oddly cadenced, but her voice was low and soft.

'Let me see your hair.'

Anarkali slowly pulled off her veil and let it float to the floor. Her golden hair was concealed beneath a tight-fitting black cap. Her eyes, the colour of amethysts in the faint candlelight and fringed by lashes darkened with kohl, looked straight into his with frank curiosity as she raised her arms to take off the cap and her hair, pale gold like corn in the moonlight, tumbled around her. Her smile told Salim, just as it had when she had been dancing, that she understood her power over men. Her confidence was deeply arousing.

'Since I saw you dance I've thought of nothing but you. I desire you.'

'If your father finds out he will be very angry with me.'

'I will tell him you were blameless – that it was all my doing. But you don't have to stay if you don't want to . . .'

299

'Your ardour flatters me. What woman in my situation would refuse a prince?'

Without waiting for Salim to say anything else Anarkali quickly undid the fastenings at the shoulder and waist of her ugly robe, and wriggled from it like a beautiful snake sloughing off its skin. Her flesh had a soft pearl-like sheen and her full, blue-veined breasts, tipped with pink, swayed a little as she came towards him. She took his hands and placed them on her silky, slender waist. Then, pressing herself yet closer so he could feel the hard tips of her nipples through his silk tunic, she ran his hands down over the rich swell of her hips and buttocks. Her skin felt just as he had imagined, warm and yielding. An uncontrollable shudder of virility ran through him and stepping back from her he began pulling off his own clothes, tearing the delicate fabric of his tunic in his haste.

'You have a warrior's body like your father, and are as quickly aroused . . .'

Salim barely heard her. He could think of nothing except burying himself in that glorious body. Taking Anarkali's hand he pulled her down on to a divan, kicking brocade cushions out of the way. Winding his hands in her long shining mass of hair, he kissed her mouth, then the velvet hollow between her breasts. He could scarcely believe the perfection of her from her delicate collarbones to the lush flesh of her rounded thighs. Sensing his urgency, she was already spreading her legs and arching her back. Her body beneath his felt slippery with sweat. 'Highness,' she was whispering, 'now . . . I am ready . . .' As Salim entered her and began to thrust, triumph and exultation surged through him – but it was not only the pleasure of taking a beautiful woman. It was taking a woman who belonged to his father.

• ◀▶ •

Salim couldn't sleep. The night seemed intolerably close and hot and the *punkah* swinging slowly back and forth over his bed barely disturbed the heavy air. Yet he knew what was really keeping him from sleep was his longing for Anarkali. The *khawajasara* had brought the Venetian to him on two subsequent nights before his father's return to Lahore but since then he had not seen her.

300

Why did she fascinate him so much? It was a hard question to answer, but he knew it was more than her beauty, more than the fact that she was his father's concubine, though both added spice. There was a spirit, a self-reliance about her, perhaps the result of her strange, turbulent life. She had told him how, when she was a young girl, pirates had attacked the ship on which she was sailing off the coast of north Africa with her merchant father, whose throat they had slit. They had taken her captive and she had been sold in the slave markets of Istanbul to a Turkish brothel owner who had had her instructed in the arts of love-making. Carefully preserving her virginity, he had sold her at the age of fifteen for a great price to a nobleman who had presented her to the Sultan. That had been four years ago.

When Salim asked whether she still thought of her homeland, Anarkali had shrugged. 'It seems long ago. I cry when I think of my poor father's fate but had we stayed in Venice who knows what my life would have been – probably a loveless marriage to some rich old man of my father's choosing. He already had such a plan. Now I live in luxury. I have jewels that would amaze the wealthiest Venetian noblewomen.' For a moment a shadow had crossed her face, but then she had smiled at him. 'And tonight a young prince strong as a stallion shares my bed – how could I be sad?'

Such smoothly flattering words came easily to Anarkali, thought Salim as sleep continued to elude him. All during their love-making she had praised his vigour and the pleasure he gave her, told him he was the greatest lover she had ever had. That everything she said must be artificial, that she probably had no real feelings for him at all, didn't dim his passion for her. That was how she had been trained and how she had survived. But perhaps at this very moment she was whispering the same words to Akbar . . .

Salim sat up. He had come to a decision. He would have Anarkali again. There must be a way and he would find it.

• ◆ •

'There is an old sandstone pavilion hidden away in thick undergrowth on the bank of the Ravi river. It's only half a mile from here. I sometimes rest in its shade while out snipe hunting. Look . . .' Salim scratched a map with charcoal on a piece of paper. 'Bring Anarkali to me there tonight while my father is with the members of the *ulama*. He will hardly call for her to dance before his mullahs.'

'Your meeting must be brief. Anarkali cannot be long gone from the *haram* while the emperor is here. And, Highness . . . this must be the last time. I cannot keep taking such risks . . . the danger is too great for us all.' The *khawajasara*'s sharp nose was almost twitching with anxiety.

Salim nodded, though in his heart he had no intention of allowing it to be the last time. He would find other ways to outwit Akbar. 'Take this. And mind you do not fail me.' He pressed a bag of gold coins into her hand. 'I will be waiting for you.'

That night, as velvet shadows stole along the riverbank, Salim pushed his way through the dry rustling reeds towards the pavilion. It must have been beautiful once. Slender columns and a shattered dome lay on the dry earth and, as he lit an oil lamp, the carving on a tumbled block of stone seemed to come to life. It was of a Hindu goddess or dancing girl, naked except for her jewels, voluptuous limbs moving in some joyful dance. It made him think of Anarkali's sleek, full body and the many positions it could assume, and his pulses quickened.

He sat down with his back against a piece of masonry and waited, listening to the rippling of the Ravi. Some small creature – a mouse perhaps – skittered over his boot-clad feet and he slapped at a mosquito as he felt its sharp bite on the side of his neck. Glancing up he saw the moon had risen. It was nearly full, casting a warm, apricot glow over the night sky, and it meant that time was passing. He strained his ears, hoping to hear a soft footfall along the riverbank, but there was nothing. Perhaps something had happened, or the *khawajasara*'s courage had finally deserted her, but he wouldn't give up yet, Salim thought. He continued to sit there, enjoying the beauty of the night and anticipating the moment when he would again bury his face beween those soft breasts. Even if the *khawajasara* had changed her mind about bringing Anarkali to him tonight he knew he could talk her round . . .

Then beyond the thick reed beds he made out a flickering light – a torch perhaps – and smiled. It was a little reckless of the *khawajasara* – surely there was enough moonlight to guide her steps – but she had never been to the pavilion before and was perhaps afraid of getting lost. Salim rose and peered harder in the direction of the light. He would go to find them. But as he picked his way out of the ruins and began pushing through the surrounding undergrowth he suddenly saw the light of several torches moving towards him. Almost simultaneously he caught the sound of male voices and of swift-moving feet crashing through the dry reeds.

What was happening? Had he been betrayed . . . ? Feeling for the dagger in his sash, Salim turned, ready to sprint off into the darkness, but found a familiar figure blocking his way.

'Highness, your father requests that you return at once to the palace.' Abul Fazl's small eyes glittered like jet in the light of the torch held by one of the guards who had just arrived behind him.

Shocked, Salim stood motionless. For once Abul Fazl wasn't bothering to disguise his feelings and Salim had never seen him so joyously triumphant. He struggled to find words to express his hatred and contempt for this man but it was Abul Fazl who spoke again.

'Highness, do you remember something you once said to me? I believe it was "I see you for what you are, and the day when my father sees it as well will be a good one." Now it seems it will be the other way round. Your father is about to see you for what *you* are . . .'

· ◆ ·

'Summon the whore.' High on his throne, dressed in robes of such deep purple they were almost black, Akbar's face as he looked down on his assembled courtiers was mask-like. Not by the flicker of a muscle did he acknowledge the presence of Salim, standing bareheaded below the dais and still dressed in the clothes in which he had gone to his rendezvous with Anarkali.

'Father, let me speak . . .'

'How dare you address me as Father when your actions show nothing but contempt for our relationship. Be silent or I will have you silenced.' Akbar's voice was full of pent-up fury.

A few minutes later, through the double doors of the audience chamber, Anarkali appeared, pushed into the room by two bulky female *haram* guards. Her hands were bound and her yellow hair streamed over her shoulders. Her face was white except where kohl had mingled with her tears to leave dark tracks. Salim could see how violently she was trembling as she advanced slowly towards Akbar and threw herself on her knees before him.

'You were my concubine, my favourite. I gave you everything you could desire yet you betrayed me as your emperor and as a man by giving yourself to this wretch who calls himself my son. There is only one penalty – death.'

Anarkali's face contorted with fear and horror. A convulsive shudder ran through her as she tried to scramble to her feet. One of the female gaurds pushed her down again, jabbing her viciously in the small of the back with the end of her long wooden staff.

'Please, Majesty . . .'

'My ears are deaf to your pleas. I have decided your punishment. You will be placed in a small cell in the palace dungeons, which will then be bricked up. As minutes turn to hours, hours to days, and death draws near, you will have time to contemplate your crime.'

'No! It was my fault, not hers. I desired her and bribed the *khawajasara* to bring her to me,' Salim burst out.

'I know,' said Akbar, at last turning his gaze on Salim. 'How do you think I learned of your despicable acts? The *khawajasara* herself came to Abul Fazl earlier tonight and confessed everything. I have been merciful to her . . . she died quickly. But this woman whom you are trying to defend has broken every rule of the imperial *haram*. She is lucky I do not have her flayed alive and her skin nailed to the palace gates.' Akbar motioned to the captain of the guard. 'Take her away.'

Two guards seized Anarkali, who began screaming and clutching at the carpet with her bound hands as if hoping that somehow she could cling on to it and delay the dreadful punishment Akbar had decreed. Salim looked away, unable to bear the sight of the beauty that had so tempted him and now as a consequence was to be destroyed. The knowledge that there was nothing he could do or say to save her overwhelmed him. Only when Anarkali's screams had finally receded and the doors had closed behind her did Salim again look up at his father. How cold he seemed, sitting there all-powerful on his glittering throne. What fate was he about to pronounce on his eldest son? Would his father take his life? For a moment Salim could almost feel the bite of cold steel on the back of his neck. He had always thought of his father, despite his faults, as honourable and just, but his terrible revenge on Anarkali had shaken that belief. Wronged as a man, he had lashed out as a man.

'Salim, as you yourself have admitted, you are the guiltiest of all.' After a pause, Akbar continued, 'How can I ever again trust a son who betrays me in such a way? Your life is worthless to me and to the Moghul empire.'

Salim felt as if his throat was constricting but if he was to die he must not show fear, so he tried to match his father stare for stare.

'You are still young and, unlike you, I place some value on our shared blood. My own mother has pleaded for you so I will be merciful. Tomorrow, you will set out for Kabul on an imperial inspection and there you will stay until I am ready to recall you. Your wives, your children and the rest of your household will remain here. Now go from my presence before I regret my mercy.'

'You're jealous of me because I am young and you are getting old. You cannot admit that you are mortal and fear that one day I will take your place on your throne as well as with your women,' Salim wanted to shout, but what was the point? Turning on his heel, he walked slowly away down the carpet that was still marked by the tracks of Anarkali's dragging feet. Was this the end of all his ambitions – if not of his life?

Chapter 24

The Indus

Driving rain lashed the roof of Salim's large tent as he tossed and turned beneath his fine cotton sheets and embroidered woollen Kashmiri blankets. His sleep was troubled as it had so often been since leaving Lahore some weeks earlier. Once more, Anarkali's lovely face swam before him, warm, vital and alive. Except that by now she would be dead. As he watched, her face seemed to tauten and her skin to shrivel away, exposing her skull, which slowly crumbled to dust, leaving only two bright blue eyes to gaze on him reproachfully for a moment before they also dissolved into the darkness.

Salim woke with a start, clutching at his bedclothes. Guilt at Anarkali's fate still weighed on him like a stone, exacerbated by his realisation after many sleepless nights that she had simply been an intoxicating plaything whom it had flattered his vanity to steal from Akbar. Perhaps if he had truly loved her his actions would seem less despicable to him. But he had carelessly and greedily helped himself to Anarkali, another human being, with no more thought than if he'd been plucking the ripest mango from the tree or the most tempting sweetmeat from the dish. Among his few comforts in his restless hours had been that – at least according to the message that had reached him from Hamida three days after he had ridden out from Lahore – Anarkali would not have suffered for long. His resourceful grandmother had written that she had found a way of smuggling a phial of poison to her as he had begged her to. He hoped this was true and that his grandmother was not merely seeking to console him.

The enormity of what had happened and its consequences swept over him once more. His melancholy thoughts turned to his own position, hundreds of miles from his family and the centre of power at the court, and on his way to banishment beyond the Khyber Pass at the very edge of the Moghul empire. Not only had he caused Anarkali's death by his lustful provoking of his father but there was little chance now that he would fulfil Shaikh Salim Chishti's prophecy that one day he would become emperor. Surely all his hopes and expectations were dust . . . If his half-brothers had even a shred of ambition they would be able to profit from his absence to promote their claims to Akbar above his. And what if his father were to die suddenly? Abul Fazl and his cronies would have settled the succession before news of his father's death had even reached him.

As the howling wind began to buffet and bow the heavy fabric of his tent Salim, in an effort to distract himself from such depressing thoughts, started to plan his onward journey. Yesterday he and his three hundred and fifty men had crossed the cold churning waters of the Indus at Attock. A young pack elephant had panicked when the raft on which it was standing had collided with another in midstream. It had tumbled in and the strong currents had carried it away, still trumpeting in terror, together with its load of precious cooking equipment. Yet despite the dangers the remainder of the party had crossed safely to the north bank.

It had been purple dusk when the last raft had been secured and unloaded. The wind had already been pushing rain clouds across the sky as he had given the order to make camp immediately among the mud banks and sandy hillocks bordering the great river. Today he would allow his men, tired by the strenuous river crossing, to sleep later than usual before breaking their makeshift camp to begin the next stage of their journey into exile – on to Peshawar and the entrance to the Khyber Pass, places familiar to him only through the tales of his grandmother and those commanders who had served in the region.

Salim's eyelids were feeling heavy, but just as he began to fall asleep a scream brought him to instant wakefulness. Was it simply some animal meeting its death in the teeth of a predator or was it human? Moments later another cry followed by a shout of 'To arms' banished all doubt. His camp was under attack.

Salim flung aside his bedding and was quickly on his feet, struggling into his clothes and grabbing a Persian sword strengthened on either side of the steel blade with gold-inlaid languets that had been a parting gift from Hamida. As he emerged from his tent some of his bodyguards were staring out into the darkness. Others were clustered, with torches guttering in the wind and rain, bending over two of their companions. One was crying pitifully as he clawed at the arrow protruding from his abdomen. The other was still.

'Extinguish those torches,' yelled Salim. 'They only serve to make you targets. More of you will be hit. Try to accustom your eyes to the darkness.'

His instructions were too late for a third guard who was struck in the back by another hail of arrows and collapsed, heels kicking convulsively, into the mud. The torches were quickly doused in some of the puddles.

'Where are Zahed Butt and Suleiman Beg?'

'I'm here, Highness,' shouted Zahed Butt, the captain of his guard.

'Me too,' called Suleiman Beg, ducking out of a neighbouring tent and buckling on his sword as he did so. All the time, other men were running up, splashing through the mud and glancing nervously around as they pulled on the last pieces of their equipment.

'What's happening? Which direction did the arrows come from?' demanded Salim.

'The arrows are coming from the east, from along the riverbank, but it's impossible to tell the enemy's strength. I've already sent some of the sentries who were guarding your tent to investigate . . .' said Zahed Butt, but before he could finish speaking two more volleys of arrows crashed into the centre of the camp through the murk and rain. As if in direct contradiction of his words, one came from the west and the other from the north. Another man fell, hit in the back of his left thigh by what could only be a lucky shot. In the wind and the darkness accuracy was impossible.

Questions raced through Salim's mind. The unknown, unseen enemy was attempting to surround his camp. Why? If they were mere dacoits wouldn't they sneak directly towards the baggage wagons and horse lines to make off with what plunder they could before escaping back into the night as quickly as possible? Could he himself be the target of the attack? Salim shuddered. Was it beyond belief that Abul Fazl, with or without his father's consent, should have sent orders for him to meet with an 'accident', just as had befallen Bairam Khan earlier in Akbar's reign?

Whatever the case, his men were looking to him for orders and they must not look in vain. Thinking quickly, he commanded, 'Let us push a new perimeter outward from here to make contact with the enemy or with any of our pickets who survive. We mustn't lose touch with each other, so it is every man's responsibility to keep his comrade on the right in view. I will lead the centre towards the baggage and horse lines. You, Suleiman Beg, command in the east while you, Zahed Butt, take the west. Make as little noise as possible.'

Quickly Salim's men sorted themselves into a rough line and drawing their weapons began to fan outwards. The two ends of the line hurried to make contact with the riverbank but the centre, led by Salim, proceeded more slowly as they slipped and scrambled up and over mud banks which suddenly loomed from the darkness in front of them. As Salim breasted the top of one large bank, his foot caught on something soft – the body of one of his sentries, sprawled face downwards. Salim stumbled and in trying to steady himself lost his balance completely and fell backwards, arms flailing, to land awkwardly in the mud. His fall probably saved his life, because as he struggled to get up arrows hissed through the air two feet above him and the men who had been on either side of him and were now on the crest were hit, one to fall forward with a strangled cry down the bank in the direction the arrows came from, the other to slump to his knees with a shaft in his shoulder.

Salim grabbed that man and pulled him down behind the mud bank. 'Take cover,' he shouted to the rest of his troops. But a great battle cry from the darkness drowned his words and suddenly assailants were rushing at his men all along the line. One giant of a man threw himself at Salim, sword outstretched. Salim parried his lunge then seized his sword arm and dragged him down on to the slope of the bank. Rolling over and over, the two men slipped down to its base. The giant had lost his weapon but was grasping with his great hands for Salim's throat. However, Salim had retained his grip on his Persian sword and as thick fingers tightened on his windpipe he thrust the blade deep into his enemy's side. Almost instantly he felt warm blood ooze from his assailant whose grip relaxed. Quickly heaving the weight of the dying body off him Salim got back to his feet, clutching his bruised throat and gasping for breath.

Everywhere the fighting was fierce and hand-to-hand. Looking up, Salim saw just to his left and above him on the top of the mud bank a tall man, obviously a commander, waving a scimitar to urge more of the enemy into the attack. Yanking a foot-long serrated throwing dagger from his belt, Salim took careful aim, pulled back his arm and sent the knife whirling end over end through the damp air towards the officer who, seeing it at the last moment, tried to dodge aside, only for it to catch him a glancing blow to the flesh of his upper left arm. Undaunted, he rushed headlong down the mud bank towards Salim, slashing with his curved sword as he came and parting the air just in front of Salim's face as he in turn leapt backwards. As the officer's impetus carried him onwards, Salim stuck out his foot to trip him and he sprawled head first into the mud. Gripping the hilt of his Persian sword with both hands, Salim brought it down vertically into the nape of his opponent's neck, killing him instantly.

Twisting out his sword and in the process severing the officer's head, Salim paused only to grab the man's scimitar to replace his throwing dagger. Then, a weapon in each hand, he ran towards where, in the growing grey light of dawn, he saw one of his Rajput bodyguards trying to hold off two attackers. Flinging himself forward, his Persian sword stretched out like a lance before him, he stabbed the first of the men in the fleshy part of his buttocks. Turning, the wounded man slashed wildly with his knife at Salim, ripping the sleeve of his tunic and grazing his right forearm. Salim swung the scimitar in

311

his left hand. Although it was a clumsy stroke with the wrong hand with an unfamiliar weapon, the scimitar's balance was good and its blade sharp. It bit deep into the man's side and he collapsed, to be finished off by the Rajput who had in the meantime disposed of his other opponent.

By now, many of the attackers were turning to flee, and as he scrambled to the top of one of the mud banks Salim saw that some of them were heading for the horse lines about a hundred yards away, where the first arrivals were already desperately trying to cut through ropes to steal mounts to hasten their flight.

'Follow me! We must drive our enemies away from the horses to prevent as many of them escaping as we can,' shouted Salim as he slipped and skidded down the steep mud bank and ran, legs pumping, through the puddles towards the long lines of horses.

Seeing him approach, a short, stocky, purple-turbaned man who had already cut the tether of a black and white horse and was struggling to sever the rope hobbling its front legs, pulled his double bow from his shoulder, fitted an arrow to the string and fired. The arrow missed Salim by inches. As the man fumbled with nervous fingers to fit another, Salim was almost upon him, but before he could grab him to grapple him to the ground he threw aside his bow and ducked beneath the horse's belly. Salim thrust at him with his sword as he went but missed.

Spooked by the noise and commotion around it, the horse skittered in fright. Suddenly the hobble on its front legs, already half cut through, snapped. Immediately the animal reared up on its hind legs, front legs lashing out wildly. One flailing hoof caught the purple-turbaned man in the pit of his stomach and he fell doubled up, only to receive another hoofblow to the back of his head which knocked off his turban, fractured his skull and left him unconscious and bleeding heavily. A quick glance showed Salim that his opponent's life was ebbing and he posed no further threat. Taking care to avoid the flailing hooves, he succeeded in grabbing the black and white horse's halter. Holding on to its threshing head with one hand and stroking its neck with the other, he spoke softly to the animal which quickly calmed. After what could have been no more than a minute or two Salim was able to scramble on to its back.

Guiding the animal as best as he could with his hands, knees and feet, he urged it after a group of his enemies riding bareback like himself towards a range of low hills two or three miles away. He was quickly joined by a dozen of his bodyguards. At first they seemed to be making no headway in closing the gap between them and their hard-galloping opponents, but then one of the leading riders' horses slipped slightly as it jumped a small stream. Since the rider had no saddle or reins it was enough to propel him over the horse's head on to the ground, where he rolled over and over. Instead of galloping on, at a shouted command from another of the foremost riders – who appeared to be the leader of the little force of no more than eight or nine men – they wheeled their mounts as best they could to attempt to rescue their fallen comrade before confronting Salim and their other pursuers.

The leader drew his sword and kicked his mount – a chestnut – towards Salim. As the two riders closed, each swung his sword at the other. Both missed and they strove to bring their mounts round in a wide circle to face each other again. Both succeeded in making the turn, and this time as they passed Salim flung himself from his horse's back and managed to pull his opponent from his mount. The two men hit the earth with a thump and the impact sent their swords flying from their hands. Salim tasted blood as he bit his tongue.

However, they quickly staggered to their feet and closed, wrestling each other. As they swayed to and fro, struggling for advantage, Salim's unknown enemy tried to pull a small dagger from his belt. Salim head-butted him hard. The man's nose broke with a satisfying crunch and he went reeling backwards. While he was still dazed, Salim grabbed the hand in which the man was still gripping the knife and with a quick twist of his wrist sent it spinning from his grasp. Then he punched him twice in his already bleeding face, splitting his lip and knocking out a tooth before kicking him with his booted foot in the groin with all the force he could muster. As his opponent doubled up, Salim brought both fists down on the back of his neck, knocking him to the ground once more. Glancing round quickly, Salim retrieved his Persian sword and held it to his anguished opponent's throat. As he did so, he saw that most of the retreating enemy riders were down or had surrendered. As far as he could make out through the bloody mess of his face, his enemy was a young man. 'Who are you?' Salim asked, stepping back a pace or two and half lowering his sword. 'And why did you attack my camp?'

'I am Hassan, the eldest son of the Raja of Galdid,' he answered, spitting out pieces of broken tooth as he did so. 'I attacked your camp because I knew that it must contain some important Moghul dignitary and I wanted to take him hostage.'

'Why?'

'To trade for my father who is imprisoned in the fortress of Murzad.'

'For what crime?'

'For loyalty to Sikaudar Shah, the rightful claimant to the throne of Hindustan. After Sikaudar Shah's death at Moghul hands, my father still refused to accept alien Moghul rule . . .' Hassan paused to wipe his bloody mouth and nose with the back of his hand before continuing, 'He took to the hills, living the life of a nomadic raider. For decades he survived, if he didn't prosper. But six weeks ago he was lured into a trap by the local Moghul commander and captured.'

'Couldn't you see your father's resistance was futile?'

'I knew it and I said so, but he is my father. I owe him my existence and my loyalty – however wrong-headed he is – just as I owed it to him to attempt to secure his release as best I could.'

'His story is true, Highness,' said Zahed Butt, who had just ridden up. 'I have many relations in this region and the family is well known.'

'Highness?' queried Hassan through a froth of blood. 'Who are you?'

'You really don't know, do you? I am Salim, son of the Emperor Akbar.'

Hearing these words Hassan reacted instantly, twisting and scrabbling towards where his knife still lay on the ground about ten feet away. Before he had covered half the distance, Salim thrust his sharp Persian sword deep into his side, sliding between his ribs. Blood spurted on to the wet ground and moments later Hassan, the loyal son, was dead. Salim was left to continue his journey into the exile inflicted by his own father for his disrespect.

• ◆ •

Snow was falling. Though it was only the first week of October, winter seemed to have come early to the lonely rocky passes south-east of Kabul. Soon the snow would block any return to Hindustan, Salim thought, even in the unlikely event that his father should relent. The previous evening a young Afghani wounded at the skirmish on the Indus had suffered frostbite in his left foot after his leg had been immobilised in a splint to allow a fracture to heal. The man – a native of Kabul – had been a fool to insist on continuing towards his homeland rather than remaining in Peshawar to recuperate. However, he had persuaded the *hakims* to use an old Afghan remedy and pack warm animal dung round the frostbitten member. Much to Salim's and the *hakims'* surprise it seemed to be working. The foot had seemed less white and blotched a few hours later.

Salim's emerald-green face cloth slipped for a moment and the bitter wind nipped his own exposed flesh. Despite his thick, *pustin,* sheepskin jacket, he felt chilled to the core and Suleiman Beg's lips looked blue with cold beneath the luxuriant dark moustache he had grown over the past weeks, of which he was inordinately proud. Snow was beginning to fall thickly now, the flakes whipping around them. The head of Salim's grey horse went down as its forelegs slipped on the frozen ground, almost unseating him. Leaning back in the saddle he pulled hard at the reins and the weary animal managed to right itself just as Salim caught what he thought was the sound of hoofbeats ahead.

'Halt. I heard something. Zahed Butt, take a detachment forward to investigate,' he yelled to the captain of his guard. 'Order the rest of the column to take up defensive positions around the baggage wagons.'

'Who do you think it is?' Suleiman Beg asked.

'I don't know, but we can't take any risks.'

As Zahed Butt cantered off into the snow at the head of a dozen soldiers, Salim frowned. Lawless bands infested these passes but surely even they might baulk at attacking an imperial force increased to five hundred well-armed men by the addition of recruits from the clans around Peshawar. War was these clansmen's trade. All were well mounted on shaggy-haired ponies bred to withstand the winter conditions, and well armed. Most carried long-barrelled muskets strapped to their saddles beside their lances. He checked his own weapons – his Persian sword and two daggers, one a throwing weapon, all slung round his waist, and a double battleaxe strapped to his saddle. A *qorchi* was carrying his musket and his bow and arrows, though in the blinding blizzard gun and bow alike would be almost useless with only fleeting indistinct shadows to aim at.

The wind was growing fiercer, howling down the narrow pass. Salim's shivering horse whinnied its discomfort and, lowering its head once more, pressed closer to Suleiman Beg's mount. Salim tightened his grip on the reins again. If anything was amiss ahead he must be ready – better prepared to meet an attack than on the Indus . . . Anxious minutes passed as he peered into the whiteness, straining his eyes and ears for any sight or sound which might betray what lay ahead. Then, above the wind, he thought he faintly made out three short blasts of a trumpet – the agreed signal that all was well. A minute or two later he heard them again, nearer and more distinct, and soon afterwards his soldiers re-emerged from the whirling snow. As they drew closer, Salim saw about a dozen newcomers riding close behind them.

'Highness.' Zahed Butt trotted up, his bushy beard and his sheepskin cap alike crusted with snow and his breath rising in frosty spirals. 'Saif Khan, the Governor of Kabul, has sent an escort to guide you on the final stages of your journey.'

Salim's shoulders dropped as he relaxed. His long ride into exile was nearly ended.

Chapter 25

The Treasurer of Kabul

The citadel's massive walls — at least ten feet thick in most places — were a good defence against the winter storms that had continued unabated since Salim's arrival in Kabul two days ago, and a fire of crackling *khanjak* logs was burning in the hearth, now and then spitting showers of red-gold sparks. All the same Salim felt chilled to his very bones. He drew closer to the fire to warm his hands as he waited for Saif Khan, who had gone to give instructions to his steward, to return.

While attendants piled yet more wood on the fire, Salim turned his head to gaze at the low platform at the far end of the long room and the throne which stood on it. Its red velvet cushions were faded and its gilded feet and high curved back a little tarnished. In the distant Moghul palaces of Lahore or Fatehpur Sikri far beyond the frozen passes such a shabby item would be unthinkable, but Salim looked at it with respect. This was where his great-grandfather, the future first Moghul emperor, had sat as the King of Kabul to dispense justice. Perhaps it was from this very seat that he had announced his intention to invade Hindustan and claim it for the Moghuls. In the flickering light of torches in sconces high on the rough stone walls, Salim could almost conjure an image of Babur deep in thought, his sword Alamgir at his waist. If Babur could leave Kabul to satisfy his ambitions perhaps it was still possible for his great-grandson to do the same and fulfil the Sufi seer's prophecy, Salim comforted himself. Just as soon as these snows eased he would visit Babur's grave in its hillside garden above Kabul . . .

The bejewelled luxury of the Moghul palaces of Hindustan with their intricately carved sandstone, scented fountains and elaborate ritual seemed separated by more than distance from this stark stronghold where Babur had nurtured his plans of conquest. Of course, the Kabul citadel, perched on a rocky promontory above the town, had never been intended as a palace to impress the cultured. It had been built to awe the local tribes and to control the trade routes. Kabul's wealth depended on the vast, swaying caravans that passed through each year with their cargos of jewels, sugar, cloth and spices, and that wealth must be protected. Even now, the Kabul revenues were important to the Moghul treasury.

'Forgive me, Highness, for leaving you alone.' Saif Khan returned with a swish of his fox-lined robes. He was a stout, genial-looking middle-aged man, though a long white scar on his left cheek and some ragged frills of shiny, pinkish flesh where his left ear had been would have shown he was a fighter even if Salim hadn't known of his years of campaigns on the empire's frontiers which had led his father to appoint him governor. 'If you will allow me, I would like to introduce the other members of my council to you.'

'Of course.'

Saif Khan whispered to an attendant who at once went to the door and ushered in the six counsellors. The governor introduced each in turn – the master-of-horse, the chief quartermaster, the commander of the garrison . . . As they bowed, Salim surveyed them with only polite interest. But then Saif Khan uttered a name that made him pay more attention. 'This is Ghiyas Beg, Treasurer of Kabul.' Ghiyas Beg . . . where had he heard that name before? Salim stared at the tall, angular man bending before him. As the man raised his head again and Salim looked into his fine-boned face – less starved than when he had last seen it but still gaunt – the years rolled back. He was a boy again, listening transfixed in Fatehpur Sikri to Ghiyas Beg standing before Akbar and telling his tale of his desperate flight from Persia, of how he had nearly abandoned his newborn daughter beneath a tree . . .

'I remember when you came to Fatehpur Sikri, Ghiyas Beg.'

'I am honoured.'

'How are your family?'

'All in good health, Highness. The mountain air of Kabul has been good for them.'

'Including your daughter?' Salim was struggling to remember her name. 'Mehrunissa, I think you called her?'

'Indeed, Highness. Mehrunissa, "Sun Among Women". She is well.'

'You've clearly prospered here. My father sent you to Kabul as an assistant but now you are the treasurer,' Salim said, and continued a little awkwardly: 'He has sent me to Kabul to satisfy myself that it is being properly governed and in particular that all the revenues are being correctly accounted for and sent to the imperial treasuries.'

'I will stake my life that not a single *shahrukki* has gone astray.'

'I am glad to hear it, but I will still need to inspect your records.'

'Of course, Highness. I can bring my ledgers here, or if you prefer, when these storms ease, perhaps you would honour my home with a visit?'

'I will.'

When Salim was alone with the governor once more he stared for a while into the flames. Something about Ghiyas Beg intrigued him, just as it had the first time he had seen him. The smooth words falling so effortlessly from his tongue could have been spoken by any courtier. However, Salim hadn't missed the look on Ghiyas Beg's face when he had questioned him about the revenues. The Persian seemed deeply protective of his honour . . . or was he being suspiciously over-vehement in his protestations of injured innocence?

Something his grandmother had once said about strange patterns in life – and about Ghiyas Beg in particular – came back to him. Hadn't she predicted that the Persian might one day become important to the Moghuls? But the question was how? For better or for worse? Looking up, he found Saif Khan watching him curiously. What was he thinking? That here was the wayward son of the emperor, sent to Kabul as punishment for his sins? He must know the tour of inspection was a mere pretence and that Salim had left the court in the deepest disgrace. Gossip travelled quickly even if Abul Fazl hadn't written to Saif Khan as Salim was sure he had, perhaps even instructed him to provide reports on his behaviour. To cover his confusion he asked, 'Tell me more about Ghiyas Beg. Is he as good and honest a treasurer as he claims?'

'The emperor has no better servant in Kabul. He has improved the way in which tolls are levied on the caravans and also the gathering of taxes from the towns and villages. During the five years that I have been governor, he has increased income by nearly a half.'

Perhaps Ghiyas Beg was as guileless as he had appeared today and in his original audience before Akbar all those years ago, Salim thought. He realised too there was nothing to be gained from continuing his inner debate about whether he was reporting on Saif Khan's conduct or the other way round. He must behave as a conscientious inspector of the collection of his father's taxes and the administration of his province. That would be his only hope of securing a return to Akbar's favour.

• ◆ •

The snow had ceased and a temporary thaw meant that the battlements of the citadel were no longer covered in ice when Salim rode down the ramp, outriders ahead and Zahed Butt and his bodyguard close behind. He had invited Suleiman Beg to go with him to Ghiyas Beg's house in the town below but his milk-brother had laughingly asked to be excused on the grounds that he had no head for figures.

A chill wind was driving small, fleecy white clouds across a pale blue winter sky as Salim approached the town walls. Beyond, smoke was rising from the caravanserais where only a few hardy travellers were billeted. When winter was over and all the passes were open again, Kabul would be teeming and walking its streets a man might hear twenty, perhaps thirty, different languages, or so Saif Khan had told him. Unlike Suleiman Beg, Saif Khan had been eager to accompany Salim, as he always was wherever he wanted to go, but Salim was suspicious of Saif Khan's motives. Was he trying to keep an eye on him? In any case, he was weary of the governor and his repetitive stories and crude jokes. He would see Ghiyas Beg alone.

Ghiyas Beg's house was a large two-storey building occupying one side of a tree-shaded square. The treasurer, turbaned in green silk and flanked by attendants, was waiting outside to greet him and Salim saw that a length of purple velvet had been spread from the marble block where he was to alight over the puddles on the thawing ground to the doors of polished chestnut wood that led into the house.

'Highness, you are welcome.' Ghiyas Beg waved away a groom and himself held Salim's right stirrup as he dismounted. 'Please follow me.'

Signalling his bodyguard and the other soldiers to remain outside, Salim accompanied Ghiyas Beg through the doors and across a courtyard into a large, luxuriously furnished chamber in which two braziers of coals were glowing. Cream brocade hangings covered the walls while bolsters and cushions of sapphire-blue velvet were set against them. The carpets were soft, thick and richly coloured, better than any in the citadel – in fact, the best Salim had seen since leaving his father's palace in Lahore.

'You live well,' he said. The magnificence of Ghiyas Beg's residence had reignited his doubts. Even if he was the best tax collector Saif Khan had ever seen, was Ghiyas Beg still creaming off some of the revenue for himself?

'I am glad you like my home. I've tried to furnish it the way my house in Persia was, importing painted and patterned tiles and so forth. So many caravans pass through Kabul, a man can find or order anything. Please, take some refreshment. The grapes grown around Kabul make good wine – almost as good as the red wines of Ghazni to the south – or perhaps some rose-flavoured sherbet? My wife is skilled at distilling the fragrance of the roses she grows so that even in the harshest months of winter we can be reminded that the summer warmth will return.'

'Thank you. Some sherbet.'

An attendant knelt before Salim with a bowl of water in which to rinse his hands and a scented towel on which to dry them while another poured some sherbet into a silver cup. Salim took the cup and drank. Ghiyas Beg was right. The sherbet indeed tasted and smelled of roses and of summer.

'I have the ledgers ready, Highness. What do you want to examine first? The caravan revenues or the village taxes?'

'A little later,' said Salim, deciding to draw Ghiyas Beg out and thus perhaps to catch him off his guard. 'First tell me about your life here. I'm curious.'

'About what aspect, Highness?'

'You are a cultured, educated man. How do you manage to live in such a place as Kabul? What possible satisfaction or interest can you find in its squabbling tribes, its blood feuds and its greedy merchants?'

'A man can find interest in anything if he sets his mind to it. And remember, Highness, I've cause to be grateful even to be in such a remote place as this. When your father sent me and my family here, he rescued us from penury and gave us hope. This may not be Isfahan or Lahore, but I have worked hard, tried to do my duty, and I have prospered. The emperor pays his servants well. By now I am wealthy enough to take my family back to Persia but my loyalty is to your father and I will stay here for as long as I can serve him well. Perhaps one day he will remember me and appoint me to a post in one of his great cities – Delhi or Agra, maybe.'

Ghiyas Beg seemed almost too good to be true, thought Salim. 'And if not?' he asked.

'I am content. When a man has seen death reaching out for himself and his family and escapes, he learns to be thankful for what he has and not to make himself unhappy by yearning for what he cannot have. That is a lesson to us all, Highness, whatever our station in life.'

Salim started. Ghiyas Beg wasn't referring to his own position, was he? The treasurer's expression remained respectful. In any case, he himself could never be that patient and philosophic, Salim thought. Every time an imperial post rider clattered up the ramp into the Kabul citadel, his leather satchel bulging with letters and despatches, he hoped that one was from his father recalling him to court, but so far he had received not one word from Akbar. The only official letters to him had been from Abul Fazl asking nitpicking questions about his reports on subjects such as the state of Kabul's defences or the condition of the road to Kandahar.

'Please try one of these sweetmeats. In Persia it is traditional to offer them to our guests. My wife made them from almonds and honey with her own hands.'

'You have only one wife?'

'She is like a part of me. I need no other.'

'You are a lucky man. Few can say that,' said Salim, thinking how much Ghiyas Beg's words reminded him of his grandmother's description of her marriage to his grandfather, Humayun. 'But doesn't your wife long to return to Persia?'

'She feels as I do that we should be content with our lot. God has been merciful.'

Salim stared at the treasurer, impressed despite himself by the man's quiet dignity and patience and again recalling Hamida and how she had often told him that their troubles had only strengthened the bonds between herself and Humayun. He could only wish that his own ties with any of his wives were so strong. But he reminded himself he had come to Ghiyas Beg's house to question him about how he carried out his responsibilities, not about his private life.

'Bring me your ledgers, Ghiyas Beg, and explain in detail how you levy the toll on the caravans that pass through Kabul. Saif Khan told me that you have made some improvements . . .'

• ◆ •

The warm night air was pungent with the smell of dung fires, spices and baking bread as the citizens of Kabul prepared their evening meal on the flat roofs of the houses Salim passed on his way through the streets. Over recent weeks as spring had blossomed he had been so many times to Ghiyas Beg's house that his grey stallion could probably find its way there blindfolded. 'What do you and that old man find to talk about? You spend more time with him than I ever did with my father,' Suleiman Beg had asked earlier that day, just as he had on many previous occasions. He was amazed that Salim sometimes preferred the Persian's company to the chance to hunt wild asses or go hawking in the hills around Kabul.

It was something Salim could not quite explain, even to himself. In Ghiyas Beg he had discovered a cultured, civilised man – a man of ideas and spiritual depth who, he sensed, felt as imprisoned and unfulfilled as he did but, unlike himself, could still find contentment. His visits to his house no longer had anything to do with checking that the treasurer was efficient and honest and indeed a great asset to his father. Ghiyas Beg had quickly proved his records accurate, and that his luxuriously furnished house had been financed by the salary due to his rank and a few trading ventures he had engaged in over the years. However, the two men had found, despite the disparity in their ages, that they shared many interests, from the natural world to the changing style of miniature painting under influences from Persia and Europe.

Tonight, however, was different. It was the first time Ghiyas Beg had invited Salim to dine at his house. Emerging from a street so narrow that the upper storeys of the timber-framed mud-brick houses on each side almost touched, Salim saw that the square where the treasurer lived was ablaze with light. Lanterns of coloured glass – red, green, blue and yellow – swayed from the boughs of budding almond and apricot trees. On either side of the entrance to the house stood giant candelabras four feet high in which burned a mass of candles. Crystals of golden frankincense smouldered in jewelled incense burners.

Ghiyas Beg was, as usual, waiting to greet him, dressed more magnificently than Salim had ever seen him. His silk robe was embroidered with flowers and butterflies and from a gold chain round his lean waist hung an ivory-hilted dagger in a coral and turquoise inlaid scabbard. On his head was a tall velvet cap like those worn by the envoys from the Shah of Persia Salim remembered seeing at Akbar's court.

'Greetings, Highness. Please follow me to where we will eat.'

Salim followed his host through the courtyard, the walls of which were covered with tiles painted with cream and mauve flowers, and down a passage leading into a second, smaller courtyard spread with

324

rugs. A silk canopy had been erected against one wall, beneath which was a low divan piled with cushions. As Salim seated himself Ghiyas Beg clapped his hands and at once servants appeared, some bringing water for Salim to rinse his hands while others spread a white damask cloth over which they sprinkled dried rose petals.

'I have had dishes prepared from my Persian homeland. I hope you will like them,' Ghiyas Beg said.

The food was some of the most delicious Salim had ever eaten. Pheasants simmered in a pomegranate sauce, lamb stuffed with apricots and pistachios, rice spiced with long golden strands of saffron and sprinkled with pomegranate seeds bright as rubies, hot wafer-thin bread to dip into pastes of smoked and pounded aubergines and chickpeas. Ghiyas Beg's attendants kept his glass filled with wine from the Khwaja Khawan Said region of Kabul, celebrated for its fire and flavour.

Salim noticed that the treasurer himself ate and drank sparingly and said little except to acknowledge Salim's frequent compliments. But when the dishes had been cleared away and grapes, musk melons and silvered almonds laid before them, Ghiyas Beg said, 'Highness, I have a favour to request. May I present my wife to you?'

'Of course,' Salim replied, realising how great a compliment this was to their friendship. Usually only male relations met the women of the household. He had been wondering whether Ghiyas Beg's wife and daughter had been watching through the fretted wooden screen he could see high in the wall opposite where he was sitting.

'You are gracious, Highness.' Ghiyas Beg whispered to an attendant, who hastened away. A few minutes later, a tall slight figure entered the courtyard through an arched doorway. She was veiled, but above the gauzy material Salim saw a pair of fine eyes and a wide, smooth forehead. She was obviously younger than Ghiyas Beg who, as she touched her hand to her breast and briefly bowed her head, said, 'Highness, this is Asmat, my wife.'

'I thank you for your hospitality, Asmat. I have not tasted better food since coming to Kabul.'

'You do us great honour, Highness. Many years ago your father the emperor saved our family from poverty, perhaps worse. I am glad to repay even a tiny portion of the debt we owe you.' She spoke court Persian as elegantly as her husband, in a voice both musical and low.

'My father acquired a good and loyal servant when he sent your husband here. There is no debt.'

Asmat looked towards her husband. 'Highness, we have another request. May our daughter Mehrunissa dance for you? Her teachers, who have trained her in the Persian style, say that she is not unskilled.'

'Certainly.' Salim lay back against the cushions and took another sip of the dark red wine. He would be intrigued to see this girl who had been abandoned beneath a tree to the jackals and the elements.

A trio of musicians – two drummers and a flautist – entered the courtyard. The drummers at once struck up a compelling rhythm, and as the piper put his instrument to his lips a languorous melody issued from it. Then came a tinkling of bells keeping perfect time with the musicians and Mehrunissa ran into the courtyard. Like her mother she was veiled but above the veil her eyes were as large and lustrous as Asmat's. She was wearing a loose robe of blue silk the colour of a kingfisher's wing. As she raised her arms and began to revolve, Salim saw that in each hand she was holding a golden ring hung with tiny silver bells.

For a moment a vision of the last woman to dance before him – Anarkali – swam before him, bringing with it the sense of shame and regret her memory still conjured. But Mehrunissa's dance was unlike anything Salim had ever seen in Hindustan, slow, graceful and controlled. Every gesture of her slender hands and fingers, the way she held her head, the stately sway of her body beneath the blue silk, the beat of her henna-painted feet on the ground, compelled attention. Salim leaned forward as the music grew louder. Mehrunissa flung back her head as if filled with the joy of the dance and then quite suddenly the music ceased and she was kneeling decorously at his feet.

'That is one of the shah's favourite dances, celebrating the coming of spring,' said Ghiyas Beg, face soft with pride.

'You are as gifted a dancer as your father said. Please rise.'

326

Mehrunissa got gracefully to her feet, but as she reached to push back a stray lock of shining black hair she caught a corner of her veil and it fell away, exposing her full mouth, a small straight nose and the soft curve of her cheeks. For a moment she looked straight into Salim's eyes before quickly refastening her veil.

· ◆ ·

'You only saw her for a few moments.'

'It was enough, Suleiman Beg.'

'Perhaps you haven't had a woman for a while.'

Salim glared at his milk-brother. Since leaving Lahore and his wives and *haram*, the memory of Anarkali's tumbling golden hair and voluptuous body – all that beauty to which he had brought such ruin – had curbed his desire, it was true, but his abstinence had certainly not been total and wasn't why he felt like this.

'Are you sure it's not because for some unfathomable reason you like her father? You think her mind might be like his and her body female perfection.' Suleiman Beg smiled and cracked a walnut between his teeth, flinging the shell out of the open casement in Salim's apartments overlooking the courtyard. 'What's really so special about her?'

'Everything. The way she moved – her grace. She was like a queen.'

'Big breasts?'

'She's not a whore from the bazaars.'

'Then I repeat my question because I just don't understand. From what you say, a veiled woman did a brief dance for you and all of a sudden your loins are on fire . . .'

'I saw her face. Suleiman Beg, it reminds me of how my grandmother speaks of Humayun's feelings when he first saw her. There was something about it . . . I can't get her out of my mind.'

'I thought you said she was veiled.'

'For a moment her veil slipped.'

'That was clever of her.'

'What do you mean?'

'She's the daughter of a petty official living in an outpost of your

327

empire.' Suleiman Beg spat a tough piece of nut on to the floor but Salim knew it was Kabul he'd really like to spit on. Suleiman Beg was bored here and couldn't wait to return to Hindustan. 'That was her chance to catch your eye. Much better to be an imperial concubine than left to fester here.'

Perhaps Suleiman Beg was right, Salim thought. In his mind's eye he recaptured that moment when her veil had slipped. Had it been by design? And had she delayed raising it again just long enough for him to see her face? If so, then all to the good. It meant she wanted him too. He stood up. 'I don't desire her merely as a concubine. I wish her to be my wife.'

Dusk was falling when an attendant brought Salim word that Ghiyas Beg had come to the citadel. As soon as the Persian was shown into his apartment, Salim said eagerly, 'Ghiyas Beg, I summoned you here not as your prince but – or so I hope – as your future son–in–law. I want to marry your daughter. Give me Mehrunissa and I will make her first among my wives and first in my heart.'

Ghiyas Beg's eyes widened. Instead of the smiles Salim had anticipated, he looked agitated.

'What is it, Ghiyas Beg?'

'Highness, what you ask is impossible.'

'I don't understand . . . I thought you would welcome my offer.'

'I do, Highness. It is a great honour, an unimaginable honour. But I must repeat what I said. It is out of the question.'

'Why?' Without realising what he was doing Salim stepped forward and grabbed Ghiyas Beg's thin arm above the elbow.

'My daughter is already promised.'

'To whom?'

'To one of your father's commanders in Bengal, Sher Afghan. As a man of honour, I cannot break off their betrothal. I am truly sorry, Highness.'

Chapter 26

Oblivion

'Highness, a letter has arrived for you from Lahore.'

Salim's *qorchi* handed him a green leather pouch secured by a twist of gold wire from which the imperial seal was dangling. Inside, Salim found a thick piece of paper folded into four and opened it to see Abul Fazl's familiar handwriting – lines and lines of it. As usual, it was only towards the bottom of the page after all the empty airy courtesies that Salim found the real meat of what his father's chronicler had to say:

His gracious Majesty the emperor, in his great and fathomless mercy commands you to return immediately to Lahore where he has fresh tasks he wishes you to undertake. He asks me to say that he hopes that from this time forward your footsteps will return to the path of righteousness and you will become a dutiful son who will never again deviate in the manner that has so distressed and disappointed him.

Salim handed the letter to Suleiman Beg, who grinned broadly as he read it. 'I was afraid we might be stuck here for years.'

'It's typical that the style and even the seals are Abul Fazl's and not my father's. Nevertheless, I didn't expect to be recalled after only eight months. I'm surprised.'

'You might look more cheerful about it. You're not still obsessed with that Persian girl, are you? When you get back to your wives and *haram* you'll realise she was no more than a passing fancy because you were bored.'

Salim considered. How did he really feel? His relationship – friendship even – with Ghiyas Beg had made his stay in Kabul much less irksome than it might have been, and after seeing Mehrunissa she had occupied his mind as much as thoughts of returning to court. But since Ghiyas Beg's rejection of his offer of marriage to her a constraint had inevitably sprung up between them. Salim's visits to the Persian's house had grown less frequent and of course he had not seen Mehrunissa again. He had, however, discovered that she was not due to wed Sher Afghan until the following year. Perhaps back in Lahore he could persuade his father to use his influence with Ghiyas Beg. If the emperor himself commanded Mehrunissa's betrothal to be broken off, Ghiyas Beg as a loyal subject could only obey . . .

• ◆ •

The long journey back down through the passes from Kabul, across the Indus and the other mighty rivers of the Punjab, had gone swiftly and well, and unencumbered by a slow baggage train Salim had reached Lahore in only six weeks. At each passing mile his spirits had risen with the heat of the plains around him. However, as he stood in Akbar's private apartments, alone before his father for the first time since his banishment, Salim felt himself trembling with a mixture of apprehension and hope.

'I am glad to see you safely returned from Kabul.' Akbar spoke first, his face inscrutable. 'I regret that we parted in anger but you left me no choice but to punish you. I hope that during your absence you reflected on the duty that a son owes to his father and that in future you will behave accordingly.'

What about the duty a father owes to his son, thought Salim, but all he said was, 'I know what is due to you and I am grateful that you have forgiven me my past errors and recalled me to the court.'

'Your errors were grave. I had intended you to stay longer in

Kabul, but your grandmother persuaded me to send for you.' Akbar's tone was still stiff.

'Father, Abul Fazl's letter mentioned you had further tasks for me. I am eager to serve you . . . I . . .'

'In due course,' Akbar interrupted him. 'You acquitted yourself well in Kabul – Abul Fazl tells me your reports were thorough and Saif Khan confirmed your good behaviour – but I have not decided what I wish you to do next.'

So Saif Khan had indeed been spying on him. Salim persisted, 'A governorship perhaps, like Murad?'

'There is no need for haste. I wish to see whether you maintain your good conduct, and I will tell you my decision about any appointment if and when the time comes.'

Salim tried not to show his disappointment but knew it must be written on his face. He had been hoping his return could mark a new beginning in his relationship with his father, but yet again it seemed he would have to be patient. Perhaps his grandmother would again use her influence on his behalf as she had to hasten his return. However, even if this was not the ideal time, there was something else he could not delay in asking Akbar, and he must ask in person.

'Father, may I request a favour?'

'What is it?' Akbar looked genuinely surprised.

'I wish to take a further wife.'

'Who?' Akbar's expression was now one of absolute astonishment.

'The daughter of Ghiyas Beg, your treasurer in Kabul,' Salim said, and before Akbar could respond continued, 'but there is a difficulty. She is already promised to one of your commanders in Bengal, Sher Afghan, and Ghiyas Beg believes it would be dishonourable to go back on the arrangement. But if you intervened, Ghiyas Beg and Sher Afghan would have to obey you and . . .'

'Enough! I had hoped that your months in exile would have taught you some sense, but I see I was wrong. It is bad enough that you want to marry a woman of obscure family – an alliance that can bring no possible benefit to our dynasty – but it beggars belief that you can then ask me to interfere in the lives of my subjects to bring it to pass.'

'It's not a passing whim. Her name is Mehrunissa. I can't get her from my mind.'

'You will have to. I will not disrupt the marriage plans of Sher Afghan, a loyal, brave fighter, so you can satisfy your insatiable lusts.'

'It's not lust . . .'

'Really? It seems to me you have developed a taste for other men's women.' Akbar's tone was brutal and his reference to Anarkali stung. Salim swallowed. What could he say in his defence that Akbar would believe? If he compared his passion to Humayun's on first seeing Hamida, as he had so often done in his own mind, it would only enrage his father.

After a moment's painful silence Akbar said wearily, 'Leave me. You make me despair. I had hoped our reunion would be happier but I can see you have not conquered your vices. You still need to learn self-control. Young as he is, your son Khurram understands the difference between right and wrong better than you.'

As Salim walked swiftly from his father's apartments tears of anger and hurt pricked his eyelids. Akbar never tried to understand him and seemingly never would. His father did, however, choose his words carefully for their effect. Was his reference to Khurram a hint that his own son was better qualified to rule than he was? Surely not . . . however well omened his birth, Khurram was no more than a precocious child.

 • ◆ •

Salim opened the painted wooden box, took out a glass jar and held it up to the light with hands that were not quite steady. Good. There were enough opium pellets to last him until morning. Flipping up the jar's silver lid, Salim tipped two pellets into a goblet then poured in some rosewater. He smiled as he watched the pellets dissolve, unleashing their smoky grey trail until only a few stubborn granules remained. He swirled the water with his index finger then raised the goblet to his lips. After a few minutes, feeling the opium begin to do its wonderful work, he took another few swallows of the strong red wine he had been drinking all day.

That felt even better. Salim lay back on a silk-covered mattress

332

by the balustrade enclosing the balcony of his apartments. The sounds of horses' hooves and men's voices rising from the courtyard below seemed to come from farther and farther away as he closed his eyes and gave himself up to the delicious languor that in recent weeks had become increasingly necessary to his well-being. It was an antidote both to his father's cold equivocation whenever he asked about an appointment and to his sons' discomfort and embarrassment whenever he broached any topic other than the most banal with them. They had changed towards him while he had been away. Though they were unfailingly polite, he sensed no warmth or intimacy.

Neither his mother Hirabai nor his grandmother Hamida had had anything constructive to offer either. His mother had voiced only contempt for Akbar and the Moghuls in general. Hamida, however sympathetic and loving her tone, had only had kind words of consolation and the advice to wait. She had reiterated how much his affair with Anarkali had hurt Akbar and how much he detested the thought that it would be the subject of common gossip among the people and damage the image they had of him as all-powerful. Consequently she had had great difficulty in securing Akbar's agreement to his return from banishment so she could do no more for the present.

The opium and the wine relaxed Salim's mind and body. They blunted painful thoughts, soothed his aching disappointments and transported him to places where nothing seemed to matter much. He felt a small insect crawl over his naked chest but the effort it would require to crush it seemed too great. Live, little creature, whatever you are, he thought and laughed softly. He readjusted his position. The soft, warm silk of the mattress felt wonderful – like the skin of a woman. Perhaps later he would go to the *haram* and make love to Man Bai or Jodh Bai, though that also seemed too much effort, particularly since they too had scarcely seemed wholehearted in their welcome to him. In fact, when he thought about it he realised he hadn't seen any of his wives or indeed his sons for days. But why should he when he was so content just lying here? For a second, Mehrunissa's striking face was before him. But Suleiman Beg was probably right. She was just another woman . . .

Still, it would be nice to have some company here, someone to share the shadowy, delightful twilight that was enveloping him. Suleiman Beg stubbornly refused his every invitation to join him. Even at the start when he'd begun experimenting with just a pellet or two, his milk-brother would not be tempted. Indeed, he'd even shown his disapproval . . . Perhaps he should invite his half-brothers Daniyal and Murad? Murad had returned to Lahore a month ago, recalled by Akbar from his governorship for having had the envoy of an important vassal flogged for showing disrespect.

Murad had probably done nothing wrong, Salim mused, despite the stories that he had been drunk when he ordered the flogging. It was just that their father was impossible to please where his sons were concerned. Even had they been perfection in every way they would never have been able to live up to his expectations, his standards and his overwhelming confidence, bolstered by his years of unbroken success, that there was only one way to do things – his. It was typical that instead of sending himself or Daniyal to replace Murad as governor, Akbar had appointed a nephew of the toadying Abul Fazl. A second insect – it felt a little larger this time – was running up Salim's arm. This time he didn't grudge the exertion but crushed it, feeling liquid ooze from its scaly body. Pity it wasn't Abul Fazl, he thought. How much fat could be squeezed from his corpulent frame? Then he closed his eyes and let his mind drift blissfully away.

Waking with a start, Salim saw that the sky above was dark and pricked with stars that seemed to be spiralling across the heavens. His head was throbbing and his mouth was so dry his tongue was sticking to his palate. Putting one hand on the stone balustrade, Salim hauled himself slowly to his feet. His legs, in fact his whole body, were trembling. He couldn't be cold. It was May, just before the monsoon rains – the hottest time of the year. This had happened to him before but he knew how to remedy it. Clearly he'd not taken enough opium. Dropping to his knees he crawled across the shadowy balcony, which was lit only by a single oil lamp, groping for the wooden box. Where was it? Panic surged through him. What would he do if he couldn't find it? He must have some more opium quickly.

334

Then he remembered he had attendants . . . tens of them. One shout would bring them running to his assistance from the corridor outside his apartments where he had ordered them to remain. But it was all right . . . here was the box.

Reaching inside he found the jar, tipped the remaining pellets into his mouth and tried to swallow them but they stuck in his dry gullet – he'd forgotten to dissolve them. He felt himself choking and tried to spit the pellets out again, but they were too firmly lodged. Fighting for breath and peering desperately into the darkness he set out on hands and knees once more, trying to find the ewer of rosewater or the bottle of wine or even one of the brass bowls of marigold petals that stood on the balcony – anything with liquid in it. Just when he thought he was about to black out he felt the cold metal of the ewer. In his haste to grab it, he knocked it over. Bending forward he greedily lapped the water from the floor and at last managed to swallow the pellets down. He could hear a harsh, ragged rasping and it was some moments before he realised it was his own breathing.

Crawling slowly back towards the mattress, he lay down again, arms folded across his chest, hands tucked beneath his armpits, anything to try to get warm. But it was no good, he couldn't stop shivering. Then he realised what it was – it wasn't cold but fear. The darkness was filled with strange and terrible creatures. He could see them whirling around him trying to get close, to stupefy him with their fetid breath and steal him away to the dank, earthy graves they inhabited. He must get away before it was too late . . . Somehow he managed to drag himself to his knees but then everything went black . . .

'Salim . . . Salim . . .' Someone was wiping his face with a cool damp cloth but he twisted away. Suppose it was one of those creatures? 'Stop fighting. It's me, Suleiman Beg . . .' Salim felt a strong hand holding him down as the wiping resumed. Forcing his eyes open, he groaned as agonisingly bright sunlight hit them and clenched the lids shut again.

'Drink this, now!' Someone was none too gently forcing his mouth open and he felt the rim of something metal against his lower lip. Then his head was being tipped back and water was gushing down his throat. He felt he was drowning, but there was no mercy till at last he heard the clang of the metal cup as it was flung to the floor and rolled away.

Opening his eyes again, this time Salim managed to keep them open and found himself staring up into Suleiman Beg's face. He had never seen his milk-brother so concerned or so strained. Salim sat up and tried to speak but couldn't harness his body to do what he wanted. His lips wouldn't move. He tried again and this time managed a little better, getting as far as 'I feel' before, suddenly and violently, a bitter, viscous fluid shot from his mouth. Ashamed, he turned aside from his friend and continued to retch on the floor until at last there was nothing left and his ribs felt as if he'd cracked them. 'I'm sorry . . .'

'What are you apologising for? Being sick or the fact that you nearly killed yourself?'

'What . . . what . . . do you mean? All I did was take opium . . .'

'How much?'

'I don't know . . .'

'And wine as well?'

Salim nodded. Putting a hand to his right temple, he found it sticky with congealed blood.

'You struck your head on the stone balustrade. Look, there's blood on it where you must have fallen against it,' said Suleiman Beg, pointing at the red-brown smears.

Salim slowly shook his throbbing head. 'I don't remember anything about that . . . All I recall is wanting more opium and not being able to find it . . . then I was choking . . .'

'Your *qorchi* heard a crash. You'd forbidden him to enter your apartments so he came to find me. I found you sprawled on the balcony, shivering and shaking and bleeding . . . I covered you with blankets and staunched your wound. Salim, you were lucky . . .'

He stared at Suleiman Beg, trying to take in what he was saying, but he was starting to feel sick again.

'I've been trying to warn you for weeks. Isn't it enough to see the state your half-brothers are in? But you've descended faster, lower and more determinedly than even they've managed. You act irrationally. You lose your temper suddenly and violently. I heard you shouting at Khusrau a few days ago for no reason at all and saw how he looked at you. You're alienating everyone around you.' Suleiman Beg sounded really angry.

Salim remained silent, still fighting down the bile that was threatening to rise in his throat.

'Why, Salim? Why do you do it?'

'Isn't the question why not?' Salim replied at last. 'At least opium and wine make me happy. I made a mistake about the quantity last night, that's all. In future I'll be more careful.'

'You haven't answered my question. Why are you setting out to ruin yourself?'

'My father has no regard for me. My life has no purpose. Murad and Daniyal have the right idea. Why not enjoy myself and forget the rest?'

'What do you mean by "the rest"? Your health, your sons, the future of your dynasty that used to matter so much to you? It's the wine and the opium speaking, not you. Have the strength and courage to give them up and then see how you feel.'

Salim scrutinised Suleiman Beg's flushed, earnest face. 'I disappoint you, I know. Just as I disappoint my father. I'm sorry.'

'Don't be sorry – do something about it. It's a good thing your father's been away on an inspection of Delhi and Agra and hasn't seen you in this state . . . You've got four weeks before he returns to Lahore. Use that time to cure yourself. You say your father despises you – well, don't give him reason to.'

'You're a good friend, Suleiman Beg . . . I know you mean well but you don't understand how hard it is. My youth's passing – my energies and talents are being wasted . . .'

'Don't lose faith. You've told me so often what Shaikh Salim Chishti said to you . . . that you wouldn't have an easy life . . . that he didn't envy you . . . but that one day everything you wanted would be yours. You should remember that. The Sufi was a wise man and your behaviour shames his memory.'

Salim could find no answer to what his milk-brother had said.

337

'And you shame me, Suleiman Beg,' he replied at last. 'You are right. I mustn't let self-pity destroy me. I will try to give up opium and drink, at least for a while, but I will need your help . . .'

'Of course. The first thing is to consult a *hakim*. I have already summoned one – a discreet man who is waiting outside.'

'You were very sure you could convince me . . .'

'No, but I hoped I could.'

Half an hour later the *hakim* had finished pulling back Salim's eyelids, checking the colour of his tongue and scraping it with a thin metal spatula, taking his pulse and running his hands over his body and back. During the examination he had said little but had looked increasingly concerned.

'Highness,' he said, closing up the leather bag in which he carried his instruments, 'I won't hide the truth from you. You tell me that last night you took a very large amount of opium. I can see that from your dilated eyes. But I can also tell that you drink to excess. You must give up both strong drink and opium, Highness, or you will become very ill. You might even die. Even now your hands are shaking.'

'No!' Salim held them out in front of him. He would show the *hakim*. But the doctor was right. They were trembling, his right hand worse than the left. However hard he tried, he couldn't control the tremors.

'Don't despair, Highness. We are in time and you are young and strong. But you must do exactly as I say. Will you put yourself in my hands?'

'How long will it take?'

'That depends on you, Highness.'

◆

Salim and Suleiman Beg were galloping along the banks of the Ravi beneath a pale November sun. Behind rode Salim's huntsmen, every man looking cheerful at the prospect of a good day's sport ahead. Suddenly a snipe flew out of the tall brown rushes. Salim rose in his stirrups and almost in a single movement reached for an arrow, fitted it to his double bow and fired. His hands were steady now and the snipe fell from the sky, wings fluttering futilely. It was six months since the night he had collapsed – six difficult months, particularly at first when his resolution had often faltered and he had returned to the twin consolations of opium and wine. However, he had struggled hard. Even now he occasionally lapsed, usually when his father had been particularly arrogant or dismissive . . . But as he replaced his bow Salim vowed he would be strong, whatever the future held, whatever disappointments and setbacks he might suffer.

Part VI

Seizer of the World

Chapter 27

A Jute Sack

'I now know my father will never give me any post of real responsibility even though, like my grandfather and my great-grandfather before him, he was emperor when he was half my age.' Pulling the ornamental dagger that hung at his waist from its scabbard, Salim stabbed at the pink silk brocade cover of the divan on which he was lounging in the late afternoon heat in the fortress-palace at Lahore. The blade had been blunted, but even so the dagger cut through the delicate cloth and penetrated the cotton padding. 'I've waited and waited and to what point? Absolutely none! No command, no governorship, no prospect of anything. Rarely even a kind word. What am I to do?' he demanded of Suleiman Beg, who was lying propped on one arm on an adjacent couch, a glass of mango juice in his other hand. 'I'm not sure,' said Suleiman Beg thoughtfully. Then, taking another sip of juice, he continued, 'But in matters of succession I've often heard it said that time and patience are the key.'

'Although he's in his late fifties, my father's health has never been better if that's what you mean. I'm not even sure he's mortal – the way he guards his power and gives no thought to his successor makes me think he at least does not recognise his mortality. Age just seems to confirm him in his belief that he alone knows best.' Salim struck at the divan again, this time more violently, raising dust as he did so.

'But if there is no immediate prospect of your father taking his place in Paradise, you cannot say the same of your half-brothers – your rivals for the succession. They've both given in entirely to alcohol, haven't they? If they continue to behave as they do, they cannot be long for the world, even if they have the constitutions of oxen.'

Salim smiled to himself as he recalled Daniyal's and Murad's behaviour ten days before. Akbar had summoned all three of his sons without prior warning to the vast dusty parade ground in front of the palace just after dawn, while the white mist still cloaked the Ravi river and only the earliest of Lahore's cocks had roused themselves to crow. Luckily the previous evening had been one of those during which Salim had steeled himself to follow the *hakim*'s advice to avoid the lure of opium and alcohol. Instead he had gone to the *haram*. Though his longing for Mehrunissa had never left him, he had determinedly pushed her from his mind. For the first time for some while he had spent the night with Jodh Bai. She had teasingly complimented him on his renewed virility as they lay together, naked and sweat-soaked, after their second bout of love-making. Salim had had to admit to himself that abstinence from alcohol and opium increased his sexual appetites. Pondering the point had rekindled his vigour, leading him to make love to Jodh Bai for a third time. Therefore he had been relaxed and sober, if tired and bleary-eyed, when he emerged on to the parade ground to answer his father's dawn summons.

As soon as they had appeared, it had been obvious that neither Murad nor Daniyal had been as abstemious as he had the previous evening. As Murad had come through the tall stone gateway on to the parade ground, one of his attendants had still been attempting to tie his sash. Murad, square jaw jutting, had brushed him aside, swearing for all to hear that he had no need of such fussing attentions while roughly knotting the sash himself. When Daniyal had entered, he had done so with the slow, exaggeratedly steady gait of the drunk trying to suggest he was anything but. He had kept his head unnaturally still and his bloodshot eyes fixed firmly in front of him as he approached his father, but he had still stumbled as he took the last few steps and tried to bend into the required low bow.

Akbar had then ordered all three of his sons to mount their horses, held ready by waiting grooms, and lead some of their bodyguards in attempting to spear watermelons from the saddle with their lances. As he tried to mount, Murad's badly tied sash had come loose and he had stumbled over the trailing cloth, entirely unable to prevent himself sprawling face down in the dust. When he had been helped up and on to his mount and had eventually set it into motion, he had galloped only a hundred yards before slipping once more from the saddle on to the ground.

Daniyal had done rather better, succeeding in mounting and getting his horse to gallop without difficulty. But then, as he attempted to bend to spear the melon, he too had fallen. Staggering to his feet, he had vomited copiously through the gloved hand with which he had tried to stem the noisome stream.

Salim meanwhile had succeeded in spearing the watermelon. His father's response had been not praise but to say, 'I see that you for once have not been drinking, Salim. Remember this will not be the last time I will put you through such a test. You are dismissed.' As Salim left the parade ground he had heard his father order his half-brothers back to their quarters and then command some of his most trusted bodyguards to make sure that the two did not leave their rooms for fourteen days and that no one took alcohol in to them. At the end of that time they were to be kept under close observation to ensure that they remained abstemious.

'Surely when their spell in confinement ends in a few days, they'll have sobered up, won't they, Suleiman Beg?'

'I doubt it. I've heard that some of their companions have managed to smuggle liquor in to them. Rumour has it Murad's fat steward wound some cow's intestines filled with spirits around him beneath his voluminous garments to do it, and that Daniyal bribed one of the guards to bring him the stuff in the blocked-off barrel of his musket.'

'The latter can't be true. My father would have a guard executed under the elephant's foot for such blatant disobedience.'

'It's surprising what risks men will take for money, but perhaps it's only a story. All I can say is that everyone is gossiping about it.'

'Maybe you're right and they've not real rivals as my father's heir, but that does not mean I have any prospect of achieving the power that is my due at this stage in my life. There is much that I could achieve for our dynasty if only my father would give me a chance.'

'Like what?'

'Well, ridding him of some of his fawning and corrupt advisers – Abul Fazl for a start.'

'But you know your father wouldn't countenance their dismissal. At the very least, you would have had to prove yourself as a good governor somewhere before criticising his own advisers and administration.'

'How can I do that when my father will give me no position of trust?' Salim thudded his dagger into the divan once more, eyes blazing. 'Sometimes I think I have no alternative but to take over the government of a province without my father's permission to demonstrate my worth!'

'But that would be rebellion.'

'Call it what you will – I might say I was using my initiative.'

'You are serious, aren't you?' said Suleiman Beg quietly.

'Yes,' said Salim, looking directly at his friend. 'It's something I've been thinking about for months in the dark hours of the night as I've fought to curb my own craving for drink. Don't look so shocked – I have many friends among the young middle-ranking commanders in our armies in the east. They too resent the dead hands of their older superiors on their shoulders – they too want power and responsibility.'

'It's true. I have heard such mutterings of discontent,' said Suleiman Beg. 'There would also be the inducements of promotion and reward . . .'

'I see that you are beginning to believe that it might be possible. Would you be prepared to join me?'

'You should know I would. We have shared so much. I owe my loyalty to you before any other.' Then after some moments' reflection, now looking as serious and intent as Salim, Suleiman Beg added, 'What's more you might well succeed in winning your father's attention and respect. If you act, what will your first steps be?'

346

'To sound out some of those young officers in the eastern army. I cannot travel there without my father's sanction, but you could . . .'

'I will go – I still have some relations in the administration in Bengal and no one will suspect if I visit them.'

'Thank you for your trust and loyalty.' Much to his surprise, as he spoke Salim heard a new-found authority in his tone – not unlike his father's. Now he had determined on action, at least the uncertainty of waiting would be ended. Whatever the outcome he would never need to reproach himself with a lack of the courage to act.

• ◆ •

As Salim looked out three months later from beneath the awning of his large tent at the centre of his camp, the sun was setting over the Chambal river. Flocks of waterfowl – dark silhouettes against the pale orange sunset – were swooping down to roost among the reeds and rushes fringing the riverbank. Under the pretext of an extended tiger hunting expedition he had left his father's court six weeks previously. For the last few days he had been anxiously scanning the landscape for approaching groups of horsemen, hoping for the return of Suleiman Beg from his clandestine mission to the east but a part of him fearing that any riders who appeared might be Abul Fazl's men coming to arrest him having discovered his plotting.

Just after noon that day, a group of horsemen had appeared. As they drew closer, emerging from the shimmering heat haze, he had seen there were too few to be an arresting party. To Salim's great relief, it had been Suleiman Beg. However, he had been so exhausted by long days in the saddle that after reassuring Salim in the broadest terms of his mission's success he had requested permission to sleep. The two had agreed to discuss the results in more detail as they ate together that night. Behind him in the tent Salim could hear his attendants beginning to make preparations for the meal.

Shading his eyes against the setting sun, he saw Suleiman Beg making his way towards him and stepped forward to greet him. The two men embraced and then, arms round each other's shoulders, ducked beneath the tent's fringed green awning and entered.

Here, a low table surrounded by silk-covered bolsters and cushions was spread with an array of foods – chicken and lamb cooked in the tandoor, stew made in the Kashmiri way with dried fruits, mild spices and yoghourt stirred into the sauce, hotter vegetable dishes made according to Gujarati recipes and fish from the Chambal. As they began to eat, dipping into the stews with pieces of nan bread, Salim dismissed the servants and spoke.

'Tell me about your discussions. How many officers can we count on in the eastern provinces?'

'Perhaps two hundred. Each new recruit suggested others who might be sympathetic to our cause. They are mostly as we expected – young men like ourselves, eager for responsibility as well as for the rewards I promised them on your behalf. But there are also some older ones disappointed by their lack of advancement or critical of the tolerance your father shows towards former enemies and those of other religions.'

'How many men do they command in total?'

'Around thirty thousand.'

'That should be enough to demonstrate to my father that I must be taken seriously and given more power.'

'Many were convinced to join us because this is your motivation, not full-scale rebellion and the usurpation of your father's throne. It reassured them that at some stage you would negotiate.'

'Then they must continue to believe so.'

'What do you mean? That is your intention, isn't it?'

'Yes . . . yes, I suppose it is. Although sometimes I indulge myself by thinking that if all went very well I might force my father's abdication now rather than wait for his death.'

'Guard against such thoughts. Your father's forces are powerful. We will have enough men to show your mettle and your worthiness for a greater role in government affairs, but never enough to succeed in a full revolt. If you tried to do so, some of our existing supporters would fall away.'

'My father is loved by the people, I know. It sometimes seems to me that he understands them better and cares more about their happiness than he does for many of those closer to him. I will doubtless negotiate. I was only suggesting we should not rule anything out while we see how the situation develops.'

'When should we take the next step? We shouldn't wait long. Abul Fazl's spies are everywhere. He has subtle ways of coaxing secrets from men and changing their loyalties.'

'Allow me to worry about Abul Fazl. He is only human, after all. But we won't delay. I've already sent messages to people I know to be loyal to me in Agra and Lahore to join me here within a month. When you're rested and we've discussed our plans in more detail you should return east and collect our forces there. Once I have assembled my own men, I'll ride with them to meet you at Allahabad. Its position at the junction of the Jumna and the Ganges will mean my father will be unable to ignore us if we make that our base.'

• ◆ •

Salim held up his hand to halt his column. The messenger he had sent to Nasser Hamid, commander of the garrison of Allahabad, now only four miles away, its domes and towers clearly visible, was galloping back towards them. As the young man reined in there was a broad smile on his face. 'Highness, Nasser Hamid has thrown open the town to you. He bids you welcome.'

Salim's shoulders dropped and he began to relax for the first time in weeks. Nasser Hamid was a friend from his youth and in secret correspondence had promised to yield Allahabad to Salim. Nevertheless, as he had ridden towards the city that morning, Salim had felt apprehensive. Everything seemed to be going almost too well. Since parting from Suleiman Beg he had succeeded in winning young officers from both Lahore and Agra to his cause. Just seven weeks ago, scarcely pausing in a conversation with Abul Fazl, Akbar had nodded his assent to his eldest son's request to leave the court and Lahore on another hunting expedition. The next day Salim had ridden out with a band of his followers on his mission to demand his father's attention and to prove his worth, as he put it to himself, although he knew others would simply call it rebellion.

As he rode he wondered whether and in what circumstances he would see Akbar again. Of more concern than the impact of his action on his father had been the fact that he could bring neither his wives nor his children with him. He felt far from close enough to any of his wives to take them into his confidence – besides, the *haram* was notorious for its loose talk. His young sons spent so much of their time with their grandfather that their departure with him would be too unusual to pass without notice. Perhaps his greatest sorrow, though, was that he had been unable to say anything to his grandmother who had worked so hard for his recall from Kabul. He knew how much it would hurt her that he was challenging his father and in such a way. She loved them both and would fear for them both, dreading their confrontation turning into all-out war. At present, however, there was no sign of that. His scouts had reported no traces of pursuit, and when a division of his father's horsemen on a routine patrol had approached, both their commander and Salim had sheered away, making sure they gave each other a wide berth. As he had ridden day after day with his growing army, Salim had begun to enjoy command and the freedom he felt from interference by his father or anyone else. He knew this would not last for ever and he would need all his abilities to secure the best outcome for himself and also, he reminded himself, for the dynasty.

Suleiman Beg had sent messengers that he and the contingent from Bengal would reach Allahabad in a fortnight. He would be glad to see his milk-brother, not just for the strong body of men he was bringing but also for his friendship, his calm, considered advice and his absolute loyalty. But for the moment he must ensure he made a good entrance into Allahabad to impress its citizens and to reinforce the confidence of his own men.

'Unfurl our banners,' he commanded, sitting straighter in the saddle. 'Order the mounted trumpeters to the front together with the elephants carrying the kettledrums and their drummers. Have our men close ranks, then sound the trumpets, beat the drums, and let us advance into Allahabad.'

◆

'Highness, an envoy has arrived from Bir Singh, the Bundela Raja of Orchha,' announced an attendant as, three months later, Salim and Suleiman Beg were standing on the tall crenellated walls of the fort at Allahabad watching Salim's cavalry drilling on the parade ground below. Nearby on the banks of the Jumna were the long, straight lines of tents which housed the fifty thousand men who by now had gathered to his banner, more than half as many again as he had originally anticipated.

'I will see him at once. Bring him to me here on the walls.'

Five minutes later a tall, thin man with large gold hoops in both ears climbed the stone staircase up to the battlements. His clothes were travel-stained, and in one hand he was carrying a jute sack around which several black flies were buzzing. When he was within a dozen feet of Salim the man placed the sack on the floor and prostrated himself.

'What news has the raja for me?'

Quickly regaining his feet, the envoy grinned, exposing uneven white teeth beneath his bushy dark moustache. 'News that will gladden your heart, Highness.'

'Go on, then.'

'Bir Singh has fulfilled your wishes.' While he spoke, the man lifted the sack once more and unpicked the series of tight knots in the cord holding it together. As he opened its folds, a sweet, sickly smell filled the still air. Then he reached inside and pulled out by the hair a decaying human head. Despite the bloated putrescent flesh, the purple splitting lips and the dry clotted blood, Salim immediately recognised the fleshy cheeks and long nose of Abul Fazl. A pale and shocked Suleiman Beg was gazing at the head, clutching his stomach as if about to vomit.

But a composed and unsurprised Salim simply said, 'The raja has done well to follow my orders. Both he and you shall have your promised rewards doubled.' Then he turned towards Suleiman Beg. 'I did not tell you in advance of my plans, Suleiman Beg, for your own protection so you would not be implicated if I was betrayed. Abul Fazl's death was necessary. He was my enemy.' He turned back to the envoy. 'Tell me how Abul Fazl perished.'

'When you alerted the raja that you expected Abul Fazl to travel through his territory while returning north to Agra from an inspection of the imperial armies fighting on the borders of the Deccan, he had the only two roads that he could use to traverse our mountainous lands carefully watched. About a month ago, he heard that Abul Fazl was approaching the westernmost one with an escort of about fifty men. Our forces — I was among them — ambushed his party as he ascended a steep and narrow pass late one afternoon. Our musketeers, hidden among boulders above the road, shot down many of Abul Fazl's bodyguards before they could even draw their weapons. However, Abul Fazl and about a dozen of his men succeeded in dismounting unhurt and took refuge in some rocks and bushes close to the road. From that cover they kept up accurate fire on any of our soldiers who approached, wounding several. Among them was one of my own brothers, who was hit in the mouth by a bullet which carried away most of his teeth and part of his jawbone. He still lives, unable to speak or to eat properly, but for his sake I pray that his death is not much longer delayed.'

After pausing, sad-eyed for a moment, the envoy continued, 'When the raja saw that Abul Fazl was completely surrounded, he sent a messenger under a flag of truce with a promise that if Abul Fazl surrendered he would spare his few surviving men. A few minutes later, Abul Fazl emerged from the scrub and throwing down his sword calmly approached the raja. His face was expressionless as he spoke. "I will not run from an unwashed, flea-ridden hill chieftain such as you. Do with me what you will but remember whom I serve."

'Enraged by his contemptuous words, the raja ran forward, drawing his serrated dagger from the scabbard at his side as he did so. He seized Abul Fazl, who did not resist, by the throat and sawed through his fat neck with his dagger. I have seen many men killed but I have never seen so much blood flow from a man as came from Abul Fazl. Then the raja had all of Abul Fazl's bodyguard who were still alive killed, whether wounded or not, and ordered all the bodies to be buried deep enough to be unreachable by the digging of even the most persistent of wild dogs.'

'Why didn't he keep his promise to spare the bodyguards?' asked Suleiman Beg.

'He could not afford to do so for fear they took word of his deed to the emperor. He knew that Akbar's love for Abul Fazl would mean that his vengeance on his killer, if known, would be harsh.'

'It was necessary, Suleiman Beg,' said Salim. 'To achieve great ends we must sometimes use harsh means – may the souls of the brave bodyguards rest in Paradise. Their only sin was to serve an evil man. Abul Fazl was constantly poisoning my father's mind against me, whispering to him of my drunkenness and my ambition, advising him to appoint his own creatures – not me or my friends – to positions of trust. Even my grandmother told me to beware of him – that he was no friend of mine. I hated him. His sneering complacent smile' – Salim's voice was rising – 'his scarcely concealed contempt . . . there were so many times I wanted to push back down his throat the patronising, hypocritical words he spoke to me before my father.'

Rage at the recollection of Abul Fazl's behaviour coursed through Salim. Suddenly he grabbed the head and in one movement kicked it over the battlements. A piece of decaying flesh flew from it as his foot struck it and the head landed with a dull thud in the rubbish-filled dry moat below. 'Good riddance to a bad man! Let the dogs gnaw out that lying flattering tongue of his and the crows peck at those fawning inquisitive eyes.'

That evening Salim and Suleiman Beg were relaxing in Salim's private apartments in the fort. Although his abstinence from opium was now complete Salim had taken to drinking wine once more. It tasted good and he had convinced himself that he was now strong enough to be its master rather than it being his. Just after an attendant had departed after bringing them another bottle, Suleiman Beg asked, 'Don't you fear your father's retribution for Abul Fazl's death? Why did you provoke him so, knowing as you must that he could crush our forces if he wished to?'

'I realise his armies are strong and loyal but he has not moved against us in the months we have been here. He has preferred to ignore my rebellion beyond issuing proclamations dismissing me as a foolish ungrateful child and threatening confiscation of the property of any who join me. Instead, he has concentrated his main armies in the Deccan to quell the rebellions on the borders of the empire. I don't expect him to change his mind and attack us now.'

'Why? Abul Fazl was his friend as well as his counsellor.'

'And I am his son. He knows he must think about the future of our dynasty. When Murad died – almost a year ago now – and with his grandsons still too young, he must have recognised that if it was to survive he has only drunken Daniyal or myself to choose from for his heir. He may have his doubts about me, but he must know he has little real choice about his successor. Now I've demonstrated to him by the death of Abul Fazl that I can act decisively and be as ruthless with my implacable enemies as he was with Hemu, Adham Khan and other traitors, he will be unable to continue to ignore me, I agree. Instead of feeling he must divert his armies from his unfinished southern campaign, I expect him to seek to conciliate me.'

'I pray for all our sakes that you've read your father aright.'

• ◆ •

'Your grandmother's caravan is no more than two miles away,' one of Salim's *qorchis* announced. Ever since her steward, the stout middle-aged Badakhshani who a few years ago had replaced the white-haired old man Salim had known all his life, had ridden through the gateway into the fortress of Allahabad the day before, Salim had been nervously awaiting Hamida's arrival. After a few hours' broken sleep, he had been pacing his apartments since dawn, steeling himself not to call for spirits or opium to calm his racing mind. He would be glad to see his grandmother, which he hadn't done since he departed from his father's court many months ago at the beginning of his bid to establish his own authority. Despite his marriages and his love for his mercurial, strong-minded mother, Hamida remained the woman he felt the greatest affection for. He had always been able to rely on her calm sympathy and sound common sense, knowing that she was motivated only by love and affection for him. However, would she understand why he had felt compelled to raise troops against his father? Had his father sent her to him? Had she come on her own initiative? Surely she must bring a message from Akbar, but what would it be? He felt much more uncertain of his father's reaction than he had claimed to Suleiman Beg when first

354

hearing of Abul Fazl's death. Soon he would find out for sure.

'Thank you. I'll come to the courtyard immediately to welcome her to Allahabad myself.'

Salim had only been standing for a few minutes beneath the green awning in the sunlit courtyard, which had been strewn with fragrant rose petals on his orders, when he saw through the open metal-bound gates the leading outriders of his grandmother's procession approach. Then, to the blaring of trumpets and the beating of kettledrums from the gatehouse, the large elephant bearing Hamida slowly entered, the fringes of its long embroidered surcoat – its *jhool* – brushing through the rose petals. The interior of the gilded and jewelled howdah was carefully screened from sun and prying eyes by thin cream gauze curtains.

As soon as the *mahout* had brought the elephant gently down on to its knees, Salim ordered all the male attendants and guards to depart. Then he walked slowly towards the howdah, mounted the small portable platform that had been placed next to it to assist its elderly occupant to descend and opened the gauze curtains. As his eyes adjusted to the dimmer light inside, he made out the familiar figure of his grandmother. Although she was now in her seventies, she was sitting as straight-backed as he remembered. Opposite her, head bowed respectfully, was one of her favourite attendants, Zubaida, his old nursemaid whom he had rescued from the ravine in Kashmir. Salim leaned forward and kissed Hamida on the forehead.

'You are most welcome to my fortress in Allahabad, Grandmother,' he said, realising as he spoke how awkward, formal and even assertive he sounded.

'I'm pleased to be here. You've been away from your proper place at the heart of our family for far too long.' Then, perhaps seeing the hardening expression on Salim's face and anticipating a tirade of exculpation, Hamida continued, 'We'll talk about that later. Now help me and Zubaida to descend.'

Towards dusk that evening, Salim walked slowly over to the women's section of the fortress where he had had the best rooms – those on the highest storey overlooking the Ganges – prepared for his grandmother's use. Claiming that she was tired after the journey and needed to wash and refresh herself and then to rest, Hamida had insisted they should not meet again until the heat of the day was dying. This had left Salim yet more time to brood on what message his grandmother might have and to try to interpret the few words they had exchanged. He had even wondered whether Hamida had brought Zubaida, now at least eighty, bent and totally white-haired, with her to remind him both of his childhood and of the times in Kashmir when he was closest to Akbar. Eventually he had abandoned such speculations as futile and filled the time first by practising swordplay with Suleiman Beg and then by luxuriating in the fort's bathhouse.

Entering the cool dark staircase leading to the top floor of the women's quarters, Salim increased his pace, once more eager to see his grandmother and hear any message she brought. As he parted the silken hangings leading into her room he saw that Hamida, neatly but not ostentatiously dressed in purple silk, was sitting on a low chair while Zubaida put the finishing touches to her still thick hair by inserting clasps set with amethysts. Seeing her grandson, Hamida asked Zubaida to leave, which she did, bowing to Salim as she went.

'Sit down on that stool, Salim, where I can see you,' said Hamida. He did so despite the pulsing tension within him which meant that he would have been far happier being free to roam the apartment. Without any more preliminaries Hamida began, her voice as soft and authoritative as he remembered.

'For the sake of the dynasty there must be no more posturing and parading of armies. You and your father must be reconciled and join together in defeating our real enemies and expanding our empire.'

'I have never intended to harm the family. I respect our lineage and the deeds of our ancestors too much. I want the empire to prosper and grow, but my father refuses to understand my desire to assist him by sharing in the imperial duties. Instead he misinterprets my actions as threats to his authority.'

'Easy enough for him to do so when you have had his chief counsellor and one of his best friends murdered.'

'I . . .'

'Don't deny it, Salim. Honesty has always been something we've shared.'

'Abul Fazl saw me as a threat to his influence and powers of patronage. I have long since despised his smooth hypocrisy and scarcely concealed corruption. His death can mark a new beginning in how the court is run.'

'And indeed perhaps in your relationship with your father. But have you got the insight to put yourself in your father's place and appreciate how much Abul Fazl's death hurt him? I think not, given all that's passed between you, so I will tell you. Imagine how you would feel if your father had Suleiman Beg murdered. After the treachery of his own milk-brother and milk-mother your father never trusted anyone fully again. I even think that their betrayal may lie behind his refusal to delegate real power to you and your half-brothers. However, over time he did begin to rely on Abul Fazl. Think then how he felt when he learned of his murder on the orders of someone else he should have been able to trust – yourself.

'Your father heard the news when he was visiting the imperial pigeon cotes, testing the speed and homing ability of some of his favourite birds. He almost collapsed and had to be helped weeping to his apartments where he remained alone for two days, refusing to see anyone or eat anything. When he emerged, red-eyed, dishevelled and unshaven, he ordered a week's court mourning for Abul Fazl. Then he went straight to reproach your mother with giving birth to such an undutiful son. She simply told him that she was glad you had a mind of your own to stand up to him.'

Salim smiled as he pictured the meeting between the two.

'Your father's grief is not a cause for amusement,' Hamida continued sternly. 'When I visited him, he broke down into tears again. He said, "I know Salim was behind this. What have I – his father – done to deserve such treatment from him? My people and my courtiers love me and respect me. Why cannot my eldest son do the same?" I tried to explain that you were still young and as such more alive to your ambitions and your need for experience than to the feelings of others. But I told him that even so, he had been harder and less sensitive and forgiving in his handling of you than of some of his

357

nobles. I reminded him his own father had died before there could be any conflict of ambitions and that in the early years of his rule he had been impatient and resentful of all restraint and advice. He acknowledged this only grudgingly at first. However, after more discussions over the succeeding days, in which I appealed to him to show to you the magnanimity and wisdom he is renowned for across the empire, he agreed to my coming here to see if you could be reconciled.'

'I am truly glad you did, but is it really in my father's character to allow me the power I crave? Isn't he more like the male tiger who consumes his own young if they should seem to threaten his authority?'

'And what about you, Salim? Can't you admit that you have been foolish and headstrong at times? You were the one to behave like a young male animal when you made love to his concubine Anarkali.'

'I was thoughtless . . . I had no concern for the consequences of my lust, only for the lust itself. I admit I was wrong . . . I cost Anarkali her life, and yes, on that occasion I strained my father's patience.'

'That is an understatement. Your father is a great man, as powerful a warrior as his ancestors Timur and Genghis Khan and a more tolerant, wiser ruler than either. I know that the parents and the children of great men often view them differently from others. However, you showed him no respect as a parent, as a man or as an emperor. You undermined the dignity that is so important to his position. A less forgiving man – one less understanding of his son's youthful lust – would have had you executed like Anarkali.'

'I know that, and I am grateful. But many other times my father has slighted me and caused me to lose face before the whole court by his dismissive treatment of me.'

'You brought him pain through your inability to control your other appetites – not just your lust. Like your half-brothers you've staggered around the court helplessly drunk or glassy-faced with opium. Your father is a proud man and very conscious of his imperial dignity. He feels your behaviour has humiliated him as well as you in the eyes of the court.'

'But I've attempted to reform my habits, unlike Daniyal – or Murad when he was alive.'

'And your father gives you credit for it.'

'Does he? And what about Abul Fazl?'

'He thinks you tried to punish him by killing his best friend but he insists he will set the ties of blood above those of friendship – and I believe he will try. Indeed, he knows he must do so. With Murad dead and Daniyal still soaked in alcohol, you and in due course your sons must be the future of the dynasty.'

A wave of relief swept through Salim. He had been right in his analysis of his father. 'So he recognises that he needs me?'

'Yes, and you should recognise that you need him more. He could crush your little rebellion if he wanted to. Even if he simply publicly disowned and disinherited you, you would find it difficult to retain your authority or your followers. You do understand that, don't you?'

Salim said nothing. His grandmother was right. His own position was not as strong as he liked to pretend. His plan to force his father's hand to give him power was going nowhere. The treasury of Allahabad was emptying fast. He would need to find more money soon if his forces were not to begin to melt away. He was isolated from the court and the nobles there, many of whom he would have to win over if he were to succeed his father. He wished to see his sons, who would have heard only their grandfather's views about his rebellion. Most important, he knew that latterly at least there had been faults on both sides in his arguments with his father. But it hurt his pride to admit it. Finally he simply said, 'Yes.'

'And you agree to be reconciled?'

'Yes . . . provided that I am not humiliated in the process.'

'You will not be. I give you my word. Your father has agreed to allow me the responsibility of organising the ceremony before the court.'

'Then I am content.'

• ◆ •

'When the trumpets sound you will enter the *durbar* hall through the right-hand door,' said Hamida. Salim had accompanied her back from Allahabad to within a day's ride from Agra, which his father had recently restored as his capital. Then he had encamped while Hamida had gone on alone to the Agra fort to tell Akbar of his son's agreement to their reconciliation and to put in hand the detailed arrangements for the ceremony.

'And you are sure that everyone will act according to your guidance?'

'Yes. Just as I am sure that you will. Now ready yourself. I must take my place behind the *jali* screen.' With a final reassuring smile and a pat on his shoulder, Hamida left the room. He had only time to look at himself briefly in the mirror and adjust the knotting of his green silk sash before the trumpets sounded. Heart thumping, he made his way towards the doors which two tall green-turbaned guards threw open for him. As he entered, he saw his father seated on his high-backed gilded throne, surrounded by his courtiers. He was dressed completely in scarlet brocade, save for his white sash and his white ceremonial turban with its two peacock's feathers held in place by four large rubies. His grandfather's sword Alamgir was at his side, and as Salim came nearer he saw that his father was wearing their ancestor Timur's ring with its snarling tiger.

When Salim was within a few feet of his father and preparing to make his low obeisance, Akbar suddenly rose and stepped down from his throne to embrace him. After some moments, he released him and turned to his courtiers.

'I call upon you to witness that my beloved elder son and I are reconciled. All our past disagreements are forgotten. See, I present him with this my ceremonial turban as a token of our reunion. Henceforth whoever acts against one of us will need to fear both.' As he spoke, Akbar removed his turban and placed it on his son's head.

Tears welled in Salim's eyes. 'I promise to honour you in all ways and to be loyal in my obedience to your every command.'

However, a quarter of an hour later, as Salim left the audience chamber, some of the euphoria had already begun to dissipate within him. Had his father's embrace been any more than an empty piece of theatre? Could he recall any warmth in Akbar's tone of voice or

360

facial expression as he had gone on to recount the initial duties, none of great significance, which Salim would be required to perform on his behalf? Would it all really be so simple?

Chapter 28

Fathers and Sons

'Ride hard, Khusrau. You can beat him,' Salim shouted across the parade ground below the Agra fort. His eldest son, mounted on an agile black pony, was swerving the animal in and out of a series of spears thrust into the hard ground. He was just behind another young man on a roan horse racing through a parallel set of spears to his left. Both were well clear of a third youth on Khusrau's right, who had already failed to negotiate one pair of spears and had to wheel his pony to try again. Khusrau had just succeeded in getting his pony's neck ahead when a minute later he crossed the finishing line, head bent low and dust billowing in his wake.

How his son had changed over the two years that Salim had spent at Allahabad and elsewhere, away from Akbar's court. When he had left, Khusrau had still been a boy. Now he was a young man of seventeen. Salim regretted more than ever that he had departed in such total secrecy that he had not felt able to take even Khusrau or Parvez with him without risking jeopardising his plans. It had been even less possible to contemplate taking young Khurram, now nearly thirteen. Since his birth he had spent most of his days with his grandfather and usually slept in Akbar's apartments at night. Even now they were standing together ten yards away. Both were vigorously applauding Khusrau, who had dismounted and was striding lithe and full of youthful strength towards Akbar who was holding a riding crop with a jewel-encrusted handle ready to present to his eldest grandson as his prize for his victory.

What a picture of familial harmony it looked, thought Salim. He had been absent from the family group for too long. Walking quickly, he reached his father and his two sons just as Khusrau took the riding crop from Akbar's outstretched hands. 'Well done, Khusrau. You have the same skill as a horseman that I had in my youth,' Akbar was saying. Then, after what Salim thought was a meaningful glance at him, he continued, 'I pray that you retain it, together with those other fine attributes that your tutors tell me you possess. Never let them be fuddled by debilitating addictions or lusts as other members of our family have.'

'I assure you I will not,' replied Khusrau, looking directly at his grandfather. Salim realised he had neither possessed nor received any encouragement from Akbar to develop such outward assurance and confidence when he was Khusrau's age.

'You did indeed ride well, Khusrau. I too congratulate you,' Salim spoke for the first time.

'Thank you, Father. It is a skill I've much improved in the time you've been away.'

'Khusrau and Khurram, would you like to accompany me to view my war elephants?' asked Akbar. 'I've some fine beasts and I know you, Khusrau, have been building up an excellent stable of your own of young elephants collected from across the empire. Perhaps you'll learn something from the training methods my *mahouts* use.'

Both Salim's sons nodded enthusiastically and followed their grandfather, who had already turned on his heel and was heading for the stables. Resisting the childish temptation to shout that he had better beasts than any of them, Salim watched three of his four closest male relations walk away from him. His father, he was almost sure, had deliberately excluded him. But had his sons, and in particular Khusrau, realised what Akbar was about and colluded with him?

• ◆ •

'What? Are you sure you are correct about what you overheard?' Salim almost shouted at Suleiman Beg in his apartments two months later.

'Yes. I'd just finished bathing in one of the *hammans* reserved for commanders to use after parade ground exercises. I was dressing in one of the side rooms when I heard two officers come in. I couldn't see them from where I was, nor, obviously, could they see me. But despite the splashing of the water in the channels as they bathed, I heard their words clearly enough. The first asked, "Have you heard that some of His Majesty's courtiers are urging him to appoint Khusrau as his heir instead of either Daniyal or Salim?" and the second replied, "No, but I can see merits in the idea. Daniyal's a useless drunk and Salim lacks the self-discipline not to relapse at any moment."'

Salim's face stiffened with anger but he said nothing as Suleiman Beg continued. 'The first spoke again. "True. In any case, Salim will seek to install his own favourites in positions of power. He is bound to prefer those who followed him in his traitorous rebellion to those of us who remained faithful to his father. We may be lucky if we escape the fate of Abul Fazl." Then some more officers entered and the two speakers broke off their conversation to talk of other matters. But I am certain I've given you the gist of their words.'

Salim still did not speak for some moments as he tried, not entirely successfully, to compose his emotions. Among his worst fears while he was at Allahabad had been that his father might promote one of his grandsons as his successor rather than himself, but such thoughts had centred around Khurram, so clearly Akbar's favourite, and he had been able to dismiss them on the grounds of Khurram's youth. Khusrau might now be a different proposition. He was older and, since his return, Salim himself had noticed that his eldest son was gathering a band of confederates around him only a little older than himself. Finally he asked, 'Is this the first time you've heard traitorous idiots speak about such a prospect?'

'In such direct terms, yes.' Suleiman Beg looked uneasy as he continued, 'But I've heard others express doubts about their own fate should you succeed. It's only natural that they should worry about the length and depth of your rift with your father and the newness of its healing. It's only a short step from that to thinking about alternatives.'

'I will not allow this,' Salim yelled, rage welling within him as he seized a jewelled dish from the low table beside him and threw it hard against the wall, dislodging some turquoise and ruby stones and denting the dish itself.

'Calm down,' said Suleiman Beg. 'You can't stop people talking or thinking about what's best for them. It's human nature. You need to exert influence yourself. Convince more people of your own virtues and suitability to rule.'

'Perhaps you're right,' said Salim, his anger subsiding a little. 'But how, after the time I've spent away?'

'Try to show you will let bygones be.'

'Maybe one way might be by offering some of the sons of my father's advisers appointments among my own counsellors.'

'Wouldn't that run the risk of introducing spies and discord amongst us?'

'Perhaps, but in truth we have little to hide. What have I done since my return? Nothing other than wait patiently again and respond willingly to every trivial request my father's made of me. I've bottled up my emotions, speaking only to you of my regret that the emperor will still not grant me more powers or give me some military command.'

'Your father might be forgiven for not wishing to put you in charge of large armies until he is more certain of your intentions.'

'I suppose I can understand that from his point of view,' Salim responded, almost smiling. After a pause his brows knitted once more. 'You don't really think my father would ever contemplate disinheriting me in favour of my son, do you?'

'To be truthful, I don't know . . . Even though he's over sixty he remains a clever and complex man well attuned to understanding the motives and concerns of those around him without ever disclosing his own. Possibly he might have considered giving a little tacit encouragement to the idea of Khusrau succeeding him, knowing that you would come to hear of it. In this way he might seek to increase the pressure on you to continue to conform to his wishes and indeed to your reformed way of life.'

'That would be typical of him and his cold machinations,' Salim shouted again, grinding his heel into one of the thick rugs covering the floor before adding more quietly, 'My father still has no regard for my feelings. Nor perhaps for those of any other of his relations. When Khusrau comes to hear of suggestions that he might succeed, it will only raise unrealistic expectations in him.'

'So what do you intend to do?'

'On the surface to ignore the rumours and continue to act the dutiful son, but privately to draw more followers to me with promises of rewards when I come to power, and to ensure I have enough officers and well-armed men to call on should the need arise. I'll want your help with this. You can talk more freely than I.'

'You will have it, Highness.'

'Meanwhile I will try to find opportunities to probe Khusrau's attitudes and ambitions . . .'

• ◆ •

Salim lost no time in arranging a meeting with Khusrau and it was only thirty-six hours later when father and son met at the archery butts. 'I'm so pleased that you could join me today,' said Salim as he put his arrow to the string of his double-curved bow and squinting along the shaft took careful aim at the straw-stuffed target, which was shaped and roughly dressed as a man. Moments later, the arrow hissed through the air to thud into the target's torso.

'Good shot, Father,' said Khusrau as he fitted his own arrow and fired, striking the target within an inch of Salim's shaft. Lowering his bow, he added, 'I am always pleased to spend time with you.'

'Good. We have been apart too long. I would not wish you to think you were absent from my mind while I was in Allahabad all those months.'

'I did not.'

'What I did I did for the good of the dynasty, for those who come to rule after me.'

Khusrau gave a wry smile. 'But my grandfather rules now. God willing it will be a long time before he is called to his reward in Paradise. Who can tell what may happen to any of us in the meantime.'

'What do you mean?' asked Salim, his tone sharper than he meant it to be as he raised his bow again and fired.

'Simply that none of us can know what may happen during the years he continues to rule. All of us are mortal. Even if we live, the passage of time changes us and others' perception of us.' Khusrau shot another arrow. This time it split Salim's last shaft as it embedded itself deep in the straw man. Was that shot simply a trick of fortune or an omen? wondered Salim, involuntarily recalling the Sikri mystic's warning to beware his sons. He fitted another arrow and fired, striking the straw man in the throat.

'You are right that our lives are subject to divine providence, but we should all wish them to follow a natural progression where sons outlive fathers and only then succeed in due order to their positions and responsibilities. None of us, I'm sure, would want it to be otherwise.'

Khusrau said nothing for a moment, then simply replied, 'I would not wish that any more than you. I agree we're all in God's hands.'

As they continued their practice, as if by mutual consent drawing back from any confrontation, father and son turned their conversation towards everyday matters of court life. However, as he packed away his bow in its rosewood case at the end of the session while Khusrau walked back across the courtyard to join his grandfather in the elephant stables, Salim knew that ambition had been sparked in the heart of his mettlesome eldest son whether by Akbar or not. He must remain on his guard both to extend his network of allies and conciliate his enemies. Above all, he must do everything he could to impress his father, even if that meant concealing his true opinions. It would not be easy, but the reward of the throne would be worth it.

• ◆ •

Tears coursed down the cheeks of both Akbar and Salim as the coffin was borne on a simple flower-decked wooden bier through a side gate of the Agra fort towards the boat that would carry it up the Jumna to Delhi for burial next to Humayun. Grief at Hamida's death was uniting the two men in a way that would have pleased

368

Hamida herself. She had slipped gently into death in her seventy-eighth year after only a few days' illness with what had at first seemed a simple cough but quickly turned into something much worse.

As Akbar and Salim had sat on either side of the low bed on which she was lying, she had bid them goodbye. As fluid wheezed in her chest she had whispered to them to love each other as she loved them both, if not for her sake then for that of their dynasty. Stretching their arms across her frail body at her request to clasp each other's hands, they had agreed to do so. Only minutes later, as the light of the crescent moon entered through the casement and a soft breeze rippled the gauze curtains, she had died. Her last words were, 'I am coming through the stars to join you in Paradise, Humayun.'

What must be going through his father's mind, Salim wondered as he fought to control his own emotions. Akbar must be growing conscious of his own mortality after the death of Gulbadan a few months previously and then Hamida's. He was the oldest member of his family now as well as – as he had long been – its head. He had lost a mother who had loved him and protected him both in the very early days after his birth at Umarkot and when, after his father's untimely death, rebellion had threatened. Hamida's love for Akbar had been unconditional, as Salim knew it had been for himself. That was why he too would miss her more than he could say, feeling as he could not help but feel that both his mother's love and that of Akbar were conditional on his adherence to their wishes, to their view of the world.

Salim glanced towards Daniyal, hunched and prematurely aged on his father's other side. His surviving half-brother had only arrived back at the court an hour before from the isolated palace near Fatehpur Sikri he occupied at Akbar's command and was visibly shaking. Salim suspected it was from either the effects of alcohol or the lack of it rather than from grief. Then Salim looked at his own three sons, Khusrau, Parvez and Khurram, standing next to him. Perhaps understandably none seemed as affected as himself and Akbar, not having known Hamida so well or for so long. Did they find him as difficult to read as he did his own father? Salim wondered, not for the first time. If they had gone to Hamida and asked her,

369

would she have told them to respect him and learn from him, as she had told him to do from Akbar many years before?

She would have been too honest to do so unreservedly. She had recognised his faults: not only his drinking, his opium taking and his lusts but also his short temper, his impatience and his unforgiving hatred and hunger for vengeance against those such as Abul Fazl who he thought mistreated him. However, despite these failings she had still believed in him and his ability to redeem his faults if he came to rule. He hoped she would have said as much to his sons too. If she ever had, Khusrau at least had shown no signs of taking the message on board. He continued to distance himself from his father, correct, formal and emotionless when they met but seeming to avoid contact whenever he could and, Salim suspected, continuing to hope to supplant him. That was perhaps how Akbar felt about himself, Salim realised. Then he looked across at his father's lined and tear-stained face and instinctively, almost involuntarily, placed his hand on his elbow in a gesture of understanding and support in his present grief. As the drums beat a slow and mournful tattoo and Hamida's body was carried carefully up the boat's gangplank, Akbar allowed his son's hand to remain on his arm while he took his leave of his mother on earth.

• ◆ •

'Suleiman Beg, you're bleeding. What's happened?' Salim exclaimed as his milk-brother pushed his way through the hangings covering the doorway into Salim's apartment, crimson blood staining his green tunic and running down his left hand and fingers to drip on to the white marble floor.

'Just a small argument about the succession and a flesh wound.'

'Come here, let me see. Should I summon the *hakim*?'

'Perhaps. Scratch though this wound is, I may require his needle and thread.' Suleiman Beg held out his hand and Salim ripped back the fabric of his tunic sleeve to reveal the wound – a three-inch-long slash to the upper arm just above the elbow. As Salim dabbed the blood away with his own neckcloth he saw that it had exposed some creamy yellow fat and some muscle but had not penetrated to the bone.

'You're right. It's a clean wound and not too deep, but you will need the *hakim*. It's bleeding a lot so hold your arm above your head to lessen the flow while I bind it.' As he wound his neckcloth around Suleiman Beg's muscled biceps, he shouted for one of his attendants to fetch the *hakim* and then asked Suleiman Beg once more, this time with a concern in his voice that went beyond his care for his closest friend, 'What happened? How do you mean, an argument about the succession?'

'I was walking through the courtyard past a band of Khusrau's youthful followers when one said to another in a voice deliberately raised for me to hear, "There goes old Suleiman Beg. I pity him. He has backed the wrong candidate to succeed the emperor. Unlike us, when Khusrau comes to power – and not his rebel of a father – he'll be left with nothing. Perhaps one of us should make him our *khutmagar*, our butler. He must know enough about wine. He'll have poured plenty for Salim." I knew the taunt was meant to provoke me but I couldn't help myself. I turned and walked up to the group, grabbed the speaker by the throat, flung him back against one of the pillars and invited him to repeat what he'd said. He spluttered that the time for my generation was past. When the emperor died we'd be passed over. It would be for the young to succeed.

'Then I told him, tightening my grip around his throat, to ask me to become his *khutmagar*, if he would. He said nothing. I squeezed harder still. His face was turning purple and his eyes were popping. If I'd persisted a minute longer he'd have been dead. Suddenly I felt a sharp stinging pain in my arm. One of his companions, bolder than the rest, had slashed me with his dagger to make me release my grip. For a moment my eyes met my assailant's, both of us appalled at what had happened and even more at what might have happened . . . Then Khusrau's little adherents ran off, hauling with them their loud-mouthed companion, who was still gasping for breath. His throat will hurt for days and he should at least think twice before provoking his betters again.'

'I couldn't have shown the restraint you did,' said Salim. 'Khusrau's followers are becoming ever bolder, posturing and strutting around and proclaiming my son's virtues and his fitness to rule. Since Daniyal's miserable death left me the only survivor of my father's sons, their clamour for the crown to skip a generation has become more intense and more open. How dare they attack you? It's as if they want to see how far they can go or perhaps even provoke me into action against them, thus alienating my father.'

'Why doesn't the emperor stop them?'

'I don't know. He's aged a lot since the deaths of his mother and Daniyal. Suddenly he looks his sixty-two years and his bouts of stomach problems have become more frequent. His greatest interest seems to be in the company of Khurram, testing and probing his abilities and teaching him in a way he never did with his sons or indeed his other grandsons.'

'Sometimes I wonder if he isn't deliberately letting Khusrau and his followers push their case to see what level of support they can muster compared to ourselves.'

'Perhaps so. I've been pleased that even some of the older nobles promoted on Abul Fazl's urgings are now beginning to cultivate my favour, perturbed by Khusrau's pressure for youth to rule experience. Maybe my father is being more astute than I give him credit for and is flushing out the preferences of his courtiers.'

'Frail as he is becoming, the emperor should never be under-estimated.'

'But then how do you explain his outbursts against me? The other day, for example, when he criticised my handling of some of the military training, suggesting in front of the whole court I had been negligent or in an opium trance just because a fool of an officer, as the man later admitted, had misheard my command and turned his squadron in the wrong direction on the parade ground.'

'All men hate to lose their grip on power. Sometimes if they feel it slipping they cannot help but lash out in frustration at their successors, raging inwardly at their debility and the transitoriness of power and even of life itself.'

'You're becoming a philosopher, Suleiman Beg,' said Salim as one of his *qorchis* appeared through the hangings of the doorway to announce *hakim*'s arrival. 'Enough. Let's talk more later. Now you must let the *hakim* perfect his embroidery on you.'

• ◆ •

'What is it, Khurram?' said Salim, surprised to see his youngest son approaching across the courtyard where he and Suleiman Beg were playing chess.

'My grandfather says that it will aid his recovery to full health to watch you and Khusrau pit your best fighting elephants one against the other.'

Salim and Suleiman Beg exchanged glances. 'When?'

'Later this afternoon when it grows a little cooler. My grandfather wishes the fight to take place on the banks of the Jumna below the fort so he can watch from the *jharoka* balcony.'

'Tell him that I am happy to obey and that I will send my favourite fighting elephant, World Shaker, against Khusrau's.'

'Yes, Father.'

'Have you spoken yet to your brother?'

'It was Khusrau who suggested holding a fight when he came to visit Grandfather today. He was praising a giant elephant he'd imported from Bengal called Damudar that has never yet been beaten.'

'It will be a good contest then. World Shaker has never lost a fight either.' Salim smiled at his son, but as soon as Khurram had left his smile faded. 'Khusrau has deliberately contrived this contest. I'm certain of it. He hopes to defeat me before all the court.'

'Perhaps he does, but how can he be sure his elephant will beat yours?'

'He is conceited enough to believe this Bengal fighter of his is invincible. But even if not, he will know that the very fact of holding the fight will suggest to the world that he and I are equals – both contenders for my father's favour. You know better than anyone the extent of his and his supporters' ambitions . . . You carry the scar. He will think victory for him will be seen as a symbol and an omen.'

'So what will you do?'

'Everything I can to make sure my elephant wins. Send for

Suraj and Basu, my best *mahouts*. We still have a few hours to prepare.'

• ◆ •

News of the elephant fight spread quickly and as the time drew near excited spectators crowded the wide, hard-baked riverbank beneath the Agra fort. The area where the fight was to take place – an enclosure two hundred feet long and fifty feet wide – had been created by piling jute sacks of earth one on top of the other to the height of a man's shoulder, leaving a gap on the west and east sides for the elephants to enter. A six-foot-high earth barrier running across width-wise divided the enclosure into two.

Salim was standing on the *jharoka* balcony with Khusrau and Khurram behind the low throne on which Akbar, wrapped in a fine embroidered Kashmiri wool shawl, was seated. Looking down, Salim noticed the purple tunics and cloth-of-silver turbans of Khusrau's men among the crowds below. He could also see the red and gold clothing of some of his own attendants, including Zahed Butt, the captain of his bodyguard. He glanced at his eldest son. Khusrau was looking very confident and something he had just said to Akbar made his grandfather laugh.

The emperor raised his hand and at the signal a trumpeter high on the battlements put his six-foot-long bronze instrument to his lips and gave three short blasts – the signal for the elephants to proceed from their stables, the *hati mahal*, down the ramp from the fort and along the riverbank. First, to the accompaniment of kettledrums booming out from above the gatehouse, came the fifteen-foot-tall Damudar, wearing a purple velvet, silver-fringed *jhool*, his great legs loosely shackled with silver chains to prevent him from bolting. His *mahout* was seated on his neck and holding the long boathook-like metal rod used to control the animal during the fight. A second *mahout* was perched immediately behind. It would be his job to take over should the first man fall or be injured. Damudar's forehead and eyes were protected by a shining steel plate that ended halfway down his trunk and his tusks were painted gold except for the tips, which were scarlet. As Damudar emerged from the fort and made his stately way towards the fight enclosure, Khusrau's supporters on the riverbank roared their approval.

Craning his neck, Salim could now see his own elephant – a gift from Jodh Bai's father – walking slowly down the ramp with Suraj sitting on his neck in front of Basu. World Shaker was smaller by nearly a foot than Khusrau's beast but his silvered tusks were longer and more curved. The Rajputs trained their elephants well and World Shaker had proved his fearlessness many times.

As soon as Damudar and World Shaker had each entered their own side of the enclosure, bags of earth were piled up behind them to close the gaps in the arena walls. While this was being done, the elephants' *jhools* had been removed and the beasts were already trumpeting angrily at each other with Khusrau's Damudar swinging his great grey head from side to side. Salim felt his blood begin to pump. Glancing at Khusrau he saw from the rapid rise and fall of his chest that he too was excited. Had he misjudged his son? Was this simply a contest between two fighting elephants to amuse the sick emperor? But watching Khusrau bend to whisper again in Akbar's ear, Salim was sure he had understood his son's motives correctly.

Youths were now darting between the elephants' legs to remove their chains. They had barely scrambled from the enclosure when with a great roar Khusrau's elephant stormed towards the central barrier and standing up on his hind legs brought his two front legs crashing down. Then he reared up again as if he couldn't wait to get at World Shaker who, guided by Suraj's gentle taps, was withdrawing slowly backwards from his own side of the barrier. Salim saw Khusrau's grin of triumph as Damudar continued to smash his way through.

Moments later, with his two riders clinging to his neck, the bellowing Damudar trampled with his great pillar-like legs the remains of the barrier and charged forward into World Shaker's half of the arena, kicking earth and dust up into the air as he went. Suraj was still holding World Shaker back, exactly as he and Salim had planned he should, to lure his opponent into making a rush attack. You could never be sure of anything in an elephant fight but it should be the right tactic, Salim thought to himself. World Shaker was smaller and nimbler than Khusrau's elephant.

As Damudar crashed forward, trunk high in the air and tusk tips horizontal, towards World Shaker, Salim wondered whether Suraj had left it too late. But at the very last moment, just as Damudar seemed about to smash into them, with a shouted command and a tap of his bar on the elephant's right shoulder Suraj made World Shaker step quickly to one side, avoiding Damudar's onrush. At the same time the elephant tossed up his head so that his tusks, filed to fine sharp points, inflicted a jagged gash to Damudar's left side as he passed. Blood at once began seeping from the wound. As Damudar stumbled off, trumpeting in pain, Suraj urged World Shaker in pursuit. He caught up with Damudar close to the earth bags enclosing the arena. There Damudar's driver, still struggling to bring his panicked and wounded beast back under full control, somehow managed to swing him round to confront World Shaker.

Urged on by their drivers and the shouts of the crowd, the two elephants rose up repeatedly on their hind legs, each seeking a way to gore the other. Within moments World Shaker had succeeded in slashing open Damudar's trunk just beneath his steel head armour. Then, as Damudar staggered back, he followed up by thrusting one of his tusks deep into his opponent's right shoulder. Khusrau was no longer looking so confident. World Shaker's victory couldn't be long delayed, Salim thought, but as the maddened elephants closed again Damudar's driver lunged forward with his metal pole. He looked as if he intended to strike his elephant but suddenly, grabbing hold of a leather strap round Damudar's neck, he leaned right out and with a quick movement hooked the curved end of his rod round Suraj's leg. Pulled off balance, Suraj teetered for a moment then fell, arms flailing, to the ground. From where he was standing Salim couldn't quite see what had happened to him but he heard the shocked gasp that a moment or two later rose up from the crowd.

'Stop the fight!' Akbar ordered.

Within moments, attendants were throwing lit fire crackers into the enclosure to frighten the elephants and drive them apart. The noisy, fizzing, smoking devices were too much for Damudar who, with his two riders still clinging to his neck, stampeded and burst right through the wall of earth-filled sacks. Trampling three spectators who were not quick enough to leap out of the way, the terrified animal bolted along the riverbank, scattering further onlookers as he ran, and then, swerving, plunged into the Jumna where he came to a halt nearly in midstream, staining the water red with his blood.

Meanwhile Basu had slid forward to take Suraj's place on World Shaker and had managed, despite the noise and the chaos, to soothe the elephant and even to slip a cotton blindfold over his eyes to quieten him further. In the very middle of the enclosure lay the mangled heap that had been Suraj. His head had been crushed to a bloody pulp by an elephant's foot and his intestines were spilled on the ground. Salim turned to his eldest son, shouting, 'Your driver realised my elephant was about to win so he cheated by attacking my *mahout,* causing the needless death of a brave man.'

'What happened was an accident.' Khusrau's face was flushed and his eyes avoided Salim's.

'You know that's not true. Since your elephant fled the arena, in the name of my dead driver I claim the victory.'

'There was no victor. It was a draw. Grandfather . . .' Khusrau turned to appeal to Akbar but the emperor wasn't attending to them. He was on his feet, supported by an attendant on either side, and peering intently over the edge of the balcony. Wondering what was claiming his father's attention, Salim stepped forward as well. The crowds below were milling around, craning to watch what remained of Suraj being gathered from the ground and carried away on a rough stretcher to await his Rajput funeral rites. But then Salim heard angry shouting and saw that scuffles were breaking out between his men and Khusrau's. As he watched, one of Khusrau's attendants pulled a dagger from his belt and slashed one of his own retainers across the face with it. Immediately more men piled into the fray on both sides, fists and weapons flying. Nearby, another group of his followers were struggling with some of Khusrau's men in the shallows of the river, throwing punches and attempting to push each other's heads beneath the water.

'Salim. Khusrau. How dare your men brawl like this in front of me! Have you no authority over them? You should both be ashamed.' Akbar was shaking with fury. 'Khurram, it seems that you are the only one I can trust. Go to the captain of the guard and order him to stop this outrage at once. Any man who drew a weapon on another is to be arrested and flogged.'

'Yes, Grandfather,' said Khurram, running to obey.

'As for you, Salim and Khusrau, go. The sight of you wearies me.' Akbar sat down again and passed a hand over his eyes.

Khusrau hurried away but Salim hesitated. He wanted to justify himself but there was no point. Whatever he said or did would only confirm his father's opinion of him. With a backward glance at Akbar, who gave him no encouragement to remain, Salim walked slowly from the balcony. At least Khusrau had incurred an equal share of Akbar's displeasure, he consoled himself, but then another thought struck him. What was it that Akbar had said to Khurram? 'You are the only one I can trust . . .'

Perhaps those words carried a deeper meaning than either he or Khusrau realised. What would Akbar say to the boy about the day's events when they were alone? That the naked rivalry between Salim and Khusrau showed that neither was fit to rule?

Chapter 29

Seizer of the World

'My *qorchi* woke me with the news that my father has been taken ill. What is wrong?' Salim asked early one morning in October 1605.

'His Majesty was seized with violent stomach cramps about three hours ago and then began vomiting,' said Akbar's chief *hakim*, an elderly, dignified-looking man dressed almost entirely in grey named Ahmed Malik. Lowering his voice and glancing over his shoulder at the guards on duty outside Akbar's bedchamber, the doctor added, 'My first thought was that he had been poisoned.'

'Poisoned? That's impossible. Everything my father eats is tasted three times and each dish sealed by the *mir bahawal*, the master of the kitchen, and escorted to his table by guards . . . even the Ganges water he is so fond of is checked again and again.'

'Ways can always be found. Remember how your great-grandfather nearly died at the hands of a poisoner here in Agra. It was my grandfather Abdul-Malik who treated him. But I now believe my suspicions were groundless. I ordered some of the vomit to be fed at once to pariah dogs but not one has shown any ill effects. Also, your father's symptoms are not developing as they would if he had been poisoned.'

'What is it then? The same stomach illness that afflicted him a few months ago?'

'Very probably, though I can't be sure yet. Whatever the malady is, it is racking your father with great virulence. My colleagues and I are doing everything we can to discover the cause, I promise you, Highness.'

'I am sure you are. May I see the emperor?'

'He is in great pain and has asked not to be disturbed.'

'Can't you relieve his suffering?'

'Of course. I offered him opium but he refused it. He says there are important issues he must decide and that to do so he must keep his mind absolutely clear, even if it costs him pain.'

Salim's eyes widened as he took in the significance of the doctor's words. There was only one reason why Akbar would have said such a thing – the choice of successor. He must think he was dying . . .

'*Hakim*, I know how much faith my father has in you. Save him.'

'I will do my best, Highness, but I must be honest. He is weaker than I have ever seen him. His pulse is faint and ragged, and I suspect he has been suffering far longer and far more than he admits from his stomach problems. Only the severity of tonight's attack induced him to summon me.'

'*Hakim* . . .' Salim began; then, hearing footsteps, broke off. Khusrau was running down the corridor towards them.

'I have just heard the news. How is my grandfather?' Khusrau's flushed face looked to Salim's cynical eyes more excited than anxious.

'He is gravely ill,' he replied shortly. 'Ahmed Malik will tell you the details. But don't let your questions detain him too long from your grandfather's bedside.'

He walked slowly away down the dimly lit corridor as he tried to collect his thoughts. A few torches still burned in their sconces but as he looked through an open casement a pale band of light on the horizon showed dawn was near. Turning a corner, he saw Suleiman Beg waiting for him.

'Well?' his milk-brother asked.

Salim slowly shook his head. 'I think the *hakim* believes my father is dying, though he didn't use those words. So, I think, does my father. But it seems incredible. I've thought about his death so many times – of what it would mean for my future. But I never believed the moment would come, never mind considered how I'd feel.'

Suleiman Beg stepped closer and put his hands on Salim's shoulders. 'You must push your feelings aside, complex as I'm sure they must be. News of the emperor's illness is already spreading and Khusrau's men are swaggering about the Agra fort as if they already own it. The talk everywhere is about who the emperor will name as his heir.'

'That's for my father to decide.'

'Of course. But none of us can predict what's going to happen. Forgive me, but the emperor might die before he has a chance to choose a successor . . . and even if he nominates you, Khusrau's men may rise in rebellion. You must prepare. The stronger you are, the quicker you can strike if you have to.'

'You're a good friend to me and are right as always, Suleiman Beg. What do you suggest I do?'

'Let me summon those commanders we know to be loyal to you to the capital with their troops.'

'Very well. But tell them to come quietly, without ostentation. I must do nothing to provoke suspicion or indeed cause anxiety to my father.'

• ◆ •

Akbar's face looked wan and his hands lay claw-like on the green silk coverlet as his attendants gently set down the chair on which they had carried him from his apartments to his private audience chamber. It was two days since he had fallen ill again and the *hakims* had still been unable to prevent him from passing and vomiting blood, although there had been some reduction in its frequency, probably because he had taken no nourishment. No wonder his skin looked almost transparent. It was hard to believe the frail old man before them had once run jubilantly round the battlements of the Agra fort, a youth clutched beneath each muscular arm.

Akbar's attendants were arranging a bolster behind his back. Salim saw his father wince with pain but after taking a moment to master himself the emperor began to speak. 'I asked you here, my loyal counsellors – my *ichkis* as my father and grandfather would have called you – to help me take perhaps the most important decision of my reign.' Akbar's voice was low but authoritative as ever. 'My illness is no secret. I will probably die soon. That is unimportant. What matters is that I leave my empire – the Moghul empire – in safe hands.' Salim noticed Khusrau, resplendent in his favourite silver and purple, edge a little further forward at his grandfather's words.

'I would have made my decision long ago but I wasn't sure whether to chose my eldest son Salim or my eldest grandson Khusrau. Convinced I still had more years to live, I decided to wait and to observe them both before judging which is better fitted to rule. But I no longer have the luxury of time. The choice will be mine alone, but before I make it I wish to hear your views. You are my advisers. Speak.'

Salim caught his breath. In the next few minutes, the course of his future life would be decided. Shaikh Salim Chishti's words echoed in his brain – 'You will be emperor' – but much had happened since that warm dark night when he had run out of the palace of Fatehpur Sikri to ask for the Sufi's help. Despite his efforts he had never fully won his father's admiration – or even his attention for long – and had allowed desperation and ambition to lure him into rash acts. He was sure Akbar had never forgiven Abul Fazl's murder even if they were now formally reconciled.

Man Singh of Amber, Khusrau's maternal uncle, stepped forward. 'Majesty, you ask our views and I will give you mine. I favour Prince Khusrau. He is young, with many years still ahead of him. Much as I respect my brother-in-law Prince Salim, he is approaching his middle years. He should advise and guide his son, not sit upon the throne himself.' As he finished, Man Singh gave a little shake of his head as if what he had just said weighed heavily upon him and had not been easy. What hypocrisy, thought Salim. It was obviously in Man Singh's interests for his nephew to become the new emperor.

'I agree,' said Aziz Koka, one of Akbar's youngest commanders. Salim's lip curled. It was common knowledge that Khusrau had promised to make him his *khan-i-khanan* when he became emperor. 'We need a young and vigorous leader to take us to yet further glories,' the man added portentously.

Silence fell in the chamber and Salim saw the courtiers exchange glances. Then Hassan Amal, whose father had ridden as a youth with Babur from Kabul stepped forward.

'No!' Although he must have been at least ten years older than Akbar, his voice was firm and resolute. 'Many times in our history brother has challenged brother for the throne, but it has never been the way of the old Moghul clans to set aside the father in favour of the son. The natural – indeed the only – successor to our great emperor must be Prince Salim. I believe I speak not only for myself but for many others gathered here who have been worried by the recent rivalry between the factions supporting the two princes. It is unseemly and it is dangerous. I am old enough to remember the days before we were secure in Hindustan – when our future here hung in the balance. Today we are undisputed masters of a great empire and must not put that at risk by breaking with custom. Justice and prudence demand that Prince Salim, the Emperor Akbar's eldest and only surviving son, succeeds to the throne. Like all of us he has made mistakes, but equally, experience has taught him many lessons. He will, I am sure, make a worthy emperor.'

'That would be my view too, as your *khan-i-khanan*,' said Abdul Rahman gently. All around heads were nodding in agreement but Salim, watching his father's face for a sign, could tell nothing. Akbar's eyes were half closed and for a moment he was afraid his father was losing consciousness. But then the emperor raised a hand.

'Hassan Amal and Abdul Rahman, I am grateful to you both for your wisdom, as I have been many times before. I can see your words have the support of the majority present. They confirm what was already in my heart. My attendants have brought the imperial turban and robes from my apartments.'

Salim tensed involuntarily and forced himself to remain calm and look at his father as Akbar continued, 'All that needs to be done is to summon the mullahs. I wish them to witness that I choose Prince Salim as my heir.'

As all eyes turned to him, massive relief overcame Salim. He would rule and fulfil his destiny. His face suffused with joy but with tears welling in his eyes, he said, 'Thank you, Father. I will be worthy of your trust. When the time comes I will need the support of all and I will rule for all.'

Twenty minutes later, before the council and the *ulama*, Abdul Rahman placed the imperial green silk turban on Salim's head, while Hassan Amal draped the imperial robes over his shoulders. Akbar looked at his son for a few moments then said, 'Before all of you gathered here, I declare my son Salim the next Moghul emperor after my death and I command your obedience to him in all things whatever your own preference may have been. Let me hear you swear your oaths.'

Throughout the chamber, voice after voice responded, pledging allegiance to Salim. Not even Aziz Koka held back.

'There is one last thing left for me to do.' Akbar reached beneath the folds of his coverlet and with a shaking hand brought out a jewelled, eagle-hilted sword. 'This is Alamgir, the sword with which my grandfather Babur extinguished his enemies and conquered an empire. Many times it saved my own life and brought me victory. Salim, I give it into your hands. Be worthy of all it represents.'

As Salim knelt by his father's side to take the sword, the eagle's ruby eyes glittered. Shaikh Salim Chishti had spoken no more than the truth. He would be emperor. His destiny was in his own hands at last.

• ◆ •

A few hours later, Akbar's *hakim* Ahmed Malik came to Salim's apartments. His expression was grave. 'Your father's condition has worsened again. However, he remains clear-minded. When he asked us how much of life was left to him, we had to tell him that none of us, his doctors, could say but that he could not survive long. It might be days but perhaps only hours. He said nothing for a minute or two. Then he calmly thanked us for our honesty and for all we had done and were doing to make him comfortable, and requested us to bring you to him again.'

'I will come at once,' said Salim, putting aside the newly completed painting of a nilgai deer he had commissioned from one of the court artists. He still retained his deep interest in nature and had asked the artist to take particular care to reproduce the muscle structure so he could study it. Only a few minutes later he had crossed the sunlit courtyard, oblivious of the beauty of the fountains bubbling in the marble water channels at its centre, and one of the bodyguards outside his father's sickroom was pulling aside the fine muslin curtains so he could go in. Neither the scent of the sandalwood and camphor burning in the incense holders nor the constant attentions of Akbar's faithful servants could quite disguise the pungent sour smell that was the inevitable consequence of the decay of Akbar's intestines.

The emperor was propped up against some brocade cushions. To his son, Akbar's pale face with its purple bags beneath the eyes remained composed as he took a sip of water held to his lips by an attendant and then said, 'Come and sit by me, Salim. My voice is weakening and I want you to hear my words.'

Obediently, Salim sat down by his father's side. As he did so Akbar continued, 'Ahmed Malik has told me that I will soon leave this world.'

'I pray that will not be the case just yet,' said Salim, realising as he spoke that there was truth behind his conventional words. Now that the crown he had craved for so long was nearly his, he felt the same apprehension as he had through much of his life. How could he measure up to his father's achievements? Quietly he added, 'But if you are to die, you do so happy and confident in your immense achievements.'

'One of the European priests once told me that a philosopher born centuries before the foundation of their Christian faith defined the essence of tragedy as being that no man could be called truly happy until he had died in peace. I have long seen the truth in these words as I have strived to arrange the affairs of our empire for the future so that my work should be built on and not dissipated after I die. Now that my death is near it would help me die in peace if you would truly listen to some parting advice from me.'

'Gladly. Over these last hours since you formally appointed me as your successor I have appreciated the enormity of the responsibility soon to fall on me. I would welcome it.'

'First, remember never to let the empire stagnate. If it does not grow and change by responding to events it can only decline.'

'I understand. I will continue the campaign in the Deccan. Our borders to north, east and west rest on rivers and mountains. The south provides the greatest opportunity for expansion.'

'Second, always be alert for rebellion.' Salim thought for a moment that Akbar was still reproaching him, but there was no hint of that in Akbar's face as he continued, 'One of my historians tells me I've overcome more than one hundred and forty rebellions during my reign. They break out when armies have no prospect of campaigns or booty to distract them from plotting.'

Salim nodded.

'Be tolerant to all, whatever their position or religion, and be merciful whenever you can. It will help unite our subjects. But when your mercy is misinterpreted or the crime heinous, act decisively and ruthlessly so that all may know your power. Avoid the mistakes of my father Humayun. It is better a few die early as an example than many later.'

'I will try not to lash out but to react firmly and with thought,' Salim replied almost mechanically. What his father was saying was obvious and certainly not new. Perhaps Akbar was congratulating himself as he reviewed his life rather than truly seeking to help him. But then, as if reading Salim's thoughts, Akbar said, 'Now for knowledge I have gleaned the hard way from my mistakes.'

Salim started. It was the first time he had heard his father admit any but the most trivial mistakes.

'Pay attention to your family. Our dynasty is now so much stronger than any potential external rival that the greatest threat to our power must come from dissension among ourselves. My father indulged his half-brothers too much. I wanted to show that power could not be shared and that my authority was absolute. I still believe that is true – that only one man can rule at a time. However, when you and your brothers grew, I expected you to develop my attributes and share my attitudes while unquestioningly obeying my instructions. I did not understand that the two were scarcely compatible. It would never have been in my own nature not to raise questions or to seek independent command if my own father had lived.'

Salim saw Akbar wince, whether through the pain in his abdomen or the recollection of his behaviour, and said, 'I will try to make allowances for the ambitions of my sons, but I have already begun to understand how difficult it is.'

'I've not helped by unsettling you all, by constantly testing which of you might be the most suitable successor. But even had I not, the longer I have lived the more clearly I have realised that the relationship between parents and children is an unequal one. The parent concentrates his future hopes as well as his love on the child and hence scrutinises and guides him closely. The child resents the burden and longs to strike out independently. He sees all his failings, faults and frustrations as due to his parents and his virtues and successes as solely his own creation. He believes he can do better than the parent if only given a chance.'

'I see that more clearly now,' Salim acknowledged, 'now that my sons are growing older. But I also felt in awe of you and your great and unique achievements. It made me awkward and surly around you. It should not have.' He paused, but then after a moment continued quietly, 'I am truly sorry for the pain I gave you.'

'And I for that I inflicted on you. But I now beg only this of you. Learn from the past but look to the future.' As he spoke, Akbar extended his dry hand towards his eldest son. Salim silently took it in his own, feeling closer to his father than he had done since his early childhood, united with him in their hopes for the dynasty.

• ◆ •

To the slow beating of kettledrums Salim mounted the steps of the marble dais to the throne that awaited him in the Hall of Public Audience in the Agra fort. On his finger was Timur's ring bearing the emblem of the tiger that he had taken gently from his dead father's hand nine days ago and placed upon his own. The eagle-hilted Alamgir hung by his side and round his neck was a triple string of uncut emeralds intertwined with pearls that had once belonged to his great-grandfather Babur. A sense of continuity with a heroic past filled Salim with pride. It was as if his ancestors were here among the ranks of his nobles and commanders, watching him claim the throne they had fought so hard for and urging him on to fresh glories.

Turning, Salim sat down on the green brocade cushions and rested his bejewelled hands on the throne's golden arms. 'I have observed nine days of mourning for my respected father, whose body now lies in his favourite gardens in Sikandra where I will construct his tomb with all the magnificence due to him. The *khutba was* read in my name on Friday in the mosques and the time has come for me to present myself to you as your new emperor.'

Salim paused and surveyed the rows of men before him as he had so often seen his father do. The world seemed a different place from here. The fate not only of those present but of million upon million of his subjects rested in his hands. It was an awesome, almost god-like responsibility, but also inspiring, and he sat up yet straighter on his throne. As he did so, his eyes met those of Suleiman Beg, standing beside the tall figure of Abdul Rahman, and the faint curve of his milk-brother's mouth told him he understood exactly how he was feeling.

Salim looked down at his sons, positioned just below the dais to his right. Eighteen-year-old Khusrau, splendid in a purple silk tunic and with diamonds flashing in his turban, was standing beside the thirteen-year-old Khurram, whose pinched face showed the marks of his continuing grief at the death of the grandfather who had meant so much to him. Sixteen-year-old Parvez was just behind them. They were all of them fine youths but it was Khusrau on whom Salim's gaze lingered longest. He must forgive Khusrau his rash ambition and find ways to reconcile this mettlesome son. There must be a way to create a bond with him and so break the cycle of frustrated ambition, envy and uncertainty that had blighted his own happiness and his relationship with his father.

Dragging his mind back to the present, Salim continued his address. 'I have chosen a new name by which I wish to be known as your emperor. It is Jahangir, 'Seizer of the World'. I have taken it because the business of kings is seizing their destiny and controlling the world. My father has left me a mighty empire. With your help, my loyal subjects, I pledge to make it mightier still.'

He rose to his feet and spread his arms, as if taking every man in the room into his embrace. All around the pillared hall rose cries of 'Long life to Jahangir!' Such sweet music to his ears.

• ◆ •

'Leave me,' Jahangir ordered his treasurer and the attendants who had accompanied him down the long flight of stone steps to the iron-bound wooden door leading into the treasure chamber concealed beneath one of the stables in the Agra fort.

'Are you sure, Majesty? It is very dark inside the chamber until the lamps are lit and the ground is dank and slippery.'

'Give me your key and leave me a torch, but I wish to be alone here.'

The treasurer handed over an intricate iron key on a leather thong while a servant passed Jahangir his burning torch of rags dipped in oil. Jahangir waited until the footsteps had receded back up the staircase and he was indeed alone in this dank, earthy-smelling place. He could still scarcely believe the extent of his wealth. The lists of imperial jewels that his treasurer had prepared for him amounted to nearly three hundred and fifty pounds in weight of diamonds, pearls, rubies and emeralds alone. 'Over six hundred and twenty-five thousand carats of the most precious gems, Majesty,' the man had pointed out, running his practised finger down the columns, 'and semi-precious gems too numerous to count, never mind all the gold and silver coin.'

It was childish of him, but Jahangir had hardly been able to contain his eagerness to visit one of his treasure houses. He turned the key in the solid, well-oiled lock, pushed the heavy wooden door open and, holding the torch high in his left hand, peered inside.

The chamber was very dark but as Jahangir entered something glimmered in the purple shadows. He held the torch yet higher and on the wall to the left of the door noticed a double row of arched niches where oil lamps had been placed. He lit the lamps from the torch, thrust the torch in a sconce, then looked around him. The chamber was larger than he'd anticipated – some thirty feet long – and the ceiling was supported by two handsome carved sandstone pillars in the middle.

389

But what caught his attention were four giant domed caskets on trestles against the back wall. Advancing slowly, he opened the lid of the first to find a mound of blood-red rubies as big as duck eggs. He took a handful and stared at them. How magnificent they were – the queen of gems. For a moment, he saw Mehrunissa's face as she had dropped her veil. Rubies would suit her and now he was emperor he could give jewels to whoever he chose . . . indeed choose anyone for his wife . . . Tipping them back in, he closed the lid and moved on. The next box contained dark green emeralds in all shapes and sizes, some cut, some uncut. The third box held sapphires and diamonds from the world's only mine in Golconda in the Deccan, while the fourth was filled with loose pearls. Plunging in his arms up to his elbows, Jahangir felt their lustrous coolness against his skin.

To the right of the trestles, Jahangir saw open sacks of corals, topazes, turquoises, amethysts and other semi-precious stones heaped casually on the ground. Even just these would be enough to finance an army for a year . . . Suddenly he was laughing aloud. This treasure house held just a tiny fraction of his wealth – it was nothing compared with those in Delhi or Lahore, the treasurer had assured him. Still laughing, Jahangir seized a sack and tipped its contents on the floor, then another, then another, mingling the different coloured gems promiscuously. Then when he had accumulated a great pile he flung himself down on them, rolling from side to side. He was emperor now. A Hindu sage had written that nothing was more disappointing than achieving your heart's desire. Well, he was wrong. Jahangir flung a fistful of gems into the air and watched them flash like fireflies in the lamplight.

An hour later, Jahangir emerged blinking into the bright April sunlight, still as light-headed as if he'd been drinking wine or taking opium, but the sight of Suleiman Beg's anxious face drove all frivolous feelings from him.

'What is it?'

'Treason, Majesty.'

'What do you mean? Who would dare . . . ?'

'Your eldest son. As you know, three days ago Prince Khusrau rode out of the Agra fort.'

'I know. He told me he was going to spend some time at Sikandra superintending the construction of my father's tomb. I gave him instructions for the builders.'

'He was lying. He never meant to go to Sikandra. He's riding north for Lahore, rendezvousing with his supporters as he goes and bribing new ones to join him. He must have planned this weeks ago. Aziz Koka is with him. The reason I know all this is that Aziz Koka tried to induce your brother-in-law Man Singh to join the rebels but he had the sense to refuse and to bring me word of the plot.'

Jahangir was barely listening as his mind raced. 'We can overtake them. Have a detachment of my fastest cavalry prepared. I myself will lead them. I have waited so long for what is mine that I'll let nobody seize it from me. Those who defy me will pay in blood, whoever they are . . .'

Historical Note

When people talk about 'the Great Moghul' it's usually Akbar they mean. He was the first Moghul emperor to be born in Hindustan. During his long and successful reign he created an empire of almost unimaginable opulence which covered two-thirds of the Indian sub-continent and had a hundred million ethnically and religiously diverse subjects. By the end of his reign he had almost trebled the size of the empire bequeathed to him by his father Humayun.

Modesty was seldom a Moghul trait and to ensure future generations appreciated his achievements Akbar employed court chroniclers. Of their works, Abul Fazl's *Akbarnama* and *Ain-i-Akbari* – together amounting to nearly four thousand pages in English translation – are outstanding sources for Akbar's reign. Despite his florid style and hagiographic language, Abul Fazl conveys Akbar's charisma and the glamour of his court. He is also meticulous, telling us not only how the emperor defeated his enemies and administered his empire but also the price the court paid for everyday commodities and the detailed arrangements for cooking, for food tasting and for the *haram*. After Abul Fazl's murder in 1602, Asad Beg, who had assisted him, took over and documented the final years of Akbar's life in his *Wikaya*. Badauni, one of Akbar's critics, also described the emperor and his court in *Muntakhab al-Tawarikh*, written in secret towards the end of Akbar's life.

Akbar's reign was also the time when growing numbers of Europeans – merchants, priests and soldiers of fortune – began making their way to the Moghul court. Father Antonio Monserrate was one of the first Jesuits to visit Akbar's court and his *Commentary on his Journey to the Court of Akbar* describes the religious debates in Akbar's *ibadat khana*. In 1584, Ralph Fitch was among the first English merchants to reach Hindustan and he describes the wonders of Agra and Fatehpur Sikri in his *Memoirs*.

Vivid and personal as many of these accounts are, I also wanted to visit – actually in most cases revisit – the places that were important to Akbar. In Delhi I sat in the walled garden and watched the sun set behind the domed sandstone and marble tomb Akbar built for his father Humayun, with its elegant symmetry and chamfered corners such an obvious forerunner to the luminous Taj Mahal. In Agra, I walked in burning heat up the steep, twisting ramp through gates studded with spikes to repel charges by armoured elephants into the sandstone fortress remodelled by Akbar. It is still encircled by the battlements around which he ran with a man clenched under each arm to show off his strength. Standing on a *jharoka* balcony I imagined how Akbar must have felt as he showed himself every dawn to the subjects clustering on the sandy riverbanks below.

Perhaps the greatest pointer to the boundless scope of Akbar's ambition and confidence is the sandstone city of Fatehpur Sikri near Agra, built and then abandoned by Akbar a few years later. Wander its courtyards, palaces and pavilions and you're surprised not to see ghosts. Bright blue tiles from Isfahan still glitter on the roof of Akbar's immense *haram* above the palace of the winds where Akbar's women sat to catch the cooling breezes. The marble platform where he sat beneath silken canopies is still there in the centre of the *Anup Talao*, Akbar's 'Peerless Pool'. The hot, dry desert air has preserved the intricate sandstone carvings while in the courtyard of the mosque people still pray at Shaikh Salim Chishti's domed white marble tomb inlaid with mother of pearl and tie twists of thread to its delicate *jali* screens as physical expressions of their innermost wishes.

In Rajasthan, the soaring fortress-palaces of Amber and Jodhpur explain Akbar's eagerness to make the proud and martial Rajputs his allies, while the ruins of the once great Rajput fortress of Chittorgarh show the consequences of refusing Akbar's overtures. I climbed up to it from the east – the direction from which Akbar's armies made their assaults. In a courtyard, a stone marks the place where, knowing that defeat by the Moghuls was inevitable, the Rajput women committed *jauhar*, hurling themselves into the flames of a great fire rather than fall into Moghul hands. It was a reminder that for all his manifold achievements, religious toleration and advanced, sophisticated view of the world, Akbar lived in and was part of a violent time and that while those who accepted Moghul rule prospered, those who resisted were crushed.

As with all the books in the Moghul Quintet, the main military, political and personal events described in *Ruler of the World* all happened. Akbar was indeed crowned on a hastily constructed brick throne after his mother and Bairam Khan concealed the death of his father Humayun to buy time; Adham Khan, Akbar's milk-brother, did attempt to kill him in the *haram*; Akbar's defeat of Hemu and his subsequent military campaigns in Rajasthan, Gujarat, Bengal, Kashmir, Sind and the Deccan all occurred; Akbar's many marriages and his hundreds of concubines are also based on fact though the names of some of his wives are unknown. Akbar's life was so rich in incident that I of course omitted some events and condensed or simplified others as well as compressing timescales in a book which covers a fifty-year period. Also because the chronicles cannot tell us everything – their writers would never have dared reveal certain things – I have used the novelist's freedom to imagine some incidents and of course to attribute motivation.

However, all the time I have tried to be true to Akbar who, as I wrote the book, became very real to me. I was moved by the dilemma of a man, outwardly so successful and beloved by his subjects, whose relationships with those closest to him often failed. Nearly all the other main characters are real too – Akbar's mother and aunt Hamida and Gulbadan, his milk-mother Maham Anga and milk-brother Adham Khan, his Persian regent Bairam Khan, his adversaries like Hemu, Shah Daud and Rana Udai Singh, his sons Salim, Murad and Daniyal and the Sufi divine Salim Chishti who predicted their birth, and his grandsons, the Persian Ghiyas Beg and his family, the Jesuit fathers Antonio Monserrate and Francisco Henriquez and the mullahs Shaikh Mubarak and Shaikh Ahmad. A few like Ahmed Khan, Akbar's *khan-i-khanan*, and Salim's confidant Suleiman Beg are composite characters.

Additional Notes

Frontispiece
The quotation from the *Akbarnama* comes from H. Beveridge's
translation (vol. I, p.631, Calcutta: Asiatic Society 1907-39)

Chapter 1
Akbar's illiteracy is well attested. He may have been dyslexic.
Humayun died in January 1556. Akbar, who was born on 15 October
1542, was proclaimed emperor on his brick throne in February
1556.
Timur, a chieftain of the nomadic Barlas Turks, is better known in
the west as Tamburlaine, a corruption of 'Timur the Lame'.
Christopher Marlowe's play portrays him as 'the scourge of God'.
Of course Akbar would have used the Muslim lunar calendar, but
I have converted dates into the conventional solar, Christian,
calendar we use in the west.

Chapter 2
The battle of Panipat against Hemu took place in November 1556.

Chapter 3
Bairam Khan was dismissed in 1560.

Chapter 4
Bairam Khan was killed in early 1561.

Chapter 5
Adham Khan killed Atga Khan and attempted to kill Akbar in May
1562. Maham Anga died soon afterwards, it is said from grief.
Akbar provided the money for a handsome tomb for them. It still
stands at Mehrauli, south of Delhi near the Qtab Minar.

Chapter 7

The Chittorgarh campaign took place in 1567–8.

Chapter 8

Although Akbar certainly married a Rajput princess of Amber (Jaipur) she was not his first wife and the chroniclers are not entirely clear on her name and give no details of the nature of her relationship with Akbar other than that she was Salim's mother. Their relationship has been fictionalised in various ways in films and novels. It is my own thought that she might have been hostile to Akbar because of his subjection of the Rajputs.

Chapter 9

Akbar visited Shaikh Salim Chishti in 1568 and Salim was born on 30 August 1569. The word *sufi* means 'those who wear rough woollen garments' and derives from the Arabic word for wool – *suf*. Sufi mystics adopted such garb as a symbol of aestheticism and poverty.

Chapter 10

Abul Fazl was born in January 1551 and entered Akbar's service in 1574.

Akbar's use of 'tens' in designating his officials as commanders of a certain number of troops was based on zero, an Indian invention. It was brought to Europe via the Middle East. Hence what we know as Arabic numerals are really Indian numerals.

Europeans wrote of how Akbar ordered sections of buildings to be prefabricated and himself laboured in the quarries cuting sandstone.

The uses of individual buildings at Fatehpur Sikri are not recorded by Abul Fazl or any other chroniclers in detail and are a fertile subject of debate among architectural historians, despite the certainty with which guides speak of them.

Chapter 11

The Gujarat campaign was in 1572.

Chapter 12

The Patna campaign and the invasion of Bengal began in 1574. Shah Daud's death was in 1576.

Chapter 13

Murad was born in June 1570, Daniyal in September 1572.

The distinction between Shia and Sunni derived from the first century of Islam and originally related to who was Muhammad's legitimate successor and whether the office should be an elected one or restricted, as the Shias claimed, to the descendants of the prophet through his cousin and son-in-law, Ali. 'Shia' is the word for 'party' and comes from the phrase 'the party of Ali'. 'Sunni' means 'those who follow the custom – *sunna* – of Muhammad'. By the sixteenth century further differences had grown between the two sects, such as the nature of required daily prayer.

The first Jesuit mission including Father Monserrate, a Spaniard, arrived at Akbar's court in 1580.

Chapter 14

Chronicles record the story of Ghiyas Beg's hazardous journey during which in 1577 Mehrunissa was born.

Chapter 16

John Newberry arrived in India with Ralph Fitch in 1584.

Some commentators have suggested that Akbar's trances, of which this was by no means the only one, were because, like Julius Caesar, he suffered from epilepsy.

Chapter 18

Many reasons have been advanced for the abandonment of Fatehpur Sikri. Lack of water is one. Another is the distance from the Jumna, a main transport artery at the time. Yet another is that Akbar moved his capital to Lahore simply to be nearer the front lines of his campaigns.

The invasion of Kashmir was in 1586.

Chapter 19

The campaign in Sind was from 1588–91.

Salim married Man Bai in 1585.

Khusrau was born in August 1587.

Chapter 21

Khurram was born on 5 January 1592 in Lahore. Parvez was born in 1589. Abul Fazl wrote in the *Akbarnama* that Akbar 'loved grandsons more than sons'. Akbar did indeed take Khurram into his own household, placing him with one of his wives, Rukhiya.

Chapter 22

The Kandahar campaign culminated in the city's fall in May 1595.

Chapter 23

The story of Salim's seduction of Akbar's concubine Anarkali was first mentioned by another English merchant William Finch who visited Hindustan between 1608 and 1611 and claimed while in Lahore to have seen a sumptuous tomb erected for Anarkali by Salim after he became emperor. Though there is no other contemporary evidence for this tragic romance, the story of Anarkali was clearly part of the oral tradition and was taken up by later Moghul writers. It is my own invention that she was Venetian.

Chapter 26

Salim indeed turned to wine, spirits and opium. His hands shook so badly he couldn't hold a glass and court physicians gave him six months to live unless he reformed.

Chapter 27

Salim left for Allahabad in July 1600. In his own memoirs the *Jahangirnama*, Salim describes Abul Fazl as 'no friend of mine' and admitted responsibility for his killing.

Murad died of drink in May 1599.

Salim returned to Agra in April 1603.

Chapter 28

Hamida died in August 1604 and Daniyal in March 1605.

Chapter 29

The western philosopher spoken of by Akbar is Sophocles.

Akbar died on 15 October 1605. According to the western calendar it was his sixty-third birthday. Intriguingly one of his most famous contemporaries William Shakespeare also died on his own birthday, 23 April 1616, at the age of fifty-two.